LOVE
LIGHTS *the* WAY

OTHER BOOKS AND BOOKS ON CASSETTE BY
MICHELE ASHMAN BELL

An Unexpected Love

An Enduring Love

A Forever Love

Yesterday's Love

Love After All

LOVE LIGHTS *the* WAY

A NOVEL

MICHELE ASHMAN BELL

Covenant Communications, Inc.

Cover illustration by Anita Kim Robbins

Cover design copyrighted 2001 by Covenant Communications, Inc.

Published by Covenant Communications, Inc.
American Fork, Utah

Printed in the United States of America
First Printing: March 2001

08 07 06 05 04 03 02 01   10 9 8 7 6 5 4 3 2 1

ISBN 1-57734-803-6

Library of Congress Cataloging-in-Publication Data

Bell, Michele Ashman, 1959-
     Love lights the way / Michele Ashman Bell.
         p.   cm.
     ISBN 1-57734-803-6
     I. Mormon women--Fiction. I. Title.
     PS3552.E5217 L695 2001
     813'.54--dc21   00-069371
                                                            CIP

This book is dedicated to
my son, Weston,
whose example
lights the way for so many.

Special thanks to
Charlene Raddon, Roger and Karen Greenwood,
and Erika and Chad Brendle
for helping in the research of this book.
And to my editor, Valerie Holladay.
Thank you is never enough.

PROLOGUE

It was the most important day of her life and Ashlyn felt like throwing up.

A formation of butterflies swooped and swirled inside her stomach. She glanced at the clock again. Someone should have come and taken her to the sealing room by now. She and Jake were already fifteen minutes late for their scheduled sealing time. The temple was booked solid in June and the temple workers kept a tight schedule.

Something was wrong.

Heavenly Father, please bless us so that everything will be okay. I'm so nervous. Please help me calm down. Bless me with Thy spirit so I can enjoy this wonderful experience. And thank you for Jake. He's the most wonderful man in the world.

The prayer helped a little, but she couldn't calm the queasiness in her middle.

She didn't dare sit for fear of crushing the satiny smooth fabric of her wedding dress, so instead, she paced the floor. Running her fingers across the dozens of pearls handsewn to the lacy bodice of the dress, Ashlyn tried to steady her breathing and relax, and force the awful thoughts away that kept clouding her mind.

She glanced in one of the dozens of mirrors in the bride's room of the Salt Lake Temple and checked her reflection for the hundredth time. Adjusting the neckline of her wedding gown, she turned sideways, pulled in her stomach, and straightened her shoulders. Then, with a sigh, she exhaled and began pacing again.

Everything's going to be okay, she told herself.

Soon, she would kneel at the altar, across from her fiancé, Jake Gerrard, and seal their love for time and all eternity. The thought sent her heart aflutter. No one had ever made her feel the way he made her feel, and she looked forward to spending forever with him. With Jake life was exciting and full of surprises, and she knew that life with him could never be boring. He was spontaneous, wild and crazy, and passionate about life. He wanted to live every day to its fullest and enjoy every minute. He was her handsome knight in shining armor.

But aside from his good looks and witty sense of humor, he had a deep, thoughtful side of him that Ashlyn found mysterious and intriguing, which explained how—only three short, romantic, and magical months after meeting him—they were now getting married. Jake said he loved her and couldn't live without her. She had never felt this way about anyone.

Her mother and stepfather had expressed their concern about her marrying Jake, but Ashlyn felt their concerns were unwarranted. They worried about her marrying someone who had dropped out of college and who didn't yet have a steady job. Even more, they were concerned that Jake didn't have any income or savings to provide for his wife after they were married. But Ashlyn had put some money away, and with her degree in journalism and a teaching certificate, she could help support them until Jake decided what he wanted to do.

Ashlyn knew it would be difficult, but she and Jake would make things work. That's what marriage was all about. There were many challenges ahead for them, but with Jake by her side, Ashlyn wasn't afraid.

They planned to honeymoon in Cozumel. Ashlyn had wanted to go to Hawaii, but Jake had assured her that Cozumel was even better. When they returned, they would move to Arizona since Jake liked the warmer climate and thought he might attend ASU. Ashlyn had just secured a job for the fall teaching English at a Salt Lake junior high school, but she knew she could find work in Arizona. Jake had already gone to Arizona to find them an apartment, and their belongings were packed in their new Land Cruiser. Since Jake had thought the larger vehicle would be more practical for them, Ashlyn had sold her Honda Accord. Besides, a Land Cruiser was a real "man's" car,

Jake insisted. With their plans made, they were all set for their new life together.

As she paced, Ashlyn thought about their first meeting. It had been at a Young Adult fireside. He'd caught her eye the minute he walked through the door into the chapel. It was a multi-stake fireside and she'd never seen him before. After the fireside, with a little effort and some finagling, she'd managed to line up behind him in the refreshment line. It was love at first sight for both of them.

They had struck up a casual conversation, which had led to a lunch date the next day. After that they saw each other every day. Within several weeks they'd confessed their love for each other and Jake had proposed.

Now they were getting married.

At least, they were supposed to be getting married. Ashlyn checked the clock again.

What in the world was going on?

She wondered if something had happened to Jake. She knew he was at the temple because they'd arrived at the same time. They'd spoken briefly. He seemed nervous and quiet, but then she was nervous, too. After all, this was their big day.

Maybe he was sick. But if he were, surely someone would have told her by now.

Finally, she couldn't stand it any longer. She had to know what was going on.

Opening the door a crack, she heard several people talking down the hall. Recognizing her mother's and stepfather's voices, she left the room to join them and find out what was causing the delay. Just when she was about to turn the corner, the mention of Jake's name caught her attention, and she stopped cold.

"I just don't know how to tell her." It was her mother's voice. "This is going to break her heart."

Ashlyn's breath caught in her chest, and a sick feeling washed over her. What was going to break her heart? What was her mother talking about?

"I'll tell her, if you want me to," her stepfather offered.

"No," her mother said softly. "I think it would be best coming from me."

"We're so sorry." The elderly voice was unfamiliar, no doubt one of the male workers at the temple. "We don't see this happen too often."

"I think I should go with you, Miranda." Ashlyn recognized the voice of Jake's mother, Barbara.

"No!" Miranda's voice came sharply. "That will just make it more painful."

Ashlyn felt tears sting her eyes. A knot formed in her throat. Backing up to the wall, she leaned against it for support. She felt faint. Something had happened to Jake.

"What are you going to say?" Garrett, her stepfather, asked.

"I don't know," Miranda cried. "How do I tell my daughter her fiancé has changed his mind and doesn't want to marry her?"

For a moment Ashlyn was stunned, not sure that she heard her mother right. Her face and hands tingled, then went numb. Then the words slowly seeped in until they speared her consciousness with a white heat. Jake had changed his mind?

He didn't want to marry her?

Suddenly the walls started melting, and the floor began to spin. Ashlyn felt her knees go weak, then everything went black.

CHAPTER ONE

Ten months later

"You didn't get the job," the woman on the phone told Ashlyn. "We hired another teacher who had more experience. I'm sorry."

Ashlyn hung up the phone with a frustrated sigh. She was tired of going to interviews and not getting hired. What was she doing wrong? She'd been offered a job once; the principal had believed her capable despite her lack of experience. But now it seemed that no one would even give her chance.

Her mother, Miranda Erickson, burst through the garage door with both hands full of grocery bags, which she deposited on the counter. Seeing the look on her daughter's face, Miranda knew instinctively that something was the matter. "What's wrong, honey?"

"I just got a call from Oakdale Elementary. They hired someone else." Ashlyn tried to speak casually, but she couldn't stop the tears that stung her eyes.

"I'm sorry, sweetie." Miranda walked over to her daughter and gave her a hug. "You'll get a job," she assured her. "You can't give up."

"Mom," Ashlyn said sharply, "that was the last opening. There are no other teaching positions available."

Miranda winced at her daughter's tone but kept her voice calm and patient. "Something will work out," she said, trying to sound positive. "You'll see."

But Ashlyn didn't believe her. Nothing had worked out for the last ten months. It was as if Jake deserting her at the temple had somehow jinxed the rest of her life.

Hoping to brighten the mood, Miranda said, "We got a letter today from Adam." Adam was Ashlyn's younger brother, who was on a mission in Portugal. He was loving every minute of it and would be home in only five more months. He and his companion had just baptized a father and mother and their two daughters.

Ashlyn listened as her mother described Adam's letter. "That's great," she said, trying to be excited for him. But she was too miserable to feel anything but sorry for herself.

Miranda made a last attempt to brighten her daughter's mood. "Hey, you didn't tell me what Camryn had to say when she called the other day. How's she doing?"

Camryn Davenport was Ashlyn's roommate from college at Southern Utah University. After a year at the University of Utah, Ashlyn had moved with friends to Cedar City in southern Utah to go to SUU, wanting the chance to live away from home and be on her own for a while. Camryn was there on scholarship and had been assigned to their dorm. She and Ashlyn had quickly become friends, and they'd grown very close. So close that Camryn would also have been Ashlyn's maid of honor, had her wedding actually taken place. Now Cami only had one more month of school before she graduated in interior design. Ashlyn didn't know how she would've made it through the last ten months without her friend.

"She's coming up to spend Easter vacation with us," Ashlyn said. "She said something about checking out the job market while she's here. I would love it if she moved to Salt Lake. Hopefully she'll have better luck finding a job than I have."

That night as Ashlyn pulled on her pajamas, she thought about her friend. She'd missed Cami and all the fun they'd had as roommates. There was nothing like a midnight run to Albertson's for Twinkies and red licorice, or Cami's interior design projects, one which had cost the girls their cleaning deposit on the apartment. They never did find out how that fire had started.

Ashlyn's gaze traveled to the corner of her room where her wedding bouquet of baby pink and powder blue roses, now shriveled and dried, hung on her wall, above a stack of boxes containing china, towels, and other trousseau items she'd collected in anticipation of her marriage to Jake Gerrard. Her mother had tried many times to get

Ashlyn to put everything away and to move on with her life, but Ashlyn felt her mother just didn't understand. Just because Jake had stopped loving her didn't mean she had stopped loving him. Ashlyn wasn't sure why, but for some reason she needed to have those things close to her. She often stayed up late at night, looking through her scrapbooks and the proofs of her engagement pictures.

Picking up one of her wedding announcements, she read for at least the hundredth time the announcement that had never come to pass.

Dr. and Mrs. David L. Gerrard
are pleased to announce the marriage of their son
Jacob Ryan Gerrard
to
Ashlyn Kensington
daughter of the late Thomas Kensington
and Garrett and Miranda Erickson.

Ashlyn wondered where Jake was, what he was doing. She'd only seen him twice in the last ten months. The first time had been on that same day he stood her up at the temple. He'd come to her house to tell her why he'd changed his mind.

"I just couldn't do it," he said, his voice a dull monotone. "I thought I loved you, but when it came down to being married for eternity, I realized I wasn't ready. It wouldn't be fair to you and it wouldn't be fair to me."

Ashlyn couldn't even respond. She'd cried the entire time he was there and for the entire week afterward. She never wanted to show her face in public again. Her heart and spirit were shattered and her pride obliterated. She felt hollow and empty inside. Many times she wondered if she would ever recover; most days she doubted it.

The one other time she'd seen him was at a University of Utah football game. Jake hadn't seen her, but she'd watched him through her stepdad's binoculars. He sat with a bunch of friends, some guys, some girls. The group appeared to be having a great time, and seeing him so happy, so obviously "over" her, seemed to reopen her wounds and rub salt into them. Which was probably the reason she didn't like to go out anymore; she didn't want to run into him again. She knew she couldn't handle it—especially if he was with another girl.

She put the wedding announcement down, then touched the feathery softness of the quill pen that guests would have used to sign their names in the wedding registry. Shutting her eyes, she remembered how hard it had been to return all the gifts that had arrived prior to the wedding day. The look of pity on people's faces when they saw her in church or ran into her at the grocery store nearly killed her. It was easier to avoid people than endure those "looks" or their questions.

She couldn't imagine going on with the rest of her life like this. At the same time she didn't know how to get over Jake. He'd left an enormous hole in her heart when he walked out on her. How would she ever repair it and go on with her life?

CHAPTER
✦ TWO ✦

Ashlyn had been anxiously watching for Cami for the past hour. She was so excited her stomach was in knots. She hadn't seen Cami since the Thanksgiving break. After waiting and watching for hours, Ashlyn saw Cami's Honda finally pull up in the driveway. Charging out the front door, Ashlyn ran to meet her friend, and the two girls hugged and laughed as they greeted each other.

"Wow," Ashlyn cried, "you've changed your hair." Cami's blonde hair had been shoulder-length and blunt cut. Basic but classy. Now it was short and wispy. Very stylish and chic.

"Thanks," Cami replied. "I felt brave one day and decided to let the hairdresser whack it all off. You sure you like it?"

"I love it," Ashlyn said.

"Me too," Cami answered with a giggle. "I feel sassy," she said, exaggerating the last word.

Ashlyn was all too aware of her plain brown hair. It had an over-abundance of natural curl to it, but it was easier to blow straight and pull back into a straggly pony tail. In the past she'd spent so much time out of doors that it always had sun-kissed streaks throughout it. Now it seemed as dull as her life was.

"You must be tired from the drive. Let's go inside. Mom and Garrett are anxious to see you."

Arm in arm the girls walked into the house. Ashlyn felt happier already, just having Cami near. She decided that she was going to do everything in her power to help Cami find a job in Salt Lake so they could move in together. Maybe that would help Ashlyn get her life back together.

"Cami!" Miranda exclaimed when the girls entered the kitchen. She put the lid back on the pot of boiling pasta and gave Ashlyn's friend a hug. "It's so good to see you. You look great."

"Thanks, Mrs. Erickson," Cami said. "Mmmm, something smells heavenly."

"Thank you. I'm baking homemade bread sticks," Miranda told her. "Ashlyn told me how much you love them."

"Hey." Garrett walked into the room. "Who's making all that noise in here?"

"Hi, Mr. Erickson." Cami turned and greeted Ashlyn's stepdad with a quick hug.

"I thought I recognized your voice. Honey," he said to Miranda, "did you remember to hide all the chocolate?"

"Garrett!" Miranda scolded.

Ashlyn and Cami giggled, remembering that last time Cami had come to visit, she'd somehow managed to be the one to eat the last brownie and the last handful of M&Ms. Ashlyn didn't know who had the bigger chocolate addiction—Cami or Garrett.

"Actually, Mr. Erickson, I brought something for you. C'mon, Ash."

After Ashlyn had helped carry in Cami's suitcase and a bag from the car, Cami dug through the bag until she found what she was looking for.

"Here it is," she announced as she pulled out a solid milk chocolate Hershey's Kiss, the size of a softball. "I brought this for your stepdad."

Ashlyn laughed. "That's perfect! Where did you get it?"

"I went to Vegas a couple of weekends ago with one of my roommates," Cami explained. "That's where she's from. Her dad was made bishop of their ward, and she wanted to be there for it. I found this in a store down there and knew I had to get it."

Ashlyn was glad to see the good rapport between her friend and her parents. "He's going to flip when he sees it," she said. "That's sure nice of you."

Cami was practically a member of the family, which was a little strange since Ashlyn didn't know much about Cami's family—just that both of her parents were dead and she'd been raised by her grandparents. Her grandmother had died a year ago. Cami never seemed overly anxious to talk about her family, and Ashlyn didn't feel comfortable asking, afraid it would appear as if she were prying. One thing she did know was that after Cami's father died, her mother had taken back the name Davenport for both of them. Ashlyn wasn't sure of the significance of that act, and Cami hadn't enlightened her.

Ashlyn had been especially glad when Cami had hit it off with Miranda and Garrett during her first visit to their house. Ashlyn hoped that her family had perhaps filled an empty spot in Cami's life.

"You've got the coolest parents," Cami said. "You're really lucky. And it's so romantic how Garrett and your mom found each other after so many years. They are so cute together." Cami put the chocolate down on Ashlyn's cedar chest and stuffed her makeup bag and hairbrush back into her suitcase. "Does it still seem weird to have him around?"

"It took a while to get used to him," Ashlyn admitted. "I mean, I was glad when they got married, but it was weird to have him stay here at first, you know."

"I can imagine." Cami nodded with understanding.

"But it feels pretty normal now," Ashlyn told her friend. "He's really great. He's more like a father to me than my dad ever was." She shrugged. "But that's all in the past. C'mon, let's give Garrett that kiss. I can't wait to see the look on his face."

⊹⊱ ❀ ⊰⊹

Later that night after a relaxing evening of popcorn and videos, Cami and Ashlyn decided to go to bed. They brushed their teeth and changed into their pajamas, then Cami pulled out some recent pictures she'd taken at school. She showed Ashlyn pictures of her trip to Las Vegas, complete with an Elvis impersonator and a visit to the Liberace museum. The two girls laughed at the pictures of Cami's roommates dressed up like Vegas showgirls, with heavy makeup and towels wrapped like turbans around their heads.

The pictures reminded Ashlyn of her own days at SUU, having fun with her roommates, trading clothes, and getting ready for dates. Fighting to use the telephone, waiting for the bathroom. It seemed like a lifetime ago.

While waiting for Ashlyn to finish getting ready for bed, Cami looked through the collection of wedding memorabilia. When she found the box containing Ashlyn's wedding veil, she lifted the filmy, sheer headpiece out of the box and placed it on her head. Then, taking Ashlyn's dried bouquet off the wall, she struck a pose.

"What do you think?" she said dramatically.

Ashlyn had to laugh. There was Cami in Hawaiian print oversized pajama pants, a wrinkled old T-shirt, a wedding veil, and a dried-up bouquet. "I don't even think Deseret Industries would accept you."

"Gee, thanks," Cami looked hurt. "It's the pants, huh?"

"Oh yeah. Everything else is fine," Ashlyn told her.

Before taking off the veil, Cami waltzed around the room as she sang, "'Here comes the bride, all dressed in white.'"

After a minute she plopped on the bed with a sigh. "Do you think either of us will ever get married?"

Ashlyn looked at her with surprise. "What makes you ask that?"

"I don't know. I'm almost twenty-three. You just turned twenty-four. Neither of us has a boyfriend."

"Well . . ." Ashlyn sat down on the bed beside her friend and rested back against the pillows. "I'm sure you'll get married, but I've decided I'm never getting married."

Cami looked surprised. "You don't want to get married?"

"Nope!" Ashlyn pulled one of the pillows onto her lap and hugged it to her chest.

"Why? Just because Jake turned out to be a jerk doesn't mean all guys are."

"I'm not so sure about that," Ashlyn said. "I mean, look at my dad. He treated my mom like garbage. And I thought Jake was the man of my dreams, you know. I mean, you think you know someone and then you find this dark, creepy side of them. I've decided I'm not taking the risk. I don't need a man in my life that bad. It hurts too much when you find out the truth."

"But—"

"Let me ask you something," Ashlyn interrupted, sitting up abruptly. "Who would you say are the majority of spouse abusers?"

"Men?" Cami guessed.

"Who are the rapists and child abusers?"

"Men," Cami admitted.

"Who are the serial killers?"

"Men," Cami answered, exasperated.

"Who—"

"Okay, okay," Cami stopped her. "I get your point. But you're forgetting, the Lord wants us to get married and have a family. That's the whole point of being on this earth. You should know that; you've been through the temple."

Ashlyn nodded, totally in agreement. "And I believe that does apply to most people," she said. "But not me. I'm fine without a man in my life. I'm going to focus on my career and helping others. I'll spend my time volunteering and giving service. Hey, I can be a Mormon Mother Teresa."

Cami rolled her eyes. "Yeah, but she was a nun. You're not."

"Yeah, well, I'd rather have fun as a nun than be miserable as a wife," she stated matter-of-factly.

"What about having children? Don't you want to know what it's like to have a baby?" Cami asked, curious.

Ashlyn sighed and her shoulders slumped in defeat. "Yeah, well, that's the one part of my plan that doesn't work. I want children more than anything. I wish there were some way to have one by myself."

"Well, you can't," Cami stated plainly, then stood up and put the veil back into its box. "Every child deserves two loving, committed parents even if it doesn't always work out that way because of divorce or—" She stopped suddenly, for no apparent reason, and then shrugged. "Anyway, you know better than that," she concluded, giving Ashlyn a hard look.

Ashlyn was quiet for a minute, then she said, "You know what? Let's change the subject. This conversation is starting to depress me. Let's talk about you moving up to Salt Lake so we can live together. We're going to have so much fun," she said, her voice rising in excitement. "We can get the paper in the morning and check the classifieds."

But Cami's expression worried Ashlyn. She knew her friend well enough to know that look meant something wasn't right.

"What?" Ashlyn asked quickly. "Is something wrong? You're still going to graduate in May, aren't you?"

Cami nodded.

"Then what?"

"Well, I . . . , uh . . . ," Cami stalled.

"What is it, Cami?" Ashlyn asked impatiently.

"I'm not going to be able to move to Salt Lake after all. I've decided to move back to Oregon."

CHAPTER THREE

"What did you say?" Ashlyn wasn't sure she'd heard her right.

"I'm moving back home after school," Cami said quickly, not meeting Ashlyn's eyes.

"Back to Oregon? But why?" Ashlyn couldn't believe it. She'd been living for the day when she and Cami could move in together. Somehow she'd felt that this was her chance to finally start over, to move on with her life. Now what was she going to do?

"My grandpa's been sick lately and I've been worried about him up there all alone. He's getting old and . . . well . . . I just feel like I should be there with him," Cami explained.

"Is he going to be okay? Did he ask you to come home?" Ashlyn asked inquisitively.

"He says he's going to be fine, and no, he didn't exactly ask me to come home, but I want to spend time with him while I can. I mean, someday he's not going to be here anymore. I would feel guilty for the rest of my life if I didn't do this." Cami hadn't looked Ashlyn directly in the eyes as she spoke, but now she looked up at her friend. "I'm sorry, I know it's hard for you to understand . . ." Cami swallowed. "This is just something I have to do."

Ashlyn nodded her head in understanding. As always, she wished Cami would open up about her family, that she would talk about her parents. At college, when she and Cami had gone out with friends and the subject of families had come up, Cami was always silent.

When asked a question, she usually gave a noncommittal answer or she managed to change the subject. Ashlyn had come to believe Cami's memories of her family had not been pleasant ones, though she knew nothing of Cami's life that would support her theory.

"I know what you mean," Ashlyn said, seeing how badly Cami felt. "I was just looking forward to us being together again."

"I know, me too." Cami's expression matched Ashlyn's.

The two girls didn't say anything for a minute. Then Cami's face lit up. Her smile was as bright as the Fourth of July fireworks. "Wait, I have an idea," she said. "You don't have a job, right?"

"Uh, no," Ashlyn grimaced. "Thanks for reminding me, though."

"No, no," Cami said. "That's great. It means you don't really have any ties here."

Ashlyn narrowed her eyes, trying to read her friend's meaning. "Cami, what are you thinking?"

"Come with me to Oregon. You'd love it." Cami grabbed her friend's hands and squeezed them excitedly. "There's plenty of room at the house, and you could probably find work there for the summer if you wanted. Or you can just hang around with me for a few months. We would have so much fun. Seamist is right on the coast. It's absolutely beautiful."

Oregon. It was something to think about.

⋅⋅⋅ 🏵 ⋅⋅⋅

On Friday Cami and Ashlyn shopped from morning until late in the afternoon. Then, famished, they stopped for a bite to eat. Looking over the menu, both girls ordered hamburgers, fries, and chocolate shakes.

As was Cami's habit, she scanned the room, giving a head count and description of every attractive male within a twenty-foot radius. Cami had developed a rating system—cute guy but self-absorbed; cute guy but undatable (usually meaning he was with a girl); and cute guy, very desirable. Cami didn't have room on her scale for anything less than cute. Of course, there was a very small percentage of guys in the upper echelon of the rating scale who fell into the drop-dead-gorgeous category. To her dismay, there were mostly "cute but undatable" guys in the restaurant tonight. After bemoaning the lack of cute, datable young men, she asked Ashlyn about Adam and his mission, and they chatted until their food arrived. Then they dove in, anxious to eat and get to a movie that started in forty-five minutes. Fortunately, the theater was just across the street from the restaurant.

"Oh, darn it!" Ashlyn exclaimed, after taking a bite of her hamburger. "The meat's red in the middle."

"Send it back," Cami said, after taking a long draw from her milk shake. She lifted her hand to attract their waiter's attention.

"No!" Ashlyn said quickly. "It's okay."

Cami lowered her hand a little and looked at Ashlyn. "If you don't like it, send it back."

"It's okay." Ashlyn reached over the table and pulled her friend's arm down. "Besides, we don't have time to send it back if we're going to catch the movie."

Cami glanced at her wristwatch. "We've got time."

"No, it's okay. Really." Ashlyn tried to make her voice firm.

Cami shrugged. "Whatever. But I don't understand why you just don't send it back."

"It's not that big of a deal," Ashlyn said, setting aside her hamburger and nibbling on her french fries.

After finishing their meal they hurried to the theater. While they were waiting in line, Cami excused herself to run to the ladies' rest room.

After standing in line a moment, Ashlyn dug into her purse to find her lipstick and a piece of gum. She looked up just in time to see three teenage boys step in line just ahead of her.

Her first impulse was to speak up and tell them that she was there before them, but she didn't. Instead she put on her lipstick and tossed the tube back into her purse, then shoved the stick of gum into her mouth and chewed angrily. She hated it when people butted in line, but she didn't like causing a scene or drawing attention to herself. So she said nothing.

"Wow, this line sure isn't moving very fast," Cami said as she joined Ashlyn. "Wait a minute—those guys weren't here earlier, were they?" She looked at Ashlyn and lifted an eyebrow. "You didn't let them butt in line, did you?"

"No," Ashlyn retorted.

Cami gave her a skeptical look.

"Well, I didn't," Ashlyn defended herself. "They just did it. I didn't 'let' them."

Cami gave her friend a stern look. "Ashlyn, it's okay to tell people that you don't appreciate their inconsiderateness."

"Their 'inconsiderateness'?" Ashlyn grinned. "Is that even a word?"

"Of course it is," Cami replied confidently. "At least I think it is. Besides, you're just trying to change the subject."

"I know," Ashlyn said and looked away, irritated.

But Cami wasn't finished with her. "I just wish you'd toughen up a little bit. You know, not let people walk all over you."

Ashlyn opened her mouth to protest, but Cami pushed onward. "You do, Ash. You let people walk all over you."

Ashlyn clamped her mouth shut. She knew Cami was right; she just didn't like having to admit it.

⋇⋇ 🕮 ⋆⋆

The next day, Saturday, they drove up to Park City. They went snowboarding for half a day, spending more time falling and laughing than they spent going down the mountain. They also had more fun than Ashlyn had had in a long time.

They continued to talk about the possibility of Ashlyn spending the summer in Oregon, and the more they talked about it, the more excited Ashlyn got. After all, there was nothing to keep her in Salt Lake but her family. She loved them and the thought of leaving them saddened her, but in her heart she felt that this move might be the one thing that would help her finally get over Jake and get on with her life.

On the way home from Park City, Cami told her about the town of Seamist. "It's paradise, pure and simple," she said. The town sat right on the ocean, and even though it was small, it still had everything a person needed. The main street of the town had some great art galleries and fun little shops. There were no traffic jams and no rush hour; the lifestyle was slow and easy.

As Cami pulled up in front of Ashlyn's house, she described her grandfather's house, which sat up on a grassy hill overlooking the coast. "You can hear the waves crashing against the shore and the seagulls overhead, and you can walk along the beach and watch the sailboats."

Ashlyn listened, entranced. "It does sound like paradise," she agreed.

"And the Coast Range mountains are right behind my house. I used to do a lot of hiking. You know, there are actually some old Indian trails we can follow."

Cami began to gather their gloves, hats, and goggles together. "That was fun. But I am going to be so sore tomorrow."

Ashlyn sat silently, staring out the car's front window.

Cami noticed the distant look in her friend's eye. "Ash? What are you doing?"

"Thinking," Ashlyn answered, not moving, her eyes still looking ahead.

"What about?"

After another moment, Ashlyn turned and looked at Cami, a devilish look in her eye. "About how much fun we're going to have together in Oregon," she announced.

Cami shrieked. "You mean it? You're coming with me?"

"Yes!" she cried, unable to conceal her own excitement. "I'm coming with you . . . if you're really serious."

"Of course I am," Cami assured her, hugging Ashlyn tightly. "This is so great. You are in for the best summer of your life."

Right now, Ashlyn thought, she needed something good in her life.

⚜

"What do you mean you're moving to Oregon?" Miranda burst out when Ashlyn told her the news.

Ashlyn was taken aback by her mother's response. Miranda seemed as upset by this news as she had the first time Ashlyn had decided to move away from home. "Mom, it's just for the summer," she tried to appease her mother. "Cami's going home and she invited me to go with her."

"But what about finding a job here? I thought you wanted a teaching position," Miranda challenged. "How can you interview for jobs if you're in Oregon?"

"Miranda." Garrett took his wife's hand and patted it comfortingly, but Miranda was too upset to be comforted.

Ashlyn looked at her friend, who had a guilty expression on her face. "Mom, please," she said. "I don't understand why you're getting so upset. It's not that big of a deal." She thought that lately her mother had been acting more emotional than usual. Miranda was the kind of person who grew teary-eyed watching Kodak commercials; she couldn't even bear her testimony without sobbing. But if it were humanly possible, she seemed to be even worse.

"But . . . but . . . ," Miranda stammered. "It was one thing to have you go away to school, but to have you move so far away . . . out of the state. When are you planning to leave?"

"The first part of May, as soon as Cami's out of school," Ashlyn answered cautiously.

Miranda remained silent, no one else daring to say a word. Finally Garrett spoke up. "Did I tell you I've been to Seamist before?" he asked Cami.

"No," Cami said, surprised. "When was that?"

"About fifteen years ago. I went to Portland on some business and drove over to the coast for the weekend. I went deep sea fishing and did some whale watching. I loved the beaches and the Misty Harbor Lighthouse."

Miranda didn't seem to hear him; she only stared down at her hands in her lap. Garrett continued, "Ashlyn, your mother and I will miss you very much, but if you feel like this is right for you, then we support you."

Smiling her thanks at her stepfather, Ashlyn breathed a sigh of relief. She'd learned to love him and appreciate him a great deal since her mother had married him. Ashlyn knew he genuinely cared about her and loved her, and she appreciated the way he added a voice of reason to her and her mother's lives. She and her mother were more emotional when they approached problems, but Garrett helped them stay focused and rational. Just as he did now.

"Have you prayed about it?" Miranda finally said.

"What?" Ashlyn thought the subject was ended.

"Have you asked the Lord what you should do?" Her mother looked at her, waiting for a response. Ashlyn was quiet. She hadn't done much praying in the last ten months although she'd always considered herself a strong member of the Church. Growing up, she'd always, *always* done what she was supposed to do; she'd gone to church and seminary, waited until sixteen to date, and even then only dated good boys. She never broke the Word of Wisdom, she read her scriptures, and she wrote in her journal every day.

At least she used to. Ever since Jake had dumped her, she didn't seem to have it in her anymore. Her mother managed to drag her to church once in a while, and she'd only attended the temple a few times in the last ten months. Something had changed in her.

She didn't know if she'd ever get it back.

CHAPTER FOUR

The two girls got ready for bed that night in silence. Miranda's reaction to Ashlyn's decision to move to Oregon had seemed to upset the whole household. Garrett tried to keep things light, but Ashlyn knew her mother struggled with her leaving. But why? It wasn't even for that long. Three months would go by fast.

Maybe her mother didn't think she was coming home. But Ashlyn had told her it was just for the summer. This was so silly. Even when Ashlyn was going to get married and move to Arizona, her mother hadn't been this upset. Why was this so different?

"I feel really bad about your mom," Cami said as she rubbed lotion on her hands and face. "She probably hates me now."

Ashlyn shook her head, still confused by her mother's reaction. "No she doesn't. But I wish I understood why this was such a big deal to her."

"How old is your mom?"

"I don't know . . . forty-two, forty-three."

"Maybe she's going through menopause. They say women get really emotional and irrational when they go through 'the change.'" Cami kicked off her slippers and kneeled down beside the bed.

"I guess that could be it. Boy, I feel sorry for Garrett then. She's going to be horrible to live with if this is how she's going to act." Ashlyn grabbed her alarm clock and began to set the time. They were all going to church the next day and then over to her grandmother's for lunch.

Cami bowed her head to pray and Ashlyn looked at her, her conscience pricked by guilt. But she ignored it; she just didn't feel like praying. She felt like the Lord had let her down and that the only person she could depend on was herself. It was up to her to make her own life work.

Cami finished her prayers and climbed into bed, and they turned out the lights and pulled up the covers.

"Ash," Cami said softly, "can I ask you something?"

"Sure," Ashlyn said, "if you promise to not hog all the covers tonight."

"I don't hog all the covers," Cami retorted.

"You do, too. I shivered all last night."

"Okay, fine," Cami said with a huff. "But you have to promise not to snore."

"What?" Ashlyn was flabbergasted. "Me? Snore? I do not!"

"Well, if it wasn't you, then you've got a snarling monster under your bed." Cami kicked her feet to loosen the sheets around her legs.

"What are you doing?" Ashlyn asked.

"The sheets are too tight. I get claustrophobic when they're like that."

"But you're messing up the bed," Ashlyn complained.

"So, we can make it in the morning."

"I know, but it's just easier if you don't mess it up during the night," Ashlyn told her.

Cami started laughing. "Are you for real? It's not normal to sleep in one position all night, like you do, unless you're in a coma."

"Well, that's better than thrashing around all night like you do. I swear you are more active at night than you are during the day," Ashlyn scolded her. "It's like aerobic sleeping."

Cami giggled. "Aerobic sleeping?"

"Yeah," Ashlyn said, starting to laugh also.

Cami sat up on one elbow. "I like that. It could be a new fitness craze. Work out while you sleep. I think it could really catch on."

"Okay, okay. Go to sleep," Ashlyn told her as she took the covers and tucked them underneath her so Cami couldn't pull them away. Cami twisted and flipped around a few times, partly to get more comfortable but mostly to try to annoy Ashlyn one more time.

"Are you about finished?" Ashlyn demanded.

"I think so," Cami answered. She kicked her foot one more time. "Okay, now I am."

"You are so weird. Maybe I don't want to move to Oregon with you," Ashlyn said grumpily.

Cami was unperturbed. "You don't have to sleep in the same bed with me. We'll have our own rooms."

"Thank goodness," Ashlyn said. "I don't remember you being so messy at school."

"I don't remember you being so neurotically organized at school," Cami returned.

Ashlyn was offended. "I am not 'neurotically organized,'" she defended herself.

"Look at your closet," Cami suggested. "Do you use a ruler to get your hangers spread exactly one inch apart?"

"No, I don't use a ruler," Ashlyn answered. "I just like having things organized. I can't help it." She didn't admit that she'd drawn lines on the closet rod with a marker so she could space her hangers evenly. But what was wrong with that? It looked nice and she liked having her closet organized. It wouldn't kill Cami to try and be a little more like her.

"Cami?" Ashlyn said. "Say something."

"I'm thinking."

"What about?" Ashlyn asked her.

"About how mad I am at Jake Gerrard."

Startled at the sudden introduction of Jake's name, Ashlyn quickly retorted, "Yeah, well join the club," she said sarcastically.

Cami wasn't finished. "He really did a number on you," she said.

Ashlyn didn't understand what she was getting at. "What does that mean?"

"I don't know. It's just that you didn't used to be so hung up about stuff before," Cami told her.

Ashlyn had always admired the way Cami spoke her mind to people. She didn't mince words. She just told people what she thought. But Ashlyn wasn't sure she liked that particular trait right now.

But she didn't say what she was thinking. Instead, Ashlyn asked. "Like what?"

"Oh, like the way everything in your room is so perfect. I mean, no one cleans every hair out of their hairbrush every time they use it. And you floss every day, sometimes twice a day. I don't even floss once a week. And your closets and drawers are, like, Martha Stewart perfect."

"I don't see why that's so bad," Ashlyn said defensively.

"I guess it's not bad," Cami said. "It's just kind of extreme. But the thing that concerns me the most . . ." She paused.

"Yeah?" Ashlyn asked, wondering if she really wanted to know.

"Well, you used to be the most spiritual person I knew. You always read your scriptures, said your prayers, went to church. You even read the Church magazines cover to cover."

Ashlyn closed her eyes, not wanting to have this conversation.

"I don't see you do those things any more. What happened? You didn't answer when your mom asked if you'd prayed about your decision to move. Have you?"

"No," Ashlyn said reluctantly.

"That's what I mean," Cami said pointedly. "I always admired the way you relied on the Spirit to guide you. You helped me so much with my testimony, just by your example. You've been through the temple. Do you even go anymore?"

Ashlyn felt like pulling the covers over her head.

"Ashlyn?" Cami wasn't going to let her get off the hook that easy.

"I don't know what to say," Ashlyn finally answered. "You don't know how hard this last year has been. I fasted and prayed and I thought I got an answer to marry Jake. I thought I knew without a doubt we were supposed to be together. Then he called off the wedding, and I doubted my ability to hear what the Spirit was trying to tell me. And now, I guess I wonder if the Lord even hears my prayers. I used to think he did, but I'll tell you what—he hasn't been listening lately, or things would definitely be different than they are now."

"You feel like the Lord has turned His back on you?" Cami asked.

"No, I feel like He's not even there anymore," Ashlyn said quietly. "I know other people have hard things to handle and big things going on in their lives and I should be grateful for all I have, but geez, Cami, it's like I'm on my own here. And to tell you the truth, I'm not doing that great of a job with my life."

"Do you go to church?"

"Yeah," Ashlyn said, then her conscience pricked her. "Once in a while."

"Do you pray? Read the scriptures?"

Ashlyn remained quiet for a moment, wondering how they'd gotten on this topic in the first place. "No," she said, not trying to hide the irritation in her voice.

"Don't you think you would feel the Spirit more in your life if you were doing the things you were supposed to? I mean, just basic things—like scripture study, prayer, and going to church."

"I don't know," Ashlyn shot back. "I did all that, and look how things have turned out."

Now it was Cami's turn to be silent.

"Okay," Ashlyn said, "So . . . ?" She left the rest of the sentence open for Cami to finish.

"So, what?"

"So, I'm waiting for your final analysis of my life. An explanation for why I do what I do, say what I say, feel what I feel. You always have the answers. You tell me—what would you do if you were me and wanted to get your life back on track?"

Cami rolled over with her back toward her friend. "You're asking the wrong person," she said wearily. "I don't have any answers. But there's Someone who does."

Ashlyn waited for Cami to go on, but she could tell that her friend was through talking.

For a moment Ashlyn thought about what Cami had said: prayer, scriptures and going to church. If it could only be that easy. She just didn't believe any of those things could help take away her pain, find her a job, and make her feel happy again.

CHAPTER FIVE

The next morning the girls got ready for church and Cami organized her suitcase. Since she was heading back to SUU after church, she wanted to get her things packed so she wouldn't have to do it later. Ashlyn took the opportunity to apologize to Cami.

"I'm really sorry about last night," she said, not looking at her friend as she carefully wrapped the cord around Cami's curling iron for her.

"Last night?"

"You know, our conversation. I didn't mean to get snotty with you," Ashlyn apologized.

Cami shook her head. "I shouldn't have said anything. It's none of my business."

"But it is," Ashlyn said quickly. "You're my friend and you care about me. I would be the same way with you if you were doing something I didn't agree with."

"Thanks, I hope so. If friends can't tell you the truth, then who can?" Cami said.

"True," Ashlyn replied thoughtfully. "Just be patient with me, okay?" Ashlyn pleaded. "This has been the hardest year of my life. I don't seem to be coping very well with things anymore."

"I know it's been hard for you," Cami acknowledged. "I'm sorry. I'll try to be better about it."

"So, you still want me to move to Oregon with you?" Ashlyn asked hopefully.

"Of course I do," Cami reassured her. "Why wouldn't I?"

"I don't know." Ashlyn handed Cami a pair of shoes to put inside her bag. "I thought maybe I made you mad last night."

"You kind of did," Cami replied. "But I know you need to work through things your own way, and my job is to support you and be there for you."

"So, we're okay? I can still move with you?" Ashlyn raised her eyebrows hopefully.

"We're okay and yes, I still want you to move home with me." As Cami tossed the rest of her stuff into her bag, Ashlyn fought the urge to fold each clothing item neatly so it wouldn't get wrinkled on the way home, but she knew Cami would kill her if she did.

⚡

In the following weeks, after Cami's visit, Ashlyn began preparing for her move to Oregon. She found herself growing more and more excited to go someplace completely new and different, to make a fresh start, and, hopefully, begin her life again.

Cami's classes ended the first week of May, followed several days later, by the school's commencement exercises. Ashlyn planned to attend Cami's graduation, especially since her grandfather couldn't make the trip down from Oregon.

As Cami's graduation got closer, Ashlyn ran to the mall to find a graduation gift for her friend. She also wanted a pair of sandals she could wear on the beach, and she needed a new camera so she could take lots of pictures to send back home.

Since her parents were going in on Cami's gift, Ashlyn was able to find a gorgeous new watch she knew Cami would love. The sandals were also easy to find, but Ashlyn was overwhelmed with the choice and selection of cameras to choose from. She wasn't much of a camera buff; she just wanted something simple and easy that still took good pictures. Deciding to try one more place to see if it would help her make up her mind, she walked into an electronics store. As she approached the counter to talk to the salesman, she stopped dead in her tracks when she saw who was behind the counter.

Jake!

Before she could turn and flee from the store, he saw her.

"Ashlyn, hi," he said. He came around from behind the counter and walked toward her. Ashlyn hadn't anticipated seeing anyone she knew and was wearing scruffy jeans, an SUU sweatshirt, and an old pair of Nikes. Her hair was pulled back in a ponytail. Of course, Jake looked like he'd just stepped off the cover of *GQ*. He had a strong, lean, muscular body and broad shoulders, which allowed him to wear clothes as if they were tailor-made for him. She'd always felt a little inferior to his cover model looks; now she felt even more inferior.

"Hi," she mumbled, embarrassed. "I didn't know you worked here."

"Started last month. I'm already the top salesman," he bragged.

Ashlyn gave him a halfhearted smile of congratulations.

"Yup, it's going great. I work here in the evenings, so I can still go skiing during the day."

"Oh," Ashlyn said, wondering how she was going to get out of there. She didn't want him to help her. He'd already "helped" her enough.

"Some friends and I are going up to Jackson Hole for the weekend for some skiing. You been up much this year?"

"A few times," Ashlyn answered, still trying to come up with a getaway plan.

"Working here has been great. I just got a great deal on a car stereo and some awesome speakers. It feels like you're right in their living room," he bragged.

"Whose living room?" she said, distracted, only half listening to his words.

"You know—the band's living room, whoever's on the CD."

"Oh, yeah," she said. She didn't care one whit about speakers, bands, or living rooms, let alone who was in them. "Well, I gotta be going."

"Wait—why did you come in?"

"I . . . um . . . ah . . . Well, I just wanted to look at your cameras. But I think I found one I like at another store— "

"Camera?" He jumped at the opportunity. "I've got a great deal right now on a camera that would be perfect for you. They're right over here."

Feeling trapped, Ashlyn stepped over to the camera display and listened as Jake rattled on and on about features and threw around technical terms that she wasn't familiar with.

"Will you be using your camera indoors or outdoors?" he asked.

"I'm moving to Oregon, so probably outdoors," she answered.

"You're moving to Oregon?" He finally stopped and really looked at her. Up until this point, he'd treated her more like a customer and potential sale than as the person he'd nearly been sealed to for eternity.

"Yeah, next week. And I want to have a good camera to take pictures of the beach and lighthouses and whales and stuff." She liked that she had his attention at last. Obviously her announcement that she was moving had caught it.

"Wow," he said, his eyebrows lifting with interest. "You're just up and moving?"

"No, I'm going with Cami. You remember her. She was going to be my . . . , uh, she was my roommate back at college."

"Oh, sure. Cami, the blonde."

Ashlyn nodded.

"Well, that's great." He bobbed his head a few times, as if he didn't know what else to say. "Hey, did I tell you I'm going to Jackson this weekend?"

"Yeah," Ashlyn said quietly. "You did."

"Oh." A little abashed, he quickly changed subjects and pointed to the cameras. "If you want my opinion, this camera right here is the simplest to use but has the best quality for your money."

Ashlyn actually liked the camera and thought the price seemed reasonable. "I'll take it," she said.

"Oh, okay." He seemed a little surprised.

She followed him back to the counter, her feelings churning inside of her. She knew part of her still loved him. She wondered if she always would. The other part of her still ached from the pain of him calling off their wedding. She doubted that many things in life would ever hurt that badly—at least she hoped there wouldn't be many. She didn't know if she could survive many more blows like that.

She watched him as he rang up the sale and ran her credit card through the machine—the dimple in his cheek, the deep blue of his eyes, the glossy sheen of his hair. His looks still had the power to stop her heart.

She swallowed as a knot began to form in her throat. Obviously he had no feelings for her at all. Nothing. And here she couldn't get through a day without thinking of him and missing him. It was stupid and she hated herself for not being stronger, but she didn't know what to do to change. She hoped this move to Oregon would accomplish that. If it didn't, she didn't know if anything could. Somehow she had to move on.

"There you go," he said, handing her the bag and her receipt.

"Thanks, Jake." She smiled quickly, then averted her eyes, afraid that the emotion bubbling up inside of her would find its way to the surface.

"Sure, anytime." His casual smile nearly tore her fragile heart in two.

"Jake," someone from the other side of the store called to him.

"I gotta go," he said. "Have fun in Oregon." With a quick wave he was off, walking away without a backward glance, just as he had at the temple, leaving her alone and empty, overcome with feelings that she'd worked so hard to push deep down inside of her.

Tears stung her eyes and she quickly left the store before Jake could see.

Would she ever get over him and get on with her life?

⁓⁓ ⚜ ⁓⁓

"What in the world are you doing?" her mother asked when she found Ashlyn downstairs, sorting out game pieces and card games that had gotten mixed up over the years.

"I'm organizing the game closet. It's a real mess." Ashlyn tossed a handful of Monopoly hotels into the compartment in the game box and began sorting money.

"I appreciate it, honey, really I do, but you don't need to do this."

"I know," Ashlyn said, working as feverishly as if she had a life-threatening deadline to meet.

"Sweetie, what's wrong?"

"Nothing." Ashlyn's hands grew still. She looked down as a rush of tears filled her eyes.

"I know you, Ash. You're a cleaner and an organizer when you get upset. What is it?"

Ashlyn blinked several times to clear her eyes as she put a rubber band around the play money. "I . . . I . . ." She sniffled and put the lid on the box. Taking a deep breath, she said, "I ran into Jake tonight at the mall."

"Oh, sweetie," Miranda said, wrapping her arms around her daughter.

At first, Ashlyn remained stiff, trying to be strong, but she quickly dissolved into tears, her body collapsing like a house of cards. "He acted like he didn't . . . even . . . care . . . ," she sobbed. "It was like I was just another . . . customerrrrrr."

She buried her head in her mother's shoulder and cried as her mother patted her back and rocked her gently.

*

After Ashlyn had dried her tears and sought refuge in her room, Miranda stood a long moment looking out the large living room window, thinking about her daughter. Miranda didn't know what to say to ease Ashlyn's broken heart. She felt her own breaking right along with Ashlyn's. It hurt to see her daughter in so much pain.

"I'm so sorry, sweetie," Miranda said softly, wondering how long her daughter would suffer because of Jake's rejection. She knew the pain that came from giving love and not having it returned. She wished she could take away the heartache her daughter was feeling, but she knew that wasn't the way it worked. Just as she herself had grown and become stronger through the pain and trials of her life, Ashlyn too, would grow stronger.

But it hurt to watch her experience the growing pains, unable to do anything to help. Especially when she was going through a challenge herself. A challenge she hadn't told anyone yet. Even Garrett.

CHAPTER
SIX

Going back to Cedar City and SUU brought back fond memories for Ashlyn. Memories of a happier, more carefree time in her life. A lifetime that seemed so long ago.

Cami's graduation was actually long and boring, and by the time it was over, the girls were anxious to get on the road and head back to Salt Lake City to pick up Ashlyn's belongings, then continue on to Oregon.

Ashlyn's stomach was in constant knots. Finally, after weeks of anticipation, the day had arrived. The day that represented the first day of Ashlyn's new life. She had anticipated this day for weeks, and she suspected that her expectations were probably unrealistic. Still, she had great hopes that, at last, in Oregon, she would be able to piece her life back together again.

Once in Salt Lake it didn't take long to finish getting Ashlyn's things together. She'd been packed for a week and was ready to leave behind all her pain and heartache.

Bright and early the next morning, after a huge farewell breakfast, Cami helped Ashlyn carry her suitcases and boxes out to her car.

"Are you sure you have everything?" her mother asked as Ashlyn tossed her overnight bag onto a pile in the backseat of Cami's car. Hooked to the back of the car was a small U-Haul, containing Cami's stuff from school, Ashlyn's three suitcases, and a garment bag.

"I think so. If I need anything, maybe you can send it or I'm sure I can buy it there," Ashlyn said.

"Okay," Miranda said, sniffing back her tears.

"You've got your cell phone turned on?" Garrett reminded the girls.

Ashlyn displayed the blinking light on the phone for him to see. "We're all set."

"Good. You call if you have any car trouble or anything," he said.

"We will," Ashlyn promised.

"And don't stop at any rest stops to use the bathroom," Miranda told them. She'd heard about a woman who had been kidnapped at a rest stop.

"We won't, Mom."

"Thanks for the watch, Mr. and Mrs. Erickson," Cami said, displaying the timepiece proudly on her wrist.

"You're welcome," Miranda said, hugging her affectionately.

Garret hugged her next. "We're sure proud of you."

Miranda then gave Ashlyn a big hug, but she couldn't stop the tears from falling. "I'll miss you," she said.

"Good luck," Garrett said, taking his turn to hug her good-bye. "Be careful and let us know when you get there."

"We will," Ashlyn said, hugging her stepfather. "Take care of Mom for me," she whispered in his ear.

"She'll be fine," he whispered back. "Don't worry."

Ashlyn knew she could never have left her mother if Garrett weren't there. He had been such a great blessing in their lives. At one time Ashlyn didn't think she could ever come to think of him as anything more than her mother's husband. But he'd truly been the father she'd never had. He was funny, supportive, and wise. And he was always there for her when she needed him. She couldn't say any of those things about her own father.

And when Adam returned from his mission, Garrett and Miranda were planning a very special occasion, one they'd been waiting for, for a long time. They were going to be sealed together as a family.

As the two girls drove out of the cul-de-sac and out of sight, Ashlyn was thinking that her mother had acted as if this was the last time they'd ever see each other. But it was only for three months, for Pete's sake. Ashlyn would be home before they even had a chance to miss her.

⁂

They arrived in Seamist around midnight. Cami's grandfather waited up for them and met them in the driveway with outstretched arms and Ashlyn felt immediately welcome.

William Davenport was an old sea dog with a spritely spirit to match. His language was colorful, bordering on offensive, but the man was so sweet, with eyes of sparkling blue that he was easily forgiven. No taller than his granddaughter, William Davenport had spent many years in the navy before working as a merchant marine. He had retired early and spent the rest of his years working for a charter company, taking tourists out to sea whale watching or deep-sea fishing. He'd lost his wife the year before, and he missed her fiercely. Cami said she'd never seen such devotion between two people as she had between her grandfather and grandmother.

The next morning Ashlyn awoke just as the sun peaked over the horizon. Even though she was still tired, she was too excited to sleep. She hadn't been able to see much of the coast the night before, and there was a whole ocean outside her window waiting for her to discover.

From outside her window, she heard the lazy creak of cedar boughs as the breeze whispered through the pines. There was a damp chill in the air, but she bravely threw back the covers and grabbed for her robe. Cinching it about the waist, she strolled to the window to look out. She pulled in a long breath of air and the salty freshness tingled in her nostrils.

At the sight, her breath caught in her throat. The view from her second story window was spectacular. Down the hill from the house was the beach, a long, wide sliver of sand stretching and winding as far as she could see. Rocky outcroppings dotted the shoreline, hugged by grassy dunes. Beyond that lay the Pacific Ocean. The waves swelled and curled, breaking white along the shore, lapping at the sand, chasing the seagulls as they hunted for their morning meal.

The sea called to her. The serenity, the beauty, the magnificence, all beckoned to her soul. Donning gray sweats, T-shirt, fleecy pullover, and windbreaker, Ashlyn put on her Nikes and headed for the back door.

The house was quiet as she tiptoed down the stairs, past the grandfather clock which tick-tocked in rhythm with her footsteps. The house was neither large nor elegant, but it was open and airy and captured the feeling of the sea. The white wainscoting and walls were covered with pictures of family and loved ones, and of the sea. Brass instruments that looked like navigational devices were mounted on the wall, and a fisherman's net hung in the corner, strewn with shells and starfish. The fireplace mantle held several more beautiful seashells as well as a few twisted pieces of weathered driftwood and a jar of polished agates.

The navy blue and red plaid couch had a cozy afghan slung over its back, and two navy blue wingback chairs flanked the fireplace. At the end of the room a large sliding glass door presented a panoramic view of the sea.

Ashlyn carefully slid open the glass door and stepped out onto the wooden deck. The distant roar of the sea and the call of seagulls floated on the air. A dove-gray sky with pink-streaked clouds caught her eye. The fresh newness of her surroundings filled her with a sense of awakening and rebirth.

Crossing the lawn, she descended the wooden steps down toward the beach. Stickery gorse grew along the bluff, along with lacy fern and horsetail grass. At the bottom of the stairs she sidestepped rocks and driftwood and stepped onto the soft, cool sand.

As she walked, her feet left shallow prints behind her. Gulls swooped and cried overhead, and the hiss and roar of waves, swelling and breaking on the shore, pulled her closer to the water's edge, where the wet sand was firm and hard under her feet. In the distance, a low mist clung to the shoreline, cloaking the rock formations in its gauzy grasp.

Ashlyn felt free.

Stretching her arms wide, she took a long breath and twirled on the sand. Then she started walking but quickly found herself jogging along the water's edge, laughing when the waves playfully caught her feet. Her lungs burned and tingled, and her muscles stretched and pumped with each stride. After several hundreds yards she slowed her pace to a walk again. Looking away from the beach, she let her gaze travel across the majestic Coast Range, which rose abruptly to the east. The forested mountains guarded the small town of Seamist, where curving fingers of land created a natural protective barrier for the Misty Harbor Bay.

She continued walking until the shore wrapped around a rocky point that dropped back into the bay itself. And there across the bay, at the edge of the cape, was the beautiful Misty Harbor Lighthouse, standing like a jewel in the brightening sky.

Cami had told her that the lighthouse was no longer active, but it was still reassuring to have the stately structure there, like an ancient protector, a guardian, keeping watch over the sea. The Victorian Italiante architecture and mesmerizing red and white fresnel lens were striking, whether or not the lighthouse was still functioning.

Ashlyn walked as far as the harbor, then decided it was probably time to head back to the house. She didn't know how far she'd walked, or how long she'd been gone, and she didn't want to worry Cami or her grandfather.

The sun was in clear view as she neared the house on the bluff. Rays of light bathed the beach, sparking the ocean with silver and aqua, emerald green and deep blue. Ashlyn stopped and looked out at the ocean, seeing nothing in front of her but water. The view was so vast, so far-reaching, she felt as if she could see the very slope of the earth itself.

"It's so beautiful," she whispered. The morning breeze had kicked up, tugging at strands of hair that had strayed from her pony tail. Tucking her hair behind her ears, she turned and climbed the wooden stairs with an energy and vigor she hadn't felt for months.

Coming through the hedge of fragrant lilacs and rhododendron bushes bursting with scarlet and fuschia blossoms, Ashlyn stopped and lingered in the shade of a flowering pear tree. There was Cami's grandfather in cowboy boots and his "Mormon underwear," getting the morning paper.

Covering her mouth, Ashlyn giggled, remembering Cami's warning. "Grandpa's liable to do just about anything, so don't be too surprised if you see him walking around in his underwear."

Sure enough, there he was, for all the world to see, not caring whether he had an audience or not. Ashlyn gave him a few moments to get back inside the house and hopefully away from the living room so she could slip back to her room unnoticed.

The twittering of birds overhead and the noisy calls of the gulls, along with the rush of breaking waves, filled the fragrant air with nature's symphony. All of her senses drank in the beauty of her surroundings. She'd never felt so alive—especially in the last ten months.

Leaving her sand-covered shoes outside on the deck, Ashlyn stepped through the sliding glass door and found Cami curled on the couch, sipping a steaming mug of hot chocolate.

"Well, good morning," Cami chirped. "Where've you been? I thought you were still in your room asleep."

Ashlyn closed the door behind her. "I couldn't sleep, so I decided to take a walk on the beach."

"How was it?"

Ashlyn collapsed into one of the navy chairs. "It's perfect! I can't believe you grew up here. I mean, you actually get to live here. And I love the room you gave me. The view of the ocean, the window seat, everything, is perfect."

Cami smiled. "That was my grandmother's favorite room. I used to find her sitting in the window seat, relaxing against all those pillows, reading a book or just looking out over the ocean. She loved to watch storms come in from the sea."

Ashlyn could well imagine the magnificence of the sight. "It sounds perfectly wonderful."

"Do you realize you've said the word 'perfect' about three times since you came through that door?" Cami asked wryly.

"I have?" Ashlyn asked. "Well, that's because it is. I want to go into town today. I want you to show me everything."

"Okay, okay," Cami laughed. "Can we have breakfast and shower first?"

"Ahoy there!" Grandpa Willy called as he entered the room. Luckily he had dressed since Ashlyn saw him last. He wore an old captain's hat, a navy polo shirt, and khaki pants, with navy deck shoes. He looked ready for an outing on the ocean.

"Have you got a charter this morning, Mr. Davenport?" Ashlyn asked.

"Aye," he said. "But you can call me Willy, my dear."

Ashlyn had always been taught to call her elders by Mr. or Mrs., or Brother and Sister. She felt uncomfortable with anything else.

"How about calling him Grandpa Willy?" Cami offered.

"Suits me fine," he said. "How 'bout you?"

Ashlyn nodded. "I like that."

"Good. I'll leave you girls then, but I'll be back around fourteen hundred hours. Maybe we can drive over to Tillamook later and take Ashlyn to the cheese factory," he suggested.

When he bid them farewell and left, the room seemed empty.

"He's so full of energy," Ashlyn commented. "Apparently he's feeling better."

"Much better," Cami agreed. "I know this sounds weird, but I think he just needed me home. Grandpa hardly ever gets sick. I can honestly say I don't remember a day that Grandpa was too sick to go to the ocean, either to sail or just hang out at the harbor. Even on Sundays, he takes a walk along the beach. It's almost like an addiction and he has to have his fix every day. My grandmother used to accuse him of having a girlfriend, he had such a passion for the sea."

"I can see how it gets into your blood," Ashlyn said, relaxing back into the chair. "The ocean seems so mystical and magical."

"You want some hot chocolate? And some cinnamon toast?"

"Sure," Ashlyn said, covering her mouth as a yawn crept up on her. "I'd better get moving or I'll fall asleep."

"Let's have breakfast, then we'll go into town," Cami said. "There are tons of people I want to introduce you to."

Forcing herself to her feet, Ashlyn followed Cami into the kitchen, where they chatted happily as they ate breakfast and planned their day.

It felt great to be excited about life again, Ashlyn thought gratefully. She didn't know what the summer held for her, but she felt there was something almost nurturing here. Maybe this would be the place she could finally heal her wounded soul and get on with her life.

CHAPTER SEVEN

Downtown Seamist was as beautiful, quaint, and clean as Ashlyn had hoped it would be. It was surrounded by spruce forests and towering mountains on one side, and the beautiful Pacific Ocean on the other.

Small shops, galleries, and restaurants with outdoor dining areas lined the main street. It was a picturesque scene of small-town Americana. Cami knew a lot about the history of Seamist. The town had been established in 1882 with the coming of the railroad. Her great-great-grandfather, Ian Scott Davenport, had been sent to organize the town at Brigham Young's request, and he had started the first logging company in the area. In time his company grew to be the main supplier of wood to the entire Pacific Northwest. In those days Seamist had been a thriving community since it was a stop along the Oregon Pacific Railroad line. The town had a school, church, hotel, sawmill, several salmon canneries, a banking house, telegraph office, and the railway depot.

In 1918 a huge fire had destroyed the logging industry, and Seamist had practically become a ghost town. Now, with all the new growth the area was seeing, many of the buildings had been torn down and rebuilt, but the feeling of the original town remained. And though the town had started off as a Mormon community, Cami explained that only half of the population was currently LDS.

Further down the road, just off the main tourist area, stood a grocery store, a dry cleaner, and a hardware store, among various other establishments. Just like Cami had told her, Ashlyn was amazed with the great variety of services the town offered.

Their first stop was the grocery store. Grandpa Willy's cupboards were full of bachelor essentials: raman noodles, cereal, chips, La Choy. The girls wanted salads, fruits, and yogurt.

"Well, well. Look who's back in town," the store owner said when he saw Cami.

"Mr. Gardner!" She rushed over to him and threw her arms around his neck. "How are you?"

He laughed, his hug lifting her off the ground. "How's my Cami girl?" he asked.

"I'm just great," she told him with a smile. Ashlyn thought the man was probably in his late fifties. He had dark hair, a dark mustache, and brown eyes that crinkled into thin slits when he smiled. He wore a white apron and a feather duster stuck out of his back pocket.

"How long are you home for this time?"

"For good," she announced. "I just graduated from college and I'm back. At least, for now anyway."

"That's wonderful. You've been gone a long time. We're glad to have you back home. And who's this?" he asked, seeing Ashlyn standing in the background.

Ashlyn stepped forward and reached out her hand as Cami introduced her.

"I dare say, all the boys in town won't know how to act with your two pretty faces around. Your Grandpa Willy better dust off his shotgun. Here," he said, locating a box of fresh pineapples. "We just got these in. Straight from Hawaii. Take one home and let it ripen. It will be just right in a few days."

As the older man rang up their groceries, they spoke about the weather, glad that it was finally warming up after the wet, cold spell they'd been having.

"Any chance you'll be dropping by to say hello?" he asked as they picked up their bags. "I know Norma would love to see you around the house—and so would the rest of the family."

Cami gave the man a shy smile and shifted her bag so she could get the car keys out of her purse. "Maybe I will." Then, almost shyly, she asked, "How is Dallin doing?"

The man seemed pleased to have her ask. "He's back from Portland and is working here in town, but he's considering a job offer from New York. I'm sure he'd love to see you," he said encouragingly.

Ashlyn waited until they were out of earshot before she asked, "What was all that about and who is Dallin?"

"You remember," Cami said as she opened the trunk of the car and the two girls stowed their grocery bags inside. "I'm sure I told you about him. Dallin and I dated all the way through high school. When he left on his mission, he said he didn't feel comfortable asking me to wait for him, but he hoped I'd still be here when he got home."

Ashlyn vaguely remembered Cami talking about it, but she was foggy on the details. "So . . . ?" she said, wanting Cami to tell her more.

"So, after high school I worked for a year to save money for school, then I got a scholarship to SUU. My grandmother said the school was academically outstanding—she grew up in Cedar City— and the campus was small enough to get involved in the activities."

"And you were at school when Dallin got home, right?" Ashlyn said, remembering a little more of the story.

As Cami shut the door to the trunk and leaned against it, a group of young teens passed by on skateboards, laughing and having a fun time. The boys wore baggy clothes and baseball caps backward on their heads.

Cami continued. "When I came home for summer break, he'd already moved to Portland to go to school. We just never seemed to connect, you know? I figured if it was right, the Lord would at least help our paths cross once in a while. But it was more like everything that could come between us to keep us apart did," she said with a shrug.

"But you've seen him since he got home from his mission, haven't you?"

Cami shielded her eyes from the sun as it crept from behind the clouds. "Yeah, once."

"And how was it?"

"Oh, you know, awkward. He was with a date, a girl who'd been my best friend since high school. I always knew she had a thing for Dallin."

"That must've hurt."

"It did," Cami admitted. "But that was a year and a half ago. I'm surprised they didn't get married."

"Maybe the time wasn't right for you two before. But maybe—"

Cami raised her hand to stop Ashlyn from going on. "Ash, don't even start. I'd rather just forget about Dallin, so if you don't mind I'm ready to change the subject, okay?" She looked down the street as if she'd remembered something. "I need to run into the hardware store and pick up some nails for Grandpa. It will just take a minute."

"It had better. We've got ice cream in the trunk," Ashlyn reminded her.

Walking next door to the hardware store, Ashlyn half expected Sheriff Taylor, Barney Fife, and Aunt Bea to stroll past. The place looked like it had been preserved in a time capsule from the 1950s. There was even a soda fountain on one end of the store and tall, chrome bar stools with shiny red vinyl seats.

"Cami Davenport!" a voice called from somewhere overhead. "Is that really you?"

The next thing Ashlyn knew, Cami was being lifted off her feet in a big bear hug by a young man, close to her age. He wore black-framed glasses and had stick-straight brown hair. He was probably six foot three and all of one hundred and fifty pounds, but what he lacked in physical presence, he made up for in enthusiasm.

"Omigosh, George. I can't believe it!" Cami squealed. "I thought you'd moved to Eugene."

"I did, but after I got married we moved back to Seamist to help my dad with the hardware store. Mitch doesn't really have much time to spend here, and with my dad's heart the way it is . . . well, he just needed the help."

"How's Gina?" Cami asked.

"Doin' great. The baby's due in August. We're really excited." He glanced at Ashlyn curiously.

"Oh." Cami realized she hadn't introduced them. "George, this is my best friend, Ashlyn. Ashlyn, this is George Bradford. We went to school together. He was the school's star basketball player. We won the state championship our senior year, thanks to George."

Ashlyn smiled at him, struggling with the image of George in a basketball uniform, tearing up the court.

"Is Mitch around?" Cami asked.

"You know Mitch. He's coaching summer league baseball games and playing on a league team of his own. I think they have a game today. He'll be in later, though."

George helped Cami find the nails she needed while she filled him in on the recent events in her life.

"It's great to see you again," George said as he put the receipt for the nails in the brown paper bag.

"Maybe we can get together sometime. I'd love to see Gina again," Cami suggested.

"Sure," George agreed. "We can have a barbecue or something. I'll have her call you."

With a wave, Cami and Ashlyn left the store and strolled back to the car.

"So," Ashlyn asked her, "do you know everyone in Seamist?"

"Just about," Cami told her. "Or at least I know someone in their family."

Several boys burst out of the grocery store right then, tossing empty pop cans and chip bags into the garbage. Ashlyn saw that it was the same group of boys on skateboards that had passed them earlier.

One of the boys pointed to Cami and said, "I know you."

Cami turned and looked at the boy. "Spencer, is that you? I think you've grown six inches since I saw you last."

"Seven," he said proudly. "Whatcha doin' back in town?"

"I graduated from college and I just moved back home."

"Cool. Have you seen Dallin?"

"Not yet. We just got here last night," Cami explained. "And this is Ashlyn. She's my best friend from college. She's staying for the summer."

Spencer nodded and two of the boys giggled and elbowed each other. Ashlyn thought she heard one of them call her a "babe," but she wasn't sure. She gave the boys a warm smile just the same.

"Well, we gotta go," Cami said. "But we'll see you guys around, okay?"

"You want me to say 'hi' to Dallin for you?"

"Sure," Cami said with a smile. "You do that."

The boys took off, but one of Spencer's friends turned around to take one last look at Ashlyn. When his board hit a bump and he nearly ran into a telephone pole, he quickly focused his attention back on his skateboarding.

"Looks like you've got a fan," Cami said.

"Me? You're the one who has every person in town doing cartwheels now that you've moved home. This is quite a reception you've gotten," she commented wryly, thinking she'd never gotten that kind of reaction in her entire life.

"Hey, these people are like family to me. I've known some of them my entire life," Cami explained as they got inside the car, which had warmed up considerably under the noonday sun. "I know it's not like Salt Lake, but hey, it's home."

"Well, I love it already," Ashlyn said wistfully. "I can see why you missed it and why you came back."

Cami looked at her for several seconds. "I'm glad you do. I knew you would, and I think you're going to fit in just great here." She smiled encouragingly at her friend. "You'll see. By the time summer ends, you'll have a hard time leaving."

⊰⊱ 🕸 ⊰⊱

After a light lunch of turkey sandwiches on sourdough bread with cream cheese and cranberry jelly, Grandpa Willy, Ashlyn, and Cami got ready for their outing to Tillamook. The day had continued clear and sunny, and Ashlyn decided to change out of her jeans into a pair of khaki-colored shorts. In her bedroom she carefully hung her jeans on a hanger and tucked her tennis shoes into their spot at the bottom of the closet, changing them for a pair of comfortable sandals.

Like the rest of the house, Ashlyn's room was open and airy. The room had one big window and a wonderful skylight that allowed even more light inside. A chest of drawers was set against one wall, and next to it sat a small desk. On the other wall was a twin bed with a bright yellow comforter and a nightstand beside it. Her favorite thing about the room was the window seat, which was covered with several pillows of different shapes, colors, and sizes.

After she got dressed, she took a moment to look out the window, drinking in the incredible view of the deep blue sea and the white sandy beach. Far in the distance she could see the white triangle of a sailboat on the ocean. On the shore, two brightly colored kites danced and soared on the breeze.

"Ash," Cami's voice called. "You ready?"

"I'll be right there," Ashlyn replied, grabbing her bag off the desk and heading downstairs.

Outside of her room a small loft overlooked the living room below. Its walls were lined with shelves heavily laden with books. Two cozy overstuffed chairs and an end table with a lamp decorated the space invitingly. A white spindled banister ran around one side of the loft and across the front, keeping the space open like the rest of the house.

She hurried down the stairs to find Cami and her grandfather in the kitchen. He was on the phone and by the tone of his voice, Ashlyn could tell it wasn't a pleasant conversation.

"Now Pearl, don't get in a dither. What in Sam Hill do you want me to do about it?" He pushed his hat back on his head, scratched his forehead, then repositioned the hat. "I know. Someone's got to do something about those dogs, but you're barking up the wrong tree," he said.

He listened for a moment, then quickly said, "Sorry, poor choice of words." He was quiet, listening, then said, "Okay, okay. If I get a chance, I'll report it. No, they don't get into my garbage, but then again, maybe my garbage isn't as interesting as yours."

He listened again.

"Fine. Good-bye." He hung the phone up with a bang.

"What was that about, Grandpa?" Cami asked.

"Criminy. That woman would make any sane person drown themselves in the nearest squall. Dang dogs are gettin' in her garbage again and she's thinkin' I can do somethin' about it." He threw both hands in the air, then banged the kitchen counter. "What in tarnation I can do about it, I'll never know. She thinks that I need to complain to the city and that if we both get to gripin', we'll see some action."

"I'm sure we'll run into someone we can talk to about it, Grandpa," Cami tried to calm him. "Now, why don't we get going? I want to show Ashlyn the coast while the weather's clear."

Still grumbling, Grandpa Willy followed them out the door to the carport. A gentle breeze blew off the water, making the air tingle with a refreshing saltiness.

With Cami driving, they headed south down Highway 101 toward Tillamook. The view was spectacular and Ashlyn rode with her mouth hanging open most of the way. Right next to fern-filled forests with moss-covered trees was the magnificent Oregon coastline, rugged, rocky, and breathtakingly beautiful. Cami drove them through other small towns and fishing villages, through thickly wooded mountain passes, and alongside sprawling white sandy beaches full of beachcombers looking for seashells, agates, and drift-wood.

As they neared another small town, they drove past a high school and a baseball diamond, where swarms of people, both players and spectators, participated in an afternoon game of baseball.

"I wonder if Mitch is here?" Cami said, driving more slowly and craning her neck to get a better look.

"Do you see Mitch playing?" her grandfather asked at the same time.

Ashlyn wondered what was so wonderful about this "Mitch" they kept mentioning. What was he—Seamist's closest thing to Mark McGwire?

"Should we stop and see?" Cami asked her grandfather.

"Why not?" he said, straightening his sweat-stained, weather-beaten hat. "We've got time."

Pulling into the parking lot, Cami looked around. "I think I see his Mustang over there," she said. The three of them climbed out of the car and made their way past the batting box to some seats directly behind home plate.

Ashlyn watched the game for a moment, noticing that the players ranged from early twenties to mid-forties, maybe even fifties. One team's jersey read *Hank's Tires;* the other read *Bradford Hardware.* By the score she surmised Bradford Hardware was behind three runs.

"There's Mitch," Cami erupted excitedly. "Look, he's up to bat."

Grandpa Willy chuckled. "Just in time, too. It's the bottom of the ninth. Bases are loaded. Everything's ridin' on him."

"If anyone can do it, Mitch can," Cami said confidently.

Ashlyn couldn't see what was so great about this guy. Okay, so he looked good in a baseball uniform. He was tall, trim, and muscular. But she couldn't see much of his face from the side view of his batter's helmet.

"Steeeeeerike one!" the umpire bellowed as Mitch swung at a low, outside pitch.

"C'mon, Mitch," Grandpa Willy hollered. "You can do it."

"Steeeeeerike two!" the umpire yelled again.

After that two balls went by, but Mitch remained calm at the plate. He tapped the bat on the inside edges of his shoes and repositioned himself. The outfielders took several steps back.

The pitcher took his windup, then let the ball fly. Mitch swung and there was a loud crack as the ball shot off like a space shuttle to the moon. The crowd turned into a mass of screaming, frenzied fans. Mitch ran, hesitating only slightly at each base as the ball continued its flight, and then landed just outside the fence.

"Grand slam," Cami cheered. "Yeeeaaayyyyyyyyyy!"

Even Ashlyn couldn't help yelling and bouncing around on the metal stands. It was quite a sight seeing all those players run into home with Mitch tearing across home plate into the outstretched arms of his teammates.

"Woo-hoo," Cami yelled. "I knew he could do it."

Mass hysteria ensued as players and Bradford Hardware fans joined together on the field and celebrated their victory. Ashlyn watched as a tall, slender woman with long, glossy black hair, teased and curled into full, bouncy layers, made her way toward Bradford's star player. She wore a slim-fitting rayon skirt in bright swirls of fuchsia, orange, and yellow, with a tight, sleeveless v-necked sweater, in the same deep fuchsia pink. She was deeply tanned and very striking. Mitch turned when he saw her and lifted her off her feet, spinning her around. They spoke briefly while the woman straightened her skirt, smoothed her sweater, and fluffed her hair. Then she made her way off the field, which wasn't easy in her spike-heeled sandals though she managed to look graceful for the most part.

Cami and Grandpa Willy approached the athlete, who let out a whoop of joy when he saw Cami before he grabbed her and twirled her around. Cami laughed gleefully and "woo-hooed" again. With a tight squeeze, he put her back on the ground.

"When did you get back?" he asked.

"Last night," Cami told him. "That was a great game."

"Don't tell anyone, but I was a little scared there for a minute." It was then he removed the batting helmet.

Ashlyn could see that he was very nice-looking, in a rugged, outdoorsy, athletic sort of way. His hair was a sun-bleached golden blonde, though she thought he wore it a little too long, nearly to his shirt collar. But his eyes were as blue as the sea, and his smile was as warm and inviting as the sun.

"Willy, how are ya? It's been a while," Mitch said, shaking the older man's hand and slapping him on the back. "Thanks for coming."

"Woulda liked to seen more," the old man complained. "Just glad we got to see the best part."

Noticing they had a third member of their party, Mitch gave Ashlyn a friendly smile, and Cami quickly introduced them. "This is my best friend, Ashlyn, from Salt Lake City. She's going to live with us for the summer."

Half expecting him to pick her up and twirl her around, and half disappointed that he didn't, Ashlyn extended her hand and he shook it warmly. "Hi, Ashlyn," he smiled, revealing straight, white teeth.

Just then someone from the other team walked by.

"Great game, Mitch, but next time I'm shutting you down," the guy teasingly threatened.

"Hey, Hot Rod, I'd like to see you try," Mitch returned. "Maybe you should let your little sister pitch for you next time. She'd have a better chance."

Hot Rod laughed and waved good-naturedly. Ashlyn was just thinking that Mitch seemed a little full of himself when a teammate called out to him.

"Hey, Mitch. We're heading over to Mo's Diner. You coming?"

"Yeah," he yelled back. "I'll be right there."

"We'll let you go," Cami said. "We're on our way to Tillamook."

"Thanks for stopping by," he said. "Maybe we can get together in the next few days, and you can catch me up on what you've been doing with yourself."

"Drop by the house anytime," Grandpa Willy offered.

Ashlyn didn't realize she was staring as he jogged off the field, until Cami's voice jarred her thoughts. "Ash?" she said loudly. "Hello, Ashlyn."

"Oh," Ashlyn came back to reality. "Sorry."

"You ready to go?"

Ashlyn nodded and followed them back to the car.

She'd met his type before, at college. Guys from small towns who thought they were a big deal because they were sports heroes in high school. But when they got to the bigger cities, they suddenly became very small fish in a much bigger pond. That's why they never moved away. They loved the attention they got from all the townspeople and didn't have what it took to live in the "real world."

Sure he was attractive and he had a certain amount of charisma. But as egos and ambition went, Mitch was just a regular small-town hick.

CHAPTER EIGHT

After the trip to Tillamook to visit the cheese factory, they browsed through some shops then stopped at the Tillamook Naval Air Station Museum, where they saw vintage aircraft housed in a World War II blimp hangar. Afterwards, they headed home tired and hungry.

Hamburgers grilled to perfection on the barbecue, a tossed green salad, and potato salad from Gardner's in-store deli made a very satisfying evening meal, which they ate on the deck as they watched the sunset. Fluffy white clouds ballooned in the distance. The brilliant colors of the setting sun made it impossible to go inside until the last streak of fiery red and orange had faded to soft pink and yellow.

Cami, Grandpa Willy, and Ashlyn watched in silence until Ashlyn gave a contented sigh. "That was beautiful," she said softly.

"Nature does a mighty fine job with God's colors, doesn't she?" Grandpa Willy agreed.

Cami wrapped a crocheted afghan around her shoulders and pulled her knees up to her chest.

"Thank you for a wonderful day," Ashlyn told her hosts. "I really enjoyed myself."

"It was fun," Cami echoed. "I just wish we could've seen more of Mitch's ball game."

"Tell me about Mitch." Ashlyn had been wanting to ask the question all day. "You both seem to think a great deal of him."

"They don't come any better than Mitch Bradford," Grandpa Willy piped right up.

"That's for sure," Cami said. "We've been friends with the Bradfords our whole lives, haven't we, Grandpa?"

"Pert'n near," he said. "Mitch's great-grandfather, Joseph Bradford, and my grandfather were two of the original settlers here in Seamist. Joseph had a shipyard in the harbor and brought in all sorts of treasure from all over the world."

"So, is Mitch related to George from the hardware store?" Ashlyn asked, wanting to know more about him than just his pedigree chart.

"They're brothers," Cami said, chuckling at Ashlyn's surprised expression. "It's true. Hard to believe they're from the same gene pool, isn't it?"

"How old is Mitch?"

"Let's see, he graduated four years before me, so that makes him twenty-seven or eight," Cami told her.

"Is he married?" Ashlyn asked, remembering the tall, dark-haired beauty who had spoken to him after the game.

Cami and her grandfather looked at each other before Cami answered. "Actually, no. He was married, though."

Ashlyn raised her eyebrows. "Does that mean he's not married anymore?"

"His wife left him a year after they got married. They met in Portland when they were both going to school. She was actually from the East, Connecticut or something, but she had a scholarship to the Portland State University. They dated a few months and then got married. After they lived in Seamist for six months, she told Mitch she couldn't stand it anymore. Either he had to move with her back East so she could be near her family and live in a bigger city, or she would go alone. So he moved. I'm not sure what happened, but the next thing we knew he was home without her. He doesn't talk about it much. That was three years ago. It's taken him a while to get back to his old self, but he seems happy now."

Ashlyn wondered if he couldn't hack the big city and being away from his family and adoring fans. "Is he pretty serious with that dark-haired girl at the game today?" she asked.

Grandpa Willy snorted. "That woman's a piranha! What Mitch sees in her, I'll never know."

"She's very beautiful," Ashlyn stated.

"Vanessa James may be beautiful," Cami told her, "but she's . . . , well, she's . . ." Cami searched for the right words. "Let's just say I don't care for her much."

Ashlyn wanted to know more about Mitch's girlfriend. "What do you mean?" she asked.

"Vanessa and her father moved here about four years ago," Cami explained. "She's into real estate; her father's a wealthy land developer, plus he's on the city council. When he first got on the council, he helped make some really good changes in the community. He was behind improvements to clean up the main street of town, and plant trees and flowers to make the downtown area more appealing. He even started the 'Festival of Lights,' a Christmas lighting ceremony on Main Street that's become a tradition. But now, he's using his leverage and power to try and push development in the surrounding area. A lot of townspeople are against it. Most people here in Seamist don't want to see our town turned into a tourist trap like some of the other towns along the coast. We want to keep it small and quaint, you know, preserve what brought settlers here in the first place. But Vanessa and her father are determined to see growth and progress. They feel it is 'essential to the future of our city.'"

"But they can't," Ashlyn objected, sitting up. "It would ruin everything."

"That's how we feel, but they claim they have a much bigger 'vision' of Seamist than most of the townspeople," Cami said wryly.

Ashlyn sat back against her chair again. "I hope they don't change a thing, I love it just the way it is."

"Me too," Cami said.

Ashlyn had another question about Mitch and Vanessa. "So, how long have Mitch and Vanessa been dating?"

Cami shrugged and released a breath of air. "About a year and a half or so, I guess. They were in the Christmas choir and sang a duet together. It was incredible and I admit, at first the two seemed made for each other."

"At first?" Ashlyn asked.

"Yeah. I mean they looked good together and seemed to have a lot in common, and it was nice to see Mitch dating again after so long," Cami said.

"And now?" Ashlyn asked.

"I can't explain it. I'm not around Vanessa very much, but she seems to have her own agenda." Seeing Ashlyn's puzzled expression, Cami went on, "It's like she's wearing a mask," she said. "She's sweet and friendly to your face, especially when she's around Mitch, but when he's not around, she acts like you don't even exist." Cami glanced toward the ocean. "Oh, look, the fog's rolling in."

The sky had grown a chalky gray, and a dark mist was moving in toward the shore, like the fingers of a lost soul at sea, reaching for the safety of the beach and the haven of the harbor.

"That's amazing," Ashlyn said breathlessly. "It happened so quickly."

"That's why they named this place Seamist and called the bay Misty Harbor. Within thirty minutes, you can go from sunshine to pitch black fog," Grandpa Willy said. "The sea, oh, she's a fickle one. She draws you in, romances you with her playful waves and her deep mysterious moods, then she changes and crushes you to her breast, to keep you in the depth of her bowels, forever."

Ashlyn listened in fascination, captivated by Grandpa Willy's poetic words.

"Many a man has fallen in love with the sea. She gets in your blood and is there forever, but many a man has died at her hand, too. She's selfish when she wants to be. She'll give of herself, to be sure, but she'll also take what she wants."

Ashlyn shivered, thinking of that black mist, swirling about in a blinding shroud of darkness. "It would be awful to be a ship caught out in that fog. How do the ships find their way back?"

"Well, in the old days, we had the Misty Harbor Lighthouse, up on the point, guiding many a mariner back to safety. Yes, she was a beauty with her red and white light beaming across the water." Grandpa Willy's voice took on a faraway tone. "After a long voyage, she was a welcome sight, her light almost like a pair of open arms, welcoming us home."

Ashlyn tried to imagine being months out to sea, then the excitement and anticipation of coming back home to family and loved ones, seeing the first glimpses of that beautiful light on the hill.

"'Course, the light doesn't do much good in the fog. That's why they use fog horns. There's no prettier sound in the middle of a thick fog than the long, low moan of the fog horn, guiding the sailors to safety." He spoke quietly, almost reverently.

"Grandpa used to tell me that the gospel is like a lighthouse," Cami told her. "The light guides us and brings us to safety. But sometimes we're surrounded by wickedness and evils of the world, like a thick fog, and we can't see the light. But the Spirit is like a fog horn. We can hear its voice in the darkness, and it will guide us back to the harbor."

"That's beautiful," Ashlyn whispered.

Cami's grandfather began to speak. "'If I take the wings of morning, and dwell in the uttermost parts of the sea; Even there shall thy hand lead me, and thy right hand shall hold me. If I say, Surely the darkness shall cover me; even the night shall be light about me. Yea, the darkness hideth not from thee; but the night shineth as the day: the darkness and the light are both alike to thee.'"

Ashlyn thought it sounded like a scripture, but she had never heard it before. She wanted to ask where the passage was found in the scriptures, but Cami answered her question before she could ask it. "That's Psalms, chapter 139, verses nine through twelve."

"'If I take the wings of morning, and dwell in the uttermost parts of the sea . . .'" Ashlyn repeated. "I've never heard such a lovely phrase before." She hadn't realized that Grandpa Willy had such a spiritual side to him.

Just then the wind kicked up, and a wind chime on the porch swayed and tinkled musically through the chilly night air.

"I think it's about time I got this old carcass into bed," Grandpa Willy said, pushing his tired body out of the Adirondack chair. "I'll see you girls in the mornin'." He leaned over and kissed his granddaughter on the forehead.

"G'night, Grandpa," she said.

"Sleep well, Grandpa Willy," Ashlyn added, and to her surprise he leaned over and kissed her on the forehead as well.

She couldn't have felt more at home in Seamist, especially in the Davenports' home, than she did right at that moment.

⁂

The next morning the sea was frothy with tumbling waves. The sky was overcast and gray, but there was no rain. Last night's fog had retreated, but the stormy morning clouds hung low on the horizon.

Still, the sea called and Ashlyn quickly dressed for her morning jog. She glanced in the mirror as she pulled her long hair back into a scrunchy and groaned at her reflection. All the moisture in the air was bringing out her natural curl. When she was little, the kids at school had called her "mop head" and "Bozo the Clown." She hated her curls, but everyone else seemed to think she was lucky to have naturally wavy hair. But she felt like it was a curse. *I look like a Brillo pad*, she said to herself.

Wondering if she was going to have to fight her hair the whole time she was in Oregon, she smoothed it back as best she could, then pulled a Nike baseball cap over it.

She hurried down the wooden stairs to the beach, anxious to start her morning with a brisk run on the beach. She'd put on a few pounds over the past months and hoped that her morning outings would remedy this.

The rhythmic pounding of the surf, the fresh sea air, and the emptiness of the beach gave Ashlyn a surge of strength and energy. After walking several hundred feet, she broke into a labored jog, her body still clinging to its sedentary comfort zone of the past few months. But Ashlyn was determined to change that, and she couldn't think of a better place to do it.

So, putting mind over matter, one foot in front of the other, she pushed herself faster and farther. As she neared the harbor, the seclusion of the beach she'd been enjoying gave way to early morning beachcombers and strolling tourists. Stopping for a few deep breaths before turning back, Ashlyn watched foaming white waves crash against breakers at the harbor's edge, their spray fanning out like a graceful fountain.

She wanted to stay and enjoy the view more, but the wind was getting colder by the minute. She turned and retraced her steps on the sand toward home.

The stiff wind that had been at her back now worked against her, and she leaned into each step, her ears feeling the bite of chill in the air.

Snatches of sound, voices, carried with each gust, swirled around her, and at one point she thought she heard her name. With her head bent, and her hands in her pockets, she trudged toward home, anticipating the warm, soothing shower that awaited her.

"Ash . . . lynnn."

She stopped. That was her name. But who was calling her?

Turning around, she saw someone running to catch up to her. As the figure drew nearer, she recognized who it was. "Mitch," she called back, amazed that he'd actually recognized her and remembered her name.

"I thought that was you," he said, rubbing his arms for warmth. "A little cold for a walk, wouldn't you say?"

"Yeah, I didn't think it would be quite this rough out here. Guess I'm not a good judge of the weather yet."

"I've lived here all my life and I still get surprised occasionally. The rule of thumb around here is plan on rain and take advantage of it when the sun shines."

"I'll have to remember that," Ashlyn said as she shivered and crossed her arms over her chest.

"Well," he noticed her trying to stay warm. "I just wanted to say hi. Good to see you again."

"You, too," she said, deciding that it was pretty nice of him to make the effort to tell her hello.

He tilted his head and studied her face for a moment. She knew she looked like a scarecrow with frizzy strands of hair poking out all over underneath her hat. The funny thing was, Mitch's hair was touseled and windblown, too, but somehow that only made him look more rugged and outdoorsy.

"Do you come jogging on the beach often?" he asked.

"Every morning," she said. "Well, for the past two mornings since I got here."

He laughed. "Maybe I'll see you again. I try to get out two or three mornings a week."

She nodded and walked away. Even though she didn't glance behind her, she still felt his eyes on her back. She broke into a jog, hurrying down the beach in hopes of escaping his gaze. Still distracted by her thoughts of meeting him out of the blue like that, she ran straight past the steps leading up to the Davenports' beach house.

As the terrain grew rockier and she had to sidestep several large weather-beaten logs, she realized she was in unfamiliar territory. Studying the coastline to the south, she wondered what was beyond the rocky outcropping ahead of her. During what was called a minus tide, Cami had said it was possible to make it around the jagged point ahead of her, but on a stormy day like today, such an attempt might prove dangerous. Some other time she would come back and explore this new area of the beach.

With the fierce wind picking up speed, she hurried back toward the sheltered cove below the beach house, then noticed a different set of steps leading to the bluff.

Thinking they might also lead to Cami's house, she climbed the wooden stairs and found herself in a thickly wooded area. A trail through the trees seemingly led the way to the Davenports' and Ashlyn eagerly followed it, anxious to get out of the wind and the cold. She was positive the heavy clouds were ready to let loose any minute.

Within the thick pines, she had some protection from the driving gusts. Thinking she was just about there, she began running down the trail until she burst out into an open area and found herself in front of an old and shabby, but still gorgeous, Victorian mansion.

"Whoa! Look at that." She stood, in awe of the sheer size of the building, saddened by its dilapidated condition. Boards were nailed across the windows, paint peeled from the eaves and wood siding, and bare patches shown on the roof where shingles had blown away. Still, the turreted home, with widow's walk and latticework trim, was a magnificent sight to behold.

"Who are you?" A cackling voice suddenly yelled at her. "Get away from here!"

Ashlyn jumped at the sound of the voice. She didn't sit around waiting to see if some spooky apparition would appear. Tearing off through the trees, she sprinted for home, leaving the house and the voice behind her.

※　※

"What in the world?" Cami turned around, startled, when Ashlyn burst through the door.

"That house . . . on the hill . . . a voice . . ." Ashlyn gasped for air, grateful to be inside where it was safe and warm.

Grandpa Willy came in from the other room to see what was going on.

"I think she found the Davenport Mansion," Cami told him.

Nodding in understanding, Grandpa Willy said, "What's this about a voice?"

"Someone, a woman, yelled at me. Told me to get out of there." Ashlyn had calmed down so she could speak now. But her knees still trembled, from the cold or from pure adrenaline racing through her veins, she wasn't sure which.

Cami and her grandfather smiled at each other.

"I'm telling you the truth!" Ashlyn said determinedly. "I distinctly heard a voice."

Neither Cami nor her grandfather said anything.

"Well?" Ashlyn demanded. "Who was it? And don't tell me it was a ghost. I don't believe in ghosts."

"Wish it were a ghost," Grandpa Willy said. "'Twould be a sight more pleasant than that old cranky pants, Pearl."

"The lady who complained about the dogs in her garbage?"

Cami rolled her eyes. "That's the one. She's an old spinster lady who lives behind the mansion. She's about as crotchety as an old bear and growls twice as loud."

"But that house . . . you said it's the Davenport Mansion. Why is she there?" Ashlyn asked.

"Who knows?" Grandpa Willy grunted. "Crazy old witch probably feels at home there."

"What about the mansion? Why is it falling apart? It's beautiful." Ashlyn finally sat down and removed her shoes, realizing she had tracked in half of the beach when she came in. "I'll sweep that up," she told Cami.

"No big deal," Cami told her. "I was sweeping the kitchen anyway."

Ashlyn waited for someone to tell her about the mansion. "Well," she finally asked again.

"Oh, the mansion." Cami leaned the broom against the door jamb, happy to give the history of the mansion. "My great-great-grandfather, Ian Scott, built the house for my great-great-grand-mother, Olivia Easton. They lived there for a number of years until about 1918. That was before the logging industry in the area was wiped out by a huge forest fire. Acres of trees burned, the saw mill burned—it took out the whole business. They tried to recover their losses but couldn't. When my great-great grandfather was forced to leave Seamist to find work further up the coast near Astoria, it broke my grandmother's heart to leave the mansion. They never sold the house, hoping someday to return, but they never did."

"Durned thing is falling apart," Grandpa Willy said. "'Twould take a fortune to do all the fixin' and repairs. I've thought about selling the place, but I just can't seem to make myself do it."

"That's so sad," Ashlyn said. "It's such a beautiful house. I'll bet from the second story you can get quite a view of the ocean."

"Nearly twenty miles each direction," Grandpa Willy said.

Ashlyn had a hard time believing that they could just let that house fall apart like that. There had to be something there worth salvaging.

⁂

Wrapping her hair in a towel, turban style, Ashlyn dressed in jeans and a soft cable-knit sweater of soft creamy white. A rain had begun to fall while she was in the shower, and it had now turned into a torrential downpour.

A tap came on her bedroom door.

"Come in," Ashlyn said as she sat on the edge of her bed to pull on a pair of socks.

Cami opened the door. "You about ready for some breakfast?"

"Mmm, yes. I'm starving." She took the towel off her head and used it to squeeze extra water out of her hair. "If we get some time, I need to run to the store and get some different conditioner. My hair is going nuts here. It's going to be hard to keep it straight with all this moisture in the air."

"Why don't you just wear it curly? I love it that way."

Ashlyn pulled a face. "Oooh, no. I look better with straight hair."

Cami's eyebrows narrowed. "Who told you that? You always used to wear your hair curly in college and it looked great. It really made your eyes stand out."

Ashlyn sidestepped the question. "No one, really. I just like it better straight."

"Well, I think you look better with it curly. It's so soft and feminine that way."

Ashlyn rolled her eyes. "Yeah, right."

"Well, it is." Cami walked around the room and stopped to look at the various pictures and trinkets arranged on top of the dresser. She picked up several pictures of Ashlyn and Jake and looked at them closely. In every picture of Ashlyn with Jake, her hair was straight.

"You know," Cami said. "Now that I think of it, you didn't start wearing your hair straight until you started dating Jake. I'll bet he told you he liked your hair better straight, didn't he?"

Letting out a frustrated huff, Ashlyn dropped the towel on the floor and went to the closet for her shoes.

But Cami wasn't going to let her drop the question. "Ash? What did he say, then?"

"Oh, all right," she said, shoving one foot into her loafer. "He said he didn't like my hair curly. He said I looked better with it straightened."

"And you believed him?"

Putting on her other shoe, Ashlyn said, "I guess so. Why shouldn't I?"

Cami thought for a moment, then said, "Tell me something, Ash. How do *you* like your hair?"

"What do you mean?"

"It's a simple question. How do you like your hair?" she repeated.

Plopping herself down on her bed, Ashlyn realized she might as well cooperate. Cami wasn't about to let her drop the subject.

"Honestly?"

Cami nodded.

"Growing up, I hated my hair. Kids used to say all sorts of mean things about it. Then in high school, perms and stuff were kind of in style, and I felt really lucky that my hair was naturally curly. All these girls were frying their hair with perms and wishing it could be like mine, and for once I realized that having naturally curly hair was okay. I even liked it, because if I ever wanted it straight, I could just blow it that way. It was like having the best of both worlds."

Cami listened with interest, which was one of the many things Ashlyn liked about her. Cami was a great listener.

"I guess I was finally comfortable with my hair after all those years. Then I started dating Jake, and one day we were going to this formal dinner with his family. I blew my hair straight and fixed it kind of elegantly, you know? And he went nuts over it. I mean, he couldn't quit telling me how beautiful I looked with my hair that way, and after that I always straightened it for him."

"Well, I think it looks great either way," Cami declared, "but I'm telling you, and I'm being totally honest, I love it when you wear it curly."

Ashlyn smiled at her friend. "Thanks," she said.

"Can I ask you something else?" Cami still held one of the pictures of Ashlyn and Jake as she sat next to Ashlyn on the bed. "Are you still in love with Jake?"

Ashlyn looked offended. "Of course not. Why would you think that?"

"Oh, it could be that you have a shrine to him in your room back home and a mini-shrine to him in your room here."

"I do not!"

"You do too. All your wedding stuff is on display in your room, like some Jake Gerrard 'Graceland' or something."

"That's rude," Ashlyn objected. She knew Cami was half kidding, but the half that was serious hurt.

"I'm sorry, but it's true," Cami said firmly, her tone not at all apologetic. "Then, after you met him, you weren't the same anymore."

Ashlyn's chin jutted out. "What do you mean?"

"When we first met, you used to wear bright, colorful clothes. You look so pretty in deep pink and blues and purple. I love you in purple. But all you wear anymore are khaki, cream, and navy blue."

Ashlyn looked at her, her expression showing the annoyance she was feeling. "And your point is . . . ?"

"I just wondered if Jake told you that he liked you in those colors, and that's why you wear them all the time now."

"Good grief, Cami!" Ashlyn jumped to her feet. "You make it sound like he completely brainwashed me and turned me into some sort of robot."

"I know, I'm sorry. It's just that he did change you in a lot of ways. You were so fun and awesome in college, but he seemed to knock the fun out of you. It's like you're too aware of everything now. Before he came along, you used to do what you wanted to do; you had confidence in yourself. It's like he made you doubt yourself and what *you* want, like you've forgotten what Ashlyn wants."

Ashlyn didn't say anything, and Cami went on.

"I guess I always thought when I met someone and fell in love, I would still be me, only a better me. That he would bring out the best in me. Not change me into someone else."

Ashlyn swallowed hard. "Do you think that's what Jake did? Turned me into someone else?"

Cami hesitated answering, but finally said, "Yes."

Ashlyn was silent as she pondered her friend's words.

"You are my best friend," Cami said earnestly, "and I love you like a sister. So if we can't be honest with each other, then what do we have? I think you are so much better off without him, Ash. I think that you should be grateful you aren't married to him. In fact, I think the Lord was really looking out for you when Jake didn't go through with your marriage."

"What?" Ashlyn couldn't believe Cami was saying this. When Jake walked out on her, part of her died. She never, ever wanted to have that kind of pain again in her life. Ever!

"I think you should be grateful it didn't work out," Cami said again, for emphasis. "I don't think Jake was the right guy for you."

Ashlyn pulled in several deep breaths, aware of the wind and rain as it slapped against the windows, the turbulence of the storm deepening. A low rumble thundered in the distance.

"Why did you wait until now to say anything?" she asked at last.

Cami replaced the picture beside the others, then turned and looked her friend directly in the eye. "Because that's what friends do. I knew your mind was made up so all I could do was support you and help you make the best of the situation. And pray. I prayed a lot for you."

"You did?"

"Yes, Ash, I did. Because more than anything I wanted you to be happy. And that's what I still want for you. I don't think Jake would have made you happy. I think you would have spent your life trying to make *him* happy."

Ashlyn let Cami's words sink in. Jake had been rather opinionated and stubborn when it came to his wants. But she'd always thought they would work things out, find ways to compromise, to meet each other halfway.

"Maybe you're right. I don't know," Ashlyn said. "All I do know is that the hardest thing I've ever had to do in my life is put myself back together and move on. I feel like Humpty Dumpty, but I don't have any king's horses or king's men to help me put myself back together again."

"I'll help you," Cami said, with a reassuring smile.

Ashlyn felt a sting of moisture in her eyes that threatened to turn into real tears. "I know," she nodded. "And I thank God for you every day of my life."

They shared a quick but heartfelt hug, then Cami said brightly, "So, you want me to help you chuck all those pictures of Jake into the ocean?"

Ashlyn laughed. "Maybe not today, but someday."

Cami smiled proudly at her friend. "Okay. That's good enough for me. Let's do some shopping and go to lunch. You haven't had any of Oregon coast's clam chowder yet."

"I don't really like clam chowder," Ashlyn told her.

"You will after we eat at Mo's. C'mon."

�== 🕸 ==⋅

"So this is Cannon Beach." Ashlyn craned her neck to see down the coast further. "It's a lot like Seamist, isn't it?"

Cami nodded and downshifted so they could turn off the main road.

"Oh, look at that big rock!" Ashlyn exclaimed. "That's incredible."

"That's Haystack Rock," Cami told her. "It's part of the reason I brought you here. I wanted you to see it ."

They parked the car and walked to the beach so Ashlyn could get a picture of the famous natural attraction, a rock monolith that towered 235 feet into the sky. Its massive size was breathtaking, and now that the clouds from the morning's storm were finally gone, the sun shone brightly on its moss-covered sides, where flocks of seagulls and herons sunned themselves and hunted for their lunch.

"What's that over there?" Ashlyn pointed to something just off the coastline northward.

"Oh, that's Tillie."

"Tillie?"

"It's officially known as the Tillamook Rock Lighthouse. It's the only lighthouse on the coast that is offshore." The two girls walked up the beach to get a closer look at the lonely lighthouse sitting a mile off shore.

"Do you think it would be possible to visit all the lighthouses along the coast before I go home?" Ashlyn asked Cami hopefully. "I'd really like that. I'm even thinking I'd like to start a collection of lighthouses."

Cami looked thoughtful. "There aren't that many, maybe eight or nine. Sure, we could probably do it. But you know what? I'm absolutely starved. That piece of toast I had for breakfast is pretty much gone. How about you?"

"I'm so hungry I'll even eat clam chowder," Ashlyn declared. "Just give me lots of crackers to go with it."

Ashlyn started with a small cup of chowder and loved it so much she followed that with a bowlful and loved every creamy bite. Cami had crab cakes that were, she said, "out of this world." And to make the meal even more enjoyable, they had an incredible view from Mo's picture window that allowed them to see the entire Cannon Beach shoreline.

After lunch they browsed through shops and galleries, admiring various local art work and enjoying the feel of the charming small town. Ashlyn bought some salt water taffy from a candy store to send back to her family in Utah and to her brother in Portugal.

As they walked past a boutique, Cami admired a brightly colored dress of soft, gauzy fabric that hung in flowing folds. "That's cute, don't you think?"

Ashlyn looked at the dress in the boutique window and immediately fell in love with it. "Wouldn't it be perfect for a Carribean Island vacation? Or a cruise to the Bahamas?"

"Let's go in and take a look at it," Cami suggested.

Ashlyn shook her head. "I'd better not. I'm sure it costs an arm and a leg, and since I don't have a job, I'm on a tight budget. Besides, I'm not going anywhere I could even wear a dress like that."

"Just a peek," Cami tempted. "Please."

"Oh, all right," Ashlyn relented, deciding she wouldn't let Cami talk her into any unwise purchases. She didn't want to have to call home for money.

The shop owner greeted them but allowed them to browse through the store on their own. Ashlyn liked the style of clothes the shop carried. Everything was lightweight and comfortable, soft and colorful, mostly imports from India.

While Cami found a skirt and peasant shirt to try on and a gorgeous linen pantsuit that was a pale, mossy green, Ashlyn debated whether or not to try on the dress hanging in the window. She'd been hoping it would be outrageously expensive so buying it would be completely out of the question. But the price was fairly reasonable, so she couldn't use that as an excuse.

"Just try it on," Cami whispered. "You don't have to buy it."

In the dressing room, Ashlyn slid into the cool, cotton fabric and adjusted the neckline and the bodice. The blouse had cute cap sleeves, a snug-fitting bodice that buttoned down the front, and a skirt that flared and billowed with yards of gauzy layers nearly to her ankles. The fuchsia, orange, khaki, and purple colors of the material added color to her cheeks and brought out the warm green of her eyes. She couldn't help twirling a little to see how the skirt billowed with movement. The dress made her feel feminine and flirty. She had to admit, she loved it.

"Are you dressed yet?" Cami tapped on her door. "I want to see. Don't you dare take it off until I —"

Ashlyn walked out of the dressing room right at that moment.

"Ohhhh," Cami said breathlessly. "That is so pretty on you." She walked around Ashlyn to look at her from all sides. "It fits you perfectly, too. How do you like it?" she asked hopefully.

Ashlyn looked at her with mock anger. "I knew I shouldn't have let you talk me into trying it on."

A smile crept onto Cami's face. "Does that mean . . ."

"I'll probably never wear it. But I love it, so I'm going to get it."

Cami clapped her hands with joy like a toddler. "You'll be glad you bought it, I'm sure of it."

Ashlyn in turn admired Cami's skirt and shirt. The skirt was colorful, too, in blues and greens, and the aqua-colored shirt nearly matched the color of Cami's eyes.

"You have to get that outfit, too," Ashlyn said. "It looks like it was made for you."

"I know," Cami agreed. "It's too cute, isn't it?"

The bell on the front door jingled and the next thing Ashlyn knew, a woman was calling Cami's name and running over to give her a hug. Ashlyn noticed that the woman was tall and stately, and very classy. Her perfume floated in with her, but wasn't overpowering.

"Ashlyn," Cami said, grabbing the woman's arm and pulling her close. "This is Catherine Bradford, Mitch and George's mom. Catherine, this is my best friend, Ashlyn, from Salt Lake City."

Mrs. Bradford stretched out her beautifully manicured hand and took Ashlyn's hand in her own. "It's so lovely to meet you, Ashlyn," she said with a smile that was exactly like Mitch's. Ashlyn could see immediately where he got his good looks; his facial structure, beautiful teeth, and deep blue eyes were just like his mother's. Ashlyn wondered if her husband looked more like George.

Cami filled Mrs. Bradford in on what was happening in her life, and Mrs. Bradford told her that she was still teaching piano and voice lessons out of her home. Ashlyn was thoroughly impressed with the woman. She was polished and elegant, yet warm and friendly.

"Well." She glanced at her watch. "I'm on my way to meet Vanessa for lunch. I just came by to pick up a dress I'd ordered." She noticed the two girls in their outfits. "You both look absolutely darling in those clothes, by the way." Looking at Ashlyn, she added, "That color is gorgeous on you. In fact, these dresses are perfect for the Fourth of July dinner and dance that Mitch is in charge of. You are coming, aren't you?"

"We'll be there," Cami answered excitedly.

"Good," Mrs. Bradford smiled. "I'd better be off, then. I don't want to keep Vanessa waiting." She pressed her cheek against Cami's. "It's good to see you, dear. Tell your grandfather hello for me. I'll have you over for dinner sometime soon so we can talk more. I'd like to get to know you better too, Ashlyn. And you can meet the rest of my family," she said proudly.

Ashlyn didn't mention she'd already met them. And even though she told herself she didn't care if she ever saw Mitch again, she knew she was kidding herself. She was definitely intrigued by him. But he appeared to have a serious relationship with someone else already, and Ashlyn couldn't imagine herself being ready for another serious relationship for a very, very long time.

CHAPTER NINE

That afternoon Ashlyn decided to call home. "Hi, Mom, it's me," she said when she heard her mother's voice on the line.

"Ash, sweetie, hi," her mother replied enthusiastically. "What a nice surprise."

"How are you? What's going on?" she asked, hoping they weren't having fun at home without her.

Her mother told her everything that was happening around their house, then described Adam's most recent letter and the astounding success he and his companion were having in a city that had been closed to missionaries for many years.

Ashlyn was happy to hear her brother was having such a great experience. In the early months of his mission he'd really had some rough time, but he'd hung in there and now seemed to be reaping the blessings of his efforts.

Her mother said they'd been doing some remodeling around the house. She and Garrett were painting some of the rooms and also getting new furniture in the living room. Ashlyn had wanted to fix up their house for years, but they'd never had the money to do it.

When her mother asked how she was, Ashlyn told her how nice everyone was and how beautiful Seamist was. She told about her walks on the beach and her decision to collect lighthouses. As she spoke, Ashlyn felt something strange in her mother's silence.

"Are you okay, Mom?" she asked.

"I've just had a hard time with you gone," Miranda admitted. "I know it's silly. I was fine when you transferred to SUU. I guess I'm just trying get used to the idea that you're grown up and on your own."

"I'll be back at the end of summer," Ashlyn reassured her, "and as busy as you are, it's going to go really fast. You'll see."

As she hung up the phone, Ashlyn swallowed hard, feeling guilty for leaving her mother to come to Seamist. *Mom is going to be fine,* she told herself firmly, then went to find Cami, who was out on the deck grilling marinated chicken breasts for dinner.

That evening the two girls went for a hike in the woods near their house. Ashlyn wanted to go by the old mansion again so she could see it under better circumstances than she had previously, with a storm beating down on her back and a crazed woman threatening her.

"There it is," Ashlyn said excitedly when she saw the turreted towers peeking over the tops of the trees. "It's so elegant and mysterious."

"Mysterious my eye," Cami remarked. "The place gives me the creeps. When I was little I was convinced the place was haunted. My grandfather always told me that the sounds I heard were the sea winds blowing through the attic, but I never believed him."

As before, Ashlyn marveled at its detailed craftsmanship and the charming latticework and scrolled gables. "What's it like inside?" she asked.

"I have no idea," Cami retorted dryly. "It's not like I've ever dared to go inside."

"It's still light enough to see inside. Let's just peek through the boards," Ashlyn coaxed. "C'mon."

"Okay, just a peek, then we're out of here," Cami agreed.

The two crept up the creaking, wooden stairs and stood on the porch. Ashlyn turned around, catching a glimpse of the ocean through the overgrown trees. She was certain that at one time, when the house was younger and inhabited, the trees had been pruned regularly and trimmed down so the ocean was still visible from where they stood.

"Will you just hurry up and take a look? I don't like it here," Cami fretted. She stood so close to Ashlyn, her breath on Ashlyn's neck made her shiver.

Pushing her friend away, Ashlyn said, "Will you stop it? I'm the one who heard a scary voice, and I'm not afraid to be here."

"Well, then, Miss Braveheart, why don't you lead the way?"

Ashlyn tiptoed to the front door, but she couldn't see through the slats in the boards. The two-by-fours nailed across the front window had some gaps in them, so she attempted to peek inside that way. But there wasn't enough room to see anything.

"Hey, this board is kind of loose. Let's pull it off. We can nail it back up later," Ashlyn suggested.

"I don't think so," Cami said, taking a step back and bumping into the railing that framed the wraparound porch.

Shaking her head at her friend's paranoia, Ashlyn reached up, grabbed hold of the board, and tugged. With a screeching groan, it moved about an inch but no more. She wiggled and tugged until the board came flying loose, nearly clobbering Cami on the side of the head.

"Sorry," Ashlyn apologized, letting the board drop to the porch floor.

"Be careful, will you?" Cami scolded her lightly. "I don't need a nail through my skull."

Ashlyn peered inside the house where small slivers of light cut through the darkness. She could make out doorways and stairways, but nothing clearly. "It looks so beautiful inside. Can't we go in? Please?"

"Are you crazy?" Cami looked alarmed and shivered at the thought of all the cobwebs and shadows inside the spooky house. "I wouldn't go in there for a million dollars."

"Please?" Ashlyn begged, sticking out her lower lip and pretending to pout.

"Oh, all right. You can stop with the lip," Cami said, rolling her eyes in defeat. "We'll ask Grandpa for the key later."

Ashlyn smiled triumphantly and took another look, wishing she could explore the interior of the house now. She'd always been fascinated with antiques and old pictures, and she wondered if any old memorabilia or belongings had been left behind. She couldn't understand how Cami could ignore this fascinating, mysterious mansion, especially when it belonged to her family.

"Can we ask when we get back?" Ashlyn begged.

"Okay," Cami relented. "Can we go now?"

"If we can come back in the morning," Ashlyn insisted.

"Do you have any idea how annoying you are when you make up your mind about something?" Cami teased.

"No," Ashlyn said innocently. "Tell me."

Walking around the house so Ashlyn could see what it looked like in the back, the girls saw that rose bushes grew all the way around, struggling to survive and bloom. The girls had just turned another corner when—

A woman jumped out in front of them and yelled, "WHAT ARE YOU DOING HERE?"

Ashlyn and Cami screamed at the top of their lungs, grabbing each other and holding on tightly.

Cami stammered and sputtered but couldn't speak. Ashlyn finally forced herself to look at the woman standing before them. She wore a bright red muumuu and hot pink thongs with plastic daisies on them. Her hair flew out in disarray from her head, and Ashlyn thought she had a crazed look about her. But when she looked closer, Ashlyn realized that the woman didn't seem threatening at all. She loosened her death grip on Cami, who relaxed a bit herself, seeing that they appeared to be in no mortal danger.

To Ashlyn's surprise, Cami addressed the woman by name. "Is that you, Pearl?"

The woman's eyes opened wide with surprise. "Who are you?" she asked suspiciously.

"I'm Cami Davenport. William Davenport's granddaughter."

"Little Cami?" The woman's face softened. "You used to bring me tomatoes from your grandmother's garden. I haven't seen you for years. What have you been doing with yourself?"

Cami told her briefly what she'd been doing and introduced Ashlyn, who shook the woman's hand warily.

"How would you girls like to come up to my place and have some dessert," Pearl invited. "I just made some blueberry tarts."

Cami raised an interested eyebrow. Casting a quick glance at Ashlyn, she said, "We'd love to."

Ashlyn sent her a look of concern, but Cami ignored her. Before she knew it, Ashlyn found herself following the old woman and Cami up a trail through the trees. Somehow she couldn't help feeling a little like Hansel and Gretel being led inside the witch's gingerbread house to have goodies so they'd grow fat and plump.

To her surprise, Ashlyn actually like the woman's cottage. The yard was meticulously cared for, with a wide variety of perennials growing and blooming in all parts of the yard. Every color of rhododendron available was also in bloom. Pearl's yard was a veritable palette of color.

Inside, the cottage was filled to the brim with knickknacks and souvenirs that appeared to have come from all over the world. There were Japanese screens, Persian rugs, a German grandfather clock, Belgian lace, and African carvings, to name only a few. At first glance, the place seemed cluttered and messy, but as Ashlyn studied the wonderful pieces of art and sculpture and the paintings and carvings, she realized that the woman's home was a museum of world travel.

"Have a seat and I'll be right back," Pearl offered, fussing over the pillows on the couch so the girls would be more comfortable.

When she had left them, Ashlyn leaned over to Cami and whispered, "Are you sure we should be here?"

"She's lonely," Cami said, "and I remember she used to make the most wonderful blueberry tarts."

Pearl was back in a flash, carrying a tray with napkins and plates and an assortment of tarts. "I'll let you get started on these, then I'll get us something to drink." She put the tray on a glass coffee table held up by two beautifully carved elephants standing back to back, then returned to the kitchen.

Ashlyn was eyeing the tarts warily, uncertain they were safe, when Pearl bustled in with another tray which held three frosty glasses of raspberry lemonade.

"This looks wonderful," Cami complimented her.

The woman beamed happily. "Please, go ahead and eat. It's so lovely having company."

Calming a little as she sipped the delicious drink, Ashlyn again admired the strange and exotic pieces of artwork in the room and was amazed at the assortment of countries represented by the woman's collection. Had Pearl collected all this stuff herself?

Pearl sat down in a zebra-striped chair across from them. "You'll have to forgive my behavior. I am just so tired of kids coming around and trying to break into the mansion. I've caught them with rocks and spray paint, and even baseball bats, smashing the windows. I didn't mean to frighten you. You must think I'm off my rocker to go around screaming like that."

"I don't think Grandpa or I realized that the house is such a target," Cami said. "I think we owe you a great deal for protecting it from vandalism all these years."

"Oh, no," Pearl protested. "You don't need to thank me. I love that house. I couldn't stand to see it ruined any more than it is."

Ashlyn took a bite of the tart's delicate, buttery crust and delicious, fruity filling. "These tarts are delicious," she complimented Pearl. "May I ask you something?"

"Of course," the older woman sat up, giving Ashlyn her full attention.

"Where in the world did you get all this stuff?"

Pearl laughed heartily. "That's exactly where I got it," she said, still chuckling. "From all over the world."

"You mean you've been to all of these places?"

The woman nodded. "Yup. I've been to every continent, even Antarctica, but there wasn't much to bring back from there," she chuckled again. "I've traveled by air, by boat, by camel, by canoe, and by yak. You name it, and I've probably eaten it, from the most disgusting, to the most elegant. I've dined with the Queen Mother and licked ants from a reed."

Ashlyn listened wide-eyed, imagining some of the amazing adventures this woman must have had in her lifetime.

"I've come close to death so many times we're on a first-name basis." She relaxed into her chair. "But of course, that's all behind me now. That was all when I was young, not much older than either of you, I suppose."

"How . . . when . . . ?" Ashlyn started to ask, but she was so overwhelmed by the woman's claims that all of her questions collided in her mind, so that nothing sensible came out of her mouth.

Pearl smiled at her. "You see," she explained, "I was just twenty-one when I met the love of my life. He was seven years older than I, but still we had eyes only for each other. Frederick was everything to me. He was a gentleman and an adventurer. He was also deeply romantic, and undeniably the most gorgeous man this side of the Mississippi and probably even the other side, too." She closed her eyes, reminiscing happily. "Oh, we had some wonderful, wonderful times."

She sighed heavily and looked at the girls. "But Frederick had a terrible habit which I tried desperately to help him overcome. He was a gambler. Every time he went away, he would promise that this would be the last time. He would win enough to come back and build me our dream home, then we would get married and he would settle down."

Ashlyn and Cami sat breathless, waiting for the rest of the story.

"The last time I saw him, he took my face in his hands and kissed me. He said, 'When I come home to you, it will be for good. Find yourself the most lovely wedding dress, and we will be married when I return.'"

"What happened?" Cami asked.

"That was the last time I saw him. He was shot during a card game, accused of cheating." Pearl's voice was barely a whisper. She looked away, but Ashlyn saw the sheen of tears in her eyes. "I didn't even go to his funeral. I didn't want to remember him that way. I wanted to remember him alive. And I have never stopped loving Frederick. Ever."

"How terrible for you," Ashlyn said softly. "I'm so sorry."

"What did you do after that?" Cami asked.

Pearl hesitated, as if trying to decide how much more to tell them. "It was very difficult after his death. I had to make decisions that I still live with today. Then, when I felt my only hope was to jump off a cliff into the ocean, Fate smiled on me and I was given the kind of job opportunity that comes only once in a lifetime." She paused and the girls waited anxiously for her to continue.

"I had studied journalism in school, you see—"

"So did I," Ashlyn piped up, then smiled apologetically for interrupting.

Pearl simply smiled at her and went on. "A teacher of mine from college had done some freelance work for a newspaper in the East. He recommended me for a job as a traveling correspondent. When I was offered the position, I knew it was my lifeline. So I took it and put every bit of effort and energy I had into that job. People thought I was crazy because I would dare to do anything, go anywhere, try everything. The way I saw it, I had nothing to lose. If I died trying to climb Mount Kilimanjaro or chasing after a tribe of Aborigines, then at least I would be with my dear Frederick again. So the prospect of death didn't frighten me."

"What about your family? Did they know about all the crazy things you did?" Ashlyn asked breathlessly, even further amazed at this woman in front of her.

"My family? Well, after Frederick died, things between us weren't good." She paused, obviously remembering those painful times. "I'm still not close to my family. What's left of them," she sighed wearily. "Anyway, when I retired, I bought this little place and I enjoy many pleasant hours in my garden."

"It's very pretty," Ashlyn said. "My mother loves to garden, too."

"It's very therapeutic," Pearl said.

"Uh oh," Cami exclaimed. "It's getting really late. Grandpa is probably worried sick about us."

"Why don't you call him and tell him you're on your way? I'll fix up a plate of these tarts and a few of my chocolate chip cookies. He'll like that."

Cami made the call while Pearl arranged the confections on a plate and covered them with plastic wrap. Ashlyn carried in the trays from the living room.

"He was just starting to wonder where we could be," Cami told them when she hung up the phone. "I'll bet he fell asleep watching the news again, like he does every night."

"Give him this and tell him I said hello," Pearl said.

The girls bid her goodnight and hurried home through the darkness. As a breeze blew in from the ocean, chilling the night air, Ashlyn was grateful she'd thought to bring a warm sweater along.

They found Grandpa Willy in the kitchen, getting an evening snack. Ashlyn had to hold her stomach when she saw he was eating dill pickles rolled up inside slices of bologna.

Cami presented her grandfather with the plateful of goodies.

"Where'd you get these?" he said gruffly.

"From Pearl. She packed them especially for you." Cami put the plate on the counter.

Ashlyn covered a yawn that snuck up on her. Getting up early to run on the beach was going to be hard if she didn't get to bed soon. "I think I'll go to bed," she announced. "I'm exhausted."

"Me too," Cami echoed. "It's been a busy day."

Ashlyn climbed the stairs, thinking about their encounter with Pearl. What a life the woman had experienced. She must have been some kind of woman to do all the things she'd done. Maybe that was what Ashlyn should do with her life. In a way, she was like Pearl, when Pearl was her age. A love gone wrong, trying to move on with life when it seemed so empty. Maybe Ashlyn needed to join the Peace Corps or the army.

She shook her head, realizing she wasn't really as adventurous and daring as Pearl. But she thought she could look into being a foreign correspondent for the news. Or maybe she could become an airline attendant. Now that might work. She would get to travel and see the world without the danger. There was a woman in her ward in Salt Lake City who was an attendant; Ashlyn decided she would talk to her when she went home.

At least Pearl had something to show for her life. All those souvenirs were reminders of her adventures and colorful past. The more Ashlyn thought about it, the more she realized that if she were going to spend the rest of her life alone, the best way to do it would be to fill it as full of fascinating experiences as she could.

The prospect of adventure and seeing the sights of the world sent little shivers of excitement through her. For the first time since Jake had left her at the altar, she could see a way out of the dark tunnel she was in. Meeting Pearl was the best thing that could have happened to her. Not that she wanted to end up exactly like Pearl. She couldn't imagine being all alone like her. She wondered why Pearl didn't get out and make friends? She was a fascinating woman once Ashlyn had gotten to know her.

Ashlyn was glad she had family and friends. The one thing she knew was that she didn't want to end up alone like Pearl.

The next morning Cami came to Ashlyn's room to wake her up for church.

"Church is at eleven," Cami said. "It's almost nine."

Ashlyn grumbled and pulled the sheets over her head. "I'll go next week," she said tiredly.

"Ash, c'mon. You'll love our ward," Cami prodded her.

Ashlyn ignored her, hoping that would give her friend the hint that she wasn't interested. She knew Cami had big plans to get her active again, but Ashlyn just didn't know where the church fit into her life anymore. She didn't really think of herself as inactive, just temporarily taking a break from the whole gospel/church thing. She needed to figure out her life first.

She could tell Cami hadn't left her room yet. So what was she doing? Unable to resist, she peeked out from under the covers.

"Ha! Caught ya!" Cami cried. "Now get up. I'm done in the shower."

Ashlyn propped herself up on one elbow. "I really don't feel like going today," she told her friend soberly. "I'm sorry. I'll try to go next week."

Cami looked at her long and hard. "Okay," she said, her disappointment evident. "But next week for sure. Promise?"

"I promise," Ashlyn said, pulling the covers back over her head.

Cami pulled the door shut and Ashlyn breathed a sigh of relief. Why was everyone freaking out about her not going to church? It wasn't like she wasn't ever going back. She would. Eventually.

But deep in her heart she knew it was more than that. Maybe she was wrong to feel as if the Lord had abandoned her when she needed Him most. Maybe it was wrong of her to wonder why He would allow her to go through the pain and humiliation of rejection on her wedding day, and for her to feel angry at the Lord for allowing it to happen. But she did.

So why would she turn to the Lord now for help? He'd let her down. She knew she lacked faith, but how was it possible to have faith in something she couldn't depend on? The only person she knew she could depend on was herself. And that's how she was determined to do it. By herself.

She was fully awake now, but she didn't want to get out of bed until Cami and Grandpa Willy left for church, just in case they tried to pressure her into going.

When she heard the car pull out of the driveway, she quickly got up, made her bed, and showered. She decided to take her camera and get some pictures of the coast and of the mansion to send home to her mother. Within half an hour she was out on the beach. Once again the clouds were low and angry looking. Not wanting to get caught in a storm, she snapped a few pictures and headed back up the ridge, hoping to get some pictures of the mansion.

Intrigued with the history and beauty of the structure, she tried to picture what it must have been like to live in the mansion back in the early 1900s. She could picture women dressed in beautiful clothes, sitting in the parlor drinking lemonade, while children played croquet out on the lawn, and the men relaxed on the porch, discussing politics and financial issues.

Perhaps someone would be cranking an old-fashioned ice cream machine, and everyone would take a turn at the handle, or a group of people might be in the kitchen, pulling taffy and singing songs.

The picture was happy and ideal. And probably unrealistic, she mused.

She was determined to get the key from Grandpa Willy so she could go inside. It was almost as if something was drawing her to the house. Some kind of need to step into the past.

With several hours to kill before the others came home, she decided to start dinner. Cami already had a roast in the oven, so Ashlyn decided to peel the potatoes and mash them.

Just as she reached the house, raindrops began to fall. Big sloppy drops of rain. No sooner did she step inside the back door than the clouds split open and poured out their load. Ashlyn was amazed at how heavy the rain was. It came down so hard, she could barely see to the end of the porch. Relieved that she had made it inside just in time, she went to the kitchen and started dinner.

"Something smells wonderful," Cami said as she stepped through the door.

Gravy was bubbling in a pan on the stove next to a pot of green beans as Ashlyn whipped boiled potatoes into fluffy, white mounds. Hoping that they weren't as hard as hockey pucks, Ashlyn had even attempted to make homemade baking powder biscuits. If they tasted half as good as they smelled, she'd be happy.

"Smells good enough to eat," Grandpa Willy said, hanging his jacket over the back of one of the dining chairs.

"Everything's ready if you want to get washed up," Ashlyn told them.

Cami ran upstairs and quickly changed her clothes, then joined Ashlyn in the kitchen to help get dinner on the table.

As soon as it was ready, they all sat down to eat. Cami told her that Mrs. Bradford had asked about her and hoped to see her next week. Cami was also excited because she'd been able to see George and his expectant wife, Gina, too. Ashlyn wanted to ask if the town's beloved Mitch was there, but she didn't have to.

"Of course, Mitch teaches Gospel Doctrine," Cami said with a laugh. "He has such a great way of teaching. Lots of humor and the Spirit is always there."

Grandpa Willy took another biscuit and smeared it with butter and honey. "Don't know that I've ever thought much about the story of how Alma and his people were delivered from bondage to the Lamanites," he said, "until I heard Mitch explain it today."

Ashlyn rolled her eyes and groaned. She was getting a little tired of hearing them praise this man on a constant basis.

"Me either," Cami agreed. "I loved how Mitch compared their burdens and being in physical bondage, to us today."

Ashlyn wasn't really interested in a religious discussion at the moment, but Cami wasn't done telling her about their lesson.

"Alma and his people had these horrible burdens to bear," she told Ashlyn, temporarily forgetting her food. "They were basically slaves to Amulon and his people. And when Alma's people complained, Amulon told them to stop or they'd be put to death. He even assigned guards to watch over them to make sure they didn't keep complaining."

"Hmm, how interesting," Ashlyn answered dryly.

Ignoring Ashlyn's response, Cami continued. "Alma and his people stopped complaining out loud, but they poured out their hearts to God. It's neat," she said emphatically, "because God answered their prayers because of their great faith." She tapped her knife on her plate. "I wish I could remember exactly what it said."

"That's okay," Ashlyn told her. "I remember the story from Institute."

"No, no, I want to tell you exactly what it said." Jumping up from her chair, she grabbed a Book of Mormon from a bookshelf. "Let me find it and I'll read it to you." She thumbed through the book a while before finding what she was looking for. "Here it is," she cried. "I love this part."

> "And I will also ease the burdens which are put upon your shoulders, that even you cannot feel them upon your backs, even while you are in bondage; and this will I do that ye may stand as witnesses for me hereafter, and that ye may know of a surety that I, the Lord God, do visit my people in their afflictions."

Cami looked up at Ashlyn as if checking her reaction, then continued.

> ". . . the Lord did strengthen them that they could bear up their burdens with ease, and they did submit cheerfully and with patience to all the will of the Lord."

Cami closed the book. "Right after that the Lord delivered them from bondage. He caused the Lamanites to go into a really deep sleep, and Alma and his people took their flocks and their food and their families and departed into the wilderness."

Not entirely sure what point Cami was trying to make, Ashlyn tried to look a little interested as she continued eating.

"This applies to us even now, in these days," Cami declared. "Even though most of us aren't in physical bondage to someone else, thank goodness, we may have other types of bondage. Some people might have physical handicaps, which places them in a sort of bondage. For others it might be a spiritual or emotional bondage. But if we just exercise faith, the Lord will lighten our burdens so we can bear them cheerfully. Then He will deliver us from the bondage that holds us back from progressing."

Ashlyn finally had something to say. "Exactly what kinds of 'other' bondage do you think it refers to?"

"Oh, gosh, all kinds. Like if someone is struggling with an illness or injury. Or if they've suffered great loss, like having a loved one die or something. Or if someone is struggling with any type of issue that they just can't seem to let go of and they can't move on with their life."

It seemed to Ashlyn that Cami emphasized her last example, so she didn't respond, not wanting any further discussion. But she thought about what Cami had said. Was it possible? Could it actually happen that way?

"I'll clean up the dishes, since you cooked," Cami offered.

"Okay." Ashlyn didn't put up much of a fight. "I guess I'll go up to my room and read for a bit. Let me know when you're done, and we can play cards or something."

"The clouds are breaking up," Cami said. "We could take a walk and say hi to Pearl later." She winked and Ashlyn wondered if she'd gotten the key to the mansion.

"Sounds good to me," Ashlyn replied. "Maybe she has some more tarts."

"Don't be bringin' any of those wicked tarts home for me," Grandpa Willy said. "Kept me up all night with the runs. She must've put something vicious in them."

"Grandpa, I told you, we ate the same ones you did," Cami said soothingly. "She didn't put anything in them."

"Well, I'm not taking my chances," he grumbled.

Ashlyn escaped to her room and relaxed in the window seat, looking out over the ocean. The dark clouds were indeed breaking up and streaks of sunlight shone through, creating spotlights on the sand. The beach was empty as wild waves curled and crashed upon the shore.

She thought about the scripture Cami had read to her and pondered the word "bondage." Bondage. Spiritual bondage. Emotional bondage. The word "bondage" sounded so foreign to her, too biblical to relate to. But when she thought about it, she wondered honestly, wasn't she herself in some type of bondage? Didn't she feel trapped at times, unable to make sense of her life and what she should do with it?

When she and Jake had been working toward a temple marriage, it seemed as though the rest of her life was mapped out for her. She would get a teaching job until they started their family, then she'd stay home and take care of her babies. Jake would finish school and get a job, then they would buy a home, settle down, and live happily ever after.

Well, she was a far cry from that life. So, the question now was, where did she go from here? She'd been trying to find the answer to that question for almost a year now.

She came back to her idea to follow in Pearl's footsteps, to travel and experience the wonders of the world, to make her life as full as possible. For her that made more sense, and it sounded a whole lot more fun than teaching and seeing the inside of a school room everyday.

"And I will ease the burdens that have been put upon your shoulders . . . "

She did feel like she had a burden on her shoulders. A heavy burden that she was tired of carrying. No matter what she did, the burden continually nagged at her, pulling her down, making it hard for her to feel free to move on.

Freedom. That's what she wanted. Freedom to live life again, to enjoy life again. Would that ever come? Could it? And if so, how?

She rose from the window seat and walked over to the chest of drawers. In the top drawer she found her scriptures. She looked at the book in her hand for a moment, trying to convince herself, especially her heart, that she should give the gospel another chance.

Not completely convinced but at least willing to look at the passage Cami had read earlier, she turned to the book of Mosiah. She found what she was looking for in chapter twenty-four. Scanning the verses until she found what she was looking for, she reread the account carefully. According to these verses, if she prayed, the Lord would lighten her load, and if she exercised faith, He would deliver her from bondage.

It seemed so easy. And yet so impossible.

A knock came at the door and Ashlyn nearly dropped her scriptures. Tucking them beneath her pillow, she sat on the bed. "Come in," she called.

Cami opened the door. "Whatcha doin'?"

"Not much. Just looking out the window. It looks like it's clearing up out there," Ashlyn commented.

"Good, because I found . . ." Cami pulled a ring of keys from her pocket and dangled them out for Ashlyn to see.

"The keys to the mansion!" Ashlyn cried. "Let's go!"

CHAPTER
TEN

"Shhhhh," Cami said quickly. "I'm not sure Grandpa would like us wandering around in there. He says the place is falling apart and is dangerous."

"Sorry," Ashlyn whispered. "When can we go?" She was anxious to get inside the mansion.

"Whenever you're ready."

"I'm ready now." Ashlyn jumped to her feet. "Just let me get my shoes and socks on."

"You'd better grab a jacket or a sweatshirt, it's kind of nippy out there."

"Oh, okay. I think I've got a sweatshirt in that third drawer down. Will you get it for me?"

The top drawer of the dresser was still open, exposing meticulously organized contents, complete with drawer divider and compartments. Cami stared at the drawer for several moments before Ashlyn broke into her thoughts.

"Okay," Ashlyn said, cinching her shoelace tightly. "I'm ready. Did you find the sweatshirt?"

Cami quickly closed the top drawer and opened the third one down. Inside that drawer, the clothes were neatly folded. Once again she stared down at the drawer.

Alarmed at her friend's silence, Ashlyn looked up at her. "Cami? Isn't the sweatshirt there? I could have sworn I put it in there."

"It's right here." Cami slowly pulled the navy blue sweatshirt from the drawer.

"What are you doing?" Ashlyn asked. "Is something wrong?" Ashlyn stood next to her and looked inside the drawer, expecting to see a bug or a snake.

"Your drawers are like, perfect," Cami said.

"No they're not," Ashlyn said with a laugh.

"They are. You don't have anything out of place. Even your junk drawer is perfect. I mean, look at this—" Cami pulled out the top drawer. "Not even a paper clip is out of place."

"It's just organized. Believe me, after I've been here a while it will get messy."

"But your closet, you've got your clothes hanging spaced apart, just like you did at home. And your shoes are all paired up so perfectly. Mine are in a big box inside my closet. I have to dig to find the mate half of the time."

Ashlyn wasn't sure what Cami was getting at. "That's why I keep them organized, so I don't have to dig."

Cami studied her closely for a moment.

"What?" Ashlyn reacted, taking a step back.

"I'm just trying to see if you are the real Ashlyn or the Stepford Ashlyn."

"Stepford Ashlyn?" Ashlyn grabbed the sweatshirt out of Cami's hands and tied it around her waist. "What's that?"

"Didn't you ever see that old show *The Stepford Wives?* About this community where the wives are all perfect? And this lady moves in and discovers that all the husbands are making robots of their wives so they can have everything perfect?"

"That sounds like a stupid movie. I'm not like that. And you know, Cami, maybe it's not that my stuff is all perfectly arranged, maybe it's just that your stuff is so messy. Do you want me to organize it all for you?" she offered.

Cami looked at her thoughtfully.

"Now what?" Ashlyn demanded, exasperated.

"I'm just trying to figure out why you're like this."

"Like what," Ashlyn said defensively.

"A perfectionist," Cami pronounced with authority. "A control freak."

"You know," Ashlyn joked, "if we were guys and you weren't my best friend, I think I'd punch you in the nose."

"I'm sorry. I don't mean to be rude," Cami laughed. "It's just that you weren't like this at college. I mean, you were definitely organized and neat, but you weren't this extreme. I just wonder if it has anything to do with the fact that when Jake stood you up at the temple, you felt like you lost control of your life. And this is your way to have some control over yourself and your things."

"Thank you, Sigmund Freud," Ashlyn said dryly. "Since when did an interior design major become such a psychologist?"

"I took a few psychology classes in college," Cami said in her own defense.

"So that makes you an expert?"

"Well, no. But I'm telling you, if I ever see 'Jake the Jerk' again, I'm going to punch *him* in the nose. I mean, even your driving is different, and I think the reason you've become a more aggressive driver is that it's the only place you feel safe venting your frustrations about your lack of control."

"Oh, *puh-leeze.*" Ashlyn rolled her eyes. "Have you spent a lot of time analyzing this, or is it just coming off the top of your head as we speak?"

"I've thought about this since the day you didn't marry that creep."

Ashlyn stared at Cami. "You think all of my problems are because of Jake and what he did to me, don't you?"

Cami met her gaze without flinching. "Ash, you were the happiest, sharpest, most together, most motivated, most awesome girl I knew at college. You knew what you wanted and where you were going, and nothing was going to stop you. You had your beliefs and values and you didn't hold back your feelings about them. Like the day you told off that kid at the student union building who was slamming Mormon kids for being stupid and brainwashed by their religion. The way you tore into him and put him in his place." Cami nodded approvingly. "That was cool."

Ashlyn hadn't thought about that in a long time. She remembered how impassioned she had been as she jumped all over that kid for his rude and thoughtless remarks. Her tirade had drawn a crowd and in the end, she'd received a round of applause. The guy had skulked away, embarrassed, and after that, she'd seriously considered going on a mission. If that was how it felt to spread the gospel, she was ready to go.

But then, she had met Jake, and everything changed after she met him. Which meant, to her horror, that Cami was right.

Now it was Cami's turn to say, "What?"

Ashlyn looked at her with an astonished realization of something she hadn't been able to face.

"Ash, is something wrong? Are you upset with me? I'm sorry. I didn't mean to hurt your feelings, really."

Ashlyn took a deep breath as reality began to sink in. She liked to think she was in charge of her own decisions, and she took responsibility for her actions. But it was obvious that there had been a pivotal moment in her life when she had begun to change. Jake leaving her seemed to set off a chain reaction of emotions stemming back to her relationship with her father.

She liked who she used to be. Her old self really was a pretty neat girl, she had to agree with Cami. So what did she do now? How did she revive the old Ashlyn? Was it possible to find her again?

"I'm not upset," she told Cami. "I'm just thinking about what you've said."

Cami wrapped her arms around Ashlyn and hugged her. "I think I need to learn to keep my big mouth shut. You're doing great and you don't need me to pretend I'm your mother or guardian angel or something."

They stepped back and smiled at each other.

"Actually, since I can't have a fairy godmother," Ashlyn joked, "I think having you as my guardian angel sounds pretty good."

"Honest?" Cami said with relief.

"Honest."

"Good. Then we're okay?" Cami asked hopefully.

"We're okay," Ashlyn replied. "Now, can we go take a look at that mansion? I've been dying all morning to go inside."

<hr />

"Are you sure none of the keys work?" Ashlyn insisted.

"Here." Cami handed her the set of keys. "See if you can get any of them to open the door." She stepped aside and let Ashlyn work on the lock. But still no luck.

"Darn it!" Ashlyn kicked the door. "I want to go inside."

"I'm sure these are the keys. Grandpa's had them hanging in the same spot for years."

They didn't hear someone come up behind them

"What are you girls doing?"

Ashlyn and Cami screamed together, scaring poor Pearl half to death.

"Good grief!" Pearl put her hand over her heart. "I think that just about reset my clock."

"Sorry," Cami cried. "You startled us, though."

"We didn't hear you," Ashlyn said apologetically, noticing that Pearl was wearing some type of sarong-looking outfit, with fabric draped around her shoulders.

"I didn't mean to scare you," Pearl said. She looked at the keys in Ashlyn's hands. "So, you're going inside?"

Cami looked at her sheepishly. "We were trying to go inside, but we couldn't get the keys to work."

"Oh," Pearl nodded her head a few times. "You seem disappointed."

Ashlyn sighed. "I was really looking forward to seeing what's in there. Maybe we could pull off the boards and go through a window?"

"Oh, that would thrill Grandpa," Cami told her sarcastically.

"Well." Ashlyn stomped her foot. "I can't help it, I'm desperate."

Pearl got a mischievous look in her eye. "If you really want to go inside, I think I can help you. Follow me."

The girls looked at each other and smiled.

Pearl led them behind the house and stopped at the back door. From behind an overgrown lilac bush flanking the door, she pulled out a piece of thin metal, about the size and shape of a ruler. Deftly she slid the metal in between the door jamb and the door and fiddled with the knob, until they heard a click.

With victory in her eyes, she proudly swung open the door.

CHAPTER ELEVEN

"Omigosh," Ashlyn exclaimed, feeling as though she had walked back through time. "Look at this place."

Even though it was dark and shadowy, they could easily see the contents of the room. They had stepped into the kitchen, which housed an old coal-burning kitchen range and banks of cupboards and cabinets along two of the walls. An island stood in the middle of the room and against one wall was a floor-to-ceiling built-in hutch. Seeing the two windows in the kitchen, Ashlyn gasped as she noticed the rectangles of stained glass above them.

"Are those roses?" She stepped closer. "They are! Look at this," she exclaimed excitedly. "Roses in the stained glass windows. It's beautiful."

"Unheard of," Pearl said. "What an extravagance."

"Wow." Cami looked at the dust-covered windows. "Think how beautiful it would be when the windows are clean and the sun comes through."

Next they found the dining room, a large spacious area where the only thing taking up space was a canvas-covered chandelier that hung low in the center of the room. Ashlyn was tempted to remove the covering.

"Do you think it would be okay if we took a peek at the chandelier?" she asked.

"I'd hate to break anything," Cami said.

"I don't think there would be any harm just taking a peek," Pearl said. "I'm a little curious myself."

She found the edge of the canvas and lifted back the fabric. "Oh my!" she exclaimed. "This is gorgeous."

"Let me see." Ashlyn crowded in and peeked up into the tent covering the chandelier. "Is it crystal?"

"I think it's Venetian," Pearl said. "This thing is worth a fortune if it is."

"Venetian?" Cami questioned. "Like from Venice?"

"I'm almost sure of it," Pearl said. They all breathed carefully as if any movement of air would cause the delicate chandelier to disintegrate. Gently Pearl replaced the cloth.

"Look at that molding." She indicated the beautiful woodwork along the edge of the ceiling and around the ceiling where the chandelier hung. "Every wall is covered with woodwork. And the fretwork is just like lace."

"Fretwork? What's that?" Ashlyn asked.

"See along there." Pearl pointed to the entry leading out into the hall. At the top were tiny spindles of wood, so delicate they were no bigger around than pencils, but much longer. In the center, the spindles fanned out, creating a half circle. In the corner between wall and ceiling, they fanned out again, like a delicate lace valance, only made of wood, hanging across the entry.

"I've never seen anything like it," Ashlyn whispered in awe.

"And you probably never will." Pearl shook her head. "This is pure artwork, from a skilled craftsman. Homes aren't built like this anymore."

In the spacious hallway, the front door also held a hint of color in the glasswork.

"Look, more stained glass," Ashlyn cried.

Sure enough, the same rose motif was shown in the gorgeous front door and sidelights.

"No wonder there are rose bushes all around the yard," Pearl said. "Whoever lived here loved roses."

Cami spoke up. "That would be my great-great-grandmother. You know, it's interesting how coming here and seeing where my great-great-grandmother and grandfather lived, makes me feel . . ."

She searched for the right words. "I don't know, close to them, I guess. It makes them seem more real to me. And it makes me feel kind of proud of how hard they worked to create this place. I've never felt like this before."

"Your great-great-grandmother must have been quite a woman in her day, to have had a home like this," Pearl commented. "A woman of distinction and class."

Cami smiled proudly. She liked that description—a woman of distinction and class.

"Wow," Ashlyn said from another room, just off the entry. "You've got to see this."

"Oh, my goodness," Pearl exclaimed as she entered the large, empty space, separated by partial walls on each side and a heavy, dust covered drape, which they carefully pulled aside to expose the back room. "A front and back parlor. And this wainscoting looks like it's made out of walnut," she said as she ran her hand down the wood paneling that came halfway up the walls in both rooms. Crown molding of the same wood framed each room and the doorways carried the same decorative molding.

The floor was covered with a threadbare carpet, the edges curling and crumbling. Tall windows that reached nearly to the ceiling adorned both rooms; and inside one of the walls was a fireplace used by both rooms, with a marbled hearth and mantle on each side.

"Why would someone have two parlors?" Cami wondered aloud.

"Oh, it was very fashionable at one time to have two parlors. That way, when the owners entertained, the ladies could converse in one room while the men played cards and smoked cigars in the other one. Or the front parlor could be used as a formal living room, for when guests came, and the back parlor could be more of a family room, for every day."

"How do you know so much about these things?" Ashlyn asked Pearl.

"When you've been around as long as I have, you pick up a lot of useless information," Pearl replied.

"I don't think it's useless," Cami said. "We learned about the Victorian era in school, but it's different being inside a home that actually shows the architecture and style of the period."

Ashlyn felt as if they'd opened a treasure chest, "I think it's fascinating. But it's such a waste to let this gorgeous home just sit here, unused."

"I agree," Cami said. "But it would take so much money and work to do all the repairs to make it livable. I don't think it even has running water or electricity."

They finished looking at the main floor, finding two bedrooms and a bathroom, complete with pedestal sink and slipper tub with classic brass claw feet.

"Let's go upstairs before it gets too dark to see," Ashlyn said anxiously.

Upstairs there was more light and they were able to examine the four bedrooms and two bathrooms. There was also a room that looked like a den, or perhaps a library, with a built-in desk and book-shelves and lovely picturesque window.

The light had grown so dim it was becoming difficult to see much more of the house, so they decided to leave and come back another time.

Pearl invited the girls to her house for apple strudel, which she had made earlier that day, and they accepted her invitation without hesitation.

"This is incredible," Ashlyn said, relishing a bite of the flaky crust and delicately seasoned apple filling. "You seem to do a lot of baking."

"I love to bake," Pearl told them. "I try to give away a lot of it, since I certainly can't eat everything I make. I think gardening and baking are my greatest passions in life."

"You certainly have a talent for it," Cami said. "Everything I've ever eaten of yours is better than anything I've ever had in a bakery or a restaurant."

"I think I missed my calling in life," Pearl said. "I could have been very happy as a chef, or better yet, a baker. Pastries are my favorite." Here eyes held a distant look as she said, "I should have stayed in France and been a pastry chef. I studied for years with John Pierre Longet, the well-known French chef."

Ashlyn and Cami looked at each other, both feeling a bit sorry for the lonely woman. She had so much ability and vitality; it seemed a waste that she had no one to share it with.

Breaking the silence, Ashlyn said brightly, "I'm certainly glad you helped us get into the mansion today. I've been dying to go inside. It's everything I'd dreamed it would be, don't you think, Cami?"

"Absolutely," Cami agreed heartily. "I thought it would be just a bunch of dust and junk, but the place is really gorgeous. And I really liked feeling close to my great-great-grandparents."

Ashlyn set her empty plate on the coffee table. "I'm sorry, but I can't believe that you and your grandfather don't want to live there. I mean, how can you let a house like that just rot away?"

Cami shook her head with a sigh. "I told you—it would cost a fortune to make it livable again. Besides, my grandfather has a beautiful home himself, and he and my grandmother lived there almost their entire married life. I don't think he would ever leave it."

"Then someone else should live in the mansion, or you should sell it so someone else could take care of it," Ashlyn insisted.

"Oh, no," Cami cried. "We could never sell it."

Ashlyn shook her head sadly, hating to see the mansion receive such a death sentence.

"If I might make a suggestion," Pearl said almost timidly. "You might consider turning it into a bed and breakfast. They're very popular, especially here on the coast. A turn-of-the-century home like this could be very popular. And there isn't anything like it in the area."

"A bed and breakfast?" Cami appeared to roll the thought over a few times in her brain to get the feel of it.

Immediately a visual image of the mansion, renovated and decorated, catering to honeymooners, or couples getting away for the weekend, popped into Ashlyn's mind. It was so clear, so perfect, that she couldn't contain her excitement any longer. She jumped to her feet.

"Pearl!" she exclaimed. "That's an absolutely brilliant idea! Cami, with your decorating degree, you could do a really wonderful job fixing it up again. And you've got so many wonderful recipes, Pearl, maybe you could do the baking for the bed and breakfast. You know, sweet rolls and muffins for breakfast, croissants and salads for lunch, classy desserts at dinner."

Pearl's face lit up. "I would love to," she exclaimed excitedly. "And I have a stuffed quail recipe that would really put us on the map."

Cami sat pensively, saying nothing. Ashlyn wondered if the money issue made it difficult for her to see the mansion's potential.

"I know you could do it," Ashlyn said. "You could get a business loan and pay it back with the money you make renting out the rooms. It wouldn't take that much to get the yard put together. All those roses in bloom . . . it would be stunning." She took in a sharp breath, feeling goose bumps run up her spine. "In fact, I have the perfect name—"

Pearl and Cami looked at her with anticipation.

"—The Sea Rose."

Cami's eyes lit up. "I love it! It's perfect!" she exclaimed.

"I do too," Pearl added enthusiastically. "The Sea Rose. Especially with all that stained glass. Oh, my goodness, it is perfect."

"You know what?" Cami said, barely able to contain her excitement. "It's a great idea."

Ashlyn's mind seemed to go into warp speed. One idea spurred another and another. Pearl began to throw out ideas, and Cami got completely carried away with the decorating possibilities.

"You know," Cami said, "my grandfather has a lot of stuff from his travels that he's collected, but they're just gathering dust in storage. I bet he'd love to see those things finally put to good use. He's got this gorgeous headboard, hand carved, from somewhere in South America."

"Well," Pearl said, "if you're thinking of something like that, I would like to make a donation to the Sea Rose Bed and Breakfast. I have so much in this house, I don't know what to do with it. You're welcome to any of it—no, you're welcome to *all* of it. It's not junk really, in fact, everything is high quality, some of it priceless. But it's just sitting here in my house gathering dust. I would get such satisfaction seeing my things in a place where others could admire their beauty and worth." She looked around at her treasured belongings. "I'd actually enjoy getting rid of it, too. I'd certainly have more room around this place."

Ashlyn couldn't believe how things were falling into place. With Cami's decorating knowledge and the exotic flavor of Pearl's collection, "The Sea Rose" would definitely be distinctive from other bed and breakfasts.

"What do you think?" Ashlyn asked her friend.

"This is quite unbelievable, to be honest," Cami said. "I know it sounds crazy, but since I got home I've tried to decide about work, you know, what I'm going to do with my degree now that I'm out of college. I'm sure I could find a job around here, but I'm just not sure I want to work for a design company.

"But this— " she smiled at both of them, " —this is incredible. It would be a ton of work, but it would also be so much fun."

Ashlyn felt her scalp tingle with excitement as little shivers ran down her spine. What a great way to spend the summer, helping fix up the mansion.

"You can certainly plan on me to help," Pearl told her. "I've puttered around this place for so long, I would love having something else to do, even if it's scrubbing walls or painting trim."

"Me too," Ashlyn said.

Then Cami's expression changed to one of concern.

"What?" Ashlyn asked.

"The only thing I have to do is convince Grandpa, and that won't be easy," she said with a sigh.

* * *

Ashlyn was so excited about the mansion she could barely sleep. She finally managed to fall asleep sometime after midnight, but she was jarred from a deep slumber when her alarm went off at six a.m. She pushed the snooze button several times in an effort to win the argument her mind was having with the rest of her body to get up and get moving. She'd made the commitment to walk at least five mornings a week, six if possible, and she knew she'd be mad at herself all day if she just didn't get up and do it.

There wasn't much light in the room when she finally coaxed herself out of bed. The sky through the skylight looked dark and stormy, but she knew most days it was just that way along the coastline. Donning leggings, a sweatshirt, a waterproof windbreaker, and her trusty baseball cap, she grabbed her running shoes and headed downstairs.

Once through the patio doors, she got a better feel for the weather conditions. Except for the usual gusty winds and low, gray clouds, it seemed like most mornings since she'd arrived.

The ever-present bite of chill got her moving quickly to stay warm. Down the wooden stairs she went and out onto the sand.

She loved the hiss and crash of waves against the shore. Even though the nip in the air brought tears to her eyes, she was glad she'd dragged herself out of bed. Feeling energized and alive, she broke into a comfortable pace. She enjoyed having the wind at her back, even knowing that on the return trip, she'd have a harder time.

In an effort to increase her distance, she ran to her usual mark and a few yards beyond. Her goal was to eventually make it clear to the harbor and back without stopping to walk.

Circling back, she began the long jog home, but to her surprise, the wind had died and she was able to run without its resistance working against her. With energy to spare, she worked her way to the stairs that led back to the house, then decided to go on to the next set of stairs and come up the back way, through the trees and past the mansion.

As she rounded the jagged point below the mansion, she slowed to a walk and spent a moment cooling down and stretching her muscles. Within the tiny cove, the waves seemed to have calmed and the air was merely a salty kiss on her cheek.

She paced the rocky beach as she allowed her breathing and heart-beat to return to normal. Drawing in several long breaths of fresh air, she noticed that the tide had retreated around the point, allowing plenty of space to walk through. Curious, she inched her way closer, wanting to see what was on the other side.

The shore line was strewn with moss-covered logs, slippery sharp-edged rocks, and ropes of seaweed and flotsam, and Ashlyn gingerly made her way around the point. Just as she hoped, there was a grand view of the coastline several miles to the south. Majestic cliffs were cloaked in deep green pines and breathtaking monoliths rose sharply out of the sea along the coastline. She could see the hint of a road—Highway 101, no doubt—peeking through the trees in several places as it wound its way down the Oregon coastline.

The view was spectacular and she wondered if the mansion was situated close enough to the edge of the cliff to offer a view from the upstairs bedrooms in each direction.

Just then a large droplet of rain landed with a *plunk* on top of her hat. Ashlyn looked up and got another one in her eye.

"Oh, great," she groaned as she realized she was about to get her morning shower.

Suddenly the wind kicked up, and so did the waves, slapping the rocks with a deafening roar. She carefully negotiated her way around the rocky point, nearly losing her footing on several of the slick rocks.

To her horror, the shoreline had completely disappeared, and she was up to her ankles in angry, choppy water.

Choosing each step carefully, she worked her way along the frothy shoreline as the rain fell faster and harder. The icy water about her feet and calves was nearly unbearable as she splashed through the waves. She was struggling to keep her balance when, from out of nowhere, a wave Cami had referred to as a "sneaker" wave, came at her like a powerful, moving wall, knocking her over into the frigid water.

Ashlyn tried to get her feet back underneath her so she could stand, but the waves kept pummeling her, tossing her in their wake, rolling her over and over. Several times she went under and when she surfaced, gasping for air, she reached out desperately, hoping to find something to grab on to.

Her ribs and back throbbed from being slammed against the pointed rocks, and her lungs burned for air. With all her strength, she fought to get above the surface of the water. Instead, she felt herself being lifted up off the ground again as another large wave picked her up.

The crash of the wave drowned out her cries for help, and once again she was lost in the depths of the angry sea, her lungs frantic for air, her senses dulled from lack of oxygen.

Struggling to get her feet under her, to free herself from the icy arms of the raging sea, Ashlyn fought with every ounce of strength she possessed. But the sea was stronger than she was. As she exerted herself to make one last, final effort, the undercurrent sucked her under and everything went black.

CHAPTER TWELVE

"Where could she be?" Cami said, pacing the floor. The storm had raged for over an hour. Ashlyn had been gone almost two. "I should have gone running with her. Just because I hate to run doesn't mean I shouldn't have gone anyway."

"She probably got down the beach a ways and got caught in the storm. I'll bet she just found cover until the worst was over," Grandpa Willy consoled her.

A knock came at the door, and Cami rushed to answer it, hoping it was Ashlyn or someone with a message from her. Instead it was Mitch Bradford.

"Morning," he said. "I hope it isn't too early. I was up the street delivering a lawnmower for my dad so I thought I'd drop in and say hello."

"Come in," Cami said, unable to hide the concern in her voice.

He was wearing a cowboy hat to keep off the rain, and took it off as he entered the house.

"Is something the matter?" he asked.

"It's Ashlyn," Cami said. "She went out running on the beach at six and she hasn't gotten home yet. She's usually back within forty-five minutes, an hour at the most."

"What in the world would make her go out in this kind of weather?" he asked.

"It didn't start raining until almost seven. She should have made it back by then," Cami insisted. She walked to the glass doors and looked out at the angry storm. "I'm going out there to find her. I can't stand it any longer."

As she went for her slicker and umbrella, Mitch shoved his hat back on his head. "Cami, I can't let you go out there. You know it's not safe. Why don't I go down and take a look? If I don't find anything, I'll come back and we'll notify the coast guard. Give me fifteen minutes and I'll be back."

With his head bent against the wind and his hat keeping out the rain, he crossed the back lawn and headed down the wooden stairs. He noted gratefully that the storm was losing its intensity. At the bottom of the stairs, he studied the beach. It looked deserted. No one in their right mind would be out in a squall like this.

He looked southward, wondering if she would have gone into the cove, then shook his head. She would have to be crazy to get herself caught in there during a storm. But how would she know that a storm was coming? She wasn't from here. She wouldn't know the signs to look for. How could she when most of the townspeople who'd lived there for years still couldn't outguess the weather?

Praying that she wasn't there, but still feeling as though he should go and look, Mitch negotiated the slippery rocks and waved-filled shore for about twenty feet before he saw the glimpse of a lime green and royal blue windbreaker next to a ten-foot log.

"Holy smoke!" he cried, breaking into a run. He slipped and nearly fell but managed to keep going. He had to get to Cami's friend. There was no doubt in his mind it was her.

"Hey," he yelled as he got closer, the noise of the waves stealing the volume from his words. "Are you okay?"

There wasn't any movement.

Hurrying to the lifeless form of the girl, he breathed a silent prayer that he wasn't too late.

"Hey," he said again, "are you okay?"

Again he received no answer, but he could tell by the bluish shade of her lips, she wasn't okay. Without stopping to feel for a pulse or check for injuries, he scooped Cami's friend up in his arms and carried her back to the safety of the beach. Laying her down on the sand, he checked for any visible injury or damage and for a pulse. It was faint but still there. Her skin was cold and clammy.

Probably in shock, he guessed as he put his ear against her nose to check for breathing and watched for the rise and fall of her chest. It was barely noticeable, but she was still breathing.

"I gotta get you home," he said, picking her back up and running nearly the entire way back to the Davenports' home. At the house, Cami opened the door as Mitch, rain-soaked and out of breath, carried Ashlyn inside.

"Put her on the couch, Mitch," Cami instructed him. Ashlyn was mumbling weakly but incomprehensibly, and although Cami felt tears sting her eyes, she knew she didn't have time to cry now.

"Call Dr. Montgomery, Grandpa," she instructed. "I'll get her some blankets. Mitch, would you mind putting some hot water on to boil? She'll need something hot to drink."

They all went to work, and within minutes the color returned to Ashlyn's cheeks. She coughed weakly, then her body became wracked with spasms.

Cami held her friend and patted her back, trying to calm her. "It's okay," Cami spoke soothingly. "Everything's going to be okay."

A knock came at the door and Grandpa Willy let Dr. Montgomery in. He was a small man, no bigger than five foot eight, and very slim. He wore tiny wire-rimmed glasses and Reeboks.

Cami explained everything while the doctor checked Ashlyn's temperature, pulse, and blood pressure. Then he examined her pupils and felt her skull and neck for signs of injury.

"Get her out of these wet clothes," he ordered. "She needs to get warm and dry. She's got a bit of hypothermia." Seeing Cami's alarmed expression, he added comfortingly, "She's going to be fine. It's her lungs I'm worried about. She probably took in a fair amount of seawater. We just need to watch her closely. Other than a few scrapes and bruises, she looks fine."

Ashlyn mumbled again.

Cami leaned in closely to her. "Ash honey, are you okay? Ash?"

"What . . . What's happening?" Ashlyn murmured.

"You got caught in the cove in the storm, but you're home, safe and sound," Cami told her.

Ashlyn slowly opened her eyes. Her gaze rested on Dr. Montgomery's face for a moment.

"This is Dr. Montgomery," Cami told her. "He said you're going to be fine. Do you hurt anywhere?"

Ashlyn nodded slowly. "Everywhere." Her body shivered as it began to get warm.

Everyone laughed except her. She was serious.

"She should have some rest and she needs to stay warm," Dr. Montgomery told Cami.

"Okay," Cami said. "We can do that."

The doctor instructed her to call if there appeared to be any more trouble or if Ashlyn complained about any pain, particularly in the head, neck, or chest.

"I'll call you later to see how she's doing," he said as he gathered up his medical supplies. He gave Ashlyn's hand a gentle squeeze. "You take care of yourself, now. No more swimming for a while."

Ashlyn smiled her thanks and Grandpa Willy walked him to the door.

"All right, young lady," Cami said in a motherly tone. "Let's get you upstairs and out of those wet things. How does a nice warm bath sound?"

"Wonderful," Ashlyn said.

"Mitch, would you help me get her up the stairs. I can take it from there."

Mitch! Ashlyn sat up with a start and looked around the room. There, in a soggy denim jacket and cowboy hat, was Mitch. What in the world was he doing here?

"Hey, there," he said. "How are you feeling?"

Smiling sheepishly, Ashlyn melted against the cushions. "Pretty good," she lied, not telling him that she felt like someone had used her for batting practice and then tried to drown her.

"It's a good thing Mitch found you when he did," Cami told her.

"Mitch found me?" *Criminy*, she thought, *I feel like such an idiot.*

"He came to the house just as I was going out to look for you," Cami explained. "Maybe after your bath you can tell us what happened out there."

Ashlyn could have soaked in the hot water forever—it felt so good to be warm and safe again. Her legs were dotted with reddish welts that would soon turn into purple bruises. She didn't have any cuts, as she imagined she might, but she did have a good-sized goose egg on the back of her head.

"You need any help in there?" Cami asked through the door.

"No, thanks. This feels wonderful," Ashlyn replied. She watched the steam rise from the water for a moment, then rested her eyes, letting the soothing warmth relax her aching body. Her mind replayed the incident in the ocean and she shivered in spite of the hot water. An ominous question tugged at the back of her mind. What if Mitch hadn't found her?

But he did, and that's what mattered. And even though she owed him a great deal for rescuing her, she hoped he would be gone when she went back downstairs. She felt stupid and embarrassed that she'd let herself get caught in such a dangerous situation, and she wasn't ready to face him.

Why was he here anyway? Especially looking like the Marlboro Man.

When the water cooled, Ashlyn finally forced her sore, stiff limbs to move and she climbed out of the tub.

Not taking time to dry her hair, she twisted it up in back and secured it with a clip, but then took it out since it hurt where the goose egg was. She let her hair hang long, loose, and wavy about her shoulders instead. She wasn't in the mood to get all dolled up and certainly wasn't out to impress Mr. Wonderful.

Cami, Grandpa Willy, and, of course, Mitch, all stopped talking and studied her closely as she came down the stairs and joined them in the living room.

"Good to see you've got some color back in your cheeks," Grandpa Willy said.

"Are you feeling any better?" Cami asked her.

"Much better, thank you," Ashlyn replied, avoiding Mitch's stare. Darn him, why didn't he just go home?

A knock came at the door. Ashlyn wondered if the doctor had forgotten something. Cami had no more than turned the knob when Pearl rushed inside, carrying a kettle in with her.

"What's this I hear about Ashlyn getting caught in the storm?" She handed the kettle, potholders and all to Cami, and hurried over to Ashlyn's side. "How are you, dear? You look a little peaked. I brought you some chicken soup to warm your insides."

"How in tarnation did you hear about Ashlyn?" Grandpa Willy demanded.

"Dr. Montgomery stopped by," she replied without looking at the old man. "What happened, dear?" she asked, focusing her attention on Ashlyn.

Realizing that she was going to have to explain her actions sometime, Ashlyn decided she might as well get it over with. Pearl sat down beside her as she related her story, trying to make herself appear smarter than her actions had been.

Shaking her head and "tsk, tsking," Pearl took Ashlyn's hand and patted it repeatedly. "That must have been terrifying for you, just terrifying. Good thing you're young and strong enough to fight the waves like you did. Those sneaker waves have been known to carry people off without a trace."

"Oh, now, Pearl," Grandpa Willy grumbled. "Don't go scarin' the poor girl to death. She's had enough for one day."

"I agree with that," Mitch said. "In fact, I think we better get you a running partner so you don't have to go out at six in the morning alone on the beach anymore."

Pearl gasped. "Good heavens, no. A young lady shouldn't be out alone on the beach, especially at that time of day."

Halfheartedly Cami raised her hand. "I'll go with her," she said, though without much enthusiasm. Not only was she not a morning person, she just plain hated to run, or for that matter, walk any faster than she could window shop.

"Cami, I don't want you to have to do that for me," Ashlyn objected. "It's not fair to you. I can just go later, or do something else—"

"Wait a minute," Mitch interrupted. "You forget. I'm down at the beach three mornings a week anyway. I wouldn't mind bumping up my workouts a few more days of the week. I'd love to have someone to go running with. That would make sure I got my lazy keister out there."

The last person Ashlyn wanted to run with was Mitch. She hated the thought of listening to him go on and on about himself mile after mile. The thought made her stomach turn.

"No, really," Ashlyn assured him. "It's kind of you to offer, but I think we can come up with another idea—"

"It's no problem," he interrupted again, insistently.

The others looked at her like they couldn't understand what the problem was. Here was the King of Seamist offering to go running with her five mornings a week. She should feel like she just won a lottery.

But she didn't. Faking a smile, she said, "I guess it's settled then. Thanks, Mitch." She nearly choked on his name.

"Now, how about that soup?" Pearl jumped to her feet. Today she was wearing some type of Peruvian skirt and shirt, brightly colored, with a handwoven sash around her ample waist. Her shoulder-length, salt-and-pepper-colored hair, which was usually worn loose and moppy, was tied back with a bright red woven strip of cloth. She looked quite exotic in the outfit, and even quite attractive in the bold colors.

Her "breakfast" of soup was a healing balm to Ashlyn's weather-beaten body.

"This is the best chicken noodle soup I've ever tasted," Ashlyn said, handing her bowl to Pearl for seconds. "What's your secret?"

"Sea salt," Pearl told her. "The flavor is unsurpassed."

Everyone at the table, even Grandpa Willy agreed, although he was hesitant until he tasted how delicious it was.

"Sea salt, huh?" Ashlyn said. "Like I need more sea salt in my body today."

The group laughed with her and she reached for the package of saltine crackers. Mitch grabbed it first. "Here you go," he said, handing it to her.

"Thanks," she mumbled, taking it. Why was he being so nice? Did he just feel sorry for the stupid city girl who nearly drowned in the ocean?

Ashlyn saw that he had taken off his cowboy hat. His unruly hair touched the collar of his denim shirt, and she couldn't help but notice how the blue of his shirt deepened the color of his eyes.

The conversation around the table drifted to several topics, none of which Ashlyn could get involved in. Mostly town politics, local gossip, and upcoming summer events. Of course, "Marvelous Mitch" was in charge of the Fourth of July celebration. He was apparently the driving force behind the city of Seamist, the city's "Golden Boy."

After breakfast Mitch needed to get back to work, but not before Grandpa Willy invited him over for a barbecue sometime.

"Whenever you say, Willy," Mitch accepted enthusiastically, pulling on his denim jacket. "Just promise me you'll make some of your famous Mormon 'kick-a-poo-joy-juice.'"

"That's much safer than Grandpa's homemade root beer," Cami said to Pearl and Ashlyn. "Mitch, do you remember last time Grandpa made root beer?"

Mitch started to chuckle, then he laughed right out loud. "Boy, do I. I think they heard the explosion clear up in Cannon Beach. I thought it was going to knock Old Tilly off her rock."

"What happened?" Ashlyn asked, amused at their obvious delight in the story.

"Now, Cami," Grandpa Willy warned.

Cami ignored him and told the story. "Grandpa makes his root beer the old-fashioned way, with sugar and yeast. He mixes all the ingredients together, puts his root beer in a gallon-sized glass juice jug, then wraps it up in a blanket and puts it somewhere warm so it will ferment just enough to make it fizzy."

"Boy, did that batch ferment," Mitch said, still laughing. "We were sitting on the deck, enjoying the sunset, when all of a sudden— BOOM! We thought we'd been struck by a meteor."

"The root . . . beer . . . had—" Cami gasped for air as she laughed, "exploded."

"Blew the cupboard door right off the hinges," Grandpa Willy said with a chuckle. "Used a mite too much yeast in that batch."

"You think?" Cami giggled. Pearl couldn't help laughing, and even though it hurt her ribs, Ashlyn found herself laughing, too. The story was funny enough by itself, but seeing Cami and Mitch cracking up was contagious.

"How about this weekend?" Grandpa Willy said. "Cami, have we got anything going Saturday night?"

"Not that I know of," Cami replied, wiping at her eyes.

Ashlyn hoped they intended to invite Pearl, now that they'd planned the dinner in front of her. To her relief, Cami said, "Pearl, you'll join us too, won't you?"

"Only if you'll let me bring something," Pearl insisted.

"I'll call you later and we'll figure out what you can bring," Cami told her.

On that note, the guests left, still snickering over the exploding root beer. Cami banished Ashlyn to her room to rest her battered bones and get some sleep while she cleaned up the kitchen and did a load of laundry.

Two and a half hours later, Ashlyn woke up to the sun streaming through her skylight. Attempting to roll over onto her back, she stopped abruptly when her muscles cramped up and refused to cooperate.

"Ow, ow, ow," she groaned as she gently and slowly straightened her arms and legs. The small bit of movement helped work out the charley horses in her legs and the stiffness in her arms. Sitting up carefully, she stretched her neck and back, but not yet trusting the strength in her legs, she kept a firm hold on the nightstand as she pushed herself to her feet. She managed a few steps then made her way across the room and looked outside at the warm, sunny day. Who would've guessed that a few short hours ago she was fighting for her life in waters that had nearly overpowered her?

Gingerly she made her way down the stairs to see what everyone was doing.

She found Cami and Grandpa Willy in the kitchen snacking on chips and salsa.

"Well, look who's been raised from the dead," Cami announced cheerfully.

"You sure you got your land legs back?" Grandpa Willy said to Ashlyn. "You still look a little green behind the gills."

"I'm kind of stiff, but I feel pretty good," Ashlyn replied, trying to smile reassuringly. She knew how much worry she'd caused them.

"You need to take it easy for a while and drink lots of fresh water," Grandpa Willy instructed. "That seawater can pickle your innards, you know."

"Aye, aye, sir," Ashlyn said, smiling at his concern. Even though he pretended to be a grumpy old cuss, he was as soft and sweet as a marshmallow, she decided.

Ashlyn joined them, dipping the chips in the salsa and savoring their salty spiciness.

When Cami mentioned putting off an errand in town until tomorrow when Ashlyn felt better, Ashlyn was quick to assure Cami that as long as they weren't doing anything too strenuous she felt good enough to go to town.

It felt good to get outside and Ashlyn felt energized after a few long breaths of fresh air.

"Mitch is such a great guy, isn't he?" Cami sang his praises as she drove the car toward town.

"Yeah, I guess," Ashlyn replied flatly.

"What do you mean, you guess?" Cami asked, a look of confusion on her face.

"I just don't know if I want to go jogging with him every morning. I mean, I'm not that fast of a runner anyway, and I don't really even know him that well."

Cami raised her eyebrows and waited for her to continue.

"I know I should feel 'lucky' that he would even consider running with me." Her tone was edged with a bit of sarcasm. "But I think it's going to be kind of uncomfortable."

Cami nodded in understanding. "We didn't give you much choice about it, did we? So, don't go with him. I'll get up and go with you in the morning. I should be doing some exercise anyway."

"You don't mind?" Ashlyn asked.

Cami shook her head.

"So what do we do about Mitch then?" Ashlyn wondered.

Cami suggested that Mitch accompany them a few times, since he was already planning on it, then they would tell him they were doing okay on their own.

With that problem resolved so easily, Ashlyn breathed a huge sigh of relief. "So what did you need to come to town for?" Ashlyn asked her friend.

"You'll see," Cami said with a mischievous smile on her face.

Moments later they pulled up in front of the bank. "Let's hope my friend Mark still works here," Cami said.

Ashlyn looked curious. "Who's he?"

"A guy I went to school with. He's a great guy and he'd do anything for us," Cami said confidently.

"And we're seeing Mark because. . ."

". . . because, we want to talk to him about a loan for the bed and breakfast," Cami told her.

Ashlyn's mouth dropped open with surprise. "Cami, really? This is so exciting."

"I know," Cami agreed. "I can't quit thinking about it."

The bank was quiet inside except for several people in line waiting for the teller to help them. Cami looked around for her friend but couldn't see him. "Maybe he's at lunch," she said.

When a young girl walked out from behind the counter toward some of the loan officers' desks, Cami called to her. "Excuse me," she said. "Is Mark Wilden in?"

"Mark? He's not here anymore. Got transferred to Portland at the first of the year." The girl kept walking, and Cami gave Ashlyn a look of pure frustration.

"Wait!" Cami stopped the bank employee. "I need to talk to someone about a loan."

"Oh, I think he's gone to lunch. You'll have to wait, " the girl said impatiently and walked away.

"Let's sit down over there," Cami suggested, pointing to several chairs near a picturesque window. "We might be here a while." She picked up the local paper and began reading.

A few minutes later a man came through the door and walked past them to a desk in the back. Cami was busy reading and didn't notice him, so Ashlyn gave her a nudge. "Hey, I think the loan officer just came back."

"He did? Where?" Cami put the newspaper down and looked in the direction that Ashlyn had indicated. The blood drained from her face, leaving her pale and white.

"What?" Ashlyn asked with alarm.

"We can't stay," Cami stood up suddenly. "We have to get out of here."

CHAPTER
THIRTEEN

"It's Dallin," Cami said quietly, pulling on Ashlyn's arm. "I don't want to see him."

"That's Dallin?" Ashlyn looked over and studied him for a minute. He was clean-cut and handsome, with short, brown hair and nice brown eyes. She didn't have a straight-on view of him, but his profile was nice. "He's cute."

"Shhhhh," Cami hissed. "Come on, let's get out of here."

"Too late," Ashlyn said, seeing the girl they'd talked to earlier approach them.

"Our loan officer is back if you'd like to talk to him now," she said, slightly more cordial than before. Apparently she'd taken a much-needed break and was in a better mood, Ashlyn thought.

"Thank you." Ashlyn jumped to her feet and put her hand on Cami's arm to keep her from running out of the building. "Come on."

"No," Cami said. "I can't. What's he doing here anyway? His father said he was thinking about moving to New York."

"Will you come on? People are starting to look at us."

"Only because you're making a scene," Cami whispered fiercely, yanking her arm out of Ashlyn's grip and sinking back down in her chair.

Ashlyn sat down beside her. "What's the big deal?"

"I don't know. I'm just afraid to see him after all this time. What if . . ." She gulped and stopped.

"What if you walk over there and have a conversation with an old friend?" Ashlyn filled in for her. "What's the worst thing that could happen?"

Cami squeezed her eyes shut. "I don't know."

"You can't just walk out of the bank." Ashlyn's tone was crisp and businesslike. "Besides, that girl has already gone over to his desk, probably to tell him we're waiting to talk to him."

"She has?" Cami looked over at Dallin's desk. Just then he looked up and did a double take when his eyes met Cami's.

"Cami, is that you?" he said, getting to his feet and hurrying toward them. "I can't believe it."

"You are so dead," Cami said under her breath to Ashlyn, who stood up, pulling Cami up with her. Cami reached out her hand for Dallin to shake, but he ignored her hand and pulled her into a hug. Ashlyn liked him already.

"You look wonderful," he told Cami as he stepped back and gave her a long, appreciative look. Ashlyn thought she saw a flicker in his eyes. He still liked Cami, she was sure of it.

"Thanks," Cami said. "You do too. I didn't know you worked here."

"Oh, it's just temporary. I've been trying to decide about a job in the East. In the meantime, Uncle John—he owns the bank, remember?" He paused and Cami nodded. "He needed some help so here I am. I guess you've finished school then?"

"I just graduated and moved back last week," Cami said, then introduced Ashlyn.

"Nice to meet you," he said, smiling.

"You too," Ashlyn smiled back, thinking that he had a nice smile. In fact, everything about him was nice. Very cute, very nice. She definitely approved.

She and Cami followed him to his desk and sat in the chairs in front of it. As Cami explained why they were there, Ashlyn looked back and forth between the two of them. In her mind she had them falling back in love, getting married, making their home in a little bungalow by the sea, and having a little baby, all by the time Cami had finished telling Dallin about their plan for a bed and breakfast.

These two belong together, Ashlyn said to herself. *He practically finishes her sentences for her. They are a perfect match.*

Dallin gave them the necessary forms to fill out, saying that he thought their idea to turn the mansion into a bed and breakfast was a great idea. When they had finished their business, Dallin walked them out to the car. He was telling them about his most recent trip to New York City when a fire engine wailed in the distance. Within minutes it was racing down the main street of town.

"Look," Cami cried. "There's Mitch." She pointed to the fire truck as it rushed by.

"What in the world is he doing in there?" Ashlyn asked.

"He's a volunteer," Dallin told her.

To Ashlyn's surprise, Cami wanted to follow the fire truck. Apparently, in a town the size of Seamist, a fire truck on its way to a disaster was a big event. Cami invited Dallin, who hopped in the car, and the next thing Ashlyn knew, they were racing down the street in the direction of the siren.

When they got to the edge of town, they found that a shed behind someone's house was smoldering, the flames having been easily doused with one quick shot from the hose.

"Mr. Durfey's shed," Cami said disappointedly. "I was hoping for something exciting."

Just then "Firefighter Mitch-Town Hero" noticed them and waved heartily. "Hey, there," he said, walking over to join them and leaning in to see everyone inside Cami's car. Ashlyn could tell he liked wearing the uniform. And even though he did look quite handsome in it, she couldn't help but wonder what exactly made this guy tick.

"Hey, Mitch," Dallin greeted him. "We just came to see what all the excitement was about."

Mitch shrugged. "Nothing much. Durfey had the barbecue too close to the shed and it caught on fire. He could've put it out with a hose, but his wife panicked. No big deal, though. The fire station hasn't seen much action the past few weeks anyway."

"Why'd they call you in?" Cami asked.

"I was over there making a delivery when the call came in. So I hopped aboard in case they needed my help." He noticed Ashlyn in the back seat. "How you feeling?" he asked.

"Fine, thank you," she said politely.

"Good," he nodded. "Are we still on for tomorrow morning, or do you need another day to recuperate?"

"No," Ashlyn said. "Tomorrow's fine." She didn't want him to think she was wimpy, although why, she couldn't have said.

"Okay. Six a.m. sharp. I'll meet you at the bottom of the stairs." One of the other firefighters yelled for him. "Oops, I gotta go. Good seein' ya, Dallin. We ought to get some of the guys together and play some basketball."

"I'd like that," Dallin said.

"Oh, and if you're still interested in getting on a baseball league, we might need a shortstop on the Bradford team. Ronnie Mitchell sprained his wrist when he fell off a roof he was shingling. We have a game at the end of the week."

The fire truck gave a loud blast from the horn. "I'll call you later," Mitch said, lifting his hand in a wave as he backed away from the car. "I gotta go. By the way—" he looked at Ashlyn, "—I like your hair that way."

The fire truck was already pulling away and Mitch sprinted after the truck. As the other men cheered, he caught up with the truck and hopped aboard. Then, with one last wave, he was gone.

Stunned, Ashlyn stared after him. Cami turned and gave her a triumphant smile. What had made Mitch say something like that to her? Ashlyn wondered.

"You heard that, didn't you?" Cami asked her.

"Yes, I heard," Ashlyn mumbled.

"What a guy," Dallin said, shaking his head.

Ashlyn swore she would throw up right there in the back seat of Cami's car if Dallin said one more thing about how "great" or "awesome" Mitch was.

As Cami put the car in gear and drove Dallin back to the bank, Ashlyn turned to her curiously. "Tell me, Cami, what is it with Mitch? Every time I see him he's wearing a different outfit. I swear he's dressed like a different one of the Village People every time I see him. If he's wearing an Indian costume next time we see him, I'm going to ask him to sing 'YMCA.'"

Dallin and Cami busted up laughing, then began to sing the old disco song as best they could remember all the way to the bank. Cami's eyes started tearing up from her laughter, and she nearly ran into the curb.

After they had composed themselves, Dallin opened the door to leave. "Thanks for coming in today. I haven't had this much fun in a long time," he told them.

"Hey," Cami said, "do you have any plans this weekend?"

"Not really." Ashlyn thought she detected a hopeful note in his voice.

"We're having a barbecue at my house Saturday night around six. We'd love it if you could come. Mitch is going to be there."

"Sure. What can I bring?" he asked.

"How about chips and salsa or something? And some pop."

"No problem." He smiled broadly. "I'll be there."

As Cami and Dallin looked at each other for a moment, Ashlyn wished she could disappear.

"It was great seeing you, Cami," he said softly.

She gave him a shy smile in return. "Yeah, you too."

"I'd better get back to work. Nice meeting you, Ashlyn," he said, then waved and went back to the bank.

Ashlyn didn't say anything as they drove home. She was waiting to see what Cami would say. But Cami was silent and finally Ashlyn couldn't stand it any longer.

"Well?" she said.

"Well, what?" Cami said, as if she didn't have a clue what Ashlyn meant.

"Dallin, that's what."

"What about Dallin?" Cami replied coolly.

"You think I didn't see the sparks flying between you two? He's definitely still in love with you. And you know what?"

"What?"

"You're still in love with him!" Ashlyn declared.

"I am not," Cami denied.

"Liar!" Ashlyn retorted. "If there were any more sparks between you two, Mr. Town Hero would have had to come and put out the fire."

"Mr. . . . ?" Cami was puzzled for a moment. "Oh, you mean Mitch?"

"Who else?"

"You don't like him very much, do you?" Cami signaled so she could change lanes and turn onto their street.

"Oh, it's not that. He seems nice enough, but this whole town acts like he's the center of the universe."

"Really?" Cami asked with surprise.

"You should hear yourselves talk about him. I'm surprised there isn't a column in the local newspaper dedicated to his daily comings and goings. *'Mitch Bradford puts out fire.' 'Mitch Bradford saves drowning visitor from ocean.' 'Mitch Bradford— walks on water.'*"

Cami rolled her eyes. "It's not that bad."

"Maybe not, but good grief, if the biggest thing people have to look forward to each day is what Mitch is doing, and *'Oooh, let's go follow Mitch on the fire truck,'* then I feel sorry for them." No sooner had the words been said, then Ashlyn realized how snotty they sounded. Seeing the crestfallen expression on Cami's face, she wished she could take them back. "I'm sorry, Cami, I didn't mean that," she apologized.

Cami's voice was subdued and she didn't look at Ashlyn as she spoke. "I thought you liked it here."

"I do. I don't know why I said that. Forgive me, okay?" Ashlyn begged. "It was mean and stupid. I think the saltwater pickled my brain not my innards."

Cami gave her a quick smile. "Okay. I guess we do act a little Mayberry around here."

"But that's part of its charm. I wouldn't want you to change a thing."

Cami was quiet as she drove, then she perked up. "Hey, let's go tell Pearl about our trip to the bank. If all goes well, and this loan gets approved, we'll be in business before we know it. Oh, and one more thing." Cami eyed Ashlyn devilishly. "Did you hear Mitch say he liked your hair that way?"

"Yes, I heard!" Ashlyn cried. "Enough with the hair already." Disgusted, she stared out the window while Cami chuckled all the way to Pearl's house.

⁂

The next morning Ashlyn woke up before her alarm went off and groaned. She was sore and stiff from her romp in the surf yesterday.

Nothing a bit of exercise wouldn't take care of, she told herself. Moving one inch at a time she slowly climbed out of bed and limped over to the window. Except for a few grayish clouds, the sky was clear and there was barely a whisper of wind. A rush of excitement filled her, then stopped. Mitch was coming with her this morning.

She groaned. Shoot, it was a perfect morning. At least it would have been.

But there was nothing she could do about it now. She resigned herself to her fate and dressed as quickly as she could. Tapping on Cami's bedroom door, she heard a low moan and the rustle of bedcovers. Taking a "best-friend liberty," she opened the door and poked her head inside. There was Cami curled up in a ball under the covers.

"Cami, you're supposed to be up and dressed. It's almost time to meet Mitch."

"I can't go," Cami groaned. "I'm dying."

"Sure, you are. Get up."

"No, really. I don't feel very good." Cami tried to lift her head but couldn't.

Ashlyn became alarmed. "What's wrong?"

"It's . . . you know, that time," Cami said.

Ashlyn had forgotten what a hard time Cami had each month when "that time" rolled around. "Oh, I'm sorry. Is there anything I can get you? Some Motrin or something?"

"I took some an hour ago and I think it's helping a little. I'll be okay," Cami assured her halfheartedly. "I'll go sit in a hot bath if I don't feel better soon."

"Maybe I should stay and take care of you," Ashlyn offered, glad to have a reason to skip her running appointment.

"No, there's nothing you can do anyway."

"I guess I'd better go then," Ashlyn said with a grimace. "Wish I had cramps."

"Believe me," Cami said. "You don't."

"Yes, I do," Ashlyn said under her breath as she pulled the door closed behind her.

"I heard that," Cami said loud enough that Ashlyn could hear her through the door.

Once she was outside it was almost possible to forget how much she dreaded going running with Mitch. The morning was breathtaking. To the east the sun was at the tip of the horizon, lighting the sky on fire, turning the clouds to a brilliant crimson, orange, and pink. The ocean lapped the shore in a calm, steady rhythm, stroking the sandy beach with gentle fingers.

Filling her lungs with fresh, lilac-scented air, Ashlyn descended the stairs and arrived at the bottom, where she found herself alone. She had thought surely Mitch would be there waiting for her. It was already after six. Noticing that once she got moving her aches and pains seemed to ease up, she jogged in place for a minute or two, then did a few calf and thigh stretches. He still hadn't arrived. Maybe something had come up.

"Well, darn," she said aloud, not in the least bit sorry. "Guess I'm on my own." Kicking up a little sand, she took off down the beach as the sky transformed itself from indigo to azure blue.

"Ashlyn!"

Hearing her name, she made a face. "Oh, pooh!" she muttered as she stopped running and turned around. There was Mitch sprinting toward her. Forcing a smile, she waited until he came within earshot, then said, "I wasn't sure you were going to make it."

"Neither was I," he said. "Sorry I'm late." He looked around. "Where's Cami?"

"Uh . . . she wasn't feeling up to it this morning."

"Too bad. It's a beautiful day. You just getting started?" he asked a bit breathlessly. She nodded. "Okay, I'm ready when you are." He unzipped his windbreaker a few inches.

"Let's go," she said, taking off at a brisk pace. They ran together silently for a minute until they found a comfortable stride for both of them.

"So," Mitch said between breaths, "you're obviously feeling better today."

"I'm still a little sore, but I'm fine," she told him.

"That's good," he huffed. "Have you found anything interesting on the beach when you've been running?"

"Not really," Ashlyn panted, wishing they could slow down just a bit. "Why?"

"Morning's the best time to find treasures on the beach that've washed ashore during the night, especially after a storm. Every once in a while you find beautiful shells or agates on the shore."

"What's an agate?"

"They're stones that have been shaped and polished by the surf. They come in all colors."

"Cami's grandfather has a jar of them on the mantle," Ashlyn remembered.

"That's right. He's even got one that has a fossil of some type of prehistoric-looking bug or something in it. Have him show it to you sometime." He pulled in a few quick breaths. "And have him show you the Japanese glass floats he's found. Those are really something."

"Japanese glass floats?" she asked, feeling as if her lungs were on fire.

"The Japanese used them to keep their fishing nets afloat," he puffed. "They come in all sizes and colors." Another puff. "Some are only four inches wide but some are up to two feet in diameter." He ended on a strangled note as he gasped for air.

"Really?" she said, feeling a sharp stab in her right side but ignoring it. "How do they get clear over here?" She was finding it hard to breathe herself.

"Some drift on the ocean for years. They show up all over the place, but the tides and trade winds bring a lot of them here." Mitch started to cough, then said, "Do you mind if we take a break for a minute? I'm not in as good a shape as I used to be."

Inside Ashlyn was dying with relief, but outside she played it cool. "Yeah, I guess so," she said. They dropped to an easy jog, not much more than a quick walking pace.

"That's better," he said. "Thanks. Did you run track in high school?"

"I ran my sophomore and junior year. I didn't have time when I was a senior." It felt good to be able to talk, move, and breathe all at the same time.

"I can tell," he said admiringly. "You've got a nice stride, and you've got the perfect build for a distance runner, long and lean."

Okay, mister, stop being so nice, she thought. *I don't plan on joining your fan club.*

"Did you do any other sports?" he asked.

"Not really," she told him. "I was a cheerleader. That didn't leave much time for anything else."

When they reached the breakers at the edge of the bay, Mitch asked, "You want to turn around or keep going?"

"We've already gone farther than I usually go," she told him honestly. "I guess we should turn around." She looked across the harbor at the lighthouse. "I don't know what it is, but there's something captivating about a lighthouse."

"I know what you mean," he said. "After my wife and I separated, I spent a lot of time at the beach. There's something therapeutic about the ocean. I just seem to think better when I'm down here." As he looked over at the lighthouse, a light wind played with locks of his hair. He had a nice profile, Ashlyn noticed. Chiseled good looks. His jaw was strong, his cheeks and eyebrows angled just right, and his nose defined to a handsome slant. She didn't know him that well, but for all the attention he got from everyone in Seamist, he didn't seem as self-absorbed as she'd first thought he'd be.

She didn't want to pry but found herself saying the words anyway. "What happened?"

"You mind if we keep walking?" he asked, indicating with a nod toward the sidewalk that curved with the shape of the harbor. "I've tried for a long time to figure out exactly what happened. You know, I thought we were a match made in heaven. Boy was I wrong."

She smiled, encouragingly, and he continued.

"It was love at first sight for both of us. We met at school and there was an immediate attraction. Like we both knew we were meant to be together. But we had such different backgrounds, I never thought she'd go out with me. I mean, she was this gorgeous coed from a very wealthy family back East. She dated all the big guys on campus. You know, the student body president, the football quarterback, guys like that. But one night I found myself standing next to her at an Institute dance. So I asked her to dance, fully expecting her to turn me down."

He stopped speaking as they sidestepped an overturned garbage can, with litter strewn about. Several steps later, they both stopped.

"You mind if we pick that up?" Mitch asked.

"I was just going to suggest the same thing."

It took about five minutes to clean up the mess, then they continued on their way.

"I'm probably boring you," Mitch said, unzipping his windbreaker all the way. The sun was above the horizon, reflecting brightly off the ocean's surface.

"Not at all," Ashlyn insisted. "I'd like to hear the rest."

"Okay, but tell me the minute you feel like diving into the water because I've bored you to death."

"I promise, I'll warn you before I jump." She cast a sidelong glance at him and smiled.

"Let's see, I was telling you about the dance?"

She nodded and tucked an errant strand of hair behind one ear.

"I guess that's where it all started. We had a great time together and danced the rest of the night together. After that we didn't go a day without seeing each other. When she left for Christmas vacation, I thought I'd go nuts without her, and when she came back for winter semester I had a ring for her. She told me she'd missed me too and said yes when I asked her to marry me. I thought that was it. We would live happily ever after."

"But you didn't?"

"Not quite. I got a business degree with an emphasis in marketing and advertising, thinking we could come back here to Seamist and live. My plan was to teach business classes at the high school and get into coaching. The school board had been holding a position open for me until I finished school. But after living here six months Tiffany decided she'd had enough. She told me either we move to Manhattan, or it was over."

Ashlyn didn't know what to say. Her heart went out to him because she knew the story didn't get better. "What happened in New York?" she asked quietly.

"We moved to Manhattan, to a brownstone her father bought for us. I found a job at a marketing firm and I actually liked it there. It was exciting and challenging, and even though living in the city was a huge change from Seamist, I liked it quite a bit. We went to all the Broadway shows and spent weekends with her family in Connecticut, and I thought things were working out great for us. Granted, I didn't really like how her father bought our home and let Tiffany use his credit cards. I was working hard to provide for us on my own, but she was determined to have the kind of life she'd always had."

He'd given up everything for this girl, Ashlyn realized. Left his home, lifestyle, and family, and uprooted himself and his dreams, to make her every wish come true. She couldn't help but think that Jake had never made any of those kinds of sacrifices for her happiness. She decided to stop that train of thought before it went any further. It would not be a good idea to start comparing Jake with Mitch.

"Then I had a business trip to Chicago and was gone overnight. And when I got home—" he swallowed hard, "—she was gone."

"What do you mean—gone?"

"I mean, furniture, clothes, dishes, towels. Gone. She'd moved out."

"Oh, Mitch," Ashlyn said sympathetically. "I'm so sorry."

"Yeah, me too. I went to her parents' house and tried to talk to her, but she wouldn't even see me. They wouldn't let me in the house. You see, she was an only child and her parents had spoiled her rotten. I knew she was spoiled and I knew they thought she'd married beneath them, but I was determined to prove myself to them and to her. And I thought I'd done a pretty good job. I mean, I got a promotion and a raise within two months after starting my job and I was on my way to a great career."

Ashlyn shook her head, wondering what was wrong with that girl. What Ashlyn would have given to have Jake care half as much for her and her feelings as Mitch had cared for Tiffany's. "So what did you do next?"

"I camped out in front of their gate, figuring they'd either let me come in and talk to my wife, or they'd run over me," he said with a smile. "After a cold night on the street, they realized I wasn't leaving and they finally let me in."

Ashlyn was completely captivated by his story. "What did she say to you?"

"She looked me square in the eye, and without even blinking, she told me she didn't love me any more and that our marriage was over." He shook his head and whistled. "Man, that hurt. Here I'd been thinking everything was going so well. I didn't even see it coming. I guess she'd been attracted to me in the beginning because I was so different from all the guys she was used to dating. Then, when we got back to her turf, so to speak, she felt like I didn't fit in with her friends and family and the big city. She even said she was embarrassed to be seen with me."

His voice was calm, but Ashlyn could tell, even after months of time and healing, the experience still hurt.

"I can't believe I just unloaded all of that on you." He laughed, unexpectedly. "And I can't believe you haven't jumped yet." He looked at the edge of the water slapping against the concrete barrier of the harbor. "I'm really sorry."

"It's okay," Ashlyn assured him. "Really."

He stopped walking. "You know, except for my parents and my brother, you're the only person I've ever told that story to."

Ashlyn was flattered that Mitch felt comfortable enough to talk to her. And even though they didn't know each other that well, she liked how easy it was to be with him.

"Hey, look, we're almost to the lighthouse. You feel like going the rest of the way? I think we can go up inside of it, if it's not too early," he invited.

"Great," she said. "I've been wanting to see the lighthouse up close." Then she realized how long she'd been gone. "But I should probably call Cami and her grandfather and let them know where I am. I don't want them to worry."

"Sure, we can use a phone at the hotel over there," he motioned to the Sea Breeze Inn. "The owner's a friend of mine."

"By the way," Ashlyn added, a little embarrassed that she hadn't really said anything before now, "thanks for rescuing me yesterday."

"You're welcome." He smiled at her and she felt her heart get all fluttery around the edges. Then to her horror she realized—it had happened.

Darn him! Darn, darn, darn him!

She didn't know how it had happened, or when, and she didn't plan on *ever* admitting it, but she'd become a fan of the irresistible and incomparable Mitch Bradford.

CHAPTER FOURTEEN

The hike through the Douglas fir and spruce trees was shady and cool, the air pungent with the smell of the damp earth and mossy undergrowth. They didn't say much as they made the climb toward the lighthouse, but the lack of conversation wasn't awkward as they absorbed the serenity of the cool green forest.

Ashlyn wondered about Mitch's current girlfriend. Did she go jogging and hiking with him? It wasn't hard to tell he loved nature. To see him cooped up in a concrete city seemed as unnatural as plucking a penguin out of the Arctic and plopping him down in Maui.

"We're almost there," Mitch called back to her. The climb had been fairly strenuous, but the last ten yards had grown extremely steep. "It's a little slick right there." He turned and reached his hand toward her. "Let me help you."

She grabbed hold of his outstretched hand and scrambled up the side of the hill. They had climbed above the tree line, and when Ashlyn turned toward the view, her breath caught in her throat.

Stretched out as far as she could see in both directions was the beautiful rocky coastline. The ocean lay before her, brilliant blue, creating a mesmerizing horizon that conjured up visions of golden galleons and white-sailed ships. The view was so broad she could see the slope of the earth, feel the magnificence of the world's creations.

A soft, playful breeze tickled her cheek. Below them, the crash and spray of waves filled the air. Along the edges of the shoreline in the distance, a soft mist hugged the beaches. It was magnificent.

"What do you think?" Mitch asked, stepping up beside her.

"It takes my breath away," she said.

"Turn around and look behind you," he told her.

She did as he said and nearly fell over backwards. There, standing like a mighty beacon, was the Misty Harbor Lighthouse, tall and powerful.

"It's beautiful," she said breathlessly. The conical structure stood at the edge of a rocky outcropping. It was nearly sixty-five feet high and was a brilliant white, with a black-roofed top that housed the gleaming ruby-red light. Mitch told her that it had 1,100,000 candle-power and could be seen as far as twenty-one miles out to sea.

"Can we go up inside?" she asked anxiously.

"If it's open." He led the way to the lighthouse and arrived just as the doors were being opened.

"Mitch, is that you?" the man asked with surprise. "What brings you up here so early?"

Mitch introduced Ashlyn to the lightkeeper, who was named Patrick McDougall, telling him that Ashlyn had wanted to see the inside of the lighthouse.

"Ye're at the Davenport place, eh?" the man said, and added, with a bit of an Irish lilt, "Ye're not taking any guff from Willy, now, are ye?"

"None at all," Ashlyn grinned, playing along. She loved his accent.

"Well, if he gives ye any trouble at all, y' let me know."

"I will." She smiled at the cute little man, whose face lit up nearly as bright as the lighthouse itself.

"And if y' have any questions, give me a holler. I'll be in th' back."

"Thanks, Patrick," Mitch said, leading Ashlyn to a spiral staircase. They wound their way up, their feet on the metal steps sending echoes through the tower. Finally, they reached the top, where Mitch pushed open the hatch to let them up inside.

He went through first, then helped Ashlyn, holding her hand until she climbed through the hatch and was steady on her feet, then for just a brief moment longer. She looked up into his eyes and felt her heart thudding in her chest again.

"Thanks," she said, trying to force a casual smile. "It's quite a climb up here."

He returned her smile, which made her heart race even faster.

"So," she said nervously, wondering what was going on inside of herself. "Tell me about the lighthouse."

"The lighthouse? Oh, yeah. Well, it was built around 1866. In 1948 they tried to tear it down, but a local historical society was determined to keep the lighthouse standing and fought hard against the city's efforts to destroy it."

He went on about the history of the lighthouse and how it was replaced by modern technology, but was still a huge tourist attraction year round. But Ashlyn wasn't listening.

What is going on with me?

She didn't like how Mitch's presence was affecting her. Just having him touch her triggered a reaction inside her she didn't expect, nor did she want to have. She'd turned off her heart and had encased it in a nice, thick protective wall. A wall she'd spent many months building. But somehow, he was getting through that wall.

And the worst problem was, he wasn't even trying.

She was mad at herself for letting him get to her. What was it about this guy that had everyone in town, even her, entranced by his spell? She had to admit, he was very handsome, and he had a great sense of humor. But it wasn't just that. Everyone—male, female, young, old—they all liked him. And with good reason, Ashlyn was beginning to realize.

He continued talking and even though she wasn't listening, she watched his face while he carefully explained the hand-ground Fresnel lens that came from Paris, France, and weighed over a ton. He had a way of communicating that made the person he was talking to feel like the most important thing in the world to him. It was obvious that he truly cared about others. It wasn't a show. It wasn't to impress anyone. He genuinely liked people.

"Isn't that amazing?" he asked, studying her face.

She nodded, coming back to the conversation. "Amazing," she answered, wondering what exactly they were talking about that was so amazing.

They looked at the view one last time, in awe at how far they could see in every direction, studying the surface of the water for any whales that might be passing by.

Mitch gave her tips on how to spot the whales, telling her to watch for the blow, which could rise as high as twelve feet. Then, as the whale began to dive, the head, dorsal fin, back ridges, and then the tail would break the surface. She squinted and studied the waves and eddies of the water's surface, hoping she would get a glimpse of one of the magnificent mammals, but she saw nothing.

"We'll have to try again. It's getting late in the season, but last week there were some whales sighted off the coast, further south by Cape Foulweather and Depoe Bay."

"I'd love to," she said, hoping that she could actually watch the whales migrate.

Mitch didn't reply, his gaze remaining fixed on the ocean. He was lost in thought and Ashlyn couldn't help but wonder what those thoughts were about. A moment later he snapped out of his trance. "You ready to go?" he asked.

She nodded. "You really do love the ocean, don't you?"

"I do. I think I would've been a sailor except for one terrible drawback when I'm on the ocean."

She lifted her eyebrows, wondering what that could be.

"I get motion sickness," he confessed.

"You do?" He didn't seem the type. He was such a rugged outdoorsman, he seemed too sturdy to be bothered by a little thing like motion sickness. She could see him as captain of a ship, sailing into the wind, battling the waves, conquering the sea.

"It's crazy. I can't even do rides at carnivals without getting queasy. I'm pretty much a landlubber. I think I would have made a good lighthouse keeper though. Since I can't sail, I could at least help the sailors get home safely."

"Grandpa Willy was talking about lighthouses once. He has a very spiritual view of them," she told him.

"I can imagine. These seamen have an amazing level of spirituality I've never understood. Maybe it's because they've experienced the elements so extremely, understood their helplessness and dependency upon the Lord during rough seas or bad storms."

Ashlyn nodded in agreement. "I'm sure he's had some experiences that have made him wonder if he would ever see dry land again."

"He's told me some hair-raising stories."

"I'll have to see if I can talk him into telling me a few of those stories."

"Willy? It won't take much persuasion to get him to talk. He loves to tell stories about his adventures on the high seas. Have him tell you about the time he encountered pirates somewhere off the coast of the Philippines."

It was a long walk home, but they enjoyed the beautiful day and the liveliness of the beach. On a clear, warm day like this, the shore was strewn with joggers, beachcombers, kite flyers, and even a few daring surfers in wetsuits.

"So, what about you?" Mitch said as they reached the final stretch home. "You know more about me than you'd probably like to know. Now tell me about yourself."

"There's not much to tell, really," Ashlyn answered, not completely comfortable with talking about herself. "After high school I went to the University of Utah for a while, then a friend talked me into going to SUU to school. That's where I got to know Cami. We were roommates, and we've been best friends ever since."

"How'd you end up in Seamist?"

"Cami was going to come to Salt Lake after she graduated from SUU, and we were going to live together. But she decided she needed to come back home and be with her grandfather."

Mitch nodded, like he understood her need to come back. "Willy's the salt of the earth," he said, then added, joking, "and the salt of the sea."

Ashlyn laughed. "He's a great guy. I'm sorry I never got to meet Cami's grandmother."

"She was an amazing woman. She worked for my father for years. Did the books at the hardware store and pretty much ran the place," Mitch told her.

Ashlyn couldn't help wondering about Cami's family. "Did they have any other children besides Cami's mother?" she asked.

"Yeah," he answered, a note of sadness in his voice. "They had a son, but he died in a car accident when he was a teenager. He was hit head-on by a drunk driver."

"How awful," Ashlyn replied. "Poor Grandpa Willy." No wonder he was so protective of Cami. He'd lost all his other loved ones. She was all he had left.

Thinking that the Davenport family had had their share of heartbreak,

Ashlyn commented, "You and Cami seem to know each other well."

"Yeah, even though I'm five years older than her—she's my brother's age—we just all kind of hung out together at the hardware store, after school and during the summer." He was quiet, as if remembering. "We had some great times. Sneaking ice cream from the fountain in my dad's store, skateboarding down main street, hiking and exploring Indian trails."

"Sounds wonderful," Ashlyn said, not remembering such a care-free childhood herself.

"Yeah, the problem was, we all grew up and went different directions. My brother got married, Cami went off to school, and of course, you know all about my life."

"Not everything," Ashlyn said, not believing that she was daring to bring up the subject.

"Oh?" he looked at her with amused surprise on his face. "What else would you like to know?"

"I understand you've got a pretty serious girlfriend now," Ashlyn baited him.

"And who told you that?" he asked, with one eyebrow raised.

"No one told me," Ashlyn replied. "I saw her at your ball game."

"Ah, yes, the ball game." He adjusted his sunglasses. "I forgot she was there."

"She's not too easy to forget," Ashlyn said. "She's very beautiful."

"That she is," he agreed.

"Did she grow up around here?" Ashlyn didn't picture the girl being a small-town bumpkin. She was much too sophisticated and glamorous.

"No, she grew up in Seattle. Her father relocated here after he and his wife got divorced. Before she moved here, she was a model in Seattle. She modeled overseas in Japan for a while, then got tired of all the traveling and came home. She's in real estate now."

He didn't answer her question about how serious the relationship was, and Ashlyn didn't feel like she could pry any further just now.

"Here we are," Mitch said as they approached the wooden steps. He let her go ahead of him and they climbed up to the Davenports' backyard.

"Ahoy there, mates," Grandpa Willy shouted from the deck when he saw them.

"Good morning, Willy," Mitch called. "How are you?"

"Dandy, Mitch. Just dandy."

Mitch and Grandpa Willy got into a conversation about Patrick McDougall over at the lighthouse, and Ashlyn excused herself and went inside.

"Whoa," she said when she saw it was almost eleven o'clock. "I had no idea it was so late."

"Ash, is that you?" Cami came around the corner from the kitchen. The wonderful smell of homemade bread followed her.

"Mmm, something smells heavenly." Ashlyn followed her back into the kitchen where several loaves of bread were cooling on racks. Ashlyn looked at the loaves in awe. "Since when did you learn to make homemade bread?" she asked with surprise.

Cami pointed to a machine in the corner on the cabinet. "Don't be too impressed. I used my grandma's breadmaker. Want a piece with butter and honey?" Cami asked, proud of her yeasty master-pieces.

"Boy, would I. I bet Mitch would, too."

"Is he still here?" Cami looked out the kitchen window.

"He's talking with your grandfather." Ashlyn went to the sink to wash her hands.

"So how was your walk?" Cami asked as she sliced thick, steaming pieces of freshly baked bread.

"Long," Ashlyn said, wiping her hands on a dish towel. "But nice. I loved seeing that lighthouse. It's so beautiful. And what a view. I wished I'd had my camera with me."

"We can go back sometime and take pictures," Cami offered.

"If we ever have another day as beautiful as today," Ashlyn said, getting several plates out of the cupboard for her friend.

"And, how did you and Mitch get along?" Cami asked in a tone that hinted at more than just mere curiosity.

"We had a nice talk."

Cami looked at her with a less than amused expression, obviously wanting more.

"Okay, he's a nice guy, I take everything back I said about him."

Cami continued "the look" until Ashlyn burst out. "What?"

"You just spent the last five hours with the man and all you can say is that he's a nice guy?"

"What else do you want me to say?"

"I don't know. Something like, you found him fascinating to talk to or you can't wait to go running with him again in the morning." Cami would have continued feeding her lines, but Ashlyn ignored her and quickly set about the task of putting the bread slices on the plates and spreading them with butter before they cooled.

"I think you've forgotten that he already has a girlfriend, and . . . ," Ashlyn said pointedly as she reached for the honey, ". . . that I am not looking for a relationship. Remember?"

Cami looked disappointed.

"You weren't trying to play matchmaker with us, were you?" Ashlyn paused, her knife hanging in mid-air. "You weren't faking this morning so Mitch and I could be together alone, were you?"

Cami looked hurt that Ashlyn would even accuse her of such a thing. "No," she said. "That was real. It's just that you were gone so long, I thought maybe a few sparks had ignited between you."

Ashlyn didn't tell her that there actually were a few sparks, if only at her end of the sparkler. But that didn't mean she was going to pursue them. Analyzing her reaction to Mitch earlier at the light-house, she reasoned that it had been only natural, given her vulnerable state after Jake. He'd left her wounded and bleeding. Of course she would respond to any kind and caring person. But Mitch already had a girlfriend and Ashlyn was going to remain unattached and uninvolved. So it was a double dead-end. Thank goodness.

⋯⋯ 🐚 ⋯⋯

The men accepted the food eagerly and each asked for seconds, along with tall, cold glasses of milk to go along with them. Then Mitch glanced down at his watch.

"I'd better shove off. I've got baseball practice at noon." He turned to Ashlyn. "Thanks for a fun morning. I hope you don't want to go that far every morning, or you may have to get yourself another workout partner."

"Don't worry," Ashlyn answered. "I'll be lucky to make it down the stairs and back in the morning."

The phone rang. "I'll get it." Cami jumped up from her chair and was through the door before the second ring. "Ash, it's for you," she called. "It's your mom."

Picking up the telephone in the kitchen, Ashlyn immediately heard the strange note in her mother's voice. *Uh-oh,* she thought, *something's up.*

"Ashlyn, honey, it's good to hear you," Miranda said.

"You too, Mom. How are you?"

"Well . . ." Her mother's voice trembled.

"Mom?"

"Oh, honey. I've been to the doctor and I have some rather shocking news for you."

Ashlyn collapsed into the nearest chair. Deep down, she'd known all along something was wrong with her mother. With a deep breath she steeled herself for the news. Was it cancer? A disease? What?

"I'm pregnant, Ashlyn."

CHAPTER
FIFTEEN

"You're what?" Ashlyn nearly choked. Her mother was almost forty-three.

"I'm pregnant," her mother replied softly.

"How can you—" she caught herself and said in a loud whisper, "*—be pregnant?*"

Cami, who had been putting away the butter and honey, accidentally missed the shelf. The butter dish and plastic bear containing the honey both clattered to the counter. Her face registered as much shock as Ashlyn's.

"Honey, are you sure you want me to answer that?" Miranda's voice held a touch of humor.

"You know what I mean. Aren't you too old to be pregnant?" Ashlyn couldn't believe what she was hearing. What was her mother thinking of? Especially at her age.

"I don't know why you're so upset, dear. Garrett and I are very excited about this," Miranda said, more calmly now in the face of Ashlyn's evident agitation.

"Excited? Mom, aren't you a little old for this?"

Cami's eyebrows raised at Ashlyn's comment. Her face reflected a different expression now, one of disappointment at Ashlyn's reaction. But Ashlyn couldn't help it. How in the world could her mother do such a thing? Didn't she have enough going on right now, with Ashlyn in Oregon and Adam on his mission? How could she take care of the two kids she already had *plus* a new baby?

In some strange way she felt like she was "losing" her mother, and the thought scared her. Her mother had always been there for her, and Ashlyn still needed her in her life. Especially now, when she was trying move on with her life and put the past behind her.

"I know this is quite a shock to you," Miranda tried to reason with her. "But I think once you get used to the idea you'll see why this is a wonderful blessing for our family. If you only knew how happy I am about this. I wanted to have more children, but your father wouldn't hear of it. I really feel like Heavenly Father—" her voice broke and Ashlyn felt the hardness in her heart begin to soften, "—like he's given me a gift. A precious, special gift."

Tears stung Ashlyn's eyes. If anyone deserved a gift from heaven it was her mother, for all the garbage, neglect, and abuse she'd had to put up with while she was married to Ashlyn's father.

"I'm sorry, Mom," Ashlyn said repentantly. "This is just the last thing I ever imagined you calling to tell me. I mean, you've been so moody and emotional, I just thought it was menopause or something."

"So did I," Miranda confessed. "My cycle was so messed up I finally went to the doctor yesterday to find out what was going on. I nearly fell off the examining table when he told me the news. Luckily Garrett was with me or I would have."

Ashlyn giggled at the thought of her mom's reaction to such an unexpected explanation for her condition. "So how are you feeling?"

"Hungry. Queasy. And very tired. I think that's the worst part. I'm so much more tired this time than I was with either of you kids. Being older does have some disadvantages," she added with a sigh.

"Well, you need to take it easy then," Ashlyn instructed her sternly.

"I will, honey," Miranda chuckled.

Ashlyn felt a twinge of guilt that she wasn't there to help her mother. "Maybe I should come home so I can help you?" she suggested.

"Heavens no," Miranda retorted promptly. "There's absolutely nothing you could do. Garrett does most of the cooking anyway, and housecleaning's no problem; the two of us don't really make that much of a mess. Really, there's nothing you could do if you did come home."

"But if you ever feel like you need my help, you know I'll be there, right?" Ashlyn insisted, feeling a combination of emotions— guilt, concern, relief, and she didn't quite know what else.

"Of course I do, dear. I'll call you if I need you. But we're doing great so far. In fact, Garrett just ran to the store to get some shrimp for me, then we're going to do some shopping. Do you realize I don't even know what kind of cribs and car seats and high chairs they have nowadays. And diapers. I've never used disposable diapers. Your father thought they were an unnecessary expense."

"I didn't think you liked shrimp," Ashlyn said.

"I don't, but it sounds good right now. With cocktail sauce. My mouth is watering just thinking about it."

Ashlyn smiled, suddenly getting a strong dose of homesickness. Maybe she should go home anyway, if not to help, just to be there with her mother.

"Mom," she asked again, "are you sure you don't want me to come home?"

"Sweetie, you know how much I'd love to see you. I miss you every day. But you'll be back in a few months, and that's going to go by so fast. I won't even be showing when you get home. I may be fifty pounds heavier, but you're not going to miss that much," she consoled Ashlyn. "If you come home, I want it to be because you want to. Don't do it for my sake, because you'll just spend all your time watching me sleep, or eat. Really—stay there and have fun. It's after the baby comes that I'm going to need your help."

Ashlyn felt better. As much as she wanted to be with her mother, she didn't want to leave Seamist quite yet. "Okay," she said. "But if you need me—"

"I'll call," Miranda said. "Now, start thinking of names for me, and give Cami and her grandfather my love."

"I will, Mom. I love you. And you know what? I am starting to feel a little excited. I hope it's a girl. I always wanted a little sister."

"I'll see what I can do," Miranda promised.

Hanging up the phone, Ashlyn sat in the quiet of the kitchen. Cami had left, wanting to give her friend some privacy.

A baby, Ashlyn mused. Her mother was going to have a baby!

Cami, Grandpa Willy, and Mitch looked up at her as she stepped through the doors out onto the deck.

"Cami said you'd received some upsetting news," Mitch said. "I decided to stay in case there was anything I could do."

That was so nice of him. Why was he such a nice guy?

"How are you doing?" Cami asked, her eyes full of concern.

Ashlyn looked at Mitch and Grandpa Willy, trying to see from their eyes if Cami had said anything. Then she looked at Cami. "Did you tell them?"

Cami nodded. "I hope that's okay."

"It was such a shock," she admitted. "And at first I felt so angry at my mother. I'm not sure why. But when she told me how excited she was to have the baby and how she felt like it was a gift from God, well," she said sheepishly, "how could I stay mad? I mean, really. I guess this is something she's wanted for a long, long time."

"This baby will be a great blessing to your entire family," Grandpa Willy said smiling, although his voice held the solemnity of both age and wisdom. "You'll see."

Mitch gave her an encouraging smile, and although she didn't know why, it made her feel better.

The girls spent some of Friday and most of Saturday getting ready for the big barbecue that night. The girls made a wonderful vegetable and pasta salad and a fruit salad, and marinated chicken breasts for the grill. Cami showed Ashlyn how to make her grandmother's famous baked beans with maple syrup and bits of bacon. Pearl was bringing dessert and asked if the girls would help her carry it down when it was time to eat.

Grandpa Willy waited patiently for them to get out of the kitchen so he could work on his concoction known as "kick-a-poo-joy-juice." Ashlyn asked Cami what went into the drink, but Cami had never been allowed into the kitchen to find out. It was Grandpa's secret, and he wasn't about to tell the ingredients to his trademark drink. Cami did ask him if they'd all have to go confess to the bishop in the morning after drinking the juice, but he just chased her out of the kitchen with a wooden spoon and a flourish. They had no choice but to let the juice remain a secret.

The girls swept the deck and arranged chairs so everyone could sit comfortably and visit during dinner. Then they brought out a card table and covered it with a bright floral print tablecloth so they could arrange the food on it.

By four o'clock in the afternoon everything was ready for the barbecue. They'd kept their fingers crossed all day that the weather would cooperate and so far the clouds stayed a harmless, fluffy white against a startlingly blue sky.

Ashlyn couldn't help feeling excited for the fun evening ahead. Grandpa Willy had grumbled a few times that he didn't know why Cami had to go and invite Pearl to the barbecue, but she had pooh-poohed his complaints and told him to go back and finish mixing his magic potion before they decided to go through the garbage can to see what exactly he had put in the drink.

With a little time to spare, the girls wandered up to see if Pearl needed any help. It took a minute for her to come to the door, and when she finally answered, they could tell she had been crying.

"Hi, girls," she said brightly, trying to blink away the moisture in her red and swollen eyes. "Come in."

"Pearl, are you okay?" Cami asked her.

"I'm fine, dear," Pearl tried to assure her, but neither Cami nor Ashlyn was convinced. Something had obviously upset her. "I've just got a few skeletons in my closet that get to rattling from time to time. I'll be fine."

Still in the dark about what was bothering their friend, Cami and Ashlyn let the subject drop, sensing that pushing the issue would most likely get Pearl even more upset.

"We came by to see if you needed any help for tonight."

"I'd love some help," she accepted gratefully, her mood brightening a little. "I've got the crusts made. I was just getting ready to make the pie filling. We can do cream pies, like coconut, banana, or chocolate. Or we can do fruit pies, like strawberry, peach, and apple."

Ashlyn thought about the choices for a moment. "I feel like I'm at Marie Callender's with so many choices. Coconut sounds wonderful, but strawberry is my favorite."

"And we have to have chocolate," Cami insisted.

"Well then," Pearl offered a compromise, "we'll mix and match them. We can do some cream pies and some fruit pies. With all three of us working, we'll have them ready in no time."

While Pearl made one more crust, Ashlyn washed and cleaned strawberries straight from Pearl's garden. Cami stirred chocolate pudding on the stove and when it was done, she started on some vanilla pudding for the coconut cream pie. Since blackberrry was Pearl's favorite, she took charge of making it.

The three women arrived with the pies just as a sleek black sports car pulled up in front of the Davenports' house. It was Dallin.

Cami handed her pie to Ashlyn and hurried over to greet him. When Dallin put his arms around Cami in an unrestrained hug, Ashlyn smiled, hoping that the two of them would have a second chance at love. Every time Ashlyn even mentioned Dallin's name, Cami got a starry look in her eye. Not that Ashlyn was anxious to have her friend up and get married on her, but she wouldn't be a true friend if she didn't want what was best for Cami. And if this was what was best, then that was all that mattered.

Taking the pies into the house, Pearl and Ashlyn put them in the fridge. Grandpa Willy had already fired up the barbecue, so Pearl helped Ashlyn carry dishes of food out to the table on the deck.

Cami and Dallin joined them bringing his bags of chips and some liters of soda pop. Hearing them laughing at something private between them, Ashlyn knew that Cami's feelings for Dallin hadn't changed. She had that love-struck, starry look in her eye, and Dallin's face reflected the same feeling. Ashlyn's heart twinged slightly in her chest as she remembered what it felt like to love and be loved, to have someone's mere presence set her heartbeat racing and send shivers running up her spine.

The doorbell rang, jarring her thoughts. Grandpa Willy and Pearl were visiting together, and Dallin and Cami appeared to be in a world of their own, so Ashlyn went to answer it. It was Mitch, dressed in khaki-colored shorts, a white polo shirt that buttoned at the neck, and a pair of Teva sandals. He looked exceptionally handsome with his tan skin, wavy blonde hair, and smiling blue eyes.

"Hey," he said, "hope you don't mind if I brought a guest along."

"No, of course—"

"Mitch!" a female voice called. "I still can't find my lipstick. Can you come help me?"

"Just a minute," Mitch said holding up one finger. "I'll be right back."

Ashlyn's heart sank. Not that she'd expected to be Mitch's dinner partner, or date, but she hadn't anticipated him bringing "what's-her-name" along.

But why shouldn't he? she reasoned. *If I were his girlfriend, I would want to be with him all the time.*

Instead of waiting for them to return, Ashlyn left the door open and went into the kitchen to see if anything else needed to be taken out to the deck. She was mad at herself for caring that Mitch wasn't alone, but she couldn't help it. Opening a can of olives, she drained the juice and dumped them onto the relish tray with the other vegetables.

"Where should I put this?"

Ashlyn turned to see Vanessa standing in the doorway of the kitchen, holding a salad bowl in her hand. She wore slim white pants, delicate strappy sandals, and a deep turquoise blue sleeveless shell that hugged every curve of her very curvy body. She was deeply tanned and her hair and makeup were "runway" perfect.

Ashlyn felt like a frumpy cow standing in the same room with her, in her denim shorts, bright yellow T-shirt, and earthy, clunky Doc Martin sandals.

"Out on the deck. There's a table for the food."

"Thank you," Vanessa said elegantly. "I don't believe we've met."

"I'm Ashlyn, Cami's friend. I'm just here for the summer."

"Nice to meet you, Ashlyn. I'm Vanessa James," she said formally, making Ashlyn feel uncomfortable and cloddy in her casual clothes. "I'm Mitch's girlfriend. I hope it's okay that I'm here." She gave a throaty laugh. "He insisted that I come along."

"We're glad to have you," Ashlyn lied. "Why don't you go out with the others and I'll finish up in here?"

Vanessa wiggled her slim fanny out of the room and headed out to the deck. Ashlyn heard everyone greet her enthusiastically.

"So glad you could come, Vanessa," Ashlyn said under her breath. *"Don't you look lovely, Vanessa. Hope you choke on an olive pit, Vanessa."*

Ashlyn loaded the sink full of dishes into the dishwasher, wiped off the counter and put away the clutter. She was sweeping the floor when Cami walked in.

"What in the world are you doing?" Cami cried.

"Uh, this would be called sweeping," Ashlyn said in her best kindergarten teacher voice.

"But why are you doing it now? The chicken's on the grill and everyone's wondering where you are."

Ashlyn paused to give her friend a look that said, "I really doubt it," then continued sweeping. "I just wanted to straighten up in here first."

"Just leave it, we can clean up later." Cami insisted.

"Okay, already. What's the big deal anyway?"

Cami pulled a face. "Oh, I'm just bugged that Mitch brought Vanessa with him," she said, her voice lowered.

Ashlyn felt better, knowing that Cami didn't want Vanessa here either.

Cami went on, after checking the doorway to make sure no one walked in on them while she was talking. "She's just so stuffy and snooty, and Mitch can't relax and be himself when she's around."

Ashlyn didn't feel the need to voice her own feelings as well; she thought Cami was doing just great on her own.

"She's just standing there, looking bored out of her mind. I've tried to make conversation with her, but she's about as much fun to talk to as a mannequin."

Outside on the deck, Willy tended the meat on the grill. Pearl, Dallin, and Mitch were having a conversation about sports. Pearl was an avid Portland Trailblazers fan, and, Vanessa, added as much life to the party as a Barbie doll, standing next to Mitch with her arm possessively entwined in his, looking just as Cami had described her—bored out of her mind.

"How's the chicken coming, Grandpa?" Cami asked.

"I think we're about there. Why don't we have a prayer and we can eat?" Grandpa Willy suggested. He asked Mitch to offer the prayer on the food, and though Mitch prayed that they would have an enjoyable evening together, Ashlyn thought silently that it would take a miracle from heaven for Vanessa to actually enjoy herself with this crowd. Just as he was closing his prayer, there was a loud explosion.

Without even saying "Amen," Cami cried, "Grandpa, you didn't?!"

Grandpa Willy looked down at his shoes like a ten-year-old in trouble for throwing a baseball through the front window. Cami covered her face in her hands and groaned. *You made root beer!"*

Ashlyn didn't waste any time. She ran into the house and skidded to a halt when she got into the kitchen. The cupboard doors beneath the sink were wide open. Brown, sticky liquid dripped from the counters and stove, and puddled on the floor. Luckily, the glass jug hadn't shattered; it had merely cracked into several large pieces. Ashlyn didn't even know where to begin to start cleaning.

"Where are the paper towels?" Mitch said behind her.

She twirled around, surprised. "In the pantry right there," she pointed.

"Let's get up as much with the paper towels as we can, then we can wipe it down," he suggested.

"You don't have to clean this up," Ashlyn told him. "Cami and I can do it."

"It's my fault Willy made the root beer in the first place. He asked me if I wanted to try some and I said yes," Mitch said, taking all the blame. "The least I can do is help clean it up."

Ashlyn heard Cami stomping through the door, grumbling, "I can't believe Grandpa made root beer again, after what happened last time—"

She gave a shriek when she stepped into the kitchen.

"Cami, it's not that bad." Ashlyn tried to settle her down. "We can clean this up in a few minutes."

"Here," Mitch grabbed two rolls of paper towels, handing one to Ashlyn. "You start on one end and I'll start on the other."

With a sigh, Cami said, "Give me some, too."

They carefully picked up the glass, then went through wad after wad of paper towels, soaking up the sticky liquid, finding it in places they hadn't expected; it had seeped into the drawers and dripped down the pantry doors clear across the room.

Cami unloaded the cleaning supplies from beneath the cupboard where the root beer bomb had detonated and washed everything off in hot, soapy water in the sink. Even Dallin came in and helped wipe off the cupboard doors and tile floor. Pearl offered to help, but they told her they had it under control. Ashlyn noticed Vanessa didn't even offer to help, which wasn't a surprise.

As for Grandpa Willy, well, Cami had banished him from the kitchen.

Within twenty minutes the kitchen was sparkling clean and back in order. Hungrily, the group descended on the food, piling their plates high with the delicious salads and crunchy chips. Everyone found a chair and began eating. Even though the chicken was a little dry from keeping warm on the back of the grill, everything else was delicious.

Vanessa sat so close to Mitch that Ashlyn wondered how he had enough room to move his arms and hands to eat. While his plate was loaded with food, Vanessa had a piece of chicken about the size of a McNugget, and a spoonful of green salad with no dressing.

Noticing Vanessa's plate, Cami exchanged an annoyed glance with Ashlyn.

"This pasta is delicious," Dallin announced.

"Cami made it," Ashlyn piped up, making sure Cami received credit for the dish.

Cami was about to get some pop for everyone when Grandpa Willy stopped her. "Wait just a minute there, Cami," he said. "Now I know the root beer didn't go over too well."

"Actually it went over with a real bang, Willy," Mitch joked.

"I guess it did at that," he laughed. "Anyway, I still have something else for you to try. It's in that cooler right there under the table."

"Grandpa—" Cami gave him a warning glare, "—this had better not explode!"

"Now, Cami girl, have a little faith in your grandfather. This is my famous 'kick-a-poo-joy-juice,' and you've never had anything so tasty in your life."

He lifted the five-gallon cooler onto the edge of the table, grabbed a paper cup, and filled it. "Guaranteed to wet your whistle and curl your toes," he said, holding the drink up for everyone to see.

"I'll give it a try," Mitch said bravely.

"Me too," Dallin jumped up to get his cupful.

Everyone, even Vanessa, watched with anticipation as Mitch took a long sip.

"Oooowee!" he exclaimed. "Willy, that's good stuff. How about a little more?"

Dallin also agreed it was delicious and Ashlyn couldn't help but be enticed to give it a try.

"Pearl, how daring do you feel tonight?" Ashlyn asked before she got up to get her own drink.

"I haven't got anything to lose," she told Ashlyn.

Mitch tried to coax Vanessa into having some of the juice, but she refused, asking him to get her a glass of ice water instead.

Ashlyn took a tentative sip and swirled the liquid around in her mouth before swallowing. It had a tangy tropical taste—pineapple juice, fruit-punch flavored Kool-Aid, and Sprite, she guessed, with a little dry ice to make it bubble and dance.

"Grandpa," Cami said, "this is actually pretty good tonight. I hope you remember how you made it this time." She explained that it tasted different every time because he reinvented the juice each time he made it. "I think this recipe is worth keeping."

"It is good," Pearl exclaimed. "Reminds me of something I drank once in Morocco."

"Morocco?" Willy said. "You've been to Morocco?"

"Several times, actually," she told him. "In Casablanca they have this wonderful dish, a lot like a shish kebab."

"I've had it," Willy exclaimed "With lamb and potatoes and leeks?"

"That's it," Pearl said excitedly. "There's a place on the market square—"

"Fami Faheem's!" Willy interrupted.

"That's it! You've been there?" Pearl asked.

The two exchanged stories of exotic places and foods and kept the group, even Vanessa, entertained trying to outdo each other with wild tales of peril and adventure. But even Willy was no match for Pearl, as she told of a boat trip down a river in an African forest where no white man had ever gone before.

With a newfound respect for his neighbor, Willy took Pearl up on her offer to show him the stuffed crocodile she got from that particularly hair-raising adventure.

Vanessa leaned over and whispered something to Mitch. She ran her fingers through the hair on the back of his neck as she talked to him, then she stood and went inside the house. Mitch and Dallin decided on one last piece of chicken. Seeing that the honey mustard sauce was gone, Ashlyn offered to get some more from the kitchen. When she walked inside, she heard Vanessa talking on the telephone.

"I know how important this is, Daddy," Vanessa's voice was insistent. "We're about done here, then I'll have Mitch bring me over. That is, if I can get him away from 'these people.'"

Ashlyn stopped in her tracks, knowing that she should turn around and leave but unable to force herself to do so.

"No, you don't need to come and get me. He can bring me in that ridiculous car of his." There was a pause in the conversation. "I don't get it either. I took him to look at BMWs in Portland, but he just wasn't interested. Sometimes he makes me so frustrated, but at least I got him to quit wearing those awful cowboy boots of his."

Ashlyn had to admit that Mitch would look good in a BMW, but she already knew from the few times she'd talked with Mitch, that it just wasn't his style.

"I'll be there in time for the conference call," she said. "I'm not about to miss that for this sorry little barbecue."

Ashlyn was about to turn around and go back outside when she decided to go on into the kitchen and surprise Vanessa. Making as much noise as possible, she entered the room. She suppressed a smile as Vanessa's head jerked her direction and she quickly ended her phone call.

Ashlyn smiled at Vanessa, then quickly found the sauce, and went back outside. Vanessa followed soon after.

After one last glass of Willy's juice, Mitch sat back and patted his stomach. "I'm so full I could pop."

"Don't do that," Cami warned. "We've had enough popping around here tonight."

Vanessa bounced her foot impatiently.

"Hey," Dallin said, "who's up for a game of Frisbee?"

Of course, Mitch, Cami, and Ashlyn accepted the offer.

"You don't mind, do you?" Mitch asked Vanessa. "Just for a couple of minutes?"

"Of course she doesn't." Pearl came to the girl's rescue. "I haven't had a chance to visit with her all evening. This will give us some time to chat."

Vanessa smiled stiffly at Pearl but remained silent as Mitch grabbed the Frisbee from the deck and headed toward the beach.

"We'll clean up when we get back, Grandpa," Cami called over her shoulder.

"How about some more of that juice, Willy?" Pearl requested, with a twinkle in her eye.

A few gray-bottomed clouds sat low on the horizon, but there was no threat of rain. Just a warm breeze and scattered sunshine.

Dallin had a great arm and could send the frisbee straight and low, while Mitch threw it in an arch, making it travel yards down the beach. Ashlyn had a horrible right hook and managed to hit the water more often than the receivers. Cami wasn't much for catching; she usually covered her face and ducked when it came her way, but she was a good sport about retrieving the frisbee and did a fairly decent job of returning the throw.

They played for twenty minutes or so until Vanessa came to the steps to announce to Mitch that it was time to go. The foursome had just figured out a game of Frisbee Football, two against two, Dallin and Cami against Ashlyn and Mitch, and the score was tied.

"Okay," Mitch called. "I'll be right there."

Ashlyn noticed Vanessa's skin turn a shade of red that matched the setting sun. Mitch's girlfriend was obviously anxious to get to her "conference call." Ashlyn was equally anxious to tell Cami all about the conversation she had overheard.

"I'll go long," Mitch told her as they geared up to receive one of Dallin's throws. "He may try and fake us out and throw short and low, so keep your head up."

"Got it," Ashlyn said.

Cami and Dallin were in some type of huddle, which they seemed to spend a lot of time doing.

"Mitch," Vanessa called again.

"C'mon, Gardner, throw the crazy thing already," Mitch yelled at their opponents.

"Keep your shirt on," Dallin hollered back.

"Here it comes, Ash," Mitch called to her. Ashlyn liked how he shortened her name. She crouched down in a ready stance and waited as Dallin stretched his arm, preparing to launch his final throw that would break the tie, one way or the other.

He rolled the Frisbee into his shoulder, then with a grunt, he sent it flying straight at Ashlyn. It came so fast she barely had time to think. Keeping her eye on it, she reached out to catch it, but it hit her hands and spiked upward.

"I got it," Mitch cried, running full steam.

"I got it," Ashlyn yelled, going for the deflected disk.

The two reached for the Frisbee simultaneously. Ashlyn caught it then felt herself slammed as if by a Mac truck and buried in the sand with Mitch's massive form crushing her.

CHAPTER SIXTEEN

"Get off!" Ashlyn gasped but he didn't seem to hear her. With the last of her ebbing strength, she reached up and grabbed his hair and pulled as hard as she could.

With an outraged cry, Mitch rolled over, but when he saw the expression on Ashlyn's face, he quickly scrambled off of her.

Oxygen—sweet, fresh, lifesaving oxygen—filled her lungs. As she gulped in huge breaths, a swirling lightheadedness came over her. Collapsing back into the sand, she allowed her body to enjoy the sensation of not being crushed and continued to breathe deeply.

Mitch knelt down beside her. "Ash, are you okay?"

"Now—" she gulped in a breath, "that you're—" and another one, "not sitting—" and one more, "—on my chest."

"I'm sorry," he said. "Let me help you up. I didn't break anything, did I?"

"Only my bones," she said, trying to joke but wondering if it were partly true.

"Is she okay?" Cami came running as fast as she could.

"I think so," Mitch told her.

"I can't believe she caught that," Dallin said, following on Cami's heels.

"Here." Mitch scooped her into his arms. "Just relax. I'll carry you."

"I caught it?" Ashlyn asked with disbelief.

"Yeah," Mitch said proudly. "You can be on my team any time."

"I think I'd rather lose," she said drolly. Mitch laughed, relieved that she was going to be okay.

"Is she okay?" Vanessa asked as they mounted the stairs.

"I think so," Mitch said.

Ashlyn felt like she could walk on her own, but she liked having Mitch carry her. She especially liked that it was in front of Vanessa and that she'd won the game!

Pearl stood up as the group approached. "Oh, my goodness," she cried. "What happened?"

Cami filled Pearl and her grandfather in on the last play of the game while Mitch set Ashlyn gently in one of the lounge chairs. "I'm fine," Ashlyn complained, sitting up. "You don't need to fuss."

"Just stay right there," Mitch commanded, pushing her shoulders back down. "I saw those stars going around your head. I hit you pretty hard."

"I'm okay, really." But Ashlyn did as she was told and relaxed against the woven straps of the chair.

"You've got sand in your hair," Mitch said, brushing at her long, sand-matted locks.

"And up my nose and in my mouth, too," Ashlyn told him.

"Somebody get her a drink of water," Mitch called protectively while he tried to brush out as much sand as he could from her hair.

Cami handed Ashlyn a glass of water. "That was quite a catch. You want to show us that again?"

Sipping the water, she paused long enough to say, "Sure, maybe later."

"Mitch," Vanessa said. "I'm really sorry, but I need to get going."

"Oh, yeah." He glanced at his watch, then dug his keys out of his shorts pocket, tossed them to her, and said, "Why don't you take my car and I'll meet up with you later. Dallin can give me a ride home, can't you?"

Vanessa looked at Dallin and Mitch levelly, then shifted her penetrating eyes to Ashlyn.

Ashlyn shrank back in her chair. Did this woman think she'd sabotaged their date on purpose? Ashlyn was crazy but not that crazy. She wasn't about to sacrifice her body just to mess up Vanessa's evening. But seeing Vanessa fume made it almost worth it.

Vanessa cleared her throat. "All right, then." She turned to Cami. "Where's my purse?"

"I think it's in here on the couch," Cami said, taking their guest inside to get her belongings. Cami returned a moment later.

Mitch took a seat in a chair next to Ashlyn. "So," he said to her, "where'd you learn to play like that?"

"My little brother," she said. "We're very competitive. He's bigger than me, but I'm tougher than him." The group laughed and the mood lightened.

"Look at that sunset, will you?" Grandpa Willy said, as his gaze caught the final rays of sun sinking below the ocean. Everyone turned and watched in silence as the clouds ignited in a fiery burst of color. Dallin turned and noticed the gables, spires, and top balcony of the Davenport mansion peeking over the trees, reflecting the crimson hues of the setting sun.

"Now there's a sight," he directed their attention to the mansion. It looked mystical and magical in the fading pink-tinged light, majestic and powerful, sitting high upon its jutting precipice, surrounded by thick pines, overlooking the ocean below. "I can see why you want to turn it into a bed and breakfast," he added.

Cami's cheerful, relaxed expression turned to one of horror.

Grandpa Willy's forehead wrinkled with confusion. "What did you say?"

"I said, I can see why—" His voice faded as he caught the panicked look on Cami's face. "Uh oh," he said quietly. "I think it's time for me to go now."

"Dessert," Pearl interjected, trying to throw the conversation off course. "We haven't had dessert." She charged toward the door to go inside and get the pies but stopped when she saw Vanessa standing there. "Oh, my goodness, you startled me."

"Vanessa," Mitch said, "what are you doing back?"

"The car won't start," she stated impatiently.

"Gotta be the Mustang," Dallin said. "Are you still trying to restore that old thing, Mitch?"

"Hey," Mitch defended his car, "that 'old thing' will be worth a fortune once it's finished."

"Did I just hear you talking about turning the Davenport

mansion into a bed and breakfast?" Vanessa inquired casually.

The moment was growing more awkward by the minute. Fortunately, Mitch seemed to recognize the need to keep the conversation off the topic of the bed and breakfast. He jumped to his feet and said to Vanessa, "I'll go out and start it for you. I've been having trouble with the starter all week."

After he had whisked her away, no one dared speak or move. Grandpa Willy asked his question again, very slowly. "Now what in tarnation is all this talk about a bed and breakfast?" He looked at Cami, who squirmed under his questioning gaze.

"Well, Grandpa, you see—"

"Here's the pie," Pearl announced as she stepped through the back door. She brought the pies out on a tray and, with Ashlyn's help, unloaded them onto the table.

Cami didn't try to avoid the topic again. It was time to confront the issue. "Grandpa, it's a shame the mansion is just sitting there, rotting away. There's just got to be some use for it. And if you really think about it, a bed and breakfast makes perfect sense. We could get a loan to fund the renovation, then rent out the rooms. I'm sure we could make enough money to pay the loan payment each month and make a profit."

His gaze narrowed. "When were you planning on telling me about this?"

"I didn't want to bother you about it until I knew funding was available. Without a loan from the bank we couldn't do any of the improvements or remodeling."

Grandpa Willy looked at Dallin. "I suppose that's where you come in?"

"Yes, sir," Dallin said respectfully.

"And, is your bank willing to give my granddaughter some money for this project?"

"Well, sir, it's too soon to tell. She hasn't turned in the paperwork yet."

"And Grandpa—" Cami couldn't keep the excitement out of her voice, "—it would be the perfect place to use some of that furniture you've been storing. We've talked about decorating it with turn-of-the-century furnishings to make it authentic, and with some of the things you've brought home from all the places you've visited, the Sea Rose Bed and Breakfast would be absolutely unique."

"The Sea Rose?" he asked, one of his bushy eyebrows arching up suspiciously.

Cami swallowed. "I think my great-great-grandmother loved roses. Nearly every window has stained glasswork above it done in roses."

"How did you see the windows behind the boards?" he asked.

Cami looked down at her hands in her lap. "We went inside and looked around."

"You what?" Grandpa Willy demanded. "Haven't I told you how dangerous it is inside there? Cami, I've told you I don't want you in that place. If anything had happened to you . . ." He stopped, unable to continue.

"I'm sorry, Grandpa. I know we shouldn't have gone in without talking to you first."

"Who's 'we'?"

"Me and Ashlyn," Cami said.

"And me," Pearl added. "And you don't need to get all in a dither over this, William. That place is still very strong and sturdy. I agree with Cami. It's a shame to let it sit like that."

Grandpa Willy gave her a stare that would have turned wood to stone. Pearl immediately clamped her mouth shut.

"Pearl even offered to let us use her things, too," Cami went on. "She has this wonderful zebra skin that would look fabulous on the wall or spread across one of the beds. We could take you over to her place and show it to you."

Grandpa Willy sat back, thinking. "I don't know," he muttered, shaking his head. "It would take so much work to restore that place. It doesn't even have any electrical wiring or indoor plumbing. It might be sound structurally, but the roof leaks and the porch is rotting."

Cami was starting to look desperate. "Grandpa, won't you at least think about the idea?" she pleaded. "We could never do it without your permission. Please?"

Ashlyn saw his rigid expression grow softer. He scratched the bald spot on top of his head thoughtfully, then looked at Dallin, "You really think something like this would go?"

Dallin didn't hesitate. "Bed and breakfasts are very popular places for people to stay when they come to the coast. And since there aren't any right here in Seamist, I don't see how it could be anything but a success."

All four faces looked anxiously at Grandpa Willy. His brow furrowed as he stared unyieldingly at them for a moment. "All right," he said. "I'm not saying I agree or that you can do it. But I'll think about it."

"Thank you, Grandpa." Cami ran over and threw her arms around his neck. She gave him a kiss on the cheek, then hugged him again.

"That's enough," he said. "Go on with you now, and get your old grandfather some of that pie."

No one could choose which type of pie to have, so they all ended up having small pieces of all four. The strawberry was Ashlyn's favorite. She loved the tart berries in sweet sauce and the delicate layer of whipped cream on top. Pearl's crust was buttery and flaky and melted right in her mouth.

Just as everyone was finishing their fourth sampling, Mitch walked through the door.

"Hey, Cruiser," Dallin said, "where've you been?"

"The car started with no problem," Mitch said, "but I decided to take Vanessa home. She said to tell you thank you for such a nice evening and that she was sorry she had to leave."

Cami and Ashlyn looked at each other, both fighting the urge to burst into laughter.

Yeah, right, Ashlyn wanted to say, *and she hopes we can get together again real soon.*

"You're just in time for pie," Pearl said. "Would you like to give one a try?"

"I'd like to give them all a try," he said, looking at the pies hungrily.

While Mitch followed their lead and sampled each of the pies, Cami told him about the plans for the mansion.

"Vanessa will be sorry she missed hearing about all of this. She was really interested in the idea of converting the house to a bed and breakfast."

When Mitch asked for another piece of strawberry pie, Ashlyn couldn't help thinking it was curious that they both liked it best. She also noticed that he was much more relaxed with Vanessa out of the picture.

As a heavy, round moon rose, bathing them in a soft glow, turning the water to silver ripples, the group enjoyed the quiet of the evening, sharing amusing stories and listening to Pearl and Willy debate over where in England one could get the best steak and kidney pie.

⁂

To Cami's surprise, Ashlyn was awake, showered, and blowing her hair dry when she got up the next morning.

"Does this mean you're going to church?" Cami asked her hopefully.

"Yes, I am," Ashlyn answered flatly, not wanting Cami to make a big deal out of it.

"Okay." Cami held up her hands innocently. "Just asking."

Ashlyn plugged in her curling iron and picked up her mascara wand. "So, how was your walk on the beach?" After the others had left the night before, Cami and Dallin had gone for a stroll on the beach. Ashlyn had been asleep before they got back.

Resting against the door frame, Cami sighed. "It is *so* good to see him again. It's like no time at all has passed since we were together. I invited him over for leftovers after church. You don't mind, do you?"

"Why would I mind?" Ashlyn blotted her lipstick with a square of toilet paper. "Besides, I told Pearl I'd come up and sort through some of her stuff. I'm curious to see what treasures she's got stored away in that house of hers."

Cami pouted. "But I want to go through her stuff with you."

"You and Dallin can come, too."

"You know," Cami said, "I couldn't believe it when Dallin said something about the bed and breakfast last night."

"I know," Ashlyn exclaimed. "I about died."

"Me too. But I'm kind of glad he did. I wasn't sure how to bring it up to Grandpa."

"He doesn't seem too freaked out about it," Ashlyn observed.

Cami nodded. "I'm keeping my fingers crossed."

"Speaking of the bed and breakfast," Ashlyn said as she sprayed a light dusting of hairspray on her hair, "Vanessa was certainly very interested when she heard about our plans."

"I noticed that, too," Cami said.

"I didn't tell you, but I happened to overhear a phone conversation she had," Ashlyn confessed.

"Ashlyn, you eavesdropped?" Cami was horrified. Then her tone quickly changed. "Good girl, what did you hear?" she asked excitedly.

Ashlyn told her as Cami listened indignantly.

"What does she mean by 'these people'?" she asked, incredulous. "We may not be the wealthiest people in town, but we're not fish bait either."

"Just consider the source," Ashlyn reminded her.

"I know," Cami sputtered, "but who does she think she is? And what does she mean by calling Mitch's car 'ridiculous'? That car means everything to him." Cami was really getting steamed. "I have a mind to tell him all of this, so he knows just what kind of 'girlfriend' she really is."

"You can't tell him," Ashlyn insisted. "They'll both know I was listening in on the conversation."

"Yeah, but we can't just let him think Vanessa's this sweet angel, when she's not."

"I know," Ashlyn agreed. "Did you see the way she clung to him last night, and batted her eyes at him every time he looked at her?"

"She makes me so nauseated," Cami said. "She puts on such a show for him. But she's only sweet on the outside. Inside, she's as sour as a lemon."

"How do you think those two ever ended up together?" Ashlyn asked. "I mean, obviously Mitch thinks he's got this gorgeous, attentive, devoted girlfriend, and the whole time Vanessa's got him completely wrapped around her little finger. But if she's got so many complaints about him, why is she bothering with him?"

"I know exactly why Vanessa has her hooks in Mitch," Cami exclaimed. "She and her father want to turn our town into a touristy resort. Her father's on the town council and Vanessa likes to gets involved in all of Mitch's projects and community efforts, so they look like this community-minded family that loves Seamist and its people and just wants what's best for everyone."

Ashlyn nodded in understanding. "I wish Mitch could see through her and learn what she's really like. What do you think he's getting out of this relationship anyway?"

"That's easy, too," Cami answered. "He's still pretty vulnerable after being rejected by his ex-wife. Vanessa's attention makes him feel better. Let's face it, Mitch probably loves having someone beautiful and talented like Vanessa in his life. As for why he can't see what Vanessa's up to, well, love is blind. He doesn't want to see her flaws."

"I swear, Cami, you should have gone into psychology," Ashlyn told her.

Cami looked at the clock on the counter. "Omigosh, look how late it is. Are you about finished? We can talk later," she said, then quickly added, "By the way, I'm really glad you're coming to church."

Ashlyn looked at her friend. "Thanks for being patient with me." She unplugged her curling iron. "Vanessa doesn't go to this ward, does she?"

"She's the music director," Cami said mischievously.

❊

They arrived for sacrament meeting just as a member of the bishopric stood to welcome everyone to church. Ashlyn recognized a few faces from town, but most people were strangers to her. And sure enough, right up in front, the star of the meeting, was Vanessa, in all her glory.

"Vanessa has a terrific voice," Cami whispered. "She's been working with Mitch's mom, who's giving her voice lessons."

Ashlyn rolled her eyes and Cami elbowed her as the organ started playing. Vanessa took her place in front, as if performing on stage, and gave her audience a Cover Girl smile. Under her guidance, the congregation sang a rousing rendition of "The Spirit of God."

Ashlyn sang but couldn't help glancing around the room. Was Mitch there, singing proudly along with his girlfriend? He was in this ward, too. He had to be here somewhere.

The song ended and Ashlyn bowed her head as the prayer began. "Our Father in Heaven . . ."

She recognized that voice! It was Mitch giving the opening prayer. She fought the urge to open her eyes and look at him.

"We pray, Father, that Thy Spirit will be with us this day, and that if there are any among us who are in special need of Thy help, whose faith is weak and testimonies are wavering, we ask that Thou wilt bless them with a witness of the truths that they will be taught. Strengthen them and help them to know once again that Thou lovest them and that Thou art mindful of them."

She felt as if Mitch were praying in her behalf. Had he seen her come in? Did he know she was there? But even if he did, he didn't know the feelings of her heart, the struggles she was having with her faith, did he?

Maybe Cami had told him.

As she watched him walk back to his seat, by his mother and his father, she thought how attractive he was in a dark navy blue suit, crisp white shirt, and maroon tie. Turning the paper with the ward announcements over, she wrote a quick note to Cami.

What have you told Mitch about me?

What do you mean? came the reply.

Did you tell him about Jake?

No, Cami wrote. *Why?*

Just wondering, Ashlyn finished scribbling just as it was time to prepare for the sacrament. She couldn't help seeing that after the sacrament part of the service, Vanessa took her seat down in the audience, right next to him. Looking back over her shoulder as the meeting progressed, Ashlyn saw that Mitch had put his arm across the back of the bench and his hand occasionally stroked the silk of Vanessa's deep wine-colored blouse.

Why are you so stupid? she asked herself. *Quit looking at them and listen to the speaker.*

Life was so confusing sometimes. How in the world was she ever going to figure it out?

After the meeting Cami went to get a drink from the drinking fountain, and when she rejoined Ashlyn, her cheeks were flushed with excitement. She told Ashlyn that one of the sisters in Relief Society had told her the stake was doing roadshows this summer. She had asked if Cami would be willing to help them out.

"Sister Francom told me they're trying to find someone to write the roadshow," Cami explained. "Sister Benchley was going to write it, but she had to go out of town for a while and doesn't know when she'll be back."

"That's too bad," Ashlyn sympathized.

"No, it's great! I love Sister Benchley, but I think it's time someone else had a turn writing the roadshow. We've always had the worst plays in the stake. For once it would be fun to do a good one. Oh, and I hope you don't mind, but I said you'd be willing to help out, too."

"Me!" Ashlyn exclaimed. "I'm not even a real member of the ward."

"I know, but they need someone who can do choreography and you said you took a lot of dance classes in high school." Cami looked apologetic. "I know I should have asked first, but I thought maybe if we get involved, then we can finally get a good show put together. It would be kind of fun."

"I guess it does sound kind of fun," Ashlyn said, remembering a roadshow she'd been in when she was in Young Women and how much fun it had been.

Putting aside all thoughts of the roadshow, she followed Cami and Grandpa Willy to Mitch's Sunday School lesson. She was eager to hear him teach since both Cami and Grandpa Willy had raved about his lesson the week before.

Mitch walked into the classroom carrying a stack of books, which he set on the table at the front of the room. Organizing his notes and several books, he finally looked out into the faces of members gathered for Sunday School. His face lit up when he saw the Davenports and Ashlyn. Leaving his post, he walked to where they sat and greeted them.

"Well, good morning," he said. "Anyone suffering from a 'kick-a-poo-joy-juice' hangover?"

They laughed.

"Is that seat taken?" someone asked. It was Dallin. Ashlyn scooted over to let him sit next to Cami.

"You know, Bradford," he challenged as he settled into his seat, "we need to set up a Frisbee rematch. We're not going down that easily, are we, Cami?"

Cami looked at Dallin like he was crazy, and Mitch shook his head. "Gee, I don't know. That's kind of up to my partner." He looked at Ashlyn. "She may want to retire after getting plowed last night. How are you anyway?"

"I'm fine," she assured him. "Believe me, my brother's tackled me worse than that a dozen times."

Mitch looked impressed.

"Listen," Ashlyn told Dallin, "I'm up to it if you are."

"Ha!" Dallin said happily. "You're on."

"We'll make arrangements after class," Mitch said. "I'd better get the lesson started."

He walked up front and just then, Vanessa strolled into the room and went directly to Mitch. She whispered something in his ear that made him smile, then took a seat on the front row next to his parents and another man who appeared to be Vanessa's father. He had an olive complexion, a head of thick, dark hair, graying at the temples, and a firm jaw line. His suit looked expensive, his tie bold yet tasteful.

Ashlyn directed her attention away from Vanessa and her father and listened as Mitch began the lesson, introducing the sons of Mosiah and Alma the Younger. She enjoyed hearing him explain the conditions of the time period and how Alma the Younger and the four sons of Mosiah went around trying to destroy the church of God and lead many of the church members to do iniquity. She sat mesmerized as he held the group captivated with the account of the angel visiting the young men, speaking with a voice of thunder that shook the earth.

Mitch spoke with strength and power as he read the angel's words from the book of Mosiah, *"Behold, the Lord hath heard the prayers of his people, and also the prayers of his servant, Alma, who is thy father; for he has prayed with much faith concerning thee that thou mightest be brought to the knowledge of the truth. . . ."*

Ashlyn wondered how many prayers had been offered up in her behalf. She knew her mother had been concerned about her struggles, her grandparents and brother, too. Had they prayed for her like Alma's father had?

"I want you to know that I know that the Lord sent an angel to visit Alma the Younger and the sons of Mosiah to turn them from their sins so that they might repent and devote their lives to missionary work and the building up of the kingdom of God," Mitch testified, looking directly at her.

Maybe it was because it was Mitch bearing his testimony, or that for once she really, *really,* listened to what the teacher was saying, but Ashlyn felt a strong sensation, a tingling, warm sensation, fill her chest. Tears stung at her eyes, which she quickly blinked away.

It was a feeling she hadn't felt for months. A feeling, she realized, that she had missed. The loving, comforting spirit that she'd kept out of her life with her pride and stubbornness. The sweetness of the Spirit, the peace it brought to her soul, even for a moment, felt like the warm rays of the sun breaking through stormy clouds.

Mitch and the other men cleared quickly out of the room as the women began preparations for Relief Society. From out of a closet came a lacy tablecloth and a colorful centerpiece. An elderly sister played quiet music on the piano and as Cami visited with several other women in the room, Ashlyn couldn't help but watch discreetly as Vanessa spent a moment talking to the Relief Society president and her counselors. She then returned to her seat and quickly engaged Mitch's mother in conversation.

She hated to admit it, but Vanessa certainly knew how to deal with people. She was gracious, poised, and outgoing. But Ashlyn didn't sense that her actions were at all sincere. She knew she was being harsh and judgmental, but she couldn't help feeling that it was all for show. *Oh Mitch,* she thought, *you deserve better than that.*

Her thoughts returned to the Sunday School lesson and what she had felt. Everyone had tried to tell her—Cami, her mother, even her brother in far-away Portugal—that the answers to her questions came from the Lord Himself. But she'd lacked the faith and the desire to seek out His will and find out what He wanted her to do with her life.

Maybe she hadn't been ready to hear His will. The pain of Jake's rejection still hurt deeply. That day had been filled with the greatest pain and humiliation of her life. Up to that point in her life, she'd never thought anything would shake her testimony. She had to admit that she'd taken her testimony for granted, but it had been a false sense of security. With the first real trial of her faith, she'd discovered that her convictions weren't as strong as they should have been.

But isn't that how life was? Isn't that how people were? Thinking that all was well and breezy during those sunny times of life. And during those times, it was easy to let prayer, scripture study, and meeting attendance become less sincere and not as meaningful as they needed to be. So that when a storm hit, or several storms, one right after the other, there was nothing to fall back on. The strength, the conviction necessary, wasn't there to serve as an anchor.

She thought of herself as a ship on the sea, drifting to and fro, wherever the wind and waves took her. Remembering Grandpa Willy's analogy of the lighthouse, she flipped her scriptures to the 139th chapter of Psalms and reread verses nine through twelve.

> *If I take the wings of the morning, and dwell in the uttermost parts of the sea; Even there shall thy hand lead me, and thy right hand shall hold me.*
>
> *If I say, Surely the darkness shall cover me; even the night shall be light about me.*
>
> *Yea, the darkness hideth not from thee; but the night shineth as the day: the darkness and the light are both alike to thee.*

That was just what she needed—for the Lord's hand to lead her, and for the night to be light around her, so she could find her way.

The answer was there right in front of her. It had been the entire time. Just like Dorothy in the *Wizard of Oz,* who'd always had the power in the ruby slippers to return to Kansas, Ashlyn had just needed someone to tell her what she needed to do.

Well, Mitch had told her, adding his testimony to those who'd already tried to tell her. All she had needed was faith.

CHAPTER SEVENTEEN

Sunday night Mitch actually called Ashlyn to make sure she was going running the next morning. This time Cami had a new excuse not to join them. She had cut her toenails too short, she said, so now it hurt to wear her running shoes.

Mitch and Ashlyn spent a few minutes walking to warm up their muscles, then they broke into a comfortable jog and headed down the long stretch of beach, north toward the harbor.

"I enjoyed your lesson yesterday," Ashlyn told him.

"Thanks. I think this is the best calling I've ever had," he told her. "I haven't learned this much about the gospel since my mission."

"Where did you go on your mission?" she asked, sidestepping a clump of seaweed tangled on the shore.

"Chicago—the best mission in the Church," he added proudly.

Ashlyn raised her eyebrows. "Don't all missionaries say that?"

"Yeah, I think so. We have to. It's in the handbook." This made Ashlyn laugh.

Changing the subject, he asked about her family and she told him that her brother was on a mission in Portugal and that her father had died in a plane crash. She didn't tell Mitch that her father had been unfaithful to her mother or that he had completely neglected his family.

"How's the stepfather thing working out?"

"Garrett's great. He's good to my mom, and he really cares about me and my brother. I wasn't real happy when she first started dating him, but once I gave him a chance, I realized what a neat guy he is."

"Kind of like your mom being pregnant?"

Ashlyn looked at him, confused at the shift in the conversation. "What do you mean?"

"Just that you weren't really sure about your mother having another baby, but with a little time and getting used to the idea, you'll realize that it's a good thing."

They ran for a moment, feeling the rush of the misty sea breeze in their faces. It looked like it might turn into another rainy day.

"What about boyfriends?" he asked next. "Do you have someone back home in Salt Lake?"

"Nope," she said abruptly, not wanting the conversation to go in that particular direction.

"That's hard to believe," he said.

She focused her attention on the beach in front of her and didn't answer.

"Seriously," he insisted, "for someone as pretty and intelligent as you are to still be single, especially in the Church, is kind of hard to believe."

Ashlyn didn't know what to say to that and finally settled on, "Thanks . . . I think."

"It's true. I can't believe that at least one guy hasn't tried to get you to marry him."

"Believe me, there are a lot of girls prettier than I am out there," she said, embarrassed they were even having this conversation.

Mitch looked at her. "Not too many," he said, then added, "especially ones who can dive for a Frisbee like you can."

"Now that *is* a compliment," she answered. "But being single at my age isn't all that unusual, in Salt Lake or even here in Seamist. I mean, look at Cami and," she paused, "Vanessa."

"Right," he said. "You're absolutely right."

"Yes, I am," she said emphatically.

"I get the feeling this topic is now closed," he said with a questioning lift of one eyebrow.

"You're very perceptive," Ashlyn said. "Hey, look, is that a shell?" Slowing down, she approached a white object poking out of the ground. She dug at it with the toe of her shoe only to reveal a small broken seashell that wasn't worth keeping. "Darn, I keep wanting to find something valuable on the beach." She kicked the sand in frustration.

"A few years ago an Asian cargo ship passed by and lost a large crate of Nike shoes," Mitch told her. "All of a sudden athletic shoes began washing up on the shore."

Ashlyn laughed, imagining the beach strewn with Nike shoes.

"There were so many shoes washing up each day that someone set up a shoe exchange so people could come and swap the shoes they found to make pairs."

"Unbelievable," she said as they continued walking, both zipping up their windbreakers against the wind. "So tell me about this fancy car of yours. What is it?"

"My Mustang?" He seemed surprised that she would ask. "Well, it's a '65, two plus two-hatchback style. It was painted red when I got it, but I've restored it back to its original light bronze metallic color. It's got a 289-cubic-inch high output engine with 225 horsepower."

"So, that means it's fast."

"It's very fast," he boasted.

"Think I could get a ride in it sometime?" she asked.

"Anytime you'd like," he said. "It still needs some work, but she's a real beauty."

"How much is a car like that worth?" she wondered aloud.

"In top condition, about sixteen thousand. Keep in mind, I bought it for three."

"Not bad," Ashlyn said, impressed.

They climbed the steps and walked through the yard to the driveway where Mitch's car was parked in front. Ashlyn liked the bronze color and the gleaming chrome bumpers. The car had a sleek back that made it look racy and quick.

"I like it," she exclaimed. "It's got a lot of style." As Mitch nodded proudly, she recalled Vanessa's complaints about his prized possession. She wondered how he'd feel if he knew his girlfriend didn't like his car. They stood side by side, admiring the car in the patchy morning sun.

"Well, thanks for getting up to run with me," she said after a few moments of silence.

"My pleasure. I've been needing an incentive to run more often. It helps to know you're expecting me." He glanced over at her.

"It helps me, too. I just don't want to keep you back. I'm not in that great of shape."

"Unless you've forgotten, I'm the one gasping for air before we turn around, not you," he reminded her.

She waved his comment away with her hand. She was as breathless as he was at the end of the run. "Still, I appreciate it," she repeated. "I'll understand, though, if you don't want to go with me every day."

"Actually, I look forward to our morning runs," he said, looking into her eyes.

Ashlyn was glad her cheeks were already flushed from their jog in the cool morning air so he wouldn't see how red they became at his words.

"I'm glad," she said lightly. "Me too."

They stared at each other for a very long moment. Then Ashlyn felt a drop of rain on her forehead and looked up. "Uh oh, it's starting to rain. I'd better go in."

Another drop, then another fell from the sky.

"I'll see you later then," he said. "Tell Cami and Willy 'hi.'"

Instead of going inside, she stood and watched him pull out of the driveway and speed off down the road. After a few minutes, her own speeding heart rate finally began to return to normal.

What was all that about? *I look forward to our morning runs.*

What did he mean by that?

Of course, she looked forward to their morning runs, too. She had to admit she liked Mitch. He was a nice guy and a lot of fun to hang around with. But . . .

But what? There were no buts. That was it. He was fun to hang around with. Period. He was involved with Vanessa, and Ashlyn didn't intend to get involved with anyone for a long time. And that's how it was going to stay.

"Let's go into town," Cami said.

It was still drizzling outside and they were bored sitting around the house.

"Okay." Ashlyn put the recliner in an upright position. "I'm game."

"Grandpa," Cami hollered. "We're running to town. Do you need anything?"

"How about some more yeast?" he teased.

"Ha, ha, very funny," she yelled back. "Like I'd let him make more root beer," she said to Ashlyn. "That's like giving a known arsonist a load of newspaper and a gallon of gasoline."

Chuckling, Ashlyn found her shoes by the door and slipped them on. She and Cami grabbed their jackets and hurried to the car. Cami suggested a quick stop at the store for bread and eggs, then a trip to the hardware store to look at paint chips and wallpaper books.

"Then," Ashlyn continued the list for her friend, "we could go to the bank and see what's happening with the loan."

"Oh, yeah, right." Cami acted as if the thought hadn't occurred to her until Ashlyn said something. "Good idea."

Ashlyn laughed inwardly. As if Cami hadn't already thought of going to the bank to see Dallin. Ha!

The stop at the grocery store only took a minute. They also bought some fresh artichokes for dinner. Their next stop was Bradford Hardware. It appeared deserted, but Cami said whoever was working would probably be back, so she and Ashlyn went straight to the paint department for some samples of paint chips for the mansion. They were ready to launch into some of the wallpaper books when they heard . . .

"Born to be wiiiiiild . . ." A voice at the other end of the store was belting out the old Steppenwolf song.

Ashlyn and Cami looked at each other and started to laugh. Obviously the person in the store didn't know anyone else was there.

"Get your motor runnin' . . ." the voice sang. *"Head out on the highway."*

The voice grew closer as the song continued. When he got to the chorus again, Ashlyn and Cami joined in. *"Born to be wiiiiiiild . . ."*

Within a second Mitch skidded to a halt in front of them, his expression one of shocked embarrassment. He pulled the earplugs from his Walkman out of his ears. "I didn't know you were in here."

"Obviously not," Cami said. Ashlyn was trying hard not to laugh but was losing the battle.

"Okay, okay," he said. "Go ahead and laugh. Get it out of your systems."

The girls dissolved into giggles. It wasn't that he wasn't a good singer. In fact, he sounded pretty good actually. But the expression on his face was priceless.

"You ought to take that act on the road," Cami told him. "You're pretty good, Mitch."

Ashlyn nodded. "But you need a couple of backup singers." On cue Cami leaned in toward Ashlyn, and they gave him a couple of cheesy smiles.

"How about a couple of chocolate sodas instead?" he offered.

"Sure, I'd love one. How about you, Ash?"

"The more chocolate-y, the better," Ashlyn said.

As Mitch whipped up three chocolate sodas at the fountain, they sat at a table loaded with wallpaper books and through several of them, occasionally bursting into peals of laughter as they recalled Mitch's song, then laughing even harder when he groaned in agony.

"What are you two doing anyway?" Mitch said as he placed the three tall sodas on the counter.

"We're looking at paint and wallpaper. We wanted to start getting ideas for decorating the mansion," Cami told him.

"So, you're pretty serious about this?" He motioned for them to come and join him.

Climbing onto the tall bar stools, Cami sat next to Mitch and Ashlyn sat next to her. Ashlyn sipped her chocolate soda, not sure if she'd ever had one before. She decided she liked the fizzy chocolate and ice cream combination.

"Mmm, this is good," she complimented Mitch.

"Thanks," he answered then took a sip of his own drink.

"We still haven't heard anything about the loan, yet," Cami explained, in answer to his question. "That's going to be our biggest obstacle. Then, of course, we have to bring everything in the house up to code, which could be like trying to rebuild the house from the inside out."

"I know quite a bit about plumbing and electrical. Of course, you'll need a professional to do the work, but I can come and take a look and give you an idea of what it will take," he offered.

"Oh, Mitch, would you?" Cami was thrilled he would volunteer.

"Sure. George ought to be back from lunch any minute, then we can go over."

While they were waiting for George, Ashlyn and Cami ran over to the bank to talk to Dallin about the loan, but he was in a meeting.

Cami left a message for him with one of the tellers, asking him to call, then they turned and left the building in a hurry, anxious to get back to the hardware store so they could take Mitch to the house.

They were barely out the door when they nearly collided with Vanessa James, who was on her way into the bank.

"Oh," she cried, jumping out of the way.

"Vanessa!" Cami exclaimed. "Sorry, we didn't see you."

"That's okay." She smoothed her slim skirt and brushed a strand of hair from her cheek and gave them a composed smile. "So, what are you girls up to today?"

Ashlyn didn't like how she referred to them as "girls." Vanessa was probably the same age as they were; she just acted as if she thought she was more sophisticated and mature. And how come, Ashlyn wanted to know, every time they saw Vanessa, she was dressed like she was on her way to a fashion shoot, and they were dressed like they were on their way to a garage sale?

"Just a little business at the bank," Cami told her, not going into any detail.

"I'll bet this is about your little bed and breakfast venture," Vanessa guessed, managing somehow to make it sound like they were opening a lemonade stand. "How is it going anyway?"

"Just fine," Cami said. As if anything had even happened yet. But Vanessa didn't need to know that.

"Well, good luck." Vanessa gave them a patronizing smile, then turned and disappeared into the bank.

"What do you think is up with her?" Ashlyn asked as they headed back to the hardware store.

"I don't know, but did you see how her eyes got all shifty?" Cami asked. "I don't trust her."

"Me either," Ashlyn said, as the same feeling of mistrust toward Vanessa settled into the back of her mind.

"Oh well," Cami shrugged. "Who cares? Let's go get Mitch and take him through the mansion. In fact, let's see if he'll help us take down some of the boards so we can get some more light in the place. If we're going to be fixing it up, we don't need to keep the place boarded up."

George was there when they arrived at the store and Mitch was ready to go. He offered to take the girls in his car.

"Why don't you go?" Cami suggested to Ashlyn. "I'll follow in my car then we won't have to come back and get it later."

Inside Mitch's car, Ashlyn ran her hand over the dashboard, amazed at how well kept everything was. There were a few tears in the upholstery and it looked like the carpet was worn in places, but for a car that was over thirty-five years old, it was aging very well.

"So," Mitch climbed inside, "how do you like her?"

"I like 'her' a lot," Ashlyn said. "Like I said, she's got a lot of style. They don't make cars like this anymore, that's for sure."

He nodded in agreement as he backed out of the parking stall and pulled onto the road. "Do you mind a little music?"

"No, not at all. You got any Steppenwolf?" she teased.

"Sorry," he replied, unamused. Turning on the radio, he tuned in to an oldies station. After a few commercials, a Beach Boys tune came on. Mitch sang along with "California Girls" and tapped his fingers in rhythm on the steering wheel. There was something fun and care-free about driving along the coastal highway that was almost like being transported back to a simpler, happier time. The clouds had broken up by now and bright rays of sun poured down from the sky.

"Mind if I roll down the window?" Ashlyn asked, wanting to feel the wind in her hair and on her face.

"Not at all," he replied, rolling his down, too. With the fresh air, catchy music, and magical feeling the car seemed to possess, Ashlyn couldn't stop smiling.

"I love this car," she told Mitch.

"Yeah," he smiled appreciatively. "Me too."

The next song that came on was, appropriately, the Beatles' "Ticket to Ride." Before she knew it, Ashlyn was singing along with Mitch at the top of her lungs. She was almost sad when they got to Cami's house. Her face must have reflected her feelings because Mitch said, "What's wrong?"

Feeling as if he'd read her mind, she quickly said, "Oh, nothing. I just wasn't ready for it to end yet."

"Tell you what. If you aren't doing anything after we're through here, I'll drive you down the coast. We can drive down the Three Capes Scenic Loop and see the Cape Meares lighthouse and stop in Oceanside for a late lunch at Roseanna's. What do you say?"

Her first reaction was to say, "Sounds wonderful." Her second was to add, "That is, if you're sure you're not busy." Her third she kept to herself. *What about Vanessa?*

"I've been working all morning and I don't have a game until this evening," he told her.

This isn't a date, Ashlyn reminded herself. Just a friendly gesture on his part to show off his car to someone who appreciated it, and to show Ashlyn the Oregon coast.

That, she told herself, was all it was.

⊷⊷ ⚙ ⊶⊶

Cami managed to unlock the back door, just as Pearl had done, and they took Mitch through the rooms they'd already explored. Mitch surprised them by finding a dumbwaiter in the kitchen. He also pointed out an area off the south parlor that was probably used for a greenhouse conservatory.

"This place is incredible," he exclaimed, commenting on the different types of wood. Cherry, mahogany, and oak had been used for the wainscoting, ceiling panels, and hardwood flooring.

"What's upstairs?" he asked, as they stood in the entry admiring the stained glass.

They led him up the stairs, and when he saw the large, spacious bedrooms, the two bathrooms, and the study, he was impressed. "This home is still rock solid. They didn't cut any corners when they built it," he observed. "Except for putting in the plumbing and electrical and replacing the porch, everything else is going to be mostly cosmetic. This place is going to be a lot of fun to fix up."

"Are you offering to help?" Cami wasn't one to let an opportunity pass by.

"I guess so," Mitch chuckled. "I'd love to work on those wood floors."

Ashlyn and Cami smiled triumphantly. With Mitch on board, the task seemed almost surmountable.

He pushed a corner of the molding that framed the panel. "This panel doesn't look like it's quite lined up with the others," he muttered. Suddenly the wall gave way, revealing a door-sized opening.

"Whoa!" Cami exclaimed. "A secret passageway. Let's go see."

Mitch smiled. "This place gets better by the minute."

Ashlyn peered into the darkness beyond the opening. "It looks pretty dark in there," she said, "and we don't have a flashlight or anything."

"Okay," Cami gave in. "I guess we can save it for next time."

As they made their way through house, Mitch threw out different ideas. "Each bedroom should probably have its own bathroom and whirlpool bath tub. We could easily convert the closets in the two bigger bedrooms into bathrooms."

Ashlyn agreed. "My mom and stepdad love to stay in bed and breakfasts, and they won't even accept a room that doesn't have a private bath and whirlpool tub."

"Each room could have a theme, too, like a mariner room, a military room, or a safari room . . . ," Cami said.

"And how about 'The Rose Room?'" Ashlyn suggested.

Cami was practically wiggling with excitement. "I can't wait to get started," she said. "I'm going to call Dallin and see where things are at with the loan. And write down some of these ideas. We need to come up with a plan so everything runs smoothly."

Leaving the library, they went downstairs and out the back door.

"Do you still want to go on that ride down Three Capes Loop?" Mitch asked Ashlyn. "Cami, you can come too, if you want."

"Thanks," Cami said, "but I'm too excited about the house. Maybe some other time, though."

"Are you sure you don't want to come?" Ashlyn asked her, not wanting to abandon her friend.

"Absolutely," Cami waved her away. "I've got tons to do. But first, I'm going to call Dallin. Maybe by the time you get back, I'll have some news for you."

"Sounds good," Ashlyn said. She was excited to ride down the coast. To their good fortune, the day had turned out sunny and warm. She and Mitch jumped in the car and took off down Highway 101. As they listened to some old Doobie Brothers' song on the radio, she gazed out the window at the gorgeous ocean, the hills covered with fern and pine trees, and the magnificently blue sky.

Her heart was light as her mind flitted to thoughts of the mansion and its view and the unexpected gift of Mitch's company. He was easygoing, fun, and friendly, and she felt so comfortable with him.

She liked how she could be herself around him, and how easy he was to talk to. With Jake, it seemed she had always tried to please him and impress him.

She wondered what was different with Mitch, why she didn't feel the need to impress him. Was it because he was just a friend and there was no romantic interest? Or was it because she knew there could never be anything but friendship between them, so there was no need to try harder?

"Hey," he said, breaking her concentration, "what are you thinking about?"

She smiled easily, pleased that he'd noticed that she'd been lost in her own thoughts. "Nothing really. Just about the house and how much work it's going to be to fix it up."

"You've got that right, but with everyone working together, it will come together fast. You'll see," he assured her.

"So, tell me where we're going."

Mitch told her about the Three Capes Scenic Route that took them from Tillamook Bay, around Cape Meares, past the Cape Meares Lighthouse, past Three Arch Rocks, down the coast by Cape Lookout, and finally south around Cape Kiwanda.

"Three Arch Rocks is one of my favorite places," he told her. "I know you'll love it."

She wondered if he took Vanessa to places like the Misty Harbor Lighthouse and Three Arch Rocks. For some reason she couldn't picture Vanessa hiking to a lighthouse or standing on the beach letting the wind blow through her hair.

She didn't have a chance to wonder for long. Another Beatles song came on the radio and soon she and Mitch were singing "Twist and Shout" as they wound their way down the coast. Even though Ashlyn never thought she had that great of a voice, it didn't seem to matter to her right now; she was having too much fun not to sing.

Except for Cami, Mitch was the only other person she'd ever met who accepted her for who she was, without any expectations or limitations. He didn't care whether she wore her hair straight or curly, if she wore the right jeans or said the right thing at the right time.

And it felt wonderful.

CHAPTER EIGHTEEN

"Cami, what's wrong?"

Ashlyn and Mitch had returned from their drive to Three Capes Loop and returned to find Cami sitting on the couch, her face wet with tears. Ashlyn hurried to her side, while Mitch took the overstuffed chair across from them.

"Dallin called." Cami wiped at her eyes with the back of her hand. "I knew it was too good to be true."

Ashlyn glanced at Mitch, who appeared equally in the dark as to Cami's meaning. "What was?" she asked.

"The bed and breakfast. The mansion," she sniffled. "He said the bank won't approve the loan, and he doesn't think we'll have a much better chance getting it approved anywhere else either."

"Why?" Ashlyn demanded to know.

"Too big of a risk," Cami said with a sniff. "The house is a fire hazard and considered unstable. It's not built to code, so unless it's brought up to standard, they won't even consider lending money to us. But we can't afford to bring it up to code if we don't have money to make the improvements." Cami smacked the cushion of the couch with her fist. "Darn it!"

"I wish I had enough money to fund the project," Mitch said. "I'd be glad to give it to you."

"Me too," Ashlyn said.

"Thanks, you guys," Cami said. She shut her eyes, forcing herself to calm down. "You know, this is so weird, because he was so sure we wouldn't have any trouble with the loan. I mean, the land alone is worth as much as the house itself. You'd think that would be enough."

Grandpa Willy walked into the room. He'd been in the kitchen trying to install several flourescent lights in the ceiling fixture.

"Mitch," Grandpa Willy said, "can I interrupt you for a minute? I can't seem to get this bulb in." Mitch jumped to his feet and followed the old man into the kitchen while Cami stared out the window.

"I'm sorry," Ashlyn told her. "I wish I could think of something."

Cami pulled her gaze away from the window and gave her friend an empty smile. "Yeah, me too. I really felt good about this. I prayed and prayed and felt like this was what I was supposed to do. Not just have a bed and breakfast, but use this as a way to honor my family and learn about my ancestors. I mean, they left me a legacy with that house. If those walls could talk, I'm sure they'd have some amazing stories to tell."

"I agree." Ashlyn gave her an encouraging smile. "And I don't think you should give up so easily. There's got to be some other way to get some money to restore the mansion. We could find outside investors. Maybe my stepfather would put up some money. And my grandfather. It's worth asking."

"You'd be willing to do that?" Cami asked, obviously touched by her friend's offer.

"I don't see how they can lose," Ashlyn told her sincerely.

"Thanks, Ash," Cami hugged her. "You're right. I'm not going to give up that easily."

A knock came at the door. "I'll get it," Ashlyn said while Cami quickly dried her eyes and blew her nose. She answered the door and found a handsome man standing on the porch. He was about six foot two with dark olive skin and thick dark hair that was neatly trimmed. He was dressed in light khaki trousers and a navy blue short-sleeved Polo shirt.

"Hi, there," he said with a dazzling smile. "I just moved in down the street, and I wondered if I could use your phone. Mine's not hooked up yet, and with all the boxes and unpacking, I seem to have misplaced my cell phone."

"Sure," Ashlyn said, inviting him inside.

"My name is Sebastian Jamison," he introduced himself.

"Nice to meet you." Ashlyn gave him a friendly smile as she introduced herself and Cami. Sebastian stared at Ashlyn until she started to squirm. "Uh, Cami's grandfather is in the kitchen," she said quickly as she turned and called for Grandpa Willy. A moment later he and Mitch came into the living room. She introduced them all and the men shook hands.

"Have we met before?" Mitch asked.

Sebastian thought for a moment. "I don't think so, unless you've been to San Francisco. That's where I'm from originally. I just bought the Henderson home down the road."

"That place has been vacant for a long time," Mitch said.

"I'm going to be traveling between here and San Francisco for the next little while, so I'll be in and out quite a bit," he explained. "I'm a writer and I plan on doing most of my writing at the beach house."

With a background in journalism and a love for writing herself, Ashlyn immediately took an interest. "What kind of writing do you do?"

"I've published several nonfiction works about the rainforests of South America, but I'm trying to break into the fiction market with a political thriller I'm working on."

"That sounds fascinating," she said.

"Maybe we can get together sometime and I can tell you more about it." He smiled at her again, his eyes showing the same interest as his voice. "But right now, may I use your phone?" He looked toward Grandpa Willy inquiringly.

"Help yourself," Grandpa Willy said. "The phone's in the kitchen."

When he left the room, Ashlyn noticed Mitch's puzzled expression.

"What is it, Mitch?"

He shook his head. "He just seems familiar, that's all. I swear I've either seen him before or met him before."

The clock on the mantel struck four o' clock.

"Oops, I'd better get going," Mitch said.

"Thanks for your help, Mitch," Grandpa Willy said.

"And thanks for coming through the house," Cami said. "I hope we get to use your ideas someday."

"We may have lost the battle, but we haven't lost the war," Mitch said. "We're not giving up yet."

Cami smiled, appreciating his pep talk. "Right!" she exclaimed with a hopeful nod.

"Thanks for the ride," Ashlyn told him before he left. "I had a lot of fun." And she really had. They'd taken off their shoes and walked on the beach. They'd had large slices of the most decadent chocolate caramel crunch pie she'd ever tasted in her life, and they'd stood at the edge of Cape Kiwanda, amazed at the vastness and beauty of the sky and the sea.

It had been a wonderful day.

"I had a lot of fun, too," he told her. "Next time we'll go north and I'll take you up through Cannon Beach to Astoria."

"I'd like that," she smiled. "Good luck in your game."

"You've got a game?" Grandpa Willy exclaimed. "Why didn't you say something? I'll be over to watch it."

"Maybe we'll come, too," Cami said.

"Great, I'll watch for you," Mitch replied with a wave.

He left just as Sebastian Jamison returned from his phone call.

"Everything okay?" Grandpa Willy asked him.

He nodded. "Yes, thank you. My only other problem is trying to decide what to do for dinner tonight. Can you recommend a good restaurant?"

He'd asked the right people. Cami and her grandfather had a dozen suggestions.

"Wait a minute, wait a minute," Sebastian laughed. "They all sound wonderful. What about that steakhouse, though? Does it really have the best lobster along the coast?"

"Son," Grandpa Willy said, "I've had my share of seafood, and nothing beats the Hillary Steak House lobster tail."

"I guess that's settled, but I really hate to dine alone. Would you care to join me for dinner? As my guests, of course."

Ashlyn caught Cami's eye. Neither of them really liked to cook, and going out to dinner with someone as handsome and refined as Sebastian Jamison was definitely a treat in and of itself.

"Why, that's awfully nice of you, Mr. Jamison," Grandpa Willy said.

"Please, call me Sebastian," he said. "Is seven o'clock too late?"

"We'll be ready," Grandpa Willy answered for them.

Sebastian left and Ashlyn and Cami both erupted with comments about their mysterious new neighbor.

"I think he likes you," Cami told Ashlyn. "The way he looked at you a couple of times, how did you stand it? I think I would have fainted right on the spot."

"I nearly did," Ashlyn exclaimed.

"Guess we better go get ready. If we're going to the ball game and then out to dinner, I'd better go iron my skirt while we have a few minutes," Cami said.

"Me too," Ashlyn said. "My blouse is all wrinkled from church on Sunday."

Grandpa Willy held up a hand to get their attention. "Just a minute, girls," he said.

Ashlyn and Cami looked at him, wondering what it was he wanted to say.

"I've made a decision." He thrust his hands into his pants pockets and jingled some change around. "I was a little surprised that the loan didn't go through for the bed and breakfast project," he said. "And, in a way, maybe it's better it didn't."

"But Grandpa—"

"Cami, let me finish." He looked at her sternly. "I know I haven't seemed real keen on the idea, but now that I've had some time to think about it, and, well, I think it is a good idea."

"Grandpa—" Cami started to speak again but he interrupted her.

"I think the bed and breakfast is a great idea, and I want you to know you have my support and my blessings on the project. And to show you how much I believe in it," he paused for a moment before going on, "I would like to loan you the money to restore it."

Cami looked at him with disbelief. "What do you mean, loan us the money?"

"I'll give you the money you need to make the improvements, and then you can pay me back as you begin to make a profit."

"But, Grandpa, that's your retirement money," Cami pointed out.

"I know. That's why this had better be successful!" he said gruffly.

Cami crushed her grandfather in a hug. "Grandpa, this is the most wonderful thing you've ever done for me. Thank you so much. I'll make you proud, I promise."

"I know you will." He patted her back. "I know you will."

.xx.xx 🐾 xx.xx.

Ashlyn had never been a huge fan of baseball; the sport was just too dull and slow at times. But Mitch's game seemed to never have a dull moment. The teams were perfectly matched, and Bradford Hardware had to be on their toes constantly. The Hirschfelder Plumbing team ran like a well-oiled machine.

With the score tied at the bottom of the ninth, Bradford Hardware had one last chance to win the game. Again, that burden and honor lay upon Mitch's shoulders.

"Come on, Mitch!" Cami yelled. "You can do it."

With runners on first and second, there was a good chance he could at least hit one of them in to pull their team ahead. The problem was that an afternoon thundershower was threatening to pour down on them at any moment. Gusts of wind kicked up all kinds of sand and dust, and drops of rain threatened to turn into buckets.

Ashlyn noticed that Mitch's girlfriend had shown up for the ball game in a sleeveless sundress in a colorful tropical print fabric, but when the weather turned ugly she had made herself scarce. She was probably tired of trying to keep the full skirt of her dress from blowing up like a hot air balloon. Ashlyn wondered if Vanessa's lack of loyalty bothered Mitch.

The stands yelled wildly as Mitch took his place in the batter's box. He took several warm-up swings, then stretched his neck and shoulders. Stepping away from the plate for a moment, he readjusted his helmet, then looked up in the stands, directly at Ashlyn. He gave her a quick smile and turned back to the plate.

It was so fast—not even Cami noticed—but the effect of that look wasn't lost on Ashlyn. Her senses tingled as if she'd been zapped by one of the bolts of lightening that flashed off in the distance.

The pitcher wound up and let the ball fly. The ball was low and outside, and Mitch didn't swing. He didn't swing at the next pitch either, instead he jumped back off the plate at the inside ball. The next pitch, high and outside, left the stands in a frenzy. Tension mounted as teammates and fans weighed the impact of Mitch's next move.

Mitch stretched his neck and shoulders again, and Ashlyn felt her stomach clench up in knots. Overhead a flash of lightening split the sky, and the smell of rain filled the air. Ashlyn felt the wind pick up speed.

Mitch took his position and readied himself for the pitch. The spectators held their breath as the pitcher wound up, then let the ball fly. It came in a little low and outside again, but this time Mitch's bat connected, and with a loud crack that sounded just as thunder crashed overhead, the ball took flight and soared over the outfielders' heads and over the fence.

A torrent of rain burst from the clouds as Mitch ran the bases. The crowd cheered and danced in the stands as they were drenched in the downpour, but no one seemed to care. The victory was worth it!

Splashing through mud and puddles, Grandpa Willy, Cami, and Ashlyn charged onto the field with the rest of the crowd to congratulate the winners. Mitch's father grabbed his son in a fierce hug and slapped him heartily on the back. The other team members smacked and punched at him as they chanted, "Bradford, Bradford, Bradford!"

When his teammates left him to find cover, Mitch turned, his gaze connecting with Ashlyn's. For one brief moment it was as if the storm, the crowds, the noise, didn't exist.

Ashlyn blinked as the rain ran into her eyes, breaking the spell. A smile broke onto Mitch's face and he rushed toward Ashlyn and the others. To her surprise, he picked her up in a hug and twirled her around. Looking up into the drenching rain, she laughed out loud.

"You did it, my boy," Grandpa Willy praised him.

Even after Mitch set her back down on the ground, it seemed as if her feet still didn't touch it. The heavens rumbled as another blast of thunder rocked the air.

"We'd better find some cover," Mitch yelled over the noise of the storm. "It's getting worse."

They headed for their cars and scrambled inside. "Wow," Cami exclaimed. "That's some storm."

"Glad I wasn't out on the water when this front hit," Grandpa Willy said. "That's a gale force wind out there."

Ashlyn was silent, watching as Mitch climbed into his Mustang and rubbed his hair dry with a towel. She thought about an article she'd read about girls who had poor relationships, or no relationships at all, with their fathers. Without the influence of a strong male figure in their lives, the girls encountered a disastrous array of problems in attempting to fill the void left by their father's absence. Some girls were willing to do just about anything to fill the emptiness.

Ashlyn had recognized some of the characteristics described in this article in herself. She realized now that her judgment wasn't sound when it came to men, and she wondered if she would ever know what her heart was really feeling. If she grew to care about someone, would she just be trying to fill that empty spot in her life, or could she trust her feelings to be normal feelings of attraction?

As Mitch waved and drove off, she wondered about the feelings she had for him. She was definitely beginning to feel an attraction for him. How could she not? He was handsome and charming in his small-town way. But she had come to see him as a friend, and she felt as at ease talking with him as she did with Cami. She'd never really known another guy in her life that she'd felt so comfortable around.

On the ride home Ashlyn turned these thoughts over in her head. She thought about Jake and the heartache she still felt whenever she thought about him. Had she truly loved him? Or had she just been trying to fill an emptiness in her life?

Darn it, Dad! she thought. *It's your fault that I'm such a mess when it comes to relationships.*

Her father had never gone to her dance recitals or cheerleading tryouts. He wasn't there for birthdays or even Christmas some years. She had missed having a father in her life. She'd yearned as a young girl to have a daddy she could run to, someone who would hold her and keep her safe, would kiss her better when she got hurt, tease her about boyfriends, and tell her when her skirts were too short or she was wearing too much makeup. Someone who would always be there for her.

But he hadn't done any of those things. He'd never been there for her. Whenever she'd tried to go to him for counsel or advice, he'd always been too busy, or on his way to an important meeting. Her mother had done a wonderful job trying to be both father and mother, but the fact remained, Ashlyn had needed a father and her brother had needed one, too.

Thank goodness they had Garrett now. He was a wonderful father figure. But he couldn't make up for the past.

When they got to the house, Ashlyn went straight up to her room. They had over an hour before they needed to meet Sebastian for dinner. Pulling off her wet things, Ashlyn wrapped up in her fleecy robe and huddled up in the window seat, looking out at the stormy sky as it shadowed the turbulent sea. Branches from the Douglas fir trees scratched at the house as the wind blew fiercely.

A knock came at the door. Cami poked her head inside. "Hey, you want some hot chocolate?"

Cami was also in her robe. She handed a steaming mug to Ashlyn then curled up on the other side of the window seat with her own mug. "What ya doin'?" she asked companionably.

Ashlyn took a sip of the cocoa. "Just thinking."

"About what?"

She sighed. "I get to thinking about my dad, and I get so mad at him for neglecting our family so much. It seems like so many of my problems are because of him."

"What do you mean?" Cami leaned back against the pillows.

"Like Jake. I really, really loved him. I mean, heart and soul. At least I thought I did. But now I wonder, was I just using him to try and replace not having a father?"

Cami just watched her and waited, listening.

"I guess what I'm trying to say is that I'm mad at my dad for not being a better father, and I'm mad at Jake for walking out on me. It's not fair, you know? My childhood and youth weren't like I thought they would be, and my life still isn't like I'd imagined it would be."

Cami was silent and Ashlyn looked at her curiously. "Cami? Did you hear anything I said?" Ashlyn asked her.

"Oh, yes. I heard you," Cami said evenly.

Ashlyn wasn't sure how to read Cami's response. "What is it?" she asked. "Did I say something wrong?"

"You know, Ash," Cami said levelly. "Ever since I've known you, you've whined about how picked on you've been because your dad wasn't around for you and your family. Then Jake dumped you and you felt like the world ended. I'm not surprised you still can't get over him. How can you forget about a person when you have so many reminders about him around you?"

Ashlyn looked over at her dresser, where the pictures and gifts Jake had given her were neatly arranged.

"I swear, Ash, you've kept every movie ticket stub and every piece of gum he ever gave you. How do you expect to get over him if you hang on to all that stuff that reminds you of him?"

Cami was holding her cup of cocoa so tightly her knuckles were white and her voice trembled with emotion. "I know your father hurt you and your family, and I know Jake also hurt you very badly. But you're letting all these events from the past decide your future. These two men still have control over you because you let them."

Ashlyn felt a swirling of confusion inside of her, shocked that Cami was talking so heartlessly. "How do you know what I'm feeling?" Ashlyn demanded. "How do you know how bad it hurts?"

Cami stood up and put her mug on the dresser next to Jake and Ashlyn's engagement picture. Turning abruptly, she said, "I know what it's like to have a rough home life, believe me. My father was an alcoholic, Ashlyn. He used to beat my mother, sometimes until she was unconscious. And then, if he wasn't too drunk, he'd come after me. Do you know what it's like to hide under your bed with your pillow over your head and still be able to hear your mother screaming, then tremble in fear because you know you might be next?

"I used to pray that my father wouldn't come home at night. That something would happen to him so I didn't have to see him again or see him beat my mother," she said, her voice toneless. She shoved her hands into her pockets and leaned against the dresser. "And then, one day, it happened. Just like that. One night he didn't come home. Or the next, or the next."

"What happened?" Ashlyn asked, stunned at this sudden revelation from the friend she thought she knew inside and out.

"We found out he came into some money somehow and took off with it. But neither my mom nor I were sad to see him go. We moved in with Grandma and Grandpa, and then my mother died within the year. She had trouble sleeping so she had a prescription. One night she took too many pills and never woke up. Not long after that I found out my father was also dead. He'd been beaten and stabbed and left to die in a gutter in Los Angeles. He'd been dealing drugs."

Ashlyn felt like her lungs had deflated. "I don't know what to say, Cami. I'm so sorry," Ashlyn told her. "Why didn't you ever tell me?"

"It's too painful to talk about. I'd rather forget about it, and I don't like people feeling sorry for me," Cami answered quickly. "Besides, I couldn't control what happened. My parents made their own choices."

Tears welled up in Ashlyn's eyes. When she'd first met Cami, she'd wondered what had happened to her parents and when Cami wouldn't talk about it, Ashlyn had stopped thinking about it. Now for the first time Cami was sharing her most private and painful feelings. Ashlyn didn't say anything; she just let her friend talk.

"Hanging onto the past doesn't do me any good," Cami continued. "It doesn't change anything. The past is over and done with. There's nothing I can do about what happened, and I don't want to waste any more of my time or energy remembering a time of my life that was so painful.

"My father was abused as a child himself so I don't blame him for the way he was. He tried to make something of his life, but he grew up on the streets and it was just too much a part of him. I guess it made sense that he would die on the streets, too."

Cami took in a deep breath, then let it out with a weary sigh. "Like I said, it's in the past and there's nothing I can do about it now except move on and try to make a better life for myself. I've been so very blessed. Grandpa and Grandma have raised me as their own. They loved me and took care of me, and I've been very secure and happy since my parents died. No, my life isn't what I thought it would be, but I know I can control my future by the decisions I make, not by what's happened to me in the past. I can make my own dreams come true. Maybe it's time you started living your life and stopped blaming someone else for it."

Cami's words stung Ashlyn like a slap in the face. Is that what she'd been doing? she wondered. Blaming all her problems on her past and letting them control her future? Cami had never talked that much about her father or mother, and now Ashlyn could see why. She felt ashamed for having complained about her trials. Yes, she'd endured some awful things, but compared to Cami's experiences, they weren't so bad.

Cami left before Ashlyn could say anything, but it was just as well because Ashlyn didn't know what to say.

·⚮·

Ashlyn didn't feel much like going out to dinner with Sebastian Jamison. She'd thought up a dozen excuses not to go, but every time she left her room to go tell Cami she was staying home, she stopped. It might have been because she didn't feel like being alone right now. Or maybe she hoped that somehow she and Cami could talk again so Ashlyn could apologize. She hated it when things weren't right between them.

At ten minutes to seven she went downstairs. Grandpa Willy was standing by the patio doors looking out at the sky. Storm clouds were slowly breaking with the help of a gusty wind.

"I heard on the radio that a cabin cruiser was caught in the storm," he said, not even turning to look at Ashlyn, but knowing she was in the room. "The weather turned bad too quickly and they couldn't get back to shore."

"Are they okay?" Ashlyn asked. She could well imagine how terrified she would feel to be out to sea during a storm.

"The ship stayed in touch with the coast guard during the whole ordeal. John Harmon, with the coast guard, is a good friend of the ship's captain, Syd Morton. They served in the navy together. John had been through a storm just like this several months back. He could tell his friend exactly what to do, since he'd been there himself. And that made all the difference. John got Syd back to shore in one piece."

"That's good news," Ashlyn said, thinking that people who lived by the sea had their own set of challenges, which actually seemed to bring them closer together.

"Yep," Grandpa Willy said. "That's what friends do for each other. They stay right by your side and tell you what you need to hear. That's the only way they can help you."

Ashlyn realized he was trying to tell her something important. She looked down at her handbag and took a deep breath.

"I'll be out in the car, waitin'," he said and left the room. At that moment Cami came down the stairs and looked up at Ashlyn, her eyes as tentative and wary as a fawn.

"Hey," Ashlyn said, "you're wearing that sweater I gave you for your birthday." It was a pale pink sweater set, with pearls embroidered around the neckline. It looked beautiful with Cami's blonde hair and tanned skin.

"And you wore your hair curly," Cami said. "It looks great."

"Thanks," Ashlyn said. "And I don't mean just for that either. I mean for everything. Especially for being a good enough friend to tell me the truth, even though I didn't want to hear it."

Cami smiled shyly. "You're not mad at me?" she asked.

"Of course I'm not mad at you," Ashlyn replied. "I thought you were mad at me."

"I'm not mad at all," she said.

"I'm glad," Ashlyn grinned.

"Me too."

The girls hugged each other and laughed until a honk from the car horn made them both jump.

"Grandpa doesn't like to be late," Cami explained. She looked at her friend searchingly. "So, we're okay now?"

"We're okay," Ashlyn said. "And I mean it, thanks. I really appreciated what you said, and I'm glad you told me about your parents. I'm really sorry about all that."

"Yeah, well," Cami grimaced. "It made it hard to write essays in English about my family."

"I'll bet," Ashlyn said with a laugh. The horn sounded again.

"C'mon." Cami grabbed Ashlyn's arm. "You don't want to keep your dinner date waiting."

"Will you stop it?" Ashlyn said. "He invited all of us."

"Yeah, but he was looking at you the whole time," Cami reminded her. "I think you may have quite a catch on the line and you just need to reel him in."

CHAPTER
NINETEEN

"I'm so glad you could join me." Sebastian was already seated at the restaurant, but he stood and greeted them when they arrived. "Mr. Davenport." He shook Grandpa Willy's hand. "Ladies," he said, helping first Cami into her chair and then finally Ashlyn. "You look very beautiful tonight," he complimented her before taking his seat again.

Ashlyn wasn't sure what it was, but as charming as he was she felt a bit uncertain about him. Maybe it was because she hadn't had a man show such obvious interest in her since Jake. She wasn't used to being the object of someone's attention.

But she had to admit she was intrigued by him. He was exotic-looking and very classy. His clothes were expensive and designed by people whose names Ashlyn couldn't even pronounce, let alone afford. And he possessed a charismatic magnetism that kept her, Cami, and Grandpa Willy completely entranced.

The waiter approached them and Sebastian immediately took over the job of making sure everyone at the table got exactly what they wanted. He was generous and lavish with his attention to detail, making sure that everything was "just right" for his guests. He praised Ashlyn on her choice of steak and prawns. She didn't know why, but it did seem that Sebastian was paying her a lot of attention.

"So, tell me all about this charming little town," he said, looking at Ashlyn.

"Since I've only been here a few weeks, I'm probably not the right person to ask," she said, and nodded at Cami and her grandfather. "They're the ones to ask."

Between Cami and her grandfather, Sebastian learned all about the town of Seamist and its fascinating history. He paid close attention to every word, appearing to enjoy their descriptions of small-town life on the beautiful Oregon coast. They told him about nature trails, about the untouched beauty of the surrounding area, the uncommercialized coastline, and the close-knit community.

"It sounds too good to be true," he said, reaching for his water glass. "But that is what I wanted when I searched for a place such as this."

"How did you find Seamist and the Henderson house?" Grandpa Willy asked.

He thought for a moment. "About a year ago I drove up the coast from San Francisco with friends, and we stopped at the grocery store to buy some food for a picnic on the beach. I immediately liked the slower pace of the town; it was so relaxed and unhurried. I kept it in the back of my mind for months. Then when a deal came through to write this novel, I decided I needed a place to go where I could just get away from my job and the city. A place to escape to. And I remembered how I felt when I was here. So I called your Chamber of Commerce to get a listing of real estate agents and I started making phone calls."

"Who are you working with?" Cami asked.

"A woman named Vanessa James," he told them.

Ashlyn nearly choked on a piece of roll as Cami kicked her leg under the table, and her eyes began to water. Fortunately no one but Cami noticed Ashlyn was choking since at that moment the waiter arrived with their dinner salads.

As they drove home after dinner, Cami told Ashlyn, "The man must have packing peanuts for brains if he's using Vanessa James as a realtor."

"You don't think she's a good realtor?" Ashlyn asked.

"I'm sure she's a decent realtor, but I don't trust her. She's a little too conniving, too manipulative, for me. I sure wish I knew why Mitch liked her so much."

Ashlyn didn't admit it out loud, but her feelings matched her friend's exactly. "You mean aside from the fact that she's incredibly gorgeous?"

"He's not that shallow," Cami said in his defense. "He wouldn't like a person just for looks alone, although I agree, it can't hurt."

"That first wife of his must've really done a number on him," Ashlyn reminded her. "It's the only thing that makes sense. Vanessa's attention must be a balm to his bruised ego."

"Yeah, I guess," Cami agreed reluctantly.

"Mitch is no fool," Grandpa Willy piped up from the back seat. "He's just killing time until the right one comes along."

Ashlyn had forgotten all about him back there and was surprised at his matter-of-fact statement.

"You think so, Grandpa?" Cami asked as she pulled into the driveway.

"No doubt in my mind," he said. "Mitch is a smart boy. He wouldn't marry someone like Vanessa. Date her, yes. Why not? But marry her, absolutely not!"

"I hope you're right, Grandpa. I'd hate to see him end up with her. He's been through enough already with his first wife. He deserves to be happy." Cami shoved the car into park and killed the lights.

"So, what did you think about Sebastian?" Ashlyn asked, changing the subject.

"I like him," Cami replied. "And apparently, he likes you. He didn't take his eyes off of you the entire night. Grandpa, tell her. Am I making this up or did Sebastian seem to have a 'thing' for Ashlyn?"

"Well," Grandpa Willy started, "if you ask me, I've seen that look before."

"Where?" Cami asked.

"On a shark just before he attacks his victim," Grandpa Willy said slyly.

Cami and Ashlyn burst out laughing. Then Ashlyn stopped. Suddenly it wasn't funny any more.

"What?" Cami said, still giggling.

"Okay, I admit, I saw him looking at me a few times," Ashlyn confessed. "What do you think it's all about?"

"It's probably nothing," Cami assured her. "He's an aggressive city guy who's used to meeting and dating aggressive city women. He's obviously attracted to you and doesn't feel the need to play any games."

"Well, I'm not interested," Ashlyn said, "and I'm not ready for another relationship." Still, she had to admit she was flattered. And Sebastian was a very attractive man, which made it all the more enjoyable.

⚬⚬⚬ 🕮 ⚬⚬⚬

"So," Mitch said the next morning as they ran the length of the beach, "Cami tells me you were engaged before."

Ashlyn nearly tripped on a piece of driftwood. "Oh, she did, did she?"

"Well, she didn't exactly volunteer the information. I asked her if you'd had any serious boyfriends," he admitted.

Ashlyn smiled inwardly. He'd been asking about her. How come Cami hadn't said anything?

"So?" he asked, his breath coming in labored puffs.

They were almost to the end of their run, which stretched to the breakers at the mouth of the harbor, nearly two miles from home. Their goal was to build more stamina each day by running back instead of walking.

"So . . . what?" she replied, nearly breathless. They stopped talking while they pushed the last twenty feet, then slowed their pace as they turned and headed back.

"So, what happened?"

The morning sun painted patches of pink and gold on the clouds above the horizon. Ashlyn's favorite part of their morning run was watching the sun rise.

"He changed his mind," she said simply, wanting to avoid the painful details.

"Just like that?" Mitch studied her expression as if he were trying to see past her words and into her heart.

"Pretty much." Ashlyn mopped at her sweaty brow with her sleeve.

"How did he tell you? That must've been pretty awful," Mitch said sympathetically.

"Yeah," she said, hoping this would be the end of the conversation. "It still hurts."

Mitch nodded, like he understood.

"Look at that sunrise," Ashlyn said as she stopped and drank in the view. The sky grew brighter and the clouds ignited in a kaleidoscope of colors, the lapping waves glistening in the brilliant rays of light.

Mitch stopped next to her, a little closer than she'd expected, and when she turned to see if he was watching the sunrise, she bumped into him.

"Oops, sorry," she said. She went to step away, but he grabbed her elbow. She didn't resist.

"He was a fool," Mitch told her softly.

Ashlyn looked at him inquiringly, wondering why he said that.

"Your fiancé," Mitch said clearly. "He must not have known what a good thing he had."

"Oh yeah, I'm sure he still regrets leaving me at the temple," Ashlyn remarked flatly.

Mitch stared at her. "He actually did that?"

She nodded. "Yup. Left me at the altar—literally." She started walking again.

"You're kidding, right?" He caught up with her.

"Not at all," Ashlyn said. "I was in my wedding dress, in the temple, waiting to go to the sealing room when I got the news." She forced herself to look at him, keeping her expression blank and the emotion out of her voice.

"Wow," Mitch said with disbelief.

"You know what they say, 'That which doesn't kill you makes you stronger,'" she said with a sarcastic laugh, still not sure whether she believed the saying or not. It hadn't killed her, but she wasn't sure yet if she was any stronger.

They continued walking, the sun showering them with warm, glowing rays.

"Are you getting stronger?" Mitch asked after a moment.

"I'm working on it," Ashlyn said.

They neared the wooden steps. Mitch stopped her before she climbed them.

"If there's anything I can ever do to help," he offered, "or if you just need a friend to talk to, or a shoulder to cry on . . ." He didn't finish.

She looked up into his eyes and smiled her thanks. Then, without any warning at all, he put his arms around her and hugged her tightly.

It was strange, Ashlyn thought. It wasn't awkward and it wasn't "weird." In fact, if anything, it felt perfectly natural. He held her close for a moment, as the quiet serenity of the cove enveloped them in a private moment. She shut her eyes, cherishing the feeling of having two strong, protective arms hold her. It had been a long time since she'd felt that.

"Thanks, Mitch," she said. "I'm really glad we're friends."

She thought she glimpsed a strange look flicker across his face, just for a moment, then it vanished. She wasn't sure what to make of it, but she could have sworn he looked hurt.

But that was nonsense. She pushed the thought from her mind and led the way up the wooden stairs towards the Davenports' house.

⋰⋰ ⚜ ⋱⋱

A loud boom Friday morning woke Ashlyn from a deep sleep. The windows rattled and all the dogs in the neighborhood began howling with a vengeance. She sat up with a start, then realized what day it was. The Fourth of July. The cannon was a city tradition to begin the day's festivities. Following another tradition, Ashlyn and Cami planned to have breakfast at the city park.

Ashlyn quickly showered and pulled on a pair of slim white walking shorts, a coral and white striped tee shirt, and white canvas shoes. Instead of fighting the natural curl in her hair, she slicked a dollop of gel through the tangles and scrunched it through her hair, letting it hang in long, full curls around her shoulders. She realized that the more she got used to seeing her hair curly again, the more she was starting to like it.

There was a tap on her bedroom door then Cami poked her head inside. "Hey, you about ready?" Cami was wearing a light blue shirt, with khaki clam diggers and sandals.

"Just about," Ashlyn answered, running a wand of clear gloss over her lips. She shut her drawers, plumped the pillow on her bed, and turned out the light. Taking one last look around her tidy room, she said, "Okay, all set."

"Don't you want to vacuum first?" Cami teased.

"I'm sorry, but I just don't like coming home to a cluttered room. Since when did it become a crime to be neat?" Ashlyn felt her defenses rising as they usually did when Cami pointed out her "neatnik" ways.

"I'm just kiddin'," Cami told her. "But one of these days I'm going to find a way to get you to leave your room with your bed unmade."

Ashlyn shook her head hopelessly at her friend. "If it's that big of a deal to you, I'll go in and mess it up right now."

"No, it's not the same," Cami said, leading the way down the stairs. "You have to do it because you just don't care if the bed's not made, or you have something much more important to do, more fun to do, than to take the time to make your bed."

"I'll work on being more of a pig," Ashlyn told her.

"Good," Cami said with a satisfied smile, "although you don't have to go quite that far. I'd settle for 'normal.'"

Ashlyn didn't respond since Grandpa Willy was waiting for them in the living room. "Pearl just called and asked if we were going down to the breakfast," he told them.

Ashlyn had wanted to invite the older woman to go with them. But she wasn't sure if Grandpa Willy would want her to go with them or not.

"I told her she was welcome to come with us," he said.

Cami smiled at her grandfather. "I'm glad you did. It will be fun having her along."

"Well, I don't know how fun it's going to be. She has to argue about everything. I swear that woman is the most disagreeable human on the planet," he complained.

"No she isn't, Grandpa," Cami defended the woman. "It's just that you two are so much alike."

"Alike!" he exclaimed. "That's a downright rotten thing to say to your grandfather. We're not a bit alike." Ashlyn wanted to back up Cami's observation, but she could see Grandpa Willy wasn't too pleased about the comparison as it was.

Pearl looked nice in a loose denim jumper with a bright red tee shirt and matching red sandals. She'd chosen a large-brimmed straw hat from her collection of at least a dozen hats and had tied a red bandana around it. Altogether she looked very festive.

When they arrived at the park, half of the town was already lined up for flapjacks, scrambled eggs, and locally made sausage. As soon as they stepped out of their car, they caught a whiff of the spicy meat and sizzling grills.

Luckily the morning was warm and clear, except for a few white clouds in the distance. The screech of a loudspeaker caught the crowd's attention, and everyone turned to the small stage, which was adorned with red, white, and blue balloons and a large American flag.

To Ashlyn's surprise, and delight, Mitch climbed up on the stand and addressed the friends and neighbors of the community.

"Welcome to the first event of our Fourth of July celebration. We're happy to have such a good turnout and expect many more to show up, so if we can have you wait until we announce it's okay to come back for seconds, that means you—Stan and Randy—" the crowd laughed, "we'd appreciate it. Enjoy the meal and the rest of your day." Mitch left the stand and the gathering townsfolk applauded.

Ashlyn greeted many familiar faces with a smile and a "good morning." Cami had told her what a friendly community Seamist was and she was right. Everyone seemed to sincerely care about everyone else.

Everyone except Pearl. Ashlyn thought she seemed nervous. She hadn't said much since they arrived at the park.

"Everything okay, Pearl?" Ashlyn asked as she picked up her paper plate, plastic utensils, and napkin, ready to go through the line.

"This is my first time at one of these," she confessed.

"Really?" Ashlyn was surprised. "Why?"

"Oh, I don't know. I've never really felt comfortable at community functions like this. I guess, it's because I've never had anyone to go with until this year." She smiled shyly at Ashlyn.

Ashlyn knew Pearl was reserved and kept to herself, but she had always assumed it was because Pearl wanted it that way. Now she was beginning to think that Pearl had kept her distance, surrounding herself with privacy, for another reason. But why?

"Bacon or sausage," asked the cute little man who was dishing up breakfast meats.

"Bacon please," Ashlyn said. She noticed down the line that Mitch was pouring paper cups of orange juice and milk.

The line moved down the serving tables.

"Care for something to drink?" he asked, before realizing who he was speaking to. He looked up for a reply and a wide smile broke onto his face. "Well, hello there."

"Morning, Mitch," Ashlyn said, returning his smile.

"Don't you clean up nicely," he complimented.

"Well," she said, dipping her chin in feigned modesty. "Thank you."

"Hey!" someone down the line shouted. "People are starving back here."

"Keep your shirt on, Harmon. There's enough food here to even fill *your* stomach," Mitch retorted. Several people in line laughed.

"I'll catch up with you later," Mitch told Ashlyn as he quickly handed out drinks to the hungry people in line.

Ashlyn and Pearl found Cami and her grandfather, who were already seated. Sebastian was seated next to Cami and signaled to the place beside him that he had saved for Ashlyn.

"Good morning." He jumped up, taking Ashlyn's plate and drink from her so she could take her seat. "Let me help you."

"Thanks," she said, wondering why he was here. Didn't he have a best-selling novel to write or something?

And again she wondered why Sebastian had taken such a strong interest in her. She was sure she wasn't his type. He needed someone sophisticated, career driven, perfectly groomed. She was none of those things.

Sebastian was his usual charming self and he repeated the story he had been telling Grandpa Willy and Cami. "When the cannon went off this morning, I forgot I was in Oregon. I thought I was back in California and that we were having an earthquake."

He continued to entertain Grandpa Willy and Cami with several other stories, although Ashlyn noticed that Pearl didn't seem as enthralled with his charm.

When Sebastian noticed that a few of them were low on orange juice, he offered to go get refills. As soon as he was gone, Ashlyn sighed. "Is it just me, or is that man getting on anyone else's nerves?"

"I think he's nice," Cami said. "And cute."

"He's an interesting fellow," Grandpa Willy commented. "I'd say he's sixty percent hot air, but he still spins a good yarn."

"Why don't you like him?" Cami asked her. "He sure seems to like you."

"It's not that I don't like him," she said. "It's just that . . ." She searched for an explanation but came up empty handed. "Oh, I don't know. Never mind."

As they ate, Ashlyn noticed several gulls swooping down to pick at the ground for food, and her gaze drifted over the crowds. The tables were still full of people happily eating and talking while children dodged and ran between tables and chairs.

Her gaze stopped when she saw Sebastian talking with Vanessa. She paused, watching them. They leaned toward each other, talking privately and laughing.

They seemed awfully friendly, she thought. At least for a business relationship. Of course, maybe their relationship was becoming more than just a business relationship. The idea intrigued her. Maybe Vanessa would move onto someone more suited to her, someone like Sebastian. She snapped out of her thoughts when she realized that Vanessa and Sebastian had finished talking with each other, and he was headed back to their table.

"Here we go," Sebastian said, handing out the cups of orange juice he had brought them.

"Looks like I'm finished." Ashlyn stood up, gathering her dishes and utensils. "I'll just take these to the garbage and be right back."

"Here." Sebastian jumped to his feet. "I'll do that for you."

"Thanks, but I can do it," she answered coolly. "I need to stretch my legs anyway."

"I'll go with you, dear," Pearl offered. "I could use a little 'leg-stretching' myself."

They tossed their plates into the garbage can and stood for a moment, looking around at the people and enjoying the beautiful sun-filled morning. Several children ran by carrying water balloons, laughing and hollering at the top of their lungs.

"I noticed you've hardly said two words to Sebastian. How come?" Ashlyn asked.

Pearl spoke bluntly, as usual. "Honey, when you've been around the world as many times as I have, you learn how to read people very quickly. I don't care how charming he is. I'm glad you're not falling for him, dearie. You're doing a good job dodging that broom of his."

Ashlyn wasn't sure what Pearl meant. "I'm what?"

"He's trying to sweep you off your feet, but you're just too bright and too quick for him." Pearl adjusted her hat further back on her head. "I think Mr. Jamison is an interesting fellow, but I'd definitely keep him at a distance," she advised.

Just then Ashlyn saw Mitch and Vanessa. She was wearing a pair of red silk trousers and a red knit pullover, with red high-heeled sandals. Her glossy, black hair was teased and full. She looked like a human Barbie doll.

"And if you ask me," Pearl said, "that girlfriend of Mitch's is someone else to stay away from. I don't trust her as far as I can throw her." But she smiled at Mitch as he approached. It was obvious that she didn't blame him for stumbling into Vanessa's web.

"So how was your breakfast?" Mitch asked them.

"Wonderful, Mitch," Pearl answered. "You've done a nice job."

"Thank you," Mitch said, obviously pleased to hear her say so. "I hope you're planning on attending the other activities. We've got a lot planned."

Vanessa stood at Mitch's side with both of her arms wrapped around one of his, looking, Ashlyn thought, exactly like a politician's wife, giving the appearance of the devoted companion and going through the motions of good citizenship just to win the devotion of the peasants.

"I'm sure you'll enjoy the parade," Vanessa told them. "Mitch and I are riding in it together."

Ashlyn bit her tongue to keep from telling Vanessa how she felt about seeing her in the parade.

"I entered my blackberry pie in the pie contest," Pearl told them. "I'll definitely be at the dinner this evening."

"Good luck in the contest," Mitch said. "Although with your pie, you won't be needing any luck."

Vanessa smiled and waved at another couple strolling by.

"Well," Mitch said, turning to Ashlyn. "Guess I'll see you around then?"

She gave him a warm smile. "Okay."

Vanessa returned her attention to Ashlyn and Pearl long enough to give them a courtesy smile and say, "Have a fun day," before she and Mitch walked off.

"Mitch could sure do a lot better than her," was all Pearl said.

Ashlyn agreed silently. Mitch's choice in girlfriends was none of her business, but she couldn't help thinking of Vanessa as a black widow spider and Mitch as a fly caught in her web.

CHAPTER TWENTY

The parade was authentic Americana, complete with a county queen and her attendants, the high school band, and Bobo the clown riding around on a unicycle, throwing handfuls of saltwater taffy at the crowd.

As chairman of the Fourth of July festivities, Mitch got to ride in a convertible car with the Grand Marshall. Of course, Vanessa was at his side, smiling as if all the people lined up on both sides of Main Street had come just to see her.

After the parade Pearl wanted to go home for a little siesta so she would be rested for the dinner and fireworks. Sebastian offered to take her home since he was going home himself for a while, and she reluctantly allowed him to give her a ride.

The Misty Harbor boardwalk was the setting for a variety of booths and activities, and Cami and Ashlyn happily surveyed the colorful scene. At some point between the dunking machine and the sand sculptures, they lost Grandpa Willy, who had hooked up with some of his sailing buddies who were sitting in the shade watching the celebration.

A stage was set up in the middle of the action, and the two girls watched a group of cloggers who were busily kicking up their heels on the stage. When the number ended, the crowd was further entertained by a barbershop quartet. The four gentlemen, all in their seventies and dressed in white straw hats and red and white striped jackets, belted out "Sweet Adeline" with gusto. When the number ended, they were rewarded with deafening applause.

"There's Mitch's dad." Cami pointed at the tall man making his way off the stage and toward them. "Hi, Mr. Bradford," she called. He stopped to say hello, and Cami introduced Ashlyn to him.

"So you're the one who has my son getting up at the crack of dawn to go jogging?" he asked.

"That would be me," Ashlyn said with a smile.

He nodded his head approvingly. "I thought he was plumb crazy to get up early like that and go running, but now I understand why. A pretty face like yours would definitely be worth the effort," he complimented her.

Ashlyn felt her face grow warm. "Thank you," she said.

He leaned toward them, lowering his voice. "Just between us, I'm glad to see him finally spending time with someone other than—"

"Vanessa James!" the announcer said over the loudspeaker.

A roar of applause filled the air as Vanessa glided onto the stage, wearing a clingy silver dress with spaghetti straps that was just short enough to show off her shapely knees. The sun's reflection off the sequins was brighter than the Misty Harbor Lighthouse's 1,100,000 candlepower. Half the audience had to shield their eyes, but she didn't notice.

"I'd like to dedicate this song to the wonderful people of Seamist and thank them for their support. And especially, to my sweetheart, Mitch Bradford." The music began and she started singing a song made famous by Whitney Houston, "I Will Always Love You."

Her voice was clear and strong, and as much as Ashlyn didn't want to admit it, Vanessa sounded great.

"Wow," Ashlyn muttered. "She can really sing."

"I guess," Cami said sourly.

Vanessa's number was a showstopper. And to top it all off, when the song ended, Mitch walked out onto the stage with a bouquet of red roses and presented them to her with a kiss. The crowd applauded wildly and Vanessa reveled in the attention. She took a deep bow, then blew kisses to the audience.

"I think I'm going to throw up," Cami said privately to Ashlyn. "Let's get out of here." Not wasting any time, the girls slipped behind a concessions stand and started down the boardwalk.

As they walked toward the jumbo slide and a ring toss booth, they heard their names being called.

"Hey, you two," Mitch said breathlessly, coming up behind them.

They stopped and turned around. "Hi, Mitch," Cami said coolly, obviously not wanting to hear about Vanessa.

"Did you hear Vanessa?" he asked. "She just performed on the grandstand."

Before Cami could answer, Ashlyn said, "Yes, we heard her. She was really good."

"She was, wasn't she?" he said, beaming proudly. "She takes voice lessons from my mother."

"Your mother's done a good job," Ashlyn said, ready to move on to the next topic. "And so have you. The celebration's really wonderful." But she had run out of fake enthusiasm for Vanessa and could only stand there silently.

"Well, I'd better get going," Mitch said uncomfortably, not sure what to make of Ashlyn's silence. "I've got to check the water at the dunking machine. I'm filling it up."

"Is Vanessa going to do that, too?" Cami asked hopefully.

Mitch didn't seem to realize that Cami wasn't kidding. "Of course not," he laughed. "She'd never do something like that."

"Too bad," Cami said, her eyes taking on a wicked spark.

"Oh, by the way," Mitch remembered, "before I forget. Dallin's looking for you. I ran into him while he was getting a chili cheese dog at the concessions stand. He's probably still there."

"Why didn't you say something earlier?" she said, getting ready to hurry off. "I'm going to run over and see if I can catch him," she hollered back at Ashlyn. "Catch up with me there."

Ashlyn nodded and waved her on. She was glad Dallin had showed up. Cami hadn't said anything all day, but from the way Cami kept a constant eye on everyone around her, Ashlyn had a hunch her friend was hoping to see him.

Mitch walked back toward the concessions stand with Ashlyn.

"So, are you guys staying for the dinner, dance, and fireworks?" he asked.

She nodded. "I'm looking forward to the fireworks."

"They're going to be really great this year. I'm glad you'll get to see them. You'll want to stake a spot on the beach early so you can get a good view. Of course, the best place to watch them would be from the lighthouse. But that's kind of out of the way."

"Looks like Cami found Dallin," Ashlyn said as they approached the concessions.

Sure enough, Cami and Dallin were sitting side by side on a wooden bench, beneath the shade of a tree. Their heads were bent close together as they talked and laughed, unaware of anyone around them. They'd obviously been able to pick up where they left off a few years ago, and the flame had quickly reignited between them. Although Ashlyn was happy for Cami, she was a little sad for herself. She hated to lose her close relationship with her friend.

"Hey, coach," a boy called, as a group of teenagers walked by.

Mitch turned around. "Hey, Scottie. Hey, guys. You boys staying out of trouble?"

"What do you think?" the same boy asked with a hint of mischief in his eye.

"I think you're looking for free food or pretty girls. Both if you're lucky," Mitch told them.

"There's free food?" another boy asked.

"Sure, down by the bake sale, they're giving out free samples. It's right next to the grandstand, and I do believe that the high school dance team is going to perform in about fifteen minutes."

One of the boys smacked the other one. "See, I told you Jessica would be here."

The group was about to leave when one of the boys said, "You got a new girlfriend, Coach?"

"New girl—?" Mitch looked confused, then he chuckled. "Oh, you mean Ashlyn, here? No, she's just a friend. She's staying with the Davenports this summer."

"Oh," the boy nodded. A couple of the boys in the back laughed and elbowed each other.

"You'd better hurry before the cookies run out," Mitch told them. "And don't forget that you've got football practice at eight in the morning, so don't stay out late tonight. Got it?"

Ashlyn smiled at them as they left. They looked like good kids, and she imagined that Mitch had a great relationship with them. He was their leader, but he was also their friend. The look of respect and admiration on their faces was obvious. Mitch was probably these boys' hero.

"There you are," a voice behind them exclaimed. "I've been looking all over for you, Mitch." Ashlyn knew who it was before she even turned around.

"Vanessa," he exclaimed when he saw her. "I thought you were changing."

"Well, I'm done, and I wondered where you went." She put her arm firmly through his.

Ashlyn didn't like how Vanessa treated Mitch and she didn't like the way Mitch took her commands and demands. Ashlyn still wondered what he saw in this woman, besides her flawless beauty and perfect body. Then she realized she'd answered her own question. She could imagine how flattered Mitch was that this beautiful woman had chosen him when she could have had anyone for the asking.

"Your parents are meeting us at the park," she said. "George and Gina are there, too." She didn't bother to acknowledge Ashlyn.

Taking her cue, Ashlyn said, "I'd better go find Cami," wanting to let Mitch off the hook so he could leave without feeling uncomfortable.

"Guess we'll see you later," he said.

Ashlyn smiled at him as he left with Vanessa, then had to cover up a chuckle when Vanessa's high heel caught on the boardwalk and she lost her footing. Ashlyn hated to admit it but she wouldn't have minded watching Vanessa go flying down the boardwalk.

Turning to look for Cami, she came face to face with Sebastian.

"Hello, Ashlyn. I was hoping I'd bump into you."

"Oh, hi Sebastian," she said tiredly. She didn't want to be rude, but she didn't want to give him any ideas that she was even the least bit interested in him. She had no use for men in her life, especially men who were full of flattery and empty compliments like Sebastian.

"What are you doing all by yourself?" he asked.

"I was just going to look for Cami," she told him pointedly, wanting to make sure he didn't think she was just standing around waiting for some Casanova like him to waltz by. Salt Lake City wasn't a huge metropolis, but it was big enough for Ashlyn to have learned that guys like Sebastian were conquerors and potential destroyers. She didn't want anything to do with him; she was still picking emotional shrapnel from her wounds after Jake.

I'm not about to be your next conquest, and I've already had my turn being demolished, thank you very much, she thought.

"I just saw her with that fellow from the bank—Dallin, I think his name is," Sebastian informed her. "They were walking along the beach toward the north breakers. They might be a while."

You are in big trouble, Cami! Ashlyn thought.

"Since you're alone, and I'm alone," he said, invitingly, "perhaps we could be alone together for a while."

Ashlyn tried to smile graciously as her mind went into hyperdrive, trying to devise an excuse why she couldn't. But nothing materialized.

"I was thinking of going through some of the art galleries. I understand there are some very good local artists," he suggested.

His offer seemed harmless enough, Ashlyn decided. In fact, maybe after a few minutes in one of the galleries, she would think of a reason to excuse herself. Then she could find Cami and head for home. She'd had about enough of this Fourth of July celebration.

Ashlyn was amazed at how many women took double takes as she and Sebastian walked toward downtown Seamist, just a block from the beach. She wasn't blind; she was well aware of how handsome he was. But she'd learned the hard way, through Jake, that looks weren't everything. If a man didn't have a good heart, he wasn't worth her time.

As she and Sebastian wandered through galleries, studying the local artwork, several beautiful paintings of the ocean and coastline caught her eye. She found one particularly breathtaking landscape and was amazed that it was priced so reasonably. A watercolor of that caliber seemed a steal at four hundred and fifty dollars.

In addition to the art collections, there was also a display of pottery and sculpture. Sebastian seemed particularly taken with a bronze sculpture of an eagle in flight. It was majestic and magnificent and seemed very real. He left his name with the dealer. He said he wanted to talk to the artist first before he seriously considered buying it.

As they browsed and discussed various pieces of work, Ashlyn found herself relaxing and actually enjoying Sebastian's company. He had a vast knowledge of art as well as a great appreciation for the creative process, having himself dabbled in watercolor and sculpture.

By the time they finished with the last gallery, Ashlyn noticed they'd been gone over an hour.

"Goodness," she exclaimed. "Look at the time. I bet Cami's wondering where I took off to."

Back at the beach, they practically ran into Cami and Dallin.

"There you are," Cami exclaimed. "We've been looking all over for you."

"You have, have you? Down by the breakers?" Ashlyn said skeptically.

Cami and Dallin looked at each other and then back at her. "Well, we went for a walk, then we started looking for you," Cami admitted, chuckling. "We were wondering if you wanted to go to the park for a picnic. We could pick up some chicken and salads at the deli and sit in the shade and eat. What do you think?"

Ashlyn looked at Sebastian. "I'd like that," he said. "How about you, Ashlyn?"

"Why not?" she shrugged.

They stopped at the store so the two girls could run in and get the food, and while they were alone, Ashlyn gave Cami the scolding of her life.

"You're right," Cami agreed as she chose some bottles of juice. "It wasn't very thoughtful of me to leave you alone. Dallin and I wanted to say hi to a friend who had a booth down at the end of the boardwalk, and we just kept walking and talking and didn't realize how far we'd gone. Really, I'm sorry. I wasn't thinking. What happened to Mitch? You were with him when we left."

"Princess Vanessa found him," Ashlyn said. "He left like a dog on a leash."

Cami shook her head. "I swear that woman has some kind of hypnotic hold over him." She added some plump, juicy red grapes to the cart next to the fried chicken, potato salad, and juice.

"I'm sorry I abandoned you," Cami said again. "I don't know what's wrong with me."

Ashlyn looked at her. "It's obvious."

"What do you mean?"

"Just what I said. It's as plain as the smudges of lipstick on your face—"

Cami snatched a small mirror out of her purse. "Why didn't you say something?" she asked as she rubbed at the smears of lipstick around her mouth.

After they'd paid for the groceries and headed for the door, Cami said, "What was it you were saying?"

"I was going to tell you what's wrong with you," Ashlyn said as she pushed the door open with her shoulder.

"Oh, yes, that's right. And what is wrong with me, oh wise one?" Cami asked.

"You're in love."

Cami opened her mouth to deny it, then seemed to change her mind. "You're right," she confessed. "And you know what? He said he loves me, too."

After the picnic, Ashlyn decided that a little break was in order. Sebastian had left, saying he had some work to do around his yard before the barbecue and fireworks that evening. Following his lead, Ashlyn borrowed Cami's keys and drove herself home. This way Cami and Dallin could have time alone together, and she could keep a safe distance from Sebastian, Mitch, *and* Vanessa.

The house was invitingly quiet as she stepped inside. She kicked off her shoes and relaxed on the couch, grabbing a magazine off the coffee table. But after skimming a few articles, she tossed the magazine back onto the table.

An effort to call her mom and Garrett in Salt Lake proved fruitless. They were no doubt at her grandparents' house. Ashlyn's grandfather made the best barbecued ribs she'd ever tasted. Her mouth watered just thinking about them. Everyone would be outside, sitting under the shade trees, enjoying glasses of cold lemonade and good company. A touch of homesickness niggled its way into her heart.

It wasn't that she was ready to leave Seamist. She didn't want to go home, not yet. But it was on days like today that she wished she could transport herself to her grandparents' backyard, just for the afternoon, to spend time with her family.

She allowed herself five minutes of self-pity then decided to do something constructive rather than sit and pull herself into an empty hole. Before she knew it she was on her way to Pearl's house. As she entered through the picket fence, she filled her lungs with the scent of fragrant flowers—tiger lily, daisies, columbine, and bleeding heart. The sweet aroma and variety of color lifted Ashlyn's spirits, taking her mind off her family.

When Pearl answered the door, her face was subdued. She brightened when she saw who was on her doorstep. "Ashlyn, dear, come in."

"Did I come at a bad time?" Ashlyn asked, noticing Pearl's swollen eyes. "Were you sleeping?"

She shook her head. "I was lying down but I wasn't asleep. I'm glad you came over. I could use a cheerful face right now."

Ashlyn took a seat on the couch, saying, "I've been wondering if you had any photo albums of your trips and adventures. I'd love to see some of the exotic places you've been to."

"Actually, I have quite a few. Let me see," she said, checking a bookshelf right there in the living room. "I think I moved them to the back bedroom. Let's check there."

Ashlyn followed her to the bedroom where boxes were stacked in the corners and the closet bulged with memorabilia.

"Wow, you really have a lot of stuff," Ashlyn commented.

"Junk is more like it," Pearl told her. "When I bought all of these things, I thought they were nice souvenirs or important art pieces to collect. But now, I can see, it's just something else to dust. I do hope this bed and breakfast works out. I'd love to donate as much of this stuff as I can. Ah, here they are," Pearl announced as she located the albums. "Let's see what's in here."

Sitting side by side on the bed, they looked through the albums slowly. Ashlyn admired a younger Pearl's spunky short haircut and leather bomber jacket. Her cameras and lenses hung around her neck, and she wore a pack around her waist, doubtless filled with more lenses and film. She was trim and shapely in denim pants and boots, and in some pictures she wore a beret, which gave her a sophisticated, continental look.

They looked at pictures of Africa, Australia, India, and Asia. There were pictures of Pearl riding on elephants, camels, yaks, and donkeys. Ashlyn admired pictures of everything from the Great Wall of China to the Taj Mahal, from the pyramids of Egypt to the base camp at Mount Everest. Ashlyn noticed that Pearl took a lot of pictures of people—both young and old, male and female. She had visited postwar Europe and had rolls of pictures of the bombings and the camps as well as earthquake disasters, floods, and tornadoes.

"This is an incredible collection of pictures," Ashlyn exclaimed. "You've documented some fascinating places and events."

"I've pretty much seen it all," Pearl said with a sigh. "Sometimes I look back on it all and think, how in the world did a farm girl from Idaho get to the top of Mount Kilimanjaro."

"You're from Idaho?" Ashlyn was surprised.

"Oh, yes, a small town in southeast Idaho called Whitney. I grew up riding my horse to school and milking cows. When I was in Primary, our service projects were hoeing beets or thinning crops for the farmers."

"Primary?" Ashlyn asked. "You're LDS?"

Pearl nodded. "I was a long time ago."

"You're not anymore?"

"Well, I guess technically I am. I'm still on the records of the Church. But I don't have much use for the Church anymore. Not that I don't still have my beliefs," she stated, "I'm just not one for meetings and going to church."

Ashlyn didn't sense much conviction in Pearl's words. In her opinion, Pearl was lonely and desperate for companionship. She wondered if Pearl had been so independent her entire adult life that now that she was older, it was hard to admit she needed other people.

"Do you mind if I ask you something, Pearl?"

"Not at all, dear." Pearl closed the cover of the photo album and looked at Ashlyn, waiting for her question.

"Do you have any regrets? I mean, you have lived one of the most incredible lives I've ever known. You've been places and seen things that I'll never get a chance to see. I look at you and see all the excitement and adventure you've experienced, and I find myself wanting the same things. I've always thought I'd like to travel the world and cover exciting stories, just like you."

Pearl looked at her long and hard as if she were carefully thinking through her response. Then she finally asked Ashlyn. "Don't you want marriage and a family?"

Ashlyn lifted her eyebrows and took a deep breath, then sighed.

"I've given love a chance, and I've decided I haven't got much use for it. It's a long story, but I'm not sure I can ever trust a man enough to actually marry him." Ashlyn traced the pattern of the quilt on the bed. "I guess I've lost faith in men." She found herself telling Pearl about her father and Jake. The pain she'd thought she'd buried so deep still managed to surface, and she felt herself grow emotional at times as she spoke. Pearl listened quietly with a patient and understanding ear.

"So," Ashlyn concluded, "I've decided that I'm going to focus on my career. I see how fulfilling your life is, how much you've achieved, and that's what I want."

Pearl's next words caught Ashlyn off guard. "You know what I was doing all those years?" she asked. "I was running."

"Running?" That didn't make sense. Ashlyn wondered what she meant.

"Yes," Pearl looked up, her eyes brimming with tears. "I was running away from myself. I felt that if I ran far enough, my past, my fears, my pain," she gulped, trying to contain her emotions, "it would all go away."

When Pearl had her emotions under control, she continued.

"You see," Pearl swallowed, "there is something about Frederick's death I didn't tell you. I was pregnant when he left. In fact, that's why he left, to try to make enough money for us to settle down and have our child and be a family. When I learned of his death, I felt that God had completely abandoned me. He took from me the only man I would ever love and left me an unwed mother."

Ashlyn took in a sharp breath. "How difficult for you," she said softly.

"It got worse," Pearl told her. "My parents were very angry when I told them. Here I was, a twenty-one-year-old woman with a college degree, and I was pregnant. I was an embarrassment to them. They were more concerned with what the ward members and townspeople would say than with my feelings. So they sent me to my grandmother's and told me that I had to give the baby up for adoption."

"Is that what you wanted to do?" Ashlyn asked.

Pearl shook her head. "Back then, people handled things differently. Attitudes weren't at all like they are today. Nowadays, I would have moved out on my own, gotten a job, and kept the baby. But back then things were kept secret. I was ashamed for my mistake and for bringing shame to my parents. I figured they knew what was best. So I went through with it.

"They never even let me see my baby," Pearl choked out. "I don't even know if it was a boy or a girl. Not a day goes by that I don't think of that child. I think of a son, like Frederick, tall and hand-some. Or of a daughter. Did she have my eyes, my knobby knees?"

Ashlyn felt tears come to her eyes and she blinked them away.

"Maybe now you can understand why I turned away from the Church," Pearl said. "I felt like the Church had turned me away. Even my bishop counseled me at the time to give away my baby. He said this would be the way for me to start a new life." She cleared her throat.

"I can't believe you've been through all of this," Ashlyn said to her. "I am so sorry."

"Thank you." Pearl patted her hand. "I haven't told many people about this. My career was the only way to get my mind off of it. That was why I was so bold and daring back then. Dying for me would have been a blessing. The pain of this life seemed too much to bear at times. In death I could at least be free from the pain and I could be with my Frederick again. But my life was spared, many times. For what, I don't really know."

"Have you ever thought of trying to find your child?"

"Oh, yes. I have tried. Many times. But you see, back then records were sealed; some were even destroyed. I think sometimes if I could have just held my baby, spent just a few moments to memorize his or her face—" her voice began to tremble, "—to at least be able to put a face with the memory . . ." She began to cry but forced herself to finish what she was saying. "Then I wouldn't have to wonder what my baby looked like."

Ashlyn put her arms around the sobbing woman and held her. It seemed as if all this pain, all this heartache, was too much for one woman to bear. Ashlyn wondered how Pearl had survived all these years alone.

When Pearl's tears dried, she looked at Ashlyn and said, "Don't run away from your problems, dear. Don't run away from your feel-ings. Work through them, face them. It will be hard, but you will be much happier in the long run. That way your heart won't be full of hate or mistrust or pain, and there will be room for love and happiness."

Just then the doorbell rang. "I wonder who that is?" Pearl said. Both women quickly pulled themselves together as they walked to the front door. It was Cami.

"I've been looking all over for you," she said. "Are you both okay?"

"I'm sorry," Ashlyn said. "I didn't think I'd be here so long. We've been talking and forgot about the time."

"Everything's fine," Pearl said. "Right, Ashlyn?"

Ashlyn nodded and smiled.

"Well, it's almost time to go back for the crab fest and the baking contest," Cami announced, "and I heard a couple of the judges talking about your blackberry pie, Pearl."

Pearl's face lit up. "What did they say?"

"It's definitely one of the favorites. Martha Fuller has won this contest every year for the past five years, and people finally quit competing against her. Your pie has been an unexpected surprise. Grandpa wants to us to be ready to leave at 5:30. You're coming with us, aren't you, Pearl?"

Pearl wanted a few minutes to freshen up, and Cami said they would wait for her to call them when she was ready.

Ashlyn turned to Pearl. "It was a wonderful afternoon. Thanks."

"And thank you, dear." They hugged each other, their bond of friendship strengthened with the sharing of their hearts.

On the way back to the house, Cami asked, "What was that all about?"

"Oh, we just had a really good talk. You know, the more I get to know Pearl, the more I grow to love her. She's quite a lady."

"She really is," Cami agreed.

"I think she's reaching out for something. She's lonely. Her life is lacking something, but she doesn't know what."

"What do you think?" Cami asked, interested.

"I think she's lonely and she needs friends, but she especially needs the gospel. She needs the Atonement. She's carried a huge burden around with her for nearly forty years. It's time for her to let it go and enjoy the rest of her life. We need to get her to church."

"To our church?" Cami asked, surprised.

"She's LDS," Ashlyn told her. "And she doesn't know it yet, but she's ready to come back."

CHAPTER TWENTY-ONE

Feeling little tingles of excitement as they drove back for the evening, Ashlyn brushed the skirt of her brightly colored new dress. Pearl also looked very attractive that evening in a brightly colored floral dress in shades of coral and purple. It was loose and flowing and complemented Pearl's olive complexion. Her thick gray hair was tied back with a bright scarf, and her cheeks were flushed with color in anticipation of the evening's festivities.

There was music in the air as they walked from their car to the blue and white striped tents where dozens of tables and chairs were set up for the dinner. A band at the end of the tent played Latin music with a catchy beat and salsa rhythm.

Pearl went immediately to the table where all the pies in the contest were located, and Cami stopped to visit with some friends. Grandpa Willy wanted to find their seats so they could be up front by the bandstand.

Ashlyn turned in a circle, looking at the decorations, the food, and the gathering townspeople full of happy chatter and laughter, enjoying the feel of the music, the ocean, and the excitement of the celebration. Then she stopped.

There, across the room, was Mitch. He stood still, looking straight at her. He had on light khaki pants, a white T-shirt, and a bright Hawaiian print shirt that he wore unbuttoned. His blonde hair and tanned skin made him look like he should have been on a tropical beach in Mexico. He looked very handsome.

As everything else faded away, she walked toward him and smiled as he made his way to her. He reached a hand toward her as they neared each other, and she took it.

"You look gorgeous," he said.

Seeing the light in his eyes, Ashlyn felt gorgeous. "Thanks," she said breathlessly. "You look very handsome yourself."

They continued to look at each other, still smiling and oblivious to everything going on around them.

"I'm glad you came. I was hoping you would," he said.

She loved how his skin crinkled around his eyes when he smiled and how one of his front teeth was just barely out of line. Perfectly imperfect.

"You're staying for the dance and fireworks, aren't you?" he asked.

She nodded.

"Will you save a dance for me?"

"Of course," she said. "I'd like that."

"Mitch! Oh Mitch," a female voice called and a cold streak zipped up Ashlyn's spine. Vanessa again!

Wearing a form-fitting, lightweight dress of seamist green, Vanessa rushed over to Mitch. Her hair was loose and full, with a beautiful orchid pinned in one side.

"I've been looking for you, darling. I need your help bringing in a few things from the car."

"I'll be right there," he told her, then turned back to Ashlyn. "I'll see you later then." Taking his arm, Vanessa didn't waste any time whisking him away.

Ashlyn saw the expression on Vanessa's face, a look intended just for her. Mitch hadn't seen it, but Vanessa had very clearly warned Ashlyn to stay away from him.

As Ashlyn watched them leave, she remembered Pearl's words. *Don't run away from your feelings.*

But she didn't have any "feelings" to run away from, she decided, and she maintained that she didn't want to get involved with anyone at this point in her life. She had bigger and better plans for her future. She may not become the world traveler Pearl had been, but it would be a lot of fun trying.

"Well, hello there, beautiful," a deep voice behind her said. She felt her back stiffen involuntarily.

"Hello, Sebastian," she said, turning around, trying to keep her expression pleasant.

His eyes were warm and appreciative. "May I say, you look very beautiful tonight," he complimented her.

For some reason, hearing it from him didn't have quite the same effect as hearing it from Mitch. But, she had to admit, he looked nice too, in a pair of white linen pants and a deep coral-colored shirt.

From a table near the bandstand, Cami called to them, inviting Sebastian and Ashlyn to join them. Dallin was seated beside her, with Pearl and Grandpa Willy next to them. Mitch's brother, George, and his wife, Gina, were also at the table, and seats were evidently being saved for George's parents, and for Mitch and Vanessa.

Isn't this just peachy? Ashlyn scowled to herself. Whether she wanted to or not, she was paired off with Sebastian purely by the process of elimination.

A screech of the microphone caught the crowd's attention, and Mitch took his place in front. "Good evening, folks. Glad you could make it tonight. There's plenty to eat and plenty of room, so grab a seat and make yourself comfortable. We'll be announcing the winner of our pie contest this evening during dinner, and the dancing will start around eight o'clock, with the fireworks over the bay around nine-thirty or so."

Ashlyn thought it odd that instead of a tablecloth, the tables were covered with newspaper, until George and Dallin brought back a large bucket of boiled crab and a wooden mallet for everyone. Ashlyn had never eaten crab this way, and it took her a moment to figure out how to smash the shell and pick out the delicious, tender meat. Shells flew, mallets pounded, and everyone had a ball eating with their hands.

Instead of being self-conscious of how messy she was, Ashlyn laughed along with everyone else. To her surprise, Sebastian dug in, obviously relishing the delicious crab meat. In fact, he seemed to be the messiest one of all.

After they'd had their fill of crab meat, everyone cleaned their hands and faces with wet wipes that had been placed on all the tables. Then, with paper plates in hand, they headed for the buffet, where an assortment of relish trays, salads, rolls, and lunch meats for sandwiches were laid out.

Ashlyn felt like all she'd done the entire day was eat, but it was difficult to refuse the delicious food. Toward the end of the meal, Mitch, Vanessa, and Mitch's parents finally joined them. Vanessa had a few carrots and celery sticks on her plate, while Mitch's plate was piled high with food.

Dallin's father took the microphone and as owner of Gardner's Groceries, announced that it was time to present the award to the winner of the baking contest. There were three categories—baked pies, cream pies, and miscellaneous desserts.

Ashlyn reached across the table and gave Pearl's hand a squeeze, and Pearl gave her an excited smile.

"Of course, being a judge for this contest is a coveted position, as most of you know. Where else do you get to taste so many delicious desserts under one roof? In fact, I've never eaten anything quite as tasty as the desserts I tasted this morning at the judging. Every one of the entries was outstanding, making the judging very difficult. But we've managed to come up with some winners. We'd first like to thank Bradford Hardware for generously providing the awards and to George Bradford for inscribing them for us."

The crowd gave a round of applause and George waved to the tent full of people.

"Now, our first award goes to Hannah Robbins, for her Caramel Chocolate Cookie Jumbles. If you haven't tried them, you don't know what you're missing." A woman came to the front of the room and received her plaque and ribbon and smiled for a newspaper cameraman.

"Our next award goes to Lois Martinelli, for her fabulous coconut cream pie." Again, the plaque was awarded and the photo taken.

"And our award for best baked pie goes to Martha Fuller, for the sixth year in a row for her strawberry rhubarb pie, a delectable treat."

Pearl's expression faded to disappointment, and Ashlyn's heart ached for her. The older woman had finally felt confident enough to be a part of the community, but this wasn't the type of welcome she'd hoped for.

However, Mr. Gardner wasn't finished yet. "This year the judges decided to give one last award to the overall best dessert in all three categories. This award goes to Miss Pearl Finlayson, for her incredible blackberry pie, made with berries picked from the very woods behind her house."

Pearl was speechless. Grandpa Willy and Mitch had to help her to her feet—she was too stunned to move. Thunderous applause accompanied her to the stage, where she was given a large trophy and a ribbon. She managed a smile for the photographer and found her way back to her chair. When Ashlyn happened to glance at Martha Fuller, she saw a distinctly displeased expression on her face as Pearl walked by.

With the completion of the awards ceremony, the crowd was welcome to help themselves to the dessert table, which featured limited quantities of the winners' entries. Pearl assured her friends seated nearby that she had several blackberry pies at home and would love to have them over for pie and ice cream after the fireworks. Her offer received an exuberant response.

While partygoers enjoyed dessert, the band began warming up for the dance. A cool night breeze tickled the air and a bright orange sun hung heavy on the horizon.

Ashlyn sat back and watched the people of Seamist enjoy themselves and their association with one another. It felt more like a family reunion than a town party. Their closeness and genuine friendliness was obvious; these people really cared for each other. Parents gathered into small groups and visited while their children sneaked back to the dessert table for more cookies or played hide and seek under the tables.

As the band swung into motion, a Latin beat filled the air, pulling couples onto the dance floor. It didn't take long for Cami and Dallin, George and Gina, and Mitch's parents to head for the dance floor. Ashlyn was happy to see Cami having so much fun with Dallin. They were a good match, and Ashlyn could easily see wedding bells in their future.

Pearl and Grandpa Willy had gravitated toward a table where people closer to their own age visited and watched the couples dancing. Mitch and Vanessa had taken off, and even Sebastian had abandoned her.

Occasionally Ashlyn caught a glimpse of Mitch, either busy getting the food cleared out and the serving tables put away, or standing with Vanessa and other friends.

Just as Ashlyn had decided to go for a walk on the beach, Sebastian showed up. She was lonely enough that she was even happy to see him.

"I didn't mean to desert you," he said, taking a seat next to her.

Not wanting him to think she was waiting around for him, she said, "I was just enjoying watching all the people." She gazed over at Cami and Dallin, who were dancing closely, contentment showing on both of their faces.

"Would you care to dance?" Sebastian invited her.

Why not, Ashlyn decided, and couldn't help but smile as several teenage girls stopped talking and stared at Sebastian when they walked out onto the dance floor.

The easy beat and catchy rhythm of the music quickly took over, and she let Sebastian twirl her around the floor. She had taken years of dance training, ballet and jazz, and had quickly picked up the one, two, one, two, three of the mamba he was doing.

"Where'd you learn to dance like this?" she asked breathlessly as he swung her out at arm's length and then pulled her back in close to him.

"Ahhh," he said with a smile. "It is in my blood. My mother is Spanish."

The music picked up and the dance floor grew crowded. Sebastian's complete attention was devoted to Ashlyn, who found herself laughing and enjoying herself much more than she'd dreamed. It seemed his charm and persistence were paying off.

As the song ended, Sebastian dipped her back in a dramatic gesture. To their amusement, several people on the dance floor applauded them. Sebastian and Ashlyn bowed to the crowd and to each other, then the bandleader announced that the band would take a short intermission and be right back.

The crowd headed to the punch bowl for a cool drink. There Ashlyn and Sebastian met up with Dallin and Cami and several other young couples. Everyone complimented Sebastian and Ashlyn on their dance moves and style, naming them the "Fred and Ginger" of the evening.

After fifteen minutes the band returned, and soon the tent was filled with music. Dallin whisked Cami right back to the dance floor.

Glancing around, Ashlyn noticed that Sebastian wasn't anywhere around. Her gaze shifted to the sun, which was disappearing below the horizon as a sprinkle of stars spread across an indigo sky. Moving to a quieter edge of the tent, she watched as the last few golden rays faded, turning the ocean to a shimmering silver.

"It's beautiful, isn't it?" a voice behind her said. With a start she turned, surprised to find Mitch.

"I love sunsets," she said wistfully. "Each one is beautiful in its own way, but every night there's something different to see."

"Are you having a good time?" he asked, stepping up beside her.

She nodded and gave him a smile. "It's been a lot of fun. You've done a marvelous job organizing all of this," she told him. "I'm really impressed. Everyone is having a great time, the food is wonderful, and the band is terrific. You've really put a lot of work into this, haven't you?"

"I've had a great committee," he said. "I've delegated most of the work and they've really done a good job."

Ashlyn glanced around quickly. "Where's Vanessa?"

"She's getting ready to do a song. She arranged with the band to let her sing for them," he said.

"Oh," Ashlyn was surprised. "That will be a treat."

Mitch didn't respond, just looked out over the water.

"You okay?" Ashlyn asked.

He paused a moment before answering. "I think I'm worn out. As much fun as it's been, it will be good to have today over with."

"You want to sit down and rest for a bit?" she offered, gesturing toward a couple of empty chairs.

"Actually, I'd like to dance," he told her. "Would you dance with me?"

She raised her eyebrows with surprise, then smiled warmly. "I'd love to."

Taking her by the hand, he guided her to the floor and took her in his arms. The music was slow and easy. He was nowhere near as graceful and fancy a dancer as Sebastian, but Ashlyn liked his smooth, fluid movements, like the gentle waves on the shore.

At first, she held herself stiffly in his arms, unsure and uncomfortable, knowing that she was in Vanessa's place. But as the song continued, and as Mitch held her close, she relaxed and allowed herself to drift and sway with him.

She looked into his eyes and found herself lost in their depths. What was it in his eyes? She couldn't read his expression, but she thought there was something beneath the surface. But what? Whatever it was, it sent her pulse soaring. The feel of his arms around her and his eyes upon her made her weak in the knees, as did his gentle smile, his sincere caring ways, his easy manner. But as much as the feeling made her senses tingle and warmed her soul, it also scared her. He wasn't supposed to have this effect on her. She didn't want to have "those" kinds of feelings for him. He was a friend. That was all. Just a friend. And, she reminded herself, he had a girlfriend.

Tearing her gaze away from his, she rested her cheek on his shoulder and closed her eyes, trying to gain control over her trembling nerves.

There was no more room in her life for pain, she told herself. But somehow, something about Mitch had softened her heart, a heart she was determined to protect and guard against any further damage.

So why didn't she walk away? Why did she stay there, in his arms?

She refused to answer herself. She didn't want to deal with it or think about it. She didn't want to be honest with herself because she was afraid of what she would see.

When the song ended, the crowd on the dance floor turned toward the bandstand. The lead singer called for everyone's attention. "We have a special number for you this evening. Vanessa James will sing, 'My Heart Will Go On,' from the movie *Titanic*."

Everyone clapped as Vanessa took the stage. Ashlyn wondered if Mitch realized he still had his arm around her waist. The house lights dimmed and a spotlight shone upon Vanessa, who stood at the microphone waiting for the music to begin.

Even though the band wasn't quite equipped to play such a dramatic song, they managed well using drums, base, and piano, and as much as Ashlyn hated to admit it, Vanessa really knew how to sell a song. Her vocal range was astonishing, with low, throaty notes as well as clear, high notes. It wasn't Celine Dion by any means, but it was darn close.

The look on Mitch's face as he gazed at Vanessa told Ashlyn that he was head over heels in love with her. And even though she was snobby and demanding, Ashlyn couldn't blame him. With her looks and talent, it was obvious, right at that moment, that every man in that room was in love with her.

The crowd went wild as the song ended, and the applause was deafening. She was a hit, without a doubt.

"Isn't she great?" Mitch said, turning to Ashlyn, who could only smile and nod, hating the little stab of jealousy she felt inside.

"Let's go find her," Mitch said to Ashlyn, which was the last thing she wanted to do.

"You know what, Mitch?" she said. "I think I'd better go find Pearl. I kind of left her alone."

"Oh, okay," he said, hesitating slightly. "Thanks for the dance."

She knew he was sincere, but she also realized she was just someone to fill in when Vanessa wasn't available. Mitch escorted her off the dance floor, and she quickly joined Pearl, Grandpa Willy, and the others seated with them.

"Wow," Pearl said to her when Ashlyn sat down next to her. "How about that song?"

"She's pretty good, isn't she?" Ashlyn admitted.

"She is," Pearl had to agree, then whispered behind her hand to Ashlyn. "Doesn't seem fair though. Talent like that is wasted on someone like Vanessa." Pearl looked over Ashlyn's shoulder and added, "Though it looks like our friend Sebastian doesn't seem to think so."

Ashlyn turned slightly to see what Pearl meant. There was Sebastian, talking to Vanessa, who wore a very pleased expression on her face.

Not for the first time, Ashlyn wondered if there was something going on between them, aside from their business relationship. They seemed awfully comfortable with each other.

"We're moving our chairs outside," Grandpa Willy announced, "so we can watch the fireworks."

"Good idea," Pearl said. "You want to come with us?" She looked at Ashlyn.

Ashlyn pulled her attention away from Sebastian and Vanessa. "Sure, why not," she said, realizing that once again, she was on her own. Cami and Dallin were inseparable. Mitch would naturally be with Vanessa.

Carrying a chair under each arm, Ashlyn helped move the party outside where the beach was beginning to fill with blankets and chairs for the big fireworks show. There was a light chill in the air and Ashlyn realized she'd left her sweater in the car.

"I'm going to grab my sweater out of the car," she told Pearl. "I'll be back in a minute."

Since Cami never locked the car doors, she walked through the crowds heading for the beach and located the car. Sure enough, the door was unlocked and she quickly retrieved her sweater. She was just about to cross the road to head back to the beach when a car horn blasted, nearly scaring her to death.

"Hey," the driver yelled, "you trying to get yourself killed?"

Her anger disappeared when she saw it was a gleaming bronze '65 Mustang. "You nearly gave me a heart attack," she hollered back, resting her hand on her chest.

"Sorry," he apologized. "I didn't mean to scare you."

"Well, you did!" she scolded him.

"What are you doing?" he asked, and the car behind them tooted its horn. Mitch pulled off to the side and let him pass.

"Just getting my sweater so I can watch the fireworks on the beach."

"Are you sitting with Dallin and Cami?" he asked.

"No, they've disappeared. I was just going to sit with Pearl and Grandpa Willy and some of the Seamist geriatric crowd."

"Sounds like a party," he teased.

"Yeah, I think someone was going to break out a bottle of Geritol," she said with a laugh. "What are you doing?"

He shrugged. "Vanessa decided not to watch the fireworks. The manager of the band wanted to meet with her about doing some more numbers with his group at their next gig."

He didn't sound as disappointed as Ashlyn would have expected.

"Good for her," Ashlyn said. She couldn't help but notice the coincidence that Sebastian wasn't around either. "Well, I guess the fireworks are probably about to start."

"Actually, they won't start until I tell them to," Mitch said, holding up a walkie-talkie type instrument.

Ashlyn was impressed. "Wow, you really are running the show."

"That's right, and I just had an idea," he smiled up at her. "How would you like to watch the fireworks with me from the lighthouse?"

"The lighthouse, really?"Ashlyn was thrilled at the possibility.

"Sure, there are still a lot of people coming. We have time to get over there. C'mon, hop in." Without waiting for her reply, he leaned over and opened the passenger side door.

What the heck? she thought. No one would miss her.

It took only a few minutes to drive through the traffic and up the winding road to the lighthouse. From there, it was only about a hundred yards from the parking lot to the overlook. A cool ocean breeze made Ashlyn shiver, and she was glad Mitch grabbed a blanket from the trunk of his car.

After giving the signal that they could begin the fireworks, Mitch turned off the two-way radio and found a grassy spot with a perfect view overlooking the harbor. He spread out the blanket and they sat down, waiting for the show to begin.

Ashlyn pulled her knees up to her chest and wrapped her arms around her legs. The night air was nippy, and she tried hard not to shiver.

"Here," Mitch said pulling the edge of the blanket up around her shoulders. "It's pretty chilly out here. Scoot over a little closer to me."

She did as he said and he pulled the blanket around her tighter and left his arm around her shoulder. "Better?" he asked.

"Yes," she said. "Thanks."

Just then they heard a pop. A few seconds later they saw an explosion of color right before their eyes.

"Ohhh, how pretty!" she exclaimed.

She remained snuggled close to Mitch as the show continued, with stunning lights and colors reflecting off the mirrored surface of the ocean. It was a breathtaking display. Toward the end of the show, the frequency and magnitude of the fireworks increased until they were right on top of each other, exploding in a myriad of shapes and colors.

Then it was silent. The only sound was the whisper of wind through the pine trees and the roar of the ocean below. The only light came from a quarter moon, hanging lazily in the sky.

Mitch and Ashlyn sat quietly in the stillness.

Ashlyn turned to tell Mitch how much she enjoyed the show, but found him staring at her, his expression solemn and serious. Her heart thumped madly in her chest. Their gazes locked. Then, without explanation or warning, the distance between them closed and their lips met.

For a kiss as sweet and gentle as this was, Ashlyn's senses exploded like the fireworks she'd just seen. Her first reaction was one of pure bliss. Mitch's kiss was tender and warm, yet magical and electrifying. Her second reaction was pure and total terror.

What in the world was she doing?!

As suddenly as it began, the kiss ended. She was glad it was dark enough so Mitch couldn't see the shock on her face or the fear in her eyes.

How could she let that happen? But on the other hand, how could she have stopped it? *Wait a minute,* she thought. *How could he let this happen?*

"Hey," he said. "You okay?"

She smiled weakly. "Yeah," she said brightly. "I'm fine."

He returned her smile, apparently satisfied with her answer.

"We'd probably better go," he said. "I have to make sure all that mess gets cleaned up."

"Okay!" She jumped to her feet with a bound, suddenly feeling anxious to get away from him. "That sure was a spectacular fireworks show," she rambled nervously. "I've never seen anything quite like it. You were right when you said it would be better from up here. How do you decide which order to let off the fireworks? Is it dangerous to let off fireworks?"

They walked to the car, with Ashlyn asking Mitch inane questions to keep their conversation in a safe place. But inside she was churning with a maelstrom of emotions. Mitch had kissed her and she'd liked it. What was going on?

When they reached the center of town, they found themselves in a traffic jam. Ashlyn watched out the window as she tried to make sense of what had just happened. Obviously Mitch was okay with it; at least he seemed fine. But Ashlyn wasn't. What about Vanessa?

"Look, there's Cami," Ashlyn exclaimed with sheer relief when she saw her friend. "Why don't you let me out here and I'll catch a ride home with her?"

He had barely slowed the car down when Ashlyn opened the door and jumped out. "Thanks, Mitch," she said hurriedly, then took off.

"I'll see you in the morning, right?" he asked, but she was gone before she could reply. She ran through the crowd to the safety of Cami's car.

Pearl and Grandpa Willy had already gone home, Cami explained. She talked nonstop all the way home, barely pausing for a breath. Things between her and Dallin were rapidly becoming serious. Both realized that their relationship was moving at a whirlwind pace, she admitted to Ashlyn, but they'd never stopped loving each other and now the timing seemed right at last.

Ashlyn let her friend chatter, relieved to not have to discuss what she and Mitch had done that evening. She was still so upset inside she needed time to let it digest first.

"Hey," Ashlyn said, "is that a fire siren?"

Cami had been so busy talking she hadn't heard the sound of the siren until Ashlyn's words stopped her cold. "I bet some kids were playing with fireworks and started a fire," she frowned. "Happens every year."

Only seconds later the lights from the fire engine truck appeared behind them, and Cami pulled over quickly to let the truck go screaming by.

"Don't you hate it when they go the direction of your house?" Cami said.

But Ashlyn didn't answer as she watched the fire engine pull off the main road, heading toward the Davenports' house.

"Ash!" Cami cried. "You don't think—"

She jammed the accelerator and hurried after the fire engine. To their relief, they saw that their house was safe, as was Pearl's, but to their horror, the outline of the mansion appeared over the top of the trees, engulfed in flames.

The next morning Ashlyn woke up early, but she didn't feel like running. After last night she was too exhausted to move, let alone run.

The stench of burning wood was still in the air. The image of that beautiful mansion going up in flames would be forever in her memory. Luckily, Pearl had arrived home just after the fireworks, and seeing the roof in flames, she'd called the fire department immediately.

Ashlyn remembered the awful, helpless feeling of watching the mansion burn, lighting the night sky with its angry flames. There had been some concern that the thickly wooded trees would catch fire, but the fire department had worked quickly and effectively, and managed to put the fire out before it spread.

Still, the mansion had sustained a lot of damage. The roof and the back side of the home were gone. It was a devastating loss.

Of course, Mitch joined them as soon as he got word of the fire. Ashlyn had watched him with the other men fighting to save the mansion. Their efforts had been nothing less than heroic, and Grandpa Willy thanked them over and over for what they did.

Rolling over and shutting her eyes against the brightening morning sky, Ashlyn tried to calm her thoughts and go back to sleep, but sleep wouldn't come. Would Mitch be down on the beach waiting for her? They'd all gone to bed so late after the fire.

She hated the thought of him showing up and her staying in bed. Plus, she was already awake and most likely wouldn't be able to fall back asleep.

"All right, fine!" she exclaimed, throwing back the covers. She pulled on her running clothes and shoved her feet into her shoes. Shoving a baseball cap onto her head, she headed outside and down to the beach, hoping he didn't show up after all. Then she'd have some time alone to sort things out, evaluate her feelings, and understand what was going on between them and inside of her.

Mitch was waiting for her when she got there.

"Hi," she said, not sure how to greet him.

"Hi," he answered. "How is everyone?"

"Pretty upset, but I think they're okay. They're grateful it wasn't worse."

"The chief is going to examine the site today to determine the cause of the fire. We're still pretty sure it was kids playing with fireworks, probably a bottle rocket on the roof."

Ashlyn nodded. They walked down the beach, neither of them ready to bump it up to a run yet. She made no attempt at conversation. She wasn't sure what to say.

"So," Mitch finally spoke. "How are you doing? Is everything okay?"

Feeling a surge of anger, she took a sharp breath as a burst of energy ignited inside of her. Without answering, she took off in a run.

"Hey," Mitch exclaimed, picking up his pace. "Wait up. What's wrong?"

Ashlyn looked straight ahead, realizing she should have stayed in bed rather than endure the awkwardness of the situation.

"Ashlyn, what is it? Why won't you talk to me?"

It was obvious he wasn't giving up until he got her to talk to him. And frankly she couldn't hold it in any longer nor could she believe he was so dense he didn't already know what was bothering her.

She stopped dead in her tracks. "Okay, fine," she blurted out. "I'll talk to you. What do you want to know?"

"You seem upset. Is it because of the fire or is there something else?"

She rolled her eyes and let out a frustrated huff. Was he serious?

"I take it that means it's something else." He shoved his hands into the pockets of his jacket and studied her face.

"What was that last night, Mitch?" she finally said. He looked confused for a second, which made her even angrier. "Last night," she said plainly. "You know, the kiss?"

His expression changed to a look of pain and embarrassment. "Oh," he said hesitantly. "The kiss."

"What was that? I mean, where did that even come from? You're in love with Vanessa, remember? What are you doing kissing me?" She was glad they were outside and that the sound of the waves was covering her voice because she was practically yelling now.

"I . . . I . . ." He dropped his chin to his chest and kicked at the sand. "Ashlyn, I'm sorry. I had no right to kiss you. It's just that, well . . ." He paused to collect his thoughts. "Lately, I've been having . . ." He didn't finish.

Ashlyn waited, but he didn't seem able to finish. "What?" she wanted to know. "You've been having what?"

"I've been having . . . feelings—for you." He raised his gaze to meet hers.

What did that mean? Ashlyn wanted to ask. A gust of wind blew at them, bringing with it a chill. Suddenly deciding that she didn't want to know, Ashlyn turned and started walking home. Mitch grabbed her arm and stopped her, pulling her around to face him.

"More than 'just friends' kind of feelings," he said.

"What do you mean by that?" she asked. *What about Vanessa?*

"I mean, that I care for you as a friend, but you seem to be on my mind a lot," he tried to explain.

"What about Vanessa?" she made herself ask. "I thought you were in love with her."

He shook his head. "I'm not sure how I feel about her. As long as I've known her and as much time as we've spent together, I just don't connect with her like I do with you. I can't explain it. When you and I talk, it's not just with our mouths, it's with our hearts, too. I've never felt that with her."

He reached up and tucked a strand of hair behind her ear. "I'm just saying that I really like being with you, Ashlyn."

A tremor of fear started in the pit of her stomach and shot through her nerves. She admitted that she was attracted to Mitch. She admired and respected him, and genuinely liked him as a person. But she didn't know how to respond to what Mitch was saying. What was he saying?

"Ash?" He stepped closer and reached for her hands. "What's wrong?"

Sudden tears welled in her eyes. She closed her eyes tightly and fought for control but lost. She felt Mitch put his arms around her and hold her, and she let the tears fall.

"It's okay," he soothed, stroking her back. "Everything is going to be okay."

She hadn't expected someone like Mitch to come along and foul up her plans. She'd been determined to carve out her life by herself. To grasp her independence and conquer the world. To stay free and clear from any further pain and heartache caused by men. To trust no one but herself and the Lord. She'd been convinced that she'd come up with a foolproof plan for happiness, a plan that would protect her from any more pain. But obviously that coat of armor around her heart wasn't impenetrable. Mitch had found a way inside.

⁕ ⁂ ⁕

Ashlyn stood with Cami and Grandpa Willy outside the Davenport mansion, surveying the damage. LaMar Denton, the fire chief of Seamist's fire department, stood beside them. "We had a couple of other brush fires last night," he told them. "We managed to get them under control with no problem. I'm positive it had to be kids playing with fireworks. A bad combination."

Ashlyn looked at the damage, seemingly worse in the noonday sun.

"Luckily there's not a lot of interior damage, mostly the roof and the east wall on the top floor," LaMar continued. "Someone down at the city office said you're thinking about renovating this place and turning it into a bed and breakfast?"

"That's right," Grandpa Willy nodded.

"Chances are you would've needed a new roof anyway," Lamar shrugged, "as old as this place is."

Grandpa Willy nodded his head. "I guess that's that, then."

"I'll file the report when I get back to the office—unless there's anything further you need from me." The fire chief looked at each of them inquiringly.

"Nope, I think it's settled," Grandpa told him. Cami and Ashlyn nodded soberly.

"So," Grandpa Willy said, as they watched him walk down the path to his truck. "What do we have to do to get this place put back together?"

Cami stared at him, surprised.

"We've been spinnin' our wheels long enough. It's time to get down to business."

"But we still don't have the city's approval," Cami said.

"We'll get the approval. I'm not worried about it," Grandpa Willy replied. "First thing we need to do is get Nils Swanson down here and get to work replacing that wall and the roof and handling any other structural problems to bring us up to code. And I've been thinking we ought to pull out some of these trees to open up the view a bit. We'll want to put in a sprinkler system—Cal Jenkins is the man for that job—and you two need to get to work on your plans for the inside. It will take a while to sort through all of my storage, and Pearl's got plenty of junk to boot."

"Grandpa!" Cami exclaimed. "What's gotten into you?"

"If we're going to do it, then dagnabbit let's do it," he said, shoving one fist into his other hand with a loud smack. "Seeing this old place nearly go up in smoke, well . . ." He swallowed and worked his jaw several times. "I guess I realized I was more attached to it than I thought."

Cami and Ashlyn exchanged smiling glances.

"Well?" he said impatiently. "Jimminywillikers, what are we doing standing around gawkin' at each other? Let's get some phone calls made and get some bodies up here. I'm not gettin' any younger. I'd like to see this place in business before I croak."

He took off through the trees and headed for home with Cami and Ashlyn behind him.

"That fire might not have been all bad," Cami whispered. "Once Grandpa sets his mind to something, nothing gets in his way."

Before the day ended they'd received a visit from Nils Swanson, a general contractor who was more than happy to take on the project. Cal Jenkins could have his men in the yard by the end of the next week, and Ashlyn and Cami had combed Victorian and antique magazines, and all the wallpaper books and paint chips at Bradford Hardware. Grandpa Willy had gotten the ball rolling and it was already starting to pick up speed.

The next morning while Cami showered for church, the phone rang. Ashlyn answered it, surprised to hear Pearl on the other end with an invitation to come to dinner that afternoon. "I saved some of that blackberry pie for dessert," she added, then asked, "What time is church over with?"

"Two o'clock," Ashlyn said.

They decided to have dinner at three, and when Ashlyn told her about the bed and breakfast plans in progress, Pearl offered to let them sort through her belongings while they were over for dinner.

Ashlyn didn't know what it was, maybe the loneliness in Pearl's voice or maybe even a prompting from heaven. Before she knew it, the words were out of her mouth. "Pearl, why don't you come to church with us?"

The line went silent.

"Pearl?" Ashlyn wondered if she'd made a mistake inviting her. "Are you there?"

"Yes, dear, I'm here." She paused a moment. "You don't think the walls would crumble, do you?"

Ashlyn chuckled, her heartbeat quickened. "Listen, if they didn't when I went, I doubt they will for you."

"It's funny you asked," she said slowly, "because I was actually thinking about going to church today. I met so many nice people at the Fourth of July celebration Friday, I think I'd enjoy going to church. I'm in the mood for a nice sermon. And I haven't sung a hymn for years."

"Then you're in for a treat," Ashlyn teased. "Vanessa's the chorister."

"Good grief. I'm going to have to watch that woman lead the music," Pearl groaned.

"I'm afraid so. But it's worth it. Mitch gives a wonderful Sunday School lesson."

"Well . . ." She considered the offer again. "Oh, all right. Why not?"

"Great," Ashlyn exclaimed. "We'll pick you up at ten forty-five."

***

Grandpa Willy didn't even fuss that Pearl was coming with them. Apparently he and Pearl had made peace with each other. They certainly weren't the best of friends, but they'd found a lot of common ground between them, and there seemed to be a mutual respect for the lives they'd led and the people they'd become.

The ever beautiful Vanessa took her place in front of the congregation as the opening song, "Battle Hymn of the Republic," was sung in honor of the Fourth of July holiday. Everyone stood to sing, and goose bumps broke out on Ashlyn's skin as the chorus of voices sang with great enthusiasm.

The topic of the talks that day were devoted to a "steadfastness in Christ." From the youth speakers, right down to the high councilman, Ashlyn couldn't recall a meeting where she felt the stirrings of the Spirit more. And she sensed that Pearl, sitting beside her and occasionally wiping at her eyes with a tissue, also felt the strong spirit of the meeting.

Ashlyn had to give credit to Vanessa for choosing such powerful songs for the meeting. When the closing song, "The Spirit of God," was sung, Pearl could barely get through the verses.

To Ashlyn's delight, many of the congregation took a moment to welcome Pearl to church, expressing their joy at seeing her there, and making her feel a part of the fold. The bishop smiled from ear to ear, seeing her there. Sister Francom, chairman of the ward roadshow, happened to pass by just then and stopped to introduce herself to Pearl, who glowed at all the attention.

After sacrament meeting, they made their way to Relief Society room for Sunday School. Mitch was writing some scripture references on the blackboard, but he turned as they came into the room and immediately lit up when he saw Pearl. Setting his chalk down, he came over and gave her a hug and welcomed her to class, then shook hands with everyone.

Of course, the moment Vanessa entered the room, she sidled up to him at the board, as she usually did, and he gave her the chalk and let her finish writing references on the board for him while he gave a final look through his lesson.

Ashlyn had prayed all through sacrament meeting that Mitch's lesson would also touch Pearl's heart and when he introduced the day's topic, "the Atonement," she knew her prayers had been answered.

In his powerful, yet gentle, way, Mitch taught about the importance and the great power of the Atonement. He explained that all who had faith in Jesus Christ, obeyed the gospel, and repented of their sins, would be forgiven and their sins would be remembered no more. Then he read a scripture from the New Testament from the third chapter of John.

"For God so loved the world, that he gave his only begotten Son, that whosoever believeth in him should not perish, but have everlasting life."

Then, to conclude the lesson, as he always did, Mitch bore his testimony of the truths that had just been taught. His words penetrated Ashlyn's soul, and the Spirit bore witness to her that what he was saying was true. Her heart and chest burned, and her pulse quickened. Ashlyn knew without a doubt that the Savior loved her and that He gave His life for her. And that He wanted her to return and live with Him in heaven.

Pearl, sitting next to her, sniffed into a handkerchief, and Ashlyn placed a hand on her arm and gave her a gentle squeeze of love and understanding.

After the closing prayer, Pearl and Ashlyn sat quietly, not wanting to lose the spirit of the meeting. Cami stepped into the hallway, looking for Dallin. He hadn't been in the Gospel Doctrine class because he was substituting in the fourteen-year-old class.

The men left the room, leaving the women to prepare for their Relief Society lesson. The Relief Society president, noticing a new face in the midst, promptly rushed over to Pearl and introduced herself. She was thrilled to meet Pearl and immediately took down Pearl's address and phone number, and set up a time to come and visit one evening that week with her counselors.

Just before the meeting started, Cami came back in and took a seat. The smile on her face told Ashlyn that she had found Dallin. But that wasn't all she was smiling about.

"I just talked to Sister Francom," Cami whispered to Ashlyn. "She was asking me about Pearl—you know, her background, her interests. Sister Francom was looking for someone to write the roadshow, remember? And she was wondering if she should ask Pearl."

Ashlyn thought about Pearl writing the roadshow. She was a journalist, so she knew how to write. She had a wonderful imagination and a lot of background to pull from. Ashlyn was sure that if Pearl would do it, it would be incredible.

It would even be a way to get Pearl involved more and feel a part of the ward.

When Relief Society was over, Pearl gave Ashlyn and Cami a hug and thanked them for letting her come to church with them. She couldn't tell them enough how good it felt to be there and how wonderful the messages were, especially Mitch's lesson.

As they walked down the hallway looking for Grandpa Willy, Brother Winegar, one of the bishop's counselors, stopped them and asked Pearl if she had a few moments to visit with him. Giving them a curious look, Pearl followed Brother Winegar to the office. Cami and Ashlyn crossed their fingers and smiled at each other.

꙳ ꙳ 🕮 ꙳ ꙳

"I can't believe they asked me—me!—to write the roadshow. I'm not even sure how to write a roadshow, or even what one is. I've never done anything like this. I don't even know why I said yes," Pearl spoke excitedly as she stirred gravy in a pot on the stove. Grandpa Willy was looking through her picture albums, and Cami and Ashlyn were helping to prepare the roast beef and mashed potatoes for dinner.

"You'll do a wonderful job," Cami exclaimed. "You've got so many experiences that can help you, and you've had so much writing experience."

"Did they give you a theme or anything?" Ashlyn asked, wanting to get a jump on ideas for choreography.

"They just said to use stories from the Book of Mormon that testify of faith in Christ. That leaves it pretty wide open, wouldn't you say?" Pearl observed. "I might just have to read the whole book now to figure out which story to use."

Cami and Ashlyn grinned at each other. It was as if the Lord had stepped into Pearl's life and was helping her find her way back.

"Willy," Pearl announced as they placed the food on the table. "Everything's ready. C'mon now."

Grandpa Willy complimented her on her pictures of Machu Picchu as he took his seat at the table.

"Oh, yes," Pearl said, remembering fondly. "That was quite a trip. It's a fascinating place, so full of mystery and wonder. I felt like I'd stepped back in time."

"And those other pictures—were those Aborigines?" he asked.

"My goodness, yes. I haven't thought about that for ages. I went on walkabout with them through the outback for an entire summer. Barefoot!" she exclaimed. "It was a 'rite of passage' so to speak, and quite an honor to be invited to go with them. I won't go into it now, but some of the things we ate, you would never believe!" She shook her head and waved her hand in front of her face.

Over dinner they talked about the bed and breakfast and offered ideas to Pearl for the roadshow. Although she was apprehensive about the task, she also seemed excited about the challenge placed before her.

Of course, the crowning moment of the afternoon was the blackberry pie, a sweet but tart taste sensation, made even better with a scoop of smooth and creamy homemade ice cream. Ashlyn felt like she'd died and gone to heaven and even took a second helping, deciding that it was worth all the extra calories.

It was dark before she, Cami, and Grandpa Willy wound their way down the path back to their house. They'd spent nearly two hours after dinner sorting through the decorations, furniture, and odds and ends Pearl was willing to donate to the decorating of the mansion. They found fascinating pieces like an antique Queen Anne settee and a lovely standing lamp with a fringed lamp shade. They also discovered some gilded picture frames with paintings that Pearl had purchased in Paris; the artists' names were unfamiliar to them but the paintings were breathtakingly lovely nonetheless. Pearl also had a gorgeous hand-carved cherry wood sleigh bed she'd found at an estate sale in Ireland, with matching wardrobe, chest of drawers, mirror, and two nightstands.

Cami and Ashlyn could barely contain their excitement as they watched a dream in the process of becoming a reality.

Ashlyn called home later that night since it had been over a week since she'd last talked to her mother. Miranda was delighted to speak with her since she'd received a letter from Adam, telling her the date of his release.

"It's the fifth of September," Miranda announced. "Can you believe it? He'll be home in just a little over a month."

Ashlyn couldn't believe her brother had been gone almost two years. It sounded as if he was having a wonderful mission. He'd had his share of hardships and successes, but in every letter he'd borne strong testimony of the importance of missionary work and of the truthfulness of the gospel. Even though Adam had been the child who'd struggled and challenged the teachings of the gospel the most, here he was, the strong one.

On the other hand, Ashlyn had never once wavered, through high school or college, until Jake had pulled the rug out from under her.

Only then had she realized how much she'd taken her testimony for granted. Coming to Seamist had been the key in bringing the gospel back into focus for her. Seeing Pearl today and the effect the Spirit could have on someone helped Ashlyn realize even more how important the gospel was in her life.

Miranda reported that her morning sickness was "terrible," but that is was "wonderful to feel terrible," something Ashlyn didn't understand at all.

"Morning sickness generally means the baby is growing strong and healthy," Miranda explained. "It should only last another month or so. Hopefully by the time Adam gets home, I'll feel a lot better."

"I still have a hard time picturing you pregnant or with a baby," Ashlyn confessed. "It will be so weird to have a baby brother or sister."

"I'm not sure I really believe it either," her mother said. "But then again, I feel so blessed to have another child. Especially when we're getting ready to go through the temple and be sealed together."

Ashlyn listened as her mother related the neighborhood and ward news. She still felt bad she wasn't at home helping her mother, but she was glad she'd come to Seamist. In a way, she felt like the Lord had directed her there. She still had scars from her father and Jake, but she felt like she was beginning to heal at last.

That night in her room she looked at her pictures of Jake and herself. She still felt a stirring in her heart when she looked at his face. She had thought he was the man of her dreams, and no one would ever understand how much it had hurt, and what she'd suffered, when he called off their marriage. It had been more than just the humiliation at the temple. His rejection had completely shattered her sense of self-worth.

But she was getting better and growing stronger. There was just one problem she didn't know how to handle.

Mitch.

CHAPTER TWENTY-TWO

The next morning when Ashlyn answered a firm knocking at the door, she was startled to see Sebastian standing there, grinning at her. Cami had gone to the grocery store, and Grandpa Willy was up at the mansion, getting things ready before the builder and landscaper showed up. Ashlyn had just showered and dressed after her morning run with Mitch. Mitch had been unusually quiet, and Ashlyn hadn't tried to draw him out. They hadn't said much more than "hello" and "see you later."

"We haven't seen you around for a few days," Ashlyn said, hesitantly inviting him inside.

"I had to run to San Francisco unexpectedly. In fact, that's why I didn't say good-bye at the dance last Friday. I got an urgent call and had to take care of some business. But everything's fine now."

"That's good," she said politely, though she hadn't missed him for a second.

"I wondered if you had any plans for lunch today. I was thinking of driving down the coast and finding some out-of-the-way place to eat. I'd love it if you joined me."

"Gosh," she said, her tone apologetic. "As tempting as that is, I already have plans. We're starting work on the Davenport Mansion today. They need me around here. In fact, we're going to be pretty involved in the remodeling for the next while," she said, hoping to deter him from further pursuits.

"Does that mean you got the go ahead with the planning commission?" He seemed surprised by the news.

"Well, no, not exactly," Ashlyn said. "But we're confident that they'll re-zone the Davenports' property and issue a Conditional Use Permit to operate their bed and breakfast. We just want to get a jump on the project. It really upset Grandpa Willy when we nearly lost the mansion in the fire the other night. So, now he's really getting things moving."

"I see," Sebastian said slowly, weighing the information in his mind.

Expecting Cami or Grandpa Willy to show up any minute, Ashlyn glanced at her watch.

"I've always wanted to see the mansion up close. Any chance of getting you to show it to me?" Sebastian asked.

Ashlyn didn't feel like playing tour guide to him, but she didn't see a way out of it. "Sure. I'm going that way, anyway."

They walked together up the path through the thicket of trees that separated the two Davenport homes and served to seclude the mansion.

"That fire did a lot of damage, didn't it?" he observed. "I feel terrible this happened to such a beautiful structure. Do they know how it started?"

"Probably some kids playing with fireworks. They haven't found any evidence, but there's been an investigation and so far nothing's turned up." Ashlyn looked around for Grandpa Willy but didn't see him anywhere.

He nodded thoughtfully, perusing the extensive fire damage and the rest of the house. "You've got your work cut out for you," he said. "This is going to be a huge project. Are you sure it wouldn't be just as easy to tear the whole thing down and start over?"

"Of course not!" Ashlyn exclaimed. "This house has a lot of sentimental value, not to mention the workmanship and quality of the structure. Yes, it's going to be a lot of work, but we're getting a lot of support and help from everyone we've called to work on it. I guess we're too excited to care about the work. In fact, that's going to be part of the fun, seeing it go from this," she pointed to the house, "to a beautifully restored bed and breakfast. Cami wants to call it 'The Sea Rose.'"

He inclined his head thoughtfully, but before he could comment, the sound of a large truck engine roared up the graveled drive that curved around the house. A jumble of voices filled the air, and before long Grandpa Willy and Cami joined Ashlyn and Sebastian. Only minutes later three men descended upon the yard and began taking measurements and drawing diagrams for the sprinkling systems.

Hearing the trucks, Pearl decided to put in an appearance, and with her help and Grandpa Willy's input, discussions on landscaping and tree removal ensued. Several more trucks pulled up the drive, bearing the logo *Swanson Builders*. Nils Swanson, a large man with white-blonde hair, arms the size of tree trunks, and tanned, leathery skin approached them. He had a deep, booming voice. "It's about time someone did something with this place," he said heartily. "I've had it in mind to buy it myself and fix it up. Hated to see the old girl go to waste."

While Grandpa Willy and Mr. Swanson continued their discussion, Ashlyn asked Sebastian if he wanted to look inside. His arms folded across his chest, he glanced over the house. "I've seen enough for now. I need to be going, but I appreciate you taking the time to show it to me."

"Anytime," she told him brightly.

With a wave he was gone, but Ashlyn couldn't help feeling curious about him. His sudden change of interest puzzled her. But maybe he'd just forgotten an important appointment or something.

Jim Fielding from the Zoning and Planning Commission showed up in the middle of the commotion to check the area for adequate parking and neighborhood traffic concerns. He explained to Ashlyn that the commission wanted to make sure that the bed and breakfast wouldn't intrude on the residents' right to privacy. All neighbors within five hundred feet would be given notice of the bed and breakfast, and asked to sign a petition for or against it. If they were against it, their concerns would be heard by the commission.

"To be honest," Jim told Ashlyn, "I'm happy to see this place get a face lift and a new life. This mansion has been here since the town was founded. I'm sure its historic significance alone is worth preserving the place, and I think it's an outstanding idea to turn it into a bed and breakfast—even though Jonathan James has voiced his opposition to this more than once."

"Jonathan James?" Ashlyn asked. Her mind made the connection. "Vanessa's father?"

"Why yes. He's been on the commission about two years now. He's certainly in favor of growth and commerce, so I don't understand why he would oppose a bed and breakfast like this. Certainly it will bring more folks to the area."

"Do the city planners want to bring in more tourism?" Ashlyn asked.

"Good question." Jim's voice was thoughtful. "Yes, we like having visitors, but we're also committed to keeping Seamist the quaint, quiet town it is. To build condominiums, hotels, and convention centers along the beach would certainly alter the beauty of our town and change the entire atmosphere here. Believe me, many have tried to turn Seamist into a tourist spot, but most of the residents and the city council are opposed to it. Still, there are a few like Mr. James who are pushing for progress. They think the future of Seamist lies in its attraction for tourists and conventions."

He glanced down at his watch. "Looks like I'm due back at the city office for a meeting. It's been nice talking to you. And don't worry. I'm sure the project will be approved. The Davenports are good people who are a big part of the community. I don't think there's any cause for concern."

Ashlyn appreciated his assurance and stepped back to watch the activity going on around her. In a large city, workers would never be able to drop what they were doing and show up at a moment's notice to take on a new project. But that's exactly what seemed to be happening. Of course, William Davenport was well respected in the community, and it wasn't surprising that people wanted to help him.

Yes, the Sea Rose was well on her way to becoming Seamist's premier attraction, the grand lady of the coast. A title she well deserved.

⚓

One evening, while Cami was on a date with Dallin, Ashlyn went to visit Pearl. She hadn't seen her around for a few days and wondered if she needed help sorting through the mass of items in back bedrooms.

Pearl was delighted to see her and together they continued sifting through her possessions, adding to the "good will" pile that was steadily growing on her porch.

"It feels good to go through all this stuff," she told Ashlyn. "I've needed to do this for so long but just couldn't get myself to do it."

"You've got so many beautiful things here," Ashlyn said, holding up a delicate hand-painted bud vase. "But you do have a lot. I can see why you've put it off."

"It certainly seems appropriate for me right now," Pearl said.

"What do you mean?" Ashlyn asked, dusting her hands on her jeans and sitting down. The two of them had been going strong for the last hour, and she was exhausted.

"Well," Pearl said, sitting in another chair and running her fingers along the edge of the picture frame she held. "Along with cleaning house and getting rid of all of this junk, I've been doing some personal 'house cleaning,' I guess. I've carried a lot of 'junk' around with me for many years. And little by little I'm getting rid of all that extra baggage."

Not sure she understood what Pearl was saying, Ashlyn simply looked at her, waiting for her to explain. Pearl chuckled at the expression on her face and continued.

"It's hard to explain, but over the years I've learned a lot, my dear, and one thing that stands out is that we're not meant to be alone. As much as I loved my Frederick, his memory hasn't been enough to keep me company all these years. I've been very lonely, and loneliness can turn a person bitter and angry. You look around and see others with their loved ones, surrounded by their families, and you begin to realize that you've made a mistake.

"I should've found someone else and gotten married. Had children. Had a life," she confessed. "I never gave anyone a chance, though. I was too busy hanging onto Frederick's memory to open my heart to any other. And there were others who tried to break through. I think of Edward, for example. He was a wonderful man, a doctor I met in Africa . . . "

She told Ashlyn all about Edward and how they'd worked side by side trying to help so many of the hungry, sick people in that country. Edward had told her he loved her, but Pearl had convinced herself that Frederick was her only true love and if she couldn't have him, she didn't want anyone.

"I was so foolish to let him go," Pearl said sadly. "He was such a gentle man and so handsome, too." She looked at her young companion with intensity, and Ashlyn heard the urgency in her voice. "Whatever you do, dear, don't spend your life alone. Learn to let go of the things that hold you back from life and love, and from those things that prevent you from letting God into your life."

Ashlyn nodded with understanding, knowing that she had sought to take the same road that Pearl had taken.

"To sit in church on Sunday for me was like breaking a forty-day fast," Pearl confided. "I think I've been emotionally starving for the last thirty-five years. Do you know that in the last three days I've read the entire Book of Mormon?"

Ashlyn stared at her. "No wonder we haven't seen you around."

Pearl smiled at her. "For the first time in my life, the scriptures came alive. Not only was I reading the words, but it was as if a movie camera was rolling through my mind. I could see the events, see the people and the places, places I'd seen in South and Central America. I've walked where these people walked." Pearl's voice softened. "As I read, it was as though I were there, witnessing everything—the wars, the sorrows, the building of those great cities and highways, and their destruction. And I could almost see the Lord's appearance to the Nephites."

Ashlyn sat quietly, mesmerized by Pearl's words, thrilled to see the difference in her in so little time.

"I feel as though I've been let out of a dark, miserable prison," Pearl went on, not seeming to notice the tears slipping down her cheeks. "I'm free from all that pain and sorrow and loneliness. And the guilt. You have no idea how much guilt I've carried around with me." She smiled at Ashlyn and her eyes shone with new hope as well as with her tears. "I haven't felt this way for a long, long time."

Ashlyn reached for her hand and gave it a squeeze. "I can tell," she said. "There's a sparkle in your eyes that wasn't there when we first met."

Pearl laughed. "Yes, there is. I can feel it." She patted Ashlyn's hand. "I've wasted so many years on anger and resentment. I suffered a great disappointment and challenge at a very young age, and instead of turning to the Lord and the gospel for strength, I tried to handle it on my own. Now I've realized that you can't do that. None of us can handle what this life dishes out on our own. The only way we can is with the Lord's help."

Pearl's words sunk deep into Ashlyn's heart. They were words she knew she needed to hear, counsel she needed to heed.

"I've fretted and mourned about giving up my baby for adoption, but I realize that it was the most unselfish thing I've ever done in my entire life. I know that child was given to a good home, with loving parents who were members of the Church. My child has been given the chance for a full and happy life. For the first time since I gave birth to that sweet baby, I'm at peace." Her eyes filled with tears again. "I'm at peace," she whispered.

Ashlyn rose from her seat and went to her friend, placing her arms around her, and together they wept.

⊶⊷ ❀ ⊶⊷

Mitch wasn't able to join her the next morning, so Ashlyn went running by herself. She found it very soothing to look out on the water as she ran. The beach and the ocean reminded her of the vastness of the world, how tiny and insignificant she felt in comparison, and how powerful the Lord was. Powerful enough to heal her wounded heart and soul. She also knew that just like Pearl, she had turned away from the one thing that could help her the most—the gospel. She knew that God was there, and always had been, but most of her prayers had been spent whining and complaining, instead of expressing gratitude or asking for help.

The waves crashed and broke in long frothy ribbons along the shore. The sky was overcast and the air was cool, but Ashlyn relished its refreshing touch. Far in the distance, shrouded by morning mist, stood the Misty Harbor Lighthouse. She thought of Grandpa Willy's analogy, how the lighthouse guided mariners to the safety of the harbor.

She had taken her eye off that guiding light. She had drifted into rough waters and treacherous passages, but now the light was back in focus and she was entering calmer waters. She was drawing near to the safety of the harbor.

That morning she'd brought along a bag with her, containing items she'd once treasured greatly. Now she realized those items represented shackles from her past that kept her from moving forward and on with her life. It was time to break free of those shackles.

Looking at the mug with its picture of her and Jake on it, she thought how he'd surprised her with it, filled with Hershey's kisses. Taking the mug, she gave it a mighty swing and threw it into the ocean. She did the same with the candle he'd given her, the one they would have burned on their wedding night, and every anniversary night after that. Next she threw into the waves the gold necklace and bracelet he'd given her for her birthday; she was aware of its value, but she knew she could never, ever wear it again without thinking of him, so she parted with it gladly, hoping his memory would sink along with those polished links.

She pictured the items sinking into the depths of the ocean or being swept out to sea, buried far away from her heart. Gone forever.

A surge of laughter bubbled up inside of her. She'd done it! It was gone. All of it.

And it felt great.

She laughed out loud, feeling free, as if the emotional bands that had been weighing her down had finally been removed. Filling her lungs, like helium in a balloon, she felt light and carefree. And happy. Truly happy.

She recalled a poem about footsteps in the sand. As she looked back at the section of beach where there was only one set of footprints, she knew it had been the Lord, carrying her, taking care of her, until she was strong enough to walk on her own again, with Him at her side.

She believed that He'd guided her here. That He'd prompted Cami to invite her to come to Seamist. For it had been here that she'd been able to let go, to move on, and finally heal.

In a way, Seamist had been a gift to her, given to her by Cami, along with her courageous example and honesty. For Ashlyn, Seamist had been a place of renewal, and she would never, ever forget it.

She walked along the shore, kicking the sand with her shoes, letting the grains drift in the wind. She would have to take a bucket of this sand home with her; she wasn't sure how she would live otherwise, without a little bit of sand in her shoes.

She laughed again. Never before had she liked sand in her shoes. Or the wind in her hair. But things were different now. She was different now. And from now on things would be different. They would be better. Much better.

Stretching her arms out wide, she twirled in a circle. Then, pulling off her baseball hat, she let her hair cascade down her back as she spun round and round.

Yes, life was definitely going to be much better!

"Hey," a male voice behind her said. "What are you doing?"

She stopped spinning, her head still swirling a bit as she turned, surprised to find Mitch there.

"My meeting got canceled," he said.

She smiled a little woozily at him, still feeling dizzy. "Good. I'm glad your meeting got canceled."

"So," he asked again, suspiciously. "What did you say you were doing?"

"Oh . . . I was just throwing some things into the ocean."

His brows knitted in concern and curiosity. "You know you can get fined for that."

"Not if you don't tattle on me." She put her hat back on, then shoved the evidence of the plastic grocery bag into the pocket of her jacket.

"Was your garbage can full at home?" he asked.

She smiled. "No, the garbage was too good for these things. I wanted to give them a proper burial."

"Ahh," he said, catching on. "I'm thinking you've just gotten rid of something from your past."

"Yup," she said with a deep, cleansing breath. "A past I'm ready to let go of. I think it's time to move on."

He looked at her appraisingly, trying to read her expression. "You okay?"

"Yes, actually, I'm doing great!" she responded, then asked, "Did you come to run or talk?"

"Both," he said.

They started off on a slow jog, warming their muscles, getting their blood moving.

"So," he said. "You want to talk about it?"

"Not much to say," she answered. "I'm finally strong enough to get rid of my past."

"How does one go about 'getting rid of the past'?" he asked, adjusting his pace to match her quicker one.

"Well, for me it was getting rid of all the reminders," she said honestly. She hadn't thought she would want to tell Mitch what she had done, but he was just so darn easy to talk to. "I had quite a fire going last night, with all the pictures and ticket stubs and wedding invitations I burned." The pride in her voice was evident and Mitch looked suitably impressed.

"How do you feel?" he asked.

She gave him a huge smile and without warning yelled at the top of her lungs, "I . . . FEEL . . . GREAT!" She raised her arms up Rocky-style and punched her fists in the air.

Mitch laughed and so did Ashlyn, then he grabbed her and swung her around. Losing his balance, he fell back, pulling her with him, and they rolled onto the sand, laughing. For a moment they lay there as gulls swooped and swirled overhead, their laughter dying in the wind.

"I'm proud of you," Mitch said.

"Thanks," Ashlyn replied. "I'm proud of me, too."

Sitting up, they watched the waves roll in until a gull's cry caught Ashlyn's attention. She followed the flight of the bird out to sea, then something caught her eye. "Mitch, look!"

He looked where she was pointing. "That's not what I think it is, is it?"

He pushed himself to his feet and helped her up, then together they ran up the shore.

"It is!" Ashlyn exclaimed. "It's a Japanese glass fishing float."

The clear blue glass ball, about the size of a cantaloupe, was partially covered with sea weed and sand, but when they retrieved it, they found it was in perfect condition.

"You know what this means, don't you?" he asked.

She shook her head, her eyes wide.

"It means you will have good luck forever. At least, that's what they say," he said, smiling. "And I can't think of a better person to receive it."

"You're going to let me keep it?"

"Sure, you found it."

Carrying the float carefully in her arms, she walked back to the house with Mitch. He asked about the mansion, and she described everything they had done and planned to do. He would be more available to help, he said, now that the Fourth of July celebration was out of the way and he wouldn't be coaching until school started at the end of August.

They stood at the front door together, both looking down at the float in Ashlyn's arms.

"I'm glad your meeting got canceled," she said.

"Me too," he replied. Then he said thoughtfully, "I mean it, Ash, I'm proud of you. It took a lot of strength to do what you did."

She took a deep breath and released it slowly. "It took me long enough," she answered. She knew she wasn't completely over Jake, but at least she was strong enough to start trying. A month ago she would have never thrown anything of his away.

"Yes, but now you're strong enough. That's what matters." He was quiet for so long that she wondered what he was thinking about, but he finally spoke before she could say anything. "Guess I'd better be on my way. I'll drop by the mansion later to see how things are going."

Ashlyn liked that he understood the strength required to do what she had done that day. She almost felt as if she'd thrown away a part of her heart with all her reminders of Jake, but she knew that what she had gained was worth the loss.

CHAPTER TWENTY-THREE

"I've got it," Pearl cried over the phone.

"Got what?" Ashlyn said with concern. Pearl sounded completely beside herself.

"The script for the roadshow. Can you and Cami come over right away?"

The girls had been out working in the yard—with Ashlyn mowing while Cami weeded the flower gardens. Now they were just getting ready to make lunch.

"If you haven't eaten, I've got some quiche over here," Pearl suggested. "In fact, I'd like you to try it. I think we could add it to the Sea Rose menu."

"Sure," Ashlyn accepted her invitation. "We'll be right over."

Over a delicious lunch, Pearl told the girls about her script. She'd worked on it through the night and all morning. It wasn't quite finished, but she was excited with the direction it was taking.

"I love the story in the Book of Mormon about the stripling warriors who went with Helaman to fight the Lamanites. They had so much faith in what their mothers taught them," Pearl told her luncheon guests. "I think it's perfect. We can involve all the young men to be warriors and have all the young women wish the boys farewell when they go off to fight with Helaman."

Ashlyn nodded eagerly, amazed at Pearl's wisdom in using an idea that would involve as many young ward members as possible.

"The way those boys go into battle, believing that the Lord will deliver them, is such a powerful story, don't you think?" Pearl asked. "And the fact that none of those boys died makes it a very powerful message about the importance of faith in the Lord Jesus Christ."

"That's wonderful," Cami complimented her. "I think this is going to be the best roadshow we've ever had."

Pearl wanted to make sure there was plenty of humor and she'd already started writing ideas for lyrics for the songs.

"Here, for instance, when Helaman is ready to take the boys into battle to defend their families and their beliefs, Helaman has a song that will stop the show," Pearl said, then stopped talking for a moment. Looking at both girls, she said hesitantly, "I don't know how else to say this, but I really think the Spirit has been helping me. Last night when I sat down, I said a prayer, asking for help, and once I got started, the words just poured onto the paper. I fell asleep at my desk, and when I woke up, this song came to me as if I'd dreamed it and I wrote the whole thing from start to finish."

Neither Cami nor Ashlyn could believe the change that had come over Pearl. It was just as she'd told Ashlyn. She'd been starving spiritually and was now enjoying a feast of the Spirit by having the gospel back in her life. It was a miracle. But then, Ashlyn decided, Pearl deserved one.

⚜

"We have less than a month to pull this off," Pearl told the ward members who'd turned out in droves to audition for parts in the road-show. "But if we buckle down and work together, I know we can have the best roadshow ever!"

An enthusiastic cheer erupted from the audience. "We've got plenty of parts for everyone, some on stage, some behind the scenes. Cami Davenport here—" Cami stood up, "—is my set director. She needs a good team to create backdrops and scenery for the show. Ashlyn Kensington—" Ashlyn stood next, "—is the choreographer. She'll be helping you with the movements and steps that go to the songs. I have spots for as many stripling warriors as we can get. If we have twenty, that's great; if we have fifty, that's even better."

They began by separating everyone by age. Ashlyn counted twenty-four young men, who would be the stripling warriors; the eighteen young women would be the young Nephite girls of the city. The mature women would be the mothers of the stripling warriors, and the older males would be townspeople or soldiers from the Lamanite army.

Pearl then asked those who were interested in solo parts to step forward. A handful of people took the stage, and while they auditioned, the costume designer began measuring cast members for the costumes.

Meanwhile Pearl and the rest of the roadshow committee began the process of casting the main roles. There were roles for youth, which were given to the six young men and young women who volunteered, with the hopes that they had some vocal ability. After five women had auditioned for the parts of the two mothers who had speaking parts and a song, Pearl made a quick change in the script to give them all speaking parts. It was her goal to get as many ward members as possible involved in the show.

"This is going to be the most difficult," Pearl whispered to Ashlyn as the three men trying out for the part of Helaman took the stage. Ashlyn knew that Pearl was looking for someone strong and handsome, who carried himself like the leader of an army, a Nephite warrior going into battle.

Brother Williams had a beautiful tenor voice, but he was barely five foot six and quite round through the middle. Brother Quincy had a pleasant voice, though not nearly as strong as Brother Williams', but he was close to six feet tall with nice, broad shoulders.

George Bradford was the last to audition for the part. As she tried to imagine him without his glasses, Ashlyn though he might be able to pull off the look with the right clothing. Cami said he'd been in several school plays and had a lot of experience on stage. To their delight, he had a beautiful singing voice, having been trained by his mother.

"I think we have our Helaman," Pearl said quietly to Ashlyn.

It wasn't easy to break the news to Brother Williams and Brother Quincy, but she gave them roles as Lamanite generals, which seemed to please them. George was completely shocked to get the role of Helaman.

"Thank you," he told Pearl, shaking her hand wildly. "Gina is going to be so excited. She wanted to be in the play, but with the baby due in three weeks, she just wasn't up to it. So my being in it will be the next best thing."

"Three weeks," Pearl exclaimed. "The play goes on in three and a half weeks. Are you sure you'll be able to be in the play with a new baby at the same time?"

George quickly assured her everything would be fine. Gina's parents lived in town and could help out if needed. He was determined to keep the role.

"All right, people," Pearl called to the cast members and crew, who quickly settled down and listened to her instructions. "We will have practices every Thursday night from seven until eleven, and later if needed. We'll also meet Saturday mornings from seven in the morning until we get kicked out of the gym."

A few of the young people groaned at the early hour, but Pearl continued relentlessly. "Those of you who have solo parts will also come Wednesday nights at nine to work on your parts. As I said, we don't have much time, but I know we can do it and it will be the best roadshow this stake has ever seen." Another cheer from the crowd told Pearl she had their support.

"All right, everyone," she concluded. "Be sure to pick up your copy of the script on your way out. I want you to read it before our next practice so you know the story and have an idea of what the show is about. Solos, please stay after for your first rehearsal. I'd like you to get started working on your numbers right away."

Ashlyn and Cami met with the rest of the committee to plan times to work on costumes and sets. Pearl and the pianist, a seventeen-year-old girl with an amazing talent—also one of Catherine Bradford's prodigies—met to go over the music with the soloists.

Pearl began with George, who was able to sight-read his number quite easily because of his previous singing and stage experience. It also helped that Pearl had mostly used familiar tunes for the songs, changing only the lyrics. George's song came from *Les Miserables,* which Ashlyn had seen in Salt Lake with Jake, but Pearl had adapted the words for the young Nephite warriors who were fighting for their beliefs and for their families. At the chorus, George sang the words "bring them home" with such passion, Ashlyn had to swallow hard several times to stop tears from coming to her eyes.

Everyone in the gym clapped loudly when the song ended. It would be the highlight of the show, there was no doubt in Ashlyn's mind. The women's song was to the tune "Sunrise, Sunset," from *Fiddler on the Roof,* and the women sang about teaching their children to have faith in the Lord.

Pearl had written many other songs as well. Some were light and fun, like the young girls singing about their "stripling warrior" to the fifties tune "Johnny Angel," and the young men singing about having no room for fear in their hearts, only faith, to the disco tune "Stayin' Alive."

The roadshow had humor, drama, romance, suspense, and a gospel message. And whether or not the roadshow won any prizes, just the look of belonging and purpose on Pearl's face made it all worthwhile.

⊰⊱

It didn't take long for Nils Swanson to get his crew moving on the house. Tearing away the burned and charred lumber, they began to reframe the roof and wall. It was either a stroke of luck or a small miracle that led Grandpa Willy to the den; looking through drawers, cupboards, and cubby holes, he was able to locate the actual blueprints for the original structure. With those in hand, construction rolled forward at near breakneck speed.

Mitch had worked for Swanson Construction as a young boy and had roofed many of the homes in Seamist, so he was a familiar face around the construction site. But Ashlyn hated seeing him up on top of the house, her fear of heights causing her stomach to clench every time he climbed up there. But the men worked carefully, and quickly, and finished the job on schedule and without incident.

Cami spent most of her time pouring over magazines, catalogues, and old photographs and other materials from the library to help her with the decorating. She wanted to make the mansion as authentic as she could, which required a lot of research. She and Ashlyn made countless trips to Bradford Hardware to locate wallpaper samples and paint chips until they had found or ordered just the right ones. A trip to Portland proved helpful in selecting light and plumbing fixtures. Down to gilded mirrors and light switch covers, Cami wanted everything just right.

At times Cami worried that she was spending too much or going overboard, but Grandpa Willy assured her, that he supported the project one hundred percent and she was not to worry about the finances.

Between their work on the mansion and the roadshow, Cami's and Ashlyn's days were full and fun. Mitch attended most of the roadshow rehearsals, helping out with set designs. His building expertise came in handy with all the props and backdrops needed to create authentic-looking Book of Mormon settings.

Ashlyn found herself truly enjoying the time she spent choreographing the musical numbers. The young boys were frustratingly uncoordinated, but she didn't give up and, with a few modifications, she was able to choreograph their number to fit all their coordination levels.

With everything progressing smoothly, Ashlyn and Cami had nearly decided their problems were behind them.

⚜

While they were downtown placing a wallpaper order, they ran into Dallin, who offered to take them to lunch. Over shrimp salads and ice water, they discussed the latest details.

"The siding and trim go up this week," Cami said jubilantly. "Then they can begin painting outside."

"Have you heard from the Zoning and Planning Committee yet?" he asked.

Cami frowned as she stabbed at the lettuce in her bowl. "Actually, no, we haven't. I'm trying not to worry, but I can't help it. I couldn't stand it if something happened now."

Dallin leaned toward them and spoke in a low voice. "There may be no connection, but . . ." He looked around to make sure no one around them was listening. "I just found out that the James Development Group is trying to pull in a few big investors to fund a convention center and resort development they want to build."

"Is that Jonathan James?" Cami asked.

"And his daughter, Vanessa," Dallin added.

"Here?" Ashlyn asked incredulously. "In Seamist?"

"I'm afraid so," Dallin answered. "They applied for a loan at the bank; that's how I found out about it."

"I didn't think the planning commission wanted to bring in resort developments like that," Ashlyn said, feeling her temperature rise. "Where is this development supposed to be built anyway?"

"I didn't have a chance to go through the paperwork. I just saw the application," Dallin told her.

"Maybe with Vanessa's father on the board, the planning commission will change its mind about the bed and breakfast," Cami worried out loud.

"The commission won't let them build a convention center here, will they?" Ashlyn asked. "It would change everything. The whole town."

"It would bring a lot of business to the community, though," Dallin said.

Ashlyn hated to see the beauty and charm of the town spoiled by commercialism and tourism. It didn't surprise her that Vanessa and her father were behind the idea.

<hr />

The first Wednesday evening in August, the Relief Society asked Pearl to give a presentation about her travels. They would follow it with a buffet offering a variety of exotic foods from around the world. Pearl asked Cami and Ashlyn to help her tote some of her prized souvenirs and mementos to the Church.

Even though she was a nervous wreck before she gave her presentation, the minute she stood up, she relaxed completely. She told about the time she and her fellow travelers were captured by a band of agitated African natives and nearly eaten alive. But the natives found a box of chocolates in the travelers' supplies that they found so delicious, they befriended Pearl and her friends instead of eating them.

The women in the room were held spellbound as Pearl eloquently wove mystical, magical tales of her adventures. When she asked if there were any questions, nearly every hand in the room went up. The meeting went over, and even when it was finished, Pearl was surrounded by the sisters, who were full of compliments and even more questions. If there was any doubt before in Pearl's mind about being accepted by the women in her ward, it had vanished.

꘎꘎ 🐝 ꘎꘎

To Cami's and Ashlyn's surprise, Grandpa Willy acted as overseer and general contractor, and managed to keep work on the mansion going full swing. The first thing he did was go out and get a cell phone so he could call workers and contractors and keep everything on schedule. It was rare to see him without his phone to his ear or in his hand.

With the reconstruction finished, the mansion was rapidly taking on a whole new look. The painters were giving it a fresh coat of paint and transforming the tired, old structure into a cheerful, colorful masterpiece. The body of the house was painted a rich taupe; the gables, brackets, and posts were painted white; the trim a deep plum; and the shutters dark forest green.

Mitch was helping to strip the hardwood floors and refinish them while the plumbing and electrical was being installed.

One morning when Ashlyn got up to go running, Mitch surprised her. She started to laugh when she saw him standing on the beach, holding the reins of two beautiful chestnut-colored horses. "What in the world are you doing?" she asked.

"Low tide," he said. "It's the perfect time to ride horses around the point."

Ashlyn had already been around the point. She remembered the experience all too well. But on horseback with Mitch, she had to admit, it did sound fun.

"I haven't ridden much," she said. "In fact, I've only ridden once. And I fell off."

He glanced at her with an amused expression but didn't comment. Instead he said, "That's okay. These two are used to inexperienced riders. This one's Dancer and this one's Prancer."

She looked at the horses closely. "But they don't have antlers," she said with mock confusion. Mitch smiled and rolled his eyes.

"Okay, okay. But are you sure this is a good idea?" She took a tentative step closer. "I'm not wearing Wrangler jeans or cowboy boots."

"Ashlyn, you have no need to worry," Mitch assured her. "Prancer's so old and gentle, they've nicknamed him 'Grandpa.'" He motioned to the magnificent animal on his right.

"Oh, all right," she relented. "But I want a saddle with seatbelts."

"You're going to be just fine," he promised again, laughing this time. "Come closer and let him smell you."

"Smell me?" Ashlyn gave him a look of distaste.

Mitch nodded, so she stood near the horse and let him sniff her.

"That's good," Mitch said in a gentle voice. "Now, pat him gently on the neck. That's right, just like that."

The horse turned and looked at her with his large brown eyes, then nibbled at her jacket sleeve. He gave a puff of warm breath and Ashlyn pulled away. "No, that's good," Mitch told her. "He likes you." Mitch pulled a carrot from his pocket. "Here, give him this."

She held the carrot toward him, holding her breath, ready to bolt if he went for her fingers. Prancer took it with his teeth, then chomped it down, and Ashlyn gave Mitch a pleased look.

"You want to try getting on now?"

She really didn't, but she wasn't about to let that stop her.

Mitch showed her how to put her foot in the stirrup and swing her leg up over the animal's back. It took a couple of tries but soon she was in the saddle, hanging onto the saddle horn with everything she had. She tried not to act scared, but she wasn't sure that the horse was convinced. It seemed like an awful long way to the ground from where she sat.

"You ready?" Mitch asked as he settled into the saddle.

"I guess," she whispered, fearful of spooking the horse by speaking too loudly.

With a gentle kick, Mitch moved his horse forward. Ashlyn tried the same technique and, to her pleasure, it worked.

As they ambled along, Mitch and Ashlyn talked about the mansion and the roadshow. Mitch said he'd been helping his brother George rehearse his part.

"Pearl has done a terrific job of putting the roadshow together, especially when there's barely a week left to get it ready," he said.

"She's amazing," Ashlyn agreed, describing Pearl's presentation at the Home and Family Enrichment Night. "Everyone loved it."

Following the shoreline past the rocky point where Ashlyn had had her first real taste of the ocean, they continued southward. This time Ashlyn drank in the beauty of the rugged coastline, the magnificence of rock formations that jutted out of the ocean, and the power of the water crashing against the southern breakers. A morning mist hugged the headlands and shoreline, creating a magical setting.

At times Mitch would smile at her, complimenting her on how well she was managing on her horse; the rest of the time they rode together in silence as gulls, widgeons, and mallards called overhead, skimming the water's surface in search of food.

Except for a tingling numbness on the insides of her legs, Ashlyn was enjoying herself immensely. The steady stride of the strong animal beneath her, coupled with the raw power of the surging surf, gave her a new appreciation for the world around her, especially this remarkably beautiful part of the world.

They didn't dare go too far, since they wanted to make it back around the point before the tide rose. When they turned around and headed back, Ashlyn had a clear view of the precipice where the Davenport mansion stood as it rose over the surrounding trees.

"That mansion has probably got the best location of any house in town," she remarked.

"When they get some of those trees cleared, the view is going to be incredible," Mitch nodded in agreement.

"I can see why Cami's great-great-grandparents chose that spot to build. I imagine there were quite a few people back then who wished they'd thought of it first," Ashlyn said.

They rode the horses back to the stables, and Ashlyn got a surprise when Mitch reached to help her down. Her legs wouldn't move.

"Owwww," she cried as she slid into his arms. He held her steady as she got her footing.

"You okay?" Mitch asked.

"I'm great," she quipped. "I just can't walk."

Mitch chuckled. "Here, let me help you." He circled an arm around her waist and escorted her to his car. It was slow going, but they finally made it. She discovered that moving her muscles actually seemed to loosen them up a bit.

"I don't think I'm going to be able to do much dancing at the roadshow rehearsal tonight," she told him.

"You'll feel better after a long soak in a hot tub," he assured her.

He was right; she did feel better. For a while. She still had trouble on stairs and getting up from her chair, but the ride had been more than worth it.

⚜

The next few days flew by as work on the mansion continued at a rapid pace. A grand opening had originally been planned for some time in early October, but if work on the house kept up the way it was going, it would be done by Labor Day. Ashlyn was ecstatic since she would still be in Seamist for the celebration, but she would have to leave the next day to be home for her brother's return from Portugal.

She missed her family terribly, especially with her mother being pregnant. But the thought of leaving gnawed at her insides. The little town had begun to feel like home, and she was positive the Lord had had a hand in guiding her there. In this place she had been able to change her outlook on life and find a new and healthier perspective untarnished by reminders of her past. Without familiar names, faces, and places to constantly throw memories in her way, she could now see the possibility of a new life, a good life.

She wasn't sure about going back to Salt Lake. Back to her old life, back to the reminders and the memories. She'd grown stronger, of that she had no doubt, but was she strong enough to continue moving forward? She couldn't imagine not having the beach close by, or hearing the call of the seagulls. She couldn't imagine not seeing her friends everyday. So much of her life here had helped her to open her mind and her heart and to reevaluate her choices. How would she continue this back home? How could she tell Cami and Grandpa Willy, and Pearl good-bye? And of course . . . Mitch.

As the roadshow neared, the pace grew hectic and poor Pearl was in a constant dither. To add to her stress, she was also trying to make all the food for an after-the-performance party. When the sisters in the Relief Society caught wind of her efforts, they sent a sign-up sheet around on Sunday to round up plenty of help and food. Everyone in the ward recognized Pearl's hard work and the many hours she'd spent on the play, and the support was overwhelming.

Everything was going smoothly with the house and the roadshow, so smoothly, in fact, that Cami and Ashlyn were unprepared when everything fell apart Wednesday morning.

The first blow came in the form of a telephone call from Jim Fielding at the city offices. Grandpa Willy took the call while they were at the table having breakfast. By the look on his face, Cami and Ashlyn could tell something was wrong.

"You're telling me, Jim, that just one signature can hold us back from getting our permit?" he demanded.

Cami and Ashlyn looked at each other.

"Well, who in tarnation is it?" He was quiet and his expression fell as he listened. "Well, I'll be dipped in horsepucky."

"Who is it, Grandpa?" Cami whispered.

He didn't answer her.

"Do you have his number there?" He listened for a reply. "I'll track him down if I have to hire a detective." There was another pause. "I know, Jim. Thanks anyway."

Cami and Ashlyn both exploded with questions when Grandpa Willy hung up the phone. He shushed them both and when they were quiet, he gave them the news.

"The permit was refused because one of our neighbors is opposed to the bed and breakfast," he said.

"What?" Ashlyn said. "No one has said anything to us. Everyone is thrilled with the idea."

"Who was it, Grandpa?" Cami insisted.

He stood quietly, looking at them, before he finally spoke. "It's Sebastian Jamison."

CHAPTER TWENTY-FOUR

Sebastian was out of town and no one had a phone number for his house in California. No one, but Vanessa James, who had sold the house to Sebastian. The problem was, they couldn't locate her either.

Ashlyn was floored at first that Sebastian had been the one who refused to sign the permit. But when she thought about it, he had acted strangely. He'd had a lot of questions about the mansion and had shown a particular interest in their plans. What did he care if the mansion was a bed and breakfast? How did that affect him? He was only here temporarily and then he would no doubt move back to California permanently.

She was in her room sorting laundry to throw into the washer when Cami knocked on the door.

"What's up?" Ashlyn asked when she walked in.

"I don't know," she said with a frustrated huff. "Grandpa is beside himself over this. I swear if Vanessa James doesn't call—" A look of total shock and surprise registered on her face.

"What?" Ashlyn exclaimed.

"I don't believe it."

Ashlyn stared at Cami in utter bewilderment. "Believe what? What are you talking about?"

"Your dresser." Cami pointed at the chest of drawers.

"What?" Ashlyn cried, looking at the dresser for signs of damage or some ugly creature that may have hidden beneath or behind it.

"It's gone!"

"No, it's not. The dresser is right here."

"I mean, your stuff," Cami explained. "All that stupid Jake stuff is gone." Her expression simultaneously registered surprise, shock, and delight. "Where is it? What happened?"

Ashlyn hated to admit that Cami had been right all along, but she finally said, "I got rid of it."

"You did? Without me? And without telling me?" Cami looked hurt.

"Yes, I did and I'm sorry to deprive you of such a riveting experience," Ashlyn apologized sarcastically.

Cami's tone was eager. "Did you burn it or what?"

"I burned the pictures and letters," Ashlyn said, "and I threw some of it in the ocean."

"Ooooh, good! I like that," Cami said. "How did it feel to finally unload all that cra—"

"Cami!" Ashlyn exclaimed, but she relented when her friend apologized. "Actually, it felt great. I felt like I was finally getting rid of a heavy weight off my shoulders. I realized you were right, that I needed to get rid of all that stuff. It just had to be the right time for me, you know?"

"And it was?"

"Yeah," Ashlyn nodded. "I finally felt strong enough to dump my past and move on with my future."

Cami walked over to her and gave her a huge hug. "I'm so proud of you. This is the happiest moment of my life," she said dramatically.

Ashlyn laughed. "Okay, okay. That's enough."

"No, really," Cami said seriously. "It really is awesome. I'm so happy you're finally healing."

When the doorbell rang, then rang again and yet again, the girls hurried downstairs to answer it. Cami opened the door, and Pearl rushed inside, completely distraught. "This is terrible. Now what am I going to do?"

"What's wrong?" Ashlyn asked.

"It's George," she said, pacing across the room.

"Oh no! Is he okay?" Cami wanted to know. "What happened to him?"

"Nothing's happened to him," Pearl cried. "It's his wife! She's in labor and we only have eight hours until the show. What if she doesn't deliver by then? He can't leave her to come do the show."

Cami and Ashlyn exchanged worried looks. "We'll figure something out," Cami said, patting the older woman's hand. "It's going to be okay. We'll just have to find a backup."

"But no one knows the songs as well as George." Pearl fought the tears threatening to spill over at any minute. "And we can't do the roadshow without Helaman."

Ashlyn remembered something. "What about Mitch?"

"Mitch! He can't learn everything by tonight," Pearl protested.

"But he already knows it," Ashlyn told her. "He told me he's been helping George rehearse, and he knows all the songs. I don't know how his voice compares to George's, but he's worth a try."

Pearl calmed down considerably, but she still looked broken-hearted. "I guess it is," she sighed.

Cami called Bradford Hardware and learned that Mitch was at the mansion, working on the floor. Hurrying to the mansion, the three women nearly scared him to death and killed themselves in the process when they burst through the front door and went sliding across the freshly sealed hardwood floor. Pearl grabbed onto Ashlyn, nearly pulling her down, and Cami fell, sliding into Mitch like a bowling ball into a nine pin.

"What in the world?" he exclaimed, irritatedly. "Didn't you see the sign on the door?"

The three women turned around and saw the "Don't Enter" sign on the front door.

"Oops," Cami said, pushing herself onto her feet. She had varnish on her hands and knees. "Sorry, but we have a huge problem."

"Is it bigger than my problem?" He pointed to the floor with his paintbrush. There were footprints all across the glossy floor. Cami ignored him.

"George's wife is in the hospital. She's going to have the baby," she told him.

"That's great. Is everything okay?"

"She's fine," Pearl assured him. "But we don't know if George will be able to perform tonight."

"Ohhh." He finally caught what they were trying to get at. "The roadshow."

"Mitch—" Pearl looked him dead in the eye—"can you do it?"

"Me?" he exclaimed with a laugh. "I know most of his part, but I've never done it with the group."

"We're having a final run through at three o'clock. You're our only hope, Mitch." Pearl's voice was pleading.

He looked around at the anxious faces staring at him. "I guess so," he said, and the women gave a collective sigh of relief. "But I can't guarantee anything. I haven't acted or sung in front of an audience since high school."

"I'm sure you'll be wonderful," Cami assured him. "Besides, you've got nicer legs than George. You'll look better in his costume." At that, Pearl went into another frenzy, realizing that George's costume would need to be altered if, in fact, Mitch ended up performing.

With the crisis somewhat resolved, Mitch shooed them out of his way so he could try to repair the damage to the floor before the three o'clock practice.

Realizing it would take a lot of faith and prayers to pull this off, Cami, Ashlyn, and Pearl went to work on the last-minute details for the play. Grandpa Willy was still busy trying to track down Vanessa and locate Sebastian's number.

It was at times like these that being bored back home in Salt Lake didn't look so bad after all, Ashlyn decided.

⊹⊹ ❀ ⊹⊹

Helping the stage crew finish painting backdrops for the show, Ashlyn and Cami didn't get a chance to see any of the rehearsal. Even when the rehearsal had ended, they were still busy painting. They finished scarcely an hour before the roadshow was to start, which barely gave them time to get cleaned up.

Returning to the gymnasium, out of breath and exhausted, Ashlyn and Cami found Pearl immediately and wished her well. She seemed to be holding up under the pressure, especially given the fact that George's wife still hadn't delivered their baby, which meant Mitch was their lead.

Finding the seats they'd saved earlier that day, Cami and Ashlyn joined Grandpa Willy and Mitch's parents. Grandpa was still trying to locate Vanessa, as was Mitch's mother, who thought Vanessa might want to know that Mitch was performing so she could come and watch.

Pearl had actually approached Vanessa about being in the road-show, but Mitch's girlfriend had informed her loftily that she didn't have time. She was busy rehearsing with a "real" band for "real" gigs.

There were six wards in the stake, and their ward was last on the program. The first ward to perform did a cute play set in the 1950s depicting a rebellious young man who looked a lot like Fonzi from the television show *Happy Days,* but he couldn't carry a tune, let alone dance. Ashlyn never did quite figure out what the story had to do with the theme, but the audience seemed to enjoy it.

The next play was a modern-day story with missionaries going out to the world to preach the gospel. It had a couple of fun songs and it was cute, Ashlyn thought.

The other plays took their turn and then it was finally time for "The Stripling Warriors."

The curtain opened to a black stage. Then the lights came on, revealing a mock battle between the Nephites and the Lamanites. The story followed the scriptural account, but Pearl had personalized it with several mothers and sons, families, and townspeople. The back-drops looked wonderful and Ashlyn couldn't help feeling proud of her contribution.

Her breath caught in her throat as Mitch strode onto the scene. He carried himself like a warrior, like a leader, tall and strong. He got a few lines wrong and had to ad-lib part of the scene, but the message still came across and for anyone in the audience who didn't know the script, Mitch's job was flawless.

Ashlyn enjoyed the charming performance by the young Nephite girls who dreamed aloud of the young men who were brave enough to go to battle, and the stripling warriors' song also went well. But the number that stopped the show and had Ashlyn's heart pounding in her chest was Mitch's song. His voice was powerful and strong when he pleaded with the Lord to protect those young men who had enough faith in their God and the things their mothers had taught them, to fight the more experienced Lamanite army.

The audience sat spellbound as Mitch sang each note clearly and with great emotion. He looked like a Nephite leader, a man of God, noble in his cause.

When he had sung the last, heartfelt note of his song, the audience burst into enthusiastic applause that lasted several minutes. Mitch took several bows, then finally left the stage so the performance could continue. Ashlyn wasn't sure, but she wondered if there might have been some heavenly intervention that caused George's wife to go into labor so that Mitch could perform the roll of Helaman so convincingly.

Cami turned to her, her face still registering amazement. "Can you believe that was Mitch up there?"

Of course, Mitch's mother beamed with pride at her son's performance. He'd had years of his mother's training and had performed in more than a few school plays, all of which had paid off stupendously in his performance here. Catherine Bradford appeared positive that if Oscars had been awarded, Mitch would have won, hands down.

At the cast party after the roadshows, Ashlyn set out the food and fussed over Pearl, who had been going nonstop most of the day. It was there that the cast presented Pearl with a dozen long-stemmed red roses. As she stood there teary-eyed but smiling happily, everyone applauded her for the wonderful job she'd done writing and directing the play. Many of the ward members who'd attended that night, and even people from other wards, were quick to admit that "The Stripling Warriors" was by far the best roadshow there that night. There was even a request to perform the play for a stake further north.

When Mitch came into the room, there was a hushed silence, then the crowd burst into applause, chanting his last name, "Bradford, Bradford, Bradford." He smiled his thanks, then made his way to the food table and filled his plate. Looking around the room for a place to sit, he saw Ashlyn and wound his way through the masses until he reached her.

"Hello there," he said, setting his plate on the chair next to her.

"Hello there, yourself," she replied. Then with a big smile she said, "Mitch, you were absolutely wonderful tonight. I had no idea you had such an incredible voice."

"It's not as good as George's, but the song wasn't too difficult," he explained modestly. "Although I did feel a little rusty. It's been a long time since I've done a solo."

Several other cast members came by to congratulate him, including a group of giggling young girls whose faces were bright red.

"You want a ride home?" he asked Ashlyn when the party started dying down. She accepted his offer and together they pitched in to help clean up the leftover food, paper plates, and cups.

"We'll finish up here," Mitch told Cami, seeing that Pearl had nearly fallen asleep in her chair. "Why don't you take Pearl home?"

After Cami left with Pearl, Mitch and Ashlyn finished cleaning and straightening the kitchen and multi-purpose room. When everything was spotless, they turned out the lights with an enormous feeling of satisfaction and exhaustion and headed for Mitch's car.

On the way to the Davenports, Ashlyn told Mitch about the bed and breakfast permit getting turned down and how Grandpa Willy and Cami had been waiting around all day for a call from Vanessa.

Mitch apparently didn't find her absence unusual. "She went to Portland for a couple of days," he said. "She has some kind of business there to take care of. But she always checks her messages at the office. I'm sure she'll call when she gets a chance."

"Did you know she and her father have put together plans for a condominium resort and convention center that they want to build here in Seamist?" she asked casually.

"*Condominium resort?*" He stopped at the stop sign and turned to look at her. His expression told Ashlyn that this information had caught him completely by surprise.

"And convention center," Ashlyn added.

His eyes narrowed as he considered her words. "Are you sure about this? She hasn't said anything to me."

Ashlyn told him about the loan application Dallin had seen at the bank, then added, "They're also looking for outside investors."

Mitch looked doubtful. "There's nowhere in Seamist to build something of that size, unless they tear down some existing structures. And the city council has pretty much determined that we don't want Seamist to become a tourist attraction."

"That's what I thought, too," Ashlyn replied. "But with her dad on the Zoning and Planning Commission, it's possible he could change some minds."

"I wonder why she hasn't said anything to me," he mused, his eyebrows drawn together. "She knows how I feel about this. Is Dallin sure about what he saw?"

Ashlyn nodded, her heart heavy at the look of confusion on Mitch's face. She had wanted Mitch to see his girlfriend for who she really was, but now that he was beginning to, she ached for him as she recognized the sense of betrayal and bewilderment in his eyes.

"I don't understand why she didn't say anything. I can't believe this. A convention center in Seamist?" he repeated thoughtfully. "Where would they put it?"

Lost in thought, he pulled into the driveway and stopped the car. Ashlyn opened the car door and climbed out.

"Good night, Mitch," she said and when he didn't respond, she spoke his name with a little more force. "Mitch!"

"What? Oh, sorry. Good night," he said absently, not looking at her.

"Are you okay?" she asked.

"Yeah," he nodded. "I'm going to call Vanessa and see what she has to say about all of this."

"I expect she has a perfectly good explanation for all of it," Ashlyn said, wondering exactly what Vanessa would say. She and Mitch seemed to have ignored the differences between them up to this point. But Ashlyn didn't see how Mitch could overlook this one.

"It's probably just a misunderstanding," Ashlyn said. She didn't honestly believe that herself, but she wanted to say something that would give him some comfort.

Mitch looked up at her then, nodding as if in agreement, but his expression lacked conviction. "I'm just . . . surprised, I guess, and curious about what's going on. I suppose I shouldn't be surprised she hasn't said anything. She's not really the kind to open up and talk about what she's thinking. It wasn't until after we'd been dating several months that I learned anything about her mother, and about the only thing Vanessa told me was that she lives on the East coast."

Ashlyn didn't respond. She couldn't think of anything she could say about Vanessa to Mitch. Besides, she had the feeling he would be learning it all on his own before too long.

Still deep in thought, Mitch didn't seem to expect her to say anything. "This is something she could've talked to me about," he continued. "Even though I'm opposed to overdevelopment here in Seamist, I'm willing to listen to what others have to say.

"But Seamist is the kind of town where people come to get away from the tourist traps. We have enough small hotels and restaurants to accommodate them; we don't need a huge resort and convention center. Her father should know this more than anyone. He's on the commission." Mitch shook his head, obviously baffled by this whole issue.

Once again Ashlyn assured him that he probably just needed to talk to Vanessa. "And when you do," she added, "could you please ask her to call Grandpa Willy? He's very anxious to get hold of Sebastian and see if he can talk him into signing the petition. Otherwise, all that hard work and money has been wasted.

"Anyway, thanks for the ride," she told him. She hoped he made it home all right; his mind definitely wasn't on his driving. She also hoped that he would finally see Vanessa's true nature. It was high time he got past that attractive veneer and discovered the "real" Vanessa.

The next morning dawned brightly as Ashlyn waited for Mitch, all the while watching the canvas before her paint itself with pink and orange streaks of clouds against the rich shades of blue sky. Every sunrise was different, every one thrilled her.

Soon, Mitch came bounding down the stairs.

"Sorry I'm late. You wouldn't believe who called just before I left."

"Vanessa?" Ashlyn asked cautiously, as they started to walk along the beach.

"It certainly was," he said grimly. "When I asked her what was going on, she tried to deny any involvement, but she finally admitted what she and her father are doing. In fact, that's why she's in Portland—to meet with investors.

"I told her they don't stand a chance of getting approval for the project, but she just laughed at me. Apparently Jonathan has made it a point to meet with each member of the commission privately and he's persuaded many of them to see things his way. She tried to convince me that their condos and convention center will fit in 'beautifully' with the coastline and the atmosphere of the town, that they would prove to be an asset to the community, not a detraction."

"Quite the sales job," Ashlyn remarked dryly. "Did she say where they were going to build it?"

"No, she sidestepped that one," he said frowning, "and it has me wondering exactly what's she's doing." He walked several yards before speaking again. "I'm seeing a completely different side to her that I would never have believed before this."

Ashlyn made no comment, since it wasn't her place to tell him, that when it came to Vanessa he had a serious blind spot. After this, she hoped, he would see Vanessa for exactly what she was.

They broke into a jog and ran the distance without much talking. They'd built their stamina and endurance to be able to run the length of the beach both ways. It wasn't a long run, but what had taken almost an hour before, they could now cover in forty minutes. Then they slowed to a walk to cool down and relax their muscles as they approached the wooden steps.

"That felt good," Mitch said, stopping to stretch his calf and thigh muscles.

Ashlyn did the same. "It sure did. I really appreciate you getting up and running with me."

"I've enjoyed it. First time in years I've had a regular workout program," he admitted.

Stretching her back, she took a few deep breaths. "I hope I keep it up when I get back home."

A flicker of panic crossed his eyes. "When are you leaving?"

"The first of September. My brother will be home from his mission and I want to be there for his report. And," she gave him a smile, "our family is going through the temple to get sealed to my stepdad."

"That's great," Mitch congratulated her. "Are you okay with that?"

"I'm more than okay with it," she said quickly. "I'm really excited."

He nodded thoughtfully. "Wow, I guess I forgot you're leaving. What about the bed and breakfast? Don't you want to be here for the grand opening?"

"I wouldn't miss it," she assured him. "I want to be their first customer. Maybe even have my family come so they can see the place. They'd love Seamist."

"So," he said, not moving, "you're going to abandon me, huh? Leave me to run on my own?"

"The weather will get cold and rainy once winter comes, won't it?" Ashlyn wrinkled her nose, but the truth was, she couldn't imagine life without seeing Mitch almost every day.

"I guess so," he sighed. "I'm really going to miss you."

"I'll miss you, too," she said before her throat tightened with emotion.

He pulled her into a hug that said more about what they were feeling than mere words ever could. She'd see him again, she told herself. She'd be back to visit. After everything they'd shared, they would always be friends. But Ashlyn knew if she let her heart speak, that wouldn't be enough.

"Whose car is that?" Mitch asked when they walked around the side of the house and saw a sleek Toyota Celica parked in the driveway.

"I don't know," Ashlyn replied. "I've never seen that car before." She didn't have to wonder long. The door to the house opened.

She gasped and stopped dead in her tracks. To her complete surprise and horror, Jake Gerrard stepped outside.

CHAPTER TWENTY-FIVE

"Surprise!" he exclaimed, moving toward her with arms outstretched. Instinctively Ashlyn took a step backwards into Mitch. Not appearing to notice, Jake grabbed her in a fierce hug. "Boy, have I missed you!"

Letting her go at last, he stepped back and took a good look at her. "Well?" he said. "Aren't you going to say something?"

"I . . . I . . . ," she stuttered. "I don't know what to say." She wanted to ask him what he was doing here after all this time, and why was he acting like he'd missed her so much and cared so much about her. The last time she'd seen him, he'd treated her exactly like any customer in his store. No more and no less.

"I knew you'd be surprised," he beamed, then looked past her to where Mitch stood. "Who's that?"

Ashlyn took Mitch's arm and pulled him forward. "This is my friend and running partner, Mitch Bradford. Mitch, this is Jake Gerrard, from Salt Lake City."

Mitch extended his hand first. Jake shook it grudgingly.

"Nice to meet you," Mitch said. Jake nodded, eyeing him appraisingly.

Just then, Cami stepped through the front door. She was scowling and Ashlyn knew exactly what she was thinking. That Jake shouldn't be here. *And she's right,* Ashlyn thought. *Why is he here? What does he want?*

"Well," Mitch excused himself politely, "I've got a floor to finish, so I'd better get home and get showered. I'll see you later." He spoke to all of them but glanced quickly at Ashlyn, as if to make sure she was okay. "Drop by the house later and I'll show you how the floor turned out. Just knock first this time," he added with a teasing smile.

"Why don't we go inside?" Jake suggested, slipping an arm around Ashlyn's shoulder. "We've got a lot of catching up to do."

Cami left them alone in the living room to talk, but before heading for the shower, she gave Ashlyn a stern, "be strong" look.

Ashlyn took a seat on the far end of the couch from where Jake sat. "What in the world brings you to Seamist?" she asked, willing her voice not to tremble.

He scooted a little closer to her. "You."

She pressed her back into the cushioned arm of the couch, wishing it were further away from him. She swallowed hard. "Me?"

"Ashlyn, I haven't stopped thinking about you since you left. I want you to know that I've spent these last few months trying to analyze my feelings. It seemed like I just couldn't quit thinking about you and more than anything I wanted to see you.

"I called your house and your mother told me you'd be back the end of summer, but I didn't want to wait. I know I could have called but—" he scooted even closer, "I wanted to see you. I needed to see you."

Ashlyn tried to look normal, but inside her stomach was flipping around like a fish out of water. She'd finally made the break with him and his memory and severed the emotional tie he had had on her—and here he was!

"I don't understand," she said. "What's changed? Why would you want to see me after all these months?"

He bowed his head briefly, then looked at her with penitent eyes. "I made a huge mistake," he confessed. "I've tried to live with the regret and the knowledge that I hurt you, and I can't any longer. I thought that if you loved me once, you might find it in your heart to forgive me and let me make it up to you."

Her mouth fell open and she clamped it shut. Make it up to her? Was he kidding? She just spent the last year in emotional hell, and he wanted to make it up to her?

In the past she would've dissolved into tears and fallen into his arms, but now she could only look at him with amazement and laugh.

"Jake, it's too late for us. You made your decision fourteen months ago. I've moved on with my life." She couldn't believe she was actually saying the words. A small part of her was tugging at her heart, shouting that he was there, that he'd come all this way for her, and that he was still as gorgeous as ever. But only a very small part. The rest of her—heart, mind, and soul—was thinking very clearly. Jake had shown that he was not the man for her, would never be the man for her, and she would be foolish to think otherwise.

"Please, Ashlyn," he pleaded. "I've come all this way. Won't you at least give us one more chance? We could spend the day together. You could show me around Seamist, and maybe drive down the coast with me. I want to hear all about your summer, what you've been doing." He scooted closer until their knees touched. "And I want to know how you're doing," he added softly.

As she reflected upon their relationship in the past, she realized that something about him did seem different. He hadn't ever thought of her and her feelings like this before. He'd been very selfish and more concerned about himself and his needs and wants. She had to admit, he did seem to have changed.

And he had come a long way to see her.

"All right," she said cautiously. "I'll spend the day with you."

He grabbed both of her hands and kissed her knuckles. "Thank you," he exclaimed between kisses. "You've made driving all those miles worth it. We'll have so much fun, you'll see."

⚜

"What do you mean you're spending the day with him," Cami hissed, following Ashlyn into her room. "Are you nuts?"

"He just wants to spend some time with me," Ashlyn said. "He's driven all the way here and I thought it was the least I could do."

Cami threw her arms around Ashlyn and tackled her to the bed. "I won't let you go. You just got him out of your life. Don't do it, Ash," she begged. "Don't go."

"It's just a ride along the coast. We'll have lunch, look at the beach, then he'll drop me off and leave," Ashlyn told her simply.

Cami shook her head. "He's got something up his sleeve. I don't trust him."

"I know, I know," Ashlyn said. "It's freaking me out having him here, too, but I can't turn him away after he's driven so far."

"I want you to take my cell phone and call me every couple of hours," Cami insisted.

"Oh, Cami," Ashlyn protested.

"No, I mean it, I won't let you go unless you promise."

"Okay, I promise. Now get out of here so I can get ready."

The minute Cami had left the room, Ashlyn immediately dropped to her knees beside her bed and prayed with all her heart.

Please, Heavenly Father, please be with me and help me to be strong. In spite of everything, there's still a place inside that cares about him. But that day in the temple was the worst day of my life and I never want to go through anything like that ever again.

So if this is all going to lead to more heartache, please let me know, be with me every step of the way. I've tried to do this alone and I realize that I can't. I need Thy help. Jake says he's changed and he seems different, but I'm different, too. I don't know that we can ever get back what we've lost, or that we should even try. I know I used to pray he would come back to me, but now that he's here, I don't think that's what I want at all. I'm just so confused.

I do know one thing, though, and I'm grateful for this knowledge. I know I can't do it without Thy help.

⁂

Jake took her to Three Arch Rocks, the beautiful rock formation at the beach by Oceanside where she and Mitch had driven earlier that summer. After lunch, Ashlyn and Jake decided to take a walk on the beach.

"Most of the time there are sea lions on those rocks," Ashlyn said, pointing. "It's a federal refuge for them."

They squinted, looking toward the rocks for any sign of the sea lions, but they couldn't tell if the light brown lumps were animal, vegetable, or mineral.

Jake reached for her hand as they walked barefoot through the sand. Ashlyn was trying desperately to stay rational, but he was showing a side of him she'd never seen before. A side she'd always wanted him to have, but he'd never seemed to possess. Yet here he was—considerate, unselfish, and completely absorbed in her.

He reached his hand up and touched her curls. "You're wearing your hair differently, aren't you?"

"The moisture in the air makes it hard to fight the natural curl," she told him. "I've decided to just let it go."

"I like it," he said. "It brings out your eyes." They stopped walking and he looked at her longingly. "I can tell you've been running, you look really great. I've forgotten how beautiful you are."

She blushed. "I haven't changed that much."

"But you have," he disagreed. "You seem different. I'm not sure exactly what it is. But I like it. Thank you for giving me today." He leaned toward her, but she quickly turned and began walking again, not wanting him to kiss her.

They decided to stop at an ice cream shop where they ordered sundaes. The teenage girl who took their order acted as if she would rather have been anywhere but there. As they looked at the menu one more time to decide what they wanted, she sighed impatiently, and then seemed quite put out when Ashlyn changed her mind from a caramel sundae with nuts to chocolate chip cookie dough ice cream with hot fudge sauce.

As they waited for their order, they watched several children flying kites on the beach and talked. Jake had changed jobs and now worked for a car dealership in Salt Lake, which was how he'd been able to afford his sleek new car with leather interior, CD player, and all the amenities and upgrades possible. He loved selling cars and the whole sales environment. He had also gone back to college, though only part time at first.

The server returned, placing Jake's sundae in front of him, then set Ashlyn's ice cream on the table before her. One look at it and Ashlyn knew it wasn't what she had ordered.

"This is mint chocolate chip," she said. "I ordered cookie dough ice cream."

The girl stared at her as if she wanted to dump the sundae on top of Ashlyn's head.

"Could you change it, please," Ashlyn added, seeing that the girl wasn't going to make it easy for her.

"Okay, okay," the girl said, grabbing the dish of ice cream so quickly the scoops flew out of the dish and into Ashlyn's lap. Ashlyn jumped up out of her chair and looked at the girl, not bothering to hide her annoyance. "I'd like to speak to your manager," she said quietly but firmly.

At this, the girl's attitude was rapidly replaced with terror, as she hurried off and disappeared in a room behind the counter.

Ashlyn hadn't meant to cause a scene, but the girl was acting like a spoiled brat. What was more, Ashlyn absolutely hated mint chocolate chip ice cream. When she was at college, she and her roommates had pigged out on Oreos and mint chocolate chip ice cream one night, then she'd come down with the stomach flu during the night. She could still remember what it had been like to throw up green ice cream and Oreo cookies. Since that night she couldn't even look at either without getting nauseous.

She wiped the mess off her khaki-colored shorts as best she could with napkins, while Jake simply stared at her, shocked at her assertiveness.

"Excuse me," an older man said. "My name is Martin Tilman. I'm the manager here."

Ashlyn shook his hand. He went on apologetically, "I'm very sorry about what happened with Kiley. She's very upset with me because she didn't want to work today. She wanted to go to a rock concert in Portland and I wouldn't let her go."

Ashlyn stared at him, thinking that most employers wouldn't put up with that kind of attitude from their workers.

"She's my daughter," Mr. Tilman clarified, "and she's mad at the world and apparently took it out on you. Kiley!" he called toward the back.

The young girl had obviously been crying, judging by her red and swollen eyes. She came around the counter and stood next to her father, her hands clasped tightly together.

"Kiley," her father said sternly.

"I'm sorry," she said to Ashlyn, her youthful voice tremulous. "I didn't mean to spill it on you."

Ashlyn smiled at her. "That's okay," she told the young girl. "No harm done."

The girl sighed with relief, then looked at her father, who offered Ashlyn another sundae—the right kind—on the house. Ashlyn told him what she'd ordered and it was brought promptly to their table.

When they left, Jake placed a five-dollar tip on the table for the young girl, who once again disappeared into the back room and didn't come out until the couple had left.

They swung by a souvenir shop, where Jake bought some seashells and starfish to take home to his younger sisters. While she waited for him, Ashlyn admired a beautiful ceramic figure of the Misty Harbor Lighthouse. The lighthouse had become a symbol of hope and recommitment for her this summer. By learning to depend upon the Lord completely, she had actually become more independent. By turning toward the light and listening to the Spirit, she'd gained the strength to stand on her own.

She gazed at it longingly, admiring the workmanship and detail and making a mental note to purchase one like it before she went home. Even though it was quite expensive, it would be something she would treasure forever.

"That's beautiful," Jake said, looking at the lighthouse over her shoulder.

"It is, isn't it?" she replied. "I've fallen in love with lighthouses since I've been here," she told him. But rather than explain more about their significance in her life, she kept her feelings to herself.

"I can see why," Jake replied, admiring the ceramic figure as well.

Putting the lighthouse back on the shelf, she excused herself to visit the restroom.

Jake was waiting for her in the lobby and to her delight and surprise, he handed her a package. He had never been one to give her many gifts, so she was surprised when she opened the box and saw the expensive ceramic lighthouse.

"Thank you so much," she said in a whisper. "You didn't have to."

"I know," he said. "But I could see from the look on your face how much you wanted it and I couldn't resist."

"Thank you," she replied, giving him a heartfelt smile. "This really means a lot to me."

They stopped at Cape Lookout for a view of the coast north toward Cape Meares, where the Cape Meares lighthouse was located, and south toward Cape Kiwanda. The day was sunny and warm, and as she took in the view, Ashlyn wondered once again how she was ever going to leave this beautiful place.

"No wonder they call this the Three Capes," Jake said, as he stepped behind her and slid his hand around her waist. She stood stiffly in his arms, not knowing exactly what to say or how to act. This was a different Jake than the man she'd nearly married over a year ago, a new and improved version. There was a softness about him. He seemed humble, more sensitive to her feelings.

"Ash," he spoke softly in her ear. He squeezed her close to him. "It's so good to be with you again."

She would have given anything to hear those words again in the past. But she'd finally turned a corner, gained enough gumption and strength to take a few baby steps forward, leaving her past behind. Why had he shown up now? Just when she'd gotten him out of her life?

He turned her around to face him. "I am amazed at how much you've changed and grown. You've become so independent." Ashlyn wasn't sure if this was meant as a compliment or not. "Back there, in the ice cream shop, you would have never said anything about the order being wrong before. But you did it. I was so proud of you." He gazed at her, obviously liking what he saw. "I like this new side of you. I like it a lot."

She looked away from his penetrating gaze, trying to gather her thoughts as her head and heart did battle. A red light in her head flashed, "Danger! Get away from this guy!" But her heart responded, "He's changed. Give him a chance."

She looked into his face again. "You've changed, too," she said.

"Have I?"

She nodded.

"I had quite a year without you," he told her, not giving details. "And all I know is that my life was never better than when I was with you. You made me a better person. You made me want to try harder to do what I was supposed to do. I've finally gotten myself together, but I've needed you, Ash. I've really needed you."

Ashlyn did not resist when he took her in his arms. She had gained enough emotional distance to not swoon at his every word, as she once would have. She was still curious to discover what exactly had changed him, but it didn't seem the time to press the issue.

He pulled back and looked into her eyes. "You're so amazing," he told her, "and you're even more beautiful than before." Running his hand through her hair, he bent down and kissed her.

Ashlyn waited for something to happen. But her heart didn't flutter and her palms didn't grow clammy. There were no goose bumps prickling her flesh.

When the brief kiss ended, they walked back to the car. He was trying so hard and she was flattered by his attention. But she was also wary. She didn't have to dig too deep to uncover the pain he'd caused her. Still, she felt she owed him a chance to do what he had come so far to do; even more, she didn't want to wonder for the rest of her life or live with any more regrets.

All the workers had gone home for the evening, so Ashlyn took Jake to the mansion and gave him the grand tour. He was impressed by the work and the beauty of the structure, and thought the idea of a bed and breakfast was brilliant.

"There's one thing that would make the mansion perfect," she said, "and I've suggested it to Cami and Grandpa Willy already. They need to build a gazebo in the garden, overlooking the ocean. The gazebo would be a perfect addition, especially for weddings and receptions." She felt only a twinge at the word "wedding," but she kept her voice steady, as if it no longer mattered that Jake had once asked her to marry him, and then had changed his mind.

After touring the house, they made plans to meet for breakfast and Jake left. He had a room at a small inn in town and with the long drive back to Salt Lake ahead of him, he needed to get to bed.

Cami was at the door to meet her. "Well? What happened?"

Ashlyn smiled at her friend and dropped her purse and package in a chair just inside the door. She kicked off her shoes and sat down on the couch.

"Ash!" Cami exclaimed. "Will you tell me what happened?"

Ashlyn shrugged and said, "Nothing, really. We had lunch, walked on the beach, shopped for souvenirs, then he brought me home."

"That's it? You promise?" she demanded.

"That's about it." Ashlyn covered a yawn. It had been a very long day.

"So what does he want? Why did he come?" she persisted.

Cami wasn't about to let up with the third degree so Ashlyn told her everything.

Cami listened skeptically as Ashlyn gave an account of the day. "Something's up," she said decisively. "I don't trust him."

"I felt the same as you for a while," Ashlyn responded, "but you know what I think now? I think something's happened to humble him. Something that made him realize what a jerk he was to call off our wedding and to walk away like he did. And, I think he can finally see that he was lucky to have me in the first place and that he let a good thing get away."

Cami looked impressed at Ashlyn's analysis. "Very good. I'm glad you can see through him."

"There's nothing to see through," Ashlyn shrugged. "He's not playing games. He's sincere."

A look of panic crossed Cami's face. "What are you saying? You believe him?"

Ashlyn laughed. "I'm not going to go running into his arms, if that's what you're worried about."

Cami placed her hand on her chest and let out a relieved sigh.

"But I am going to hear what he has to say," Ashlyn told her. "If not for his sake, then for mine. I need to hear him apologize for what happened. I mean, not just apologize, but actually grovel a bit. I'd like to hear him beg for forgiveness." She smiled at Cami. "I know that sounds cruel, but after what he did to me, I deserve it."

"Well, I guess I worried all day for nothing," Cami replied. "It sounds like you've kept your head about this."

"Of course I have," Ashlyn told her. "I haven't enjoyed this last year, but I have learned a lot through the process, about life and about me, and I'm not going to make the same mistake twice. You can count on that."

CHAPTER TWENTY-SIX

Ashlyn didn't go running with Mitch the next morning. She knew she wouldn't have time before meeting Jake at the diner for breakfast.

Jake met her in the lobby, looking handsome in a soft, butter-yellow polo shirt and navy blue slacks. Ashlyn couldn't help but admire his fresh, all-American look, very athletic but classy. He'd always dressed nicely and worked out regularly. She also liked his thick brown hair and gold-flecked hazel-green eyes. He greeted her with a warm smile and a hug.

"I'm so glad you came," he said, as if relieved that she'd actually shown up. They followed the hostess to their seats, and Ashlyn noticed that the three waitresses working the dining room all watched as Jake walked by.

The hostess led them to a corner table that had a view of the Misty Harbor Bay, but the lighthouse was covered in early morning fog. Looking out at the beach, Ashlyn wondered if Mitch would be there, running alone.

They ordered their meal, then talked about things in general while they waited. He asked about her family and she told him about Adam. "We're going through the temple when Adam gets home," she said proudly.

Jake held her hand the entire time they talked, stroking her knuckles with his thumb. He listened intently to everything she had to say, as if it was the most important thing in the world to him.

Ashlyn didn't want to seem naive, but she honestly believed this was no act. Something inside of her told her he was truly sincere. He was different.

Their food came, but neither of them ate much.

"So, you'll be home in a few weeks," he asked.

"I guess so," she replied, hating the thought of leaving, and he commented that she obviously loved the area.

"I really do," she agreed. "This is a great place and the people are wonderful." She thought about Grandpa Willy and his exploding root beer, crazy Cami, and Pearl. She thought of Mitch. How could she tell him good-bye?

Jake toyed with his food. "So what are you going to do when you get home?" he asked.

"Get a job," she replied with a laugh. "I haven't worked all summer. I've just been draining my savings and I'm nearly out."

"You'll still have some time to date when you get home, won't you?" he asked hopefully.

She smiled at him. "I'm sure I will." He grinned back at her, and Ashlyn realized for the first time since he'd come, that they'd connected. Up until now there had been a formal awkwardness, an uncomfortable tension, that ran like an undercurrent between them. But they'd finally moved past that. They'd broken the barriers of their old relationship and let it slip behind them.

He paid the bill and they walked to his car, stopping just outside the driver's side door.

"Thanks for spending time with me," he said. "I'm really glad I came."

She was quiet, not knowing how to respond. In a way she was glad, too. She realized she had grown stronger, especially when it came to her feelings for Jake. But having him back in her life only made it more complicated. She didn't want to encourage him but she wasn't sure she wanted to discourage him either. She didn't know what she wanted.

"It was good to see you," she finally said. "I hope you have a safe trip home."

They stood in silence for a moment, neither of them knowing what to say next.

"I guess I'd better be going," he finally said.

Ashlyn let him hug her but stepped back before he got any ideas about kissing her. She wasn't comfortable with that idea, especially on the main street of town.

She watched as he climbed into the car and started the engine. He gave her one last look, and she waved good-bye as he pulled away. She didn't feel sad he was leaving, but she did feel as though old wounds had been exposed. But finally, hopefully, now they would heal.

As his taillights disappeared, she realized that she was okay.

With a lilt to her step, she headed toward Cami's car. The sky was starting to clear and a beautiful day was shaping up. She felt like doing something fun, like going on a hike and having a picnic, or flying a kite on the beach, or having a Frisbee rematch with Mitch, Dallin, and Cami.

As if thinking of Mitch had summoned him up in reality, she caught a glimpse of him a few blocks away. He was walking across the street.

"Mitch," she called. She waved, trying to get his attention, but he was too far away and didn't hear her. She hurried down the sidewalk to catch up to him. He turned the corner and headed toward the town square, which had a little park, some benches, and a statue of Lewis and Clark.

Ashlyn rounded the corner and froze. She'd found Mitch all right.

In Vanessa's arms.

And they were kissing.

CHAPTER TWENTY-SEVEN

Ashlyn drove home, angry at herself. She didn't like seeing Mitch and Vanessa together, but what really bugged her was *how much* she didn't like it. It wasn't that she had feelings for him, she reasoned in her mind. It was just that he deserved better than Vanessa. Ashlyn had been sure that after everything he'd learned about her, their relationship would be over.

Had Vanessa worked her charms on him and convinced him to reconsider the resort complex? Ashlyn wouldn't believe it. But what else could explain their being together like that?

Later that afternoon, while she and Cami were doing housework, mopping floors and cleaning windows, the phone rang and Ashlyn answered it. Her stomach tensed when she heard Vanessa's voice on the other end asking for William Davenport.

"He's not here right now. Would you like to talk to Cami?" Ashlyn asked, trying to be civilized. Since that morning, the picture of Vanessa and Mitch had become etched in her memory, an image she wished she didn't see every time she shut her eyes.

There was a deep sigh as Vanessa managed to convey what an imposition it was that Mr. Davenport wasn't home for her to talk to. "I suppose so," she said, sounding both superior and irritated.

Cami took the phone and said a few yeses and okays, and ended with, "Thank you, I'll be sure to tell my grandfather," before she hung up.

"Well," Cami said, looking at Ashlyn. "She called to say she can't seem to find Mr. Jamison's telephone number in San Francisco, but as soon as she does, she'll have her secretary call and give it to us."

"Yeah, I'll bet she misplaced it," Ashlyn scowled, thinking of her. "I'll just bet she misplaced it on purpose. She probably told Sebastian not to sign the petition."

"Why do you say that?" Cami grabbed her cleaning cloth and glass spray and stored them under the kitchen sink.

"I don't know. It just seems like something she wouldn't be above doing."

"Are you saying she's conniving?" Cami asked.

"Are you saying she isn't?" Ashlyn replied.

"I think 'manipulative' would be the word I'd use," Cami stated.

Ashlyn nodded in agreement. "I still can't get the picture of Mitch and Vanessa together, kissing, out of my head," she said with frustration. "I don't get it. He didn't seem very happy with her when we last talked, and the next thing I know they're kissing!"

"I'm sure she's just doing everything in her power to make up with him," Cami said, attempting to console her.

"I didn't get the impression he was putting up much of a fight!" Ashlyn snorted.

"Come on," Cami brightened. "We need to get your mind off of this. Let's go take a look at the house. They were supposed to get the porch painted and the windows replaced today."

The workers had indeed finished both projects. Having the windows sparkling and clean, instead of boarded over and broken, made a huge difference in the appearance of the mansion. Now it looked inviting and warm. It was turning into a real beauty.

Cami noticed Pearl out in the yard talking to the landscapers who were putting in the sprinkling system. While Cami went to see what they were discussing, Ashlyn followed the wraparound porch to the side of the house, where a window stood open to let the fresh afternoon breeze inside. She heard voices through the window and recognized one as Mitch's.

"Isn't it about time you and Vanessa tied the knot?" one of the workers asked him. "You two have dated long enough."

"It hasn't been that long," Mitch said. His voice sounded strained over the sound of sanding.

"Vanessa told my wife that you two were talking marriage," the man said.

"Hand me that flat-head screwdriver, would you?" Mitch said. Ashlyn heard a shuffling of feet.

"Well?" the man kept at him.

"Well, what?" Mitch said impatiently.

"Are you two going to get married or not?"

"Tell you what, Dave," Mitch retorted. "As soon as I get engaged, you'll be the first to know."

Someone from another room called Dave's name and Ashlyn heard the sound of heavy boots on the floor. Then Mitch began to whistle as he continued working.

Marriage? Mitch couldn't possibly be talking about marriage to Vanessa, could he?

Ashlyn didn't know what to think. Mitch hadn't told Dave marriage had been discussed, but then he hadn't said marriage to Vanessa was out of the question either. Ashlyn walked away, feeling even more confused than before.

She would be going home before much longer. Then she wouldn't have to worry about Mitch or Vanessa ever again.

⁂

When Cami took off for the rest of the day with Dallin, Ashlyn assured her she would be happy to stay home and take care of dinner for Grandpa Willy and herself, then spend the evening relaxing in front of the televison.

But before too long, a restless longing to be outside finally forced her to head outdoors. Dark clouds were rolling in low on the water, and a light breeze was blowing, but she knew it would grow stronger as the storm front approached. Drawn to the beach, she descended the stairs and began walking. The rays of the late afternoon sun streaked through breaks in the clouds and shone like spotlights on the water's choppy surface.

She found herself at the edge of the harbor adjacent to the lighthouse, which stood tall and strong in the face of the storm. She recited the psalm in her mind, the one Grandpa Willy had told her at the beginning of summer, and found comfort in its words.

"If I take the wings of the morning, and dwell in the uttermost parts of the sea; Even there shall thy hand lead me."

Ashlyn thought of the boats that set off with clear skies and calm waters, then get caught in sudden storms. But, with the help of a guiding light, they could return to the safety of the harbor. Ashlyn felt like one of those ships, surrounded by dark, rolling clouds, not knowing what direction to take. The Lord had promised that He would guide her. She just had to hang on and have faith. But sometimes it was so hard. Not knowing why things had to happen, not knowing the outcome—it seemed so terribly difficult, if not downright impossible.

She stood on the breakers as waves crashed and sprayed below her. There was a strange beauty in the storm that was threatening to beat down upon her at any time. Even as droplets of rain started to fall, she watched the white caps and troughs in the waves, rolling and curling to the shore.

A flash of lightening split the sky, startling Ashlyn. Almost immediately a roar of thunder followed, then the rain began. Ashlyn knew she'd pushed her luck and should have headed home long before now.

Breaking into a run, she headed for home, with the rain pelting her, stinging her cheeks and hands, drenching her from head to toe. Her lungs burned as she pushed herself faster and further until she reached the steps leading to the house. She looked back and could barely tell where the ocean ended and the clouds began. It was all one thick, swirling, furious wall of gray.

Finding shelter underneath a rocky overhang, Ashlyn watched the storm beat down upon the coastline as it unleashed its strength and fury. She hugged her arms across her chest, shivering at the biting cold wind, but standing in awe of the magnificence of nature. She thought of the Lord's strength and power, which was far beyond what she saw before her and felt her understanding and faith grow deeper. The Lord knew her, He loved her, He cared about her. Her life was in His hands.

Questions concerning her future and matters of her heart swirled through her mind like the storm around her. It seemed that no matter how much she'd tried to cut off her emotions, she hadn't been able to. She hadn't wanted to admit her feelings to anyone, even to herself, but she couldn't continue to disregard them as she had been trying to for the past several weeks. Even though nothing would or could change, she had to at least admit that she did have feelings for Mitch. She liked him and was attracted to him. She wanted to stay in Seamist, where she could see him and talk to him everyday. But that wasn't possible.

She was leaving and he was involved with somebody else.

At one time these feelings would have consumed her. Months ago she would have fretted and stewed over the questions plaguing her mind. But she had grown stronger these last few months, and she had the peace, the self-assurance, that everything would work out. There were no answers, but there was also no fear.

The steady rain became a torrential downpour, and angry waves crept closer and closer to where she stood. After her last dousing in the ocean, Ashlyn had no desire to get caught in those waves again, so bracing herself, she ran from her shelter to the stairs and across the lawn to the house, stopping on the deck to send a prayer of thanks heavenward. Even in the darkest of storms, the light of Christ still shone brightly, and she vowed that she would never take her eyes off that light again.

⁂

"I'll get it," Ashlyn called to Grandpa Willy as the phone rang for the second time. They were watching an old Cary Grant movie on television, and she was making popcorn to snack on while they watched.

Ashlyn was surprised to hear her mother's voice since they had spoken only a few days earlier. "Honey, I know it's short notice," Miranda said, "but your brother just called. It seems that one of the elders from his mission needs knee surgery and is coming back to the states to have it done. Since Adam is coming home in two weeks anyway, the mission president asked if Adam would escort him."

"When is he coming?"

"In two days."

Ashlyn's heart fell. Two days. She couldn't leave Seamist in two days. She wasn't ready. It was too soon.

"Honey?" her mother asked. "Are you there?"

"I'm still here," Ashlyn said slowly, trying to sort out her jumbled feelings. Of course, she was thrilled to see Adam again. And her mother. And of course Garrett. She just hadn't anticipated leaving Seamist so soon. She forced herself to listen to what her mother was saying.

"I've already checked and there's a flight from Portland that will get you to the airport an hour before Adam's flight arrives. We could meet you first, then we'd be there when he comes in," her mother said excitedly. "Isn't that terrific timing?"

Ashlyn couldn't match her mother's enthusiasm. "That does work out nicely, doesn't it?"

"Honey, I know it cuts your summer short, but you have to be here when he gets home."

"I know," Ashlyn said. She knew there was no choice. She did her best to hide her disappointment. "I'm sure Cami can drive me to the airport."

"Good. I'll take care of the arrangements. It will be so wonderful to have you home again." Miranda talked about the fun they'd have shopping for the baby and decorating the nursery, then went on to tell how the whole family—grandparents, aunts, uncles, and cousins—was planning a huge welcome home party for Ashlyn and Adam.

"And before I forget," Miranda said happily, "I called the temple to see if there's any way we could move up the sealing. They were more than happy to accommodate us. We're scheduled for next Thursday."

Ashlyn didn't want to burst her mom's bubble of excitement, so she went along with the conversation, all the while feeling empty and sick inside. She would barely have time to pack her bags before she had to leave.

After she hung up, Ashlyn looked at the bowl of popcorn and sighed. Suddenly she wasn't hungry any more. Walking slowly up the stairs, she went to her room and sat in the window seat and looked out into the stormy night.

Was this really how it was going to end, with barely enough time to pack and not enough time to say good-bye?

But she hadn't been to all the lighthouses. She hadn't been to Astoria or south to Florence. Grandpa Willy was going to take her and Cami out sailing, too.

Tears came to her eyes. She wasn't ready to go home. She didn't want this mystical, magical, beautiful time to end, and she was afraid that if she left, all the wonderful feelings she felt would go away and she'd never get them back.

Two weeks wouldn't have been long enough to prepare to leave, let alone two days.

She grabbed a pillow and hugged it to her chest, then as more and more tears came, she buried her face in her hands and cried.

The next morning Cami came bursting into Ashlyn's room and woke her up. Ashlyn hadn't gone running because there was a downpour outside and the threat of one inside. Even though she'd cried a bucket of tears last night, she knew there were still more where those had come from.

"I was hoping you'd be up last night when I got home." Cami bounced on her bed annoyingly.

"I gave up after midnight," Ashlyn said dully.

"Yeah, I guess it was pretty late when I got in. We had such a wonderful time, Ash. I'm telling you, I think this is it. Dallin told me he isn't about to let me go again. He didn't exactly ask me to marry him, but I know that's what he meant." She gazed up at the ceiling with a love-struck expression on her face.

"Wonderful," Ashlyn said, rolling over and pulling the covers over her head.

"What did you do last night?" Cami said, pulling them back down.

"Nothing," Ashlyn said, knowing that she had to tell Cami about her mother's phone call.

"I was thinking we could drive to Tillamook today and do some shopping. There's hardly anything in the cupboards, and I've got a bunch of errands we could run."

"Maybe you should do that tomorrow since we have to go that way anyway," Ashlyn told her, propping herself up on her elbows.

"Why are we going that way, anyway? Where are we going?"

"Portland. You need to drive me to the airport," Ashlyn said quietly. She had to fight to keep from dissolving into tears.

Cami's smile disappeared. "What do you mean, 'the airport'?"

"Um," Ashlyn swallowed, a knot of emotion clogging her throat. "My mom called to tell me that Adam's coming home early from his mission."

"How early?" Cami asked with alarm.

"He's coming home Friday. My plane arrives in Salt Lake just before his does."

Cami shot up off the bed. "You're serious?"

Ashlyn nodded.

"Ash, you can't leave now. The mansion's not done. We have to do the roadshow again for the north stake next week. The summer's not over yet."

Ashlyn looked at Cami, pleading for her to stop as tears gathered in the corners of her eyes.

"Okay, okay," Cami said quickly, seeing how close Ashlyn was to tears. "You can go. You should be there for your brother's welcome home. You'll just have to come back, that's all."

Ashlyn wiped at her eyes with the corner of her sheet and shrugged. "I don't know about that."

"What do you mean you don't know? You have to come back. In fact, you should just come back and find a job here and live permanently. I know you could get a job teaching in the schools here. I bet Mitch could get you a job. I think he's on the school board or something." Cami looked at her soberly. "Ash, you have to come back. You just have to."

"I'll have to see what happens when I get home," she said. She felt her lips trembling and she pressed them together, trying to get control of her emotions. "Oh, Cami, it's going to be so hard to leave."

⚜

She spent the morning washing clothes and packing since they would have to leave early the next morning to get to the airport on time. That afternoon Cami and Ashlyn went to Pearl's so Ashlyn could tell her good-bye.

"I can't believe you're leaving. I'm going to miss you so much," Pearl told Ashlyn tearfully. "You're coming back, aren't you? Especially for the grand opening of the Sea Rose."

"I wouldn't miss it for the world," she said, giving her a huge hug.

"I want to give you something," Pearl said. "Wait here." Pearl went into the back room and returned with a small box in her hand. "I have one for each of you girls. You've been so wonderful to me. Without you I don't think I would have ever discovered what wonderful people we have in the town and especially in this ward. I finally feel like this is home, and you are all my family."

She opened the box and said, "Since I will never have any daughters of my own, I would like to give you these." She pulled two dainty pearl rings from the box and handed one to Ashlyn and the other to Cami. "We can get them sized if they don't fit. I got these in Hong Kong over twenty years ago."

Ashlyn and Cami admired the antique-style rings surrounding the glossy white pearls. They were delicate and feminine and exquisitely beautiful. "Pearl, this is so wonderful," Ashlyn said, giving the older woman a grateful hug. "Thank you. I'll never forget you."

"And I'll never forget you," Pearl responded. "But this really isn't good-bye, is it? Because you'll be back soon, won't you?"

"You bet," Ashlyn nodded her head fervently.

"Maybe you can bring your family sometime," Pearl invited. "I'd love to meet them."

Ashlyn promised to do just that, trying to smile although her heart was sad and heavy. Then she and Cami left Pearl's house.

"You want to stop and take one last look at the house?" Cami suggested. "We might see Mitch there. You do want to tell him good-bye, don't you?"

"Sure," Ashlyn said, trying to sound as normal as possible. She didn't want to tell him good-bye; she thought it would kill her. But neither could she leave without seeing him one last time.

The house, with its colorful turrets, gleaming white gables and railings, and welcoming windows caused her to stop in her tracks. For one last mesmerizing moment, she took in the house, thinking how far it had come since she'd first seen it. She loved this house. It had a heart and a history that were going to be brought alive. And she was going to miss it all.

Fresh tears misted her eyes. "Come on," she said, grabbing Cami's arm. "Let's get this over with."

They greeted some of the workers and stepped into the kitchen where the hardwood floor was finally finished. "Where's Mitch?" Cami asked looking around her.

"Oh, he's gone," one of the workers told them.

"Do you know where he is?" Cami questioned.

"He won't be back until Saturday. Said something about going to Portland with Vanessa for a couple of days." The man got a roguish smile on his face. "If you ask me, those two are going to come back engaged, if not married."

Cami scowled at him and said "thanks" as she pulled a stunned Ashlyn out of the room.

"He doesn't know what he's talking about," Cami assured her. "Mitch is not about to up and marry that wench!"

But Ashlyn wasn't sure who to believe. All she knew was that Mitch wasn't there and she'd be gone when he returned. Maybe it was best this way. But it still hurt.

The next morning Cami finally went jogging with her. They didn't talk much, but Ashlyn appreciated her coming along for this last run along the beach. Ashlyn slowed her own pace to what seemed like a crawl, but Cami hadn't had the benefit of daily running as she had.

"You are so lucky," Ashlyn told her. "This is yours for the rest of your life." She gestured toward the beach and the ocean. "I'm going to miss it so much."

"I still think you need to come back and make this your home," Cami said. "I know your family is in Salt Lake City, but we're your family, too."

Ashlyn gave her friend a brave smile. "You've been so awesome, Cami. The whole town has. I've lived here barely three months and I'm more sad to go back to Salt Lake than I was to leave it in the first place."

After their run, they paused at the top of the stairs so Ashlyn could take one long, last look at the coastline. She strained to see the lighthouse, but it was covered with clouds. Waves crashed below by the rocky point where she'd nearly drowned the first week she'd arrived. She couldn't help smiling at the memory. That was the day she really noticed what a wonderful person Mitch was.

"It's getting late, Ash," Cami broke into her thoughts. "We'd better get going."

Ashlyn turned and walked away, without looking back. She knew if she did, she would never be able to leave. She was glad when it began to rain, washing away the tears that streamed down her face.

As Cami loaded Ashlyn's bags in the car, Ashlyn went back to her room, checking the room one last time to make sure she'd gotten everything.

She'd grown to love this bedroom, with the skylight, window seat, and bright, cheerful colors. She checked the closet and drawers and came up empty. She even checked under the bed and behind the door.

Convinced that she had all her belongings, she looked out the window. She was going to miss seeing that stretch of beach every morning when she woke up, and wished that she could memorize the view and take it home with her.

As a gift to Cami, Ashlyn made sure she left the bed in disarray, with the drawers partly open and her wet towels from her shower in a heap on the floor. Swallowing the lump in her throat, she glanced around the room, pulled the door shut behind her, and didn't look back.

CHAPTER TWENTY-EIGHT

At the airport Cami and Ashlyn kept the conversation light, talking about anything and everything, except for Ashlyn's departure. Ashlyn was afraid if the topic came up, she would dissolve into tears right there in the waiting area.

"You feel like a candy bar or something?" Cami asked. "I'm in the mood for Junior Mints."

Ashlyn still had twenty-five minutes before her flight. "Sure," she said, getting to her feet.

They walked down the concourse looking for a shop that sold candy. Cami was trying to explain to Ashlyn about some change Grandpa Willy wanted to make in the kitchen of the mansion to provide more lighting, when Ashlyn looked up and gasped. She grabbed Cami's arm and jerked her into the ladies room.

"What are you doing?" Cami hissed. "You about pulled my arm off."

"Sebastian and Vanessa," Ashlyn answered breathlessly.

"What about Sebastian and Vanessa?" Cami insisted.

"They're out there. Together."

"What? Where?" Cami exclaimed, heading out of the bathroom.

"Wait!" Ashlyn grabbed her again. "We don't want them to see us."

"Oh, yeah," Cami said. Then a puzzled look crossed her face. "Why not? I want to talk to him and find out why he didn't sign that petition!"

"I know. Me too, but I think there's a better way to see what they're up to." Ashlyn thought for a moment. "Why would those two be together at the airport? He's supposed to be in California."

Cami's eyes narrowed. "I have no idea, but I want to find out. Let's go take a peek and see what they're doing."

They walked slowly into the crowded concourse and scanned the swarms of people for Vanessa and Sebastian. Ashlyn couldn't see them anywhere.

"Shoot! They're gone," she complained.

"Wait a minute," Cami said, "I think I see them. Yes, it's them."

Ashlyn looked where Cami was pointing and sure enough, Vanessa and Sebastian were seated side by side, their backs to them.

"Put on your sunglasses," Ashlyn said, taking her own pair out of her purse. "And here," she gave Cami part of the newspaper she'd purchased to read on the plane. "Use this in case you need to hide your face."

Cami gave her a disbelieving smirk. "What are you planning on doing?"

"I don't know, but maybe we can get close enough to hear what they're talking about."

"What if they catch us?" Cami questioned nervously.

"I don't know. I'll come up with something. Come on, before they leave. Just follow me."

They walked together toward the row of chairs just behind Sebastian and Vanessa. Sebastian turned his head in their direction, and the girls froze, whipping their papers in front of their faces, but he didn't notice them and continued his conversation with Vanessa.

Ashlyn had to coax Cami to keep walking, and a few hurried steps put them at the chairs right behind Sebastian and Vanessa. Ashlyn knew they were taking a huge chance of getting caught, but she didn't care. She had a feeling something was going on and she wanted to find out what it was.

Sebastian addressed Vanessa in a disgruntled tone. "I told you I was leaving after that investors' meeting. I can't take any more time off work, Vanessa, and frankly, I'm tired of playing this little game of yours."

As they pretended to be busily reading their newspapers, Ashlyn and Cami glanced slyly at each other, their eyebrows raised.

"Listen, Sebastian, we've almost got them where we want them. Just one more week," Vanessa insisted.

"I've had enough," Sebastian said firmly. "My desk is piled so high with work, you can't even see the desk. I've got to get back. Besides, the Davenports are nice people, and I would never have agreed to go along with this if I would've known that. And I'm not sure I agree with what you and Uncle Jonathan are doing, anyway."

Ashlyn's mouth dropped open. She looked over and saw that Cami's mouth was also hanging open. Cami mouthed the word, "Wow," and slid down a little in her chair. They definitely didn't want to get caught now. This was much bigger than they'd expected.

"And as for that fire," Sebastian said. "I don't ever want my name connected with what happened that night, and I'll deny having anything to do with it to my dying day. I'm an attorney, for heaven's sake, not an arsonist. "

The airline announced that they were boarding passengers for the flight to San Francisco. "That's me. I've got to go," he said.

"Wait, Sebastian," Vanessa pleaded.

Ashlyn could hear the plastic seat creak as he stood up. There was the sound of rustling papers as he gathered his things.

"I can't miss my plane, Vanessa," he said sternly.

"Well," she huffed, apparently also standing up. "I hope you don't plan on getting in on this project after we've signed and sealed the deal for the convention complex. All we need is one more investor and we've got all the backing we need to go ahead."

"Don't worry. I won't," he assured his cousin. "Besides, I don't think the city will ever give you permission to build your complex. I can't imagine that the citizens of Seamist want to see their town turned into a west coast Atlantic City."

"We'll see about that," Vanessa said icily. "I've almost got Mitch convinced to support the project, and once he's on board, it's a done deal. Everyone in that city loves him, and they'll go for anything he suggests. Why do you think I've spent so much time on him?"

At this Cami and Ashlyn's eyes nearly popped out of their sockets, they were so surprised.

"I know you think you've got him fooled, but he's not stupid," Sebastian said.

"No, he's not, but when it comes to me, he'll do anything." Vanessa's tone was supremely confident.

"Good-bye, Vanessa," Sebastian said wearily. Vanessa didn't answer. Instead she released a frustrated sigh and walked away. Cami and Ashlyn didn't move, waiting until Sebastian was on the plane and Vanessa was out of sight.

⋅⋅⋅ ✿ ⋅⋅⋅

Ashlyn's neck and shoulders were in knots by the time her plane landed and taxied to the gate. She waited until nearly everyone had left the plane, then grabbed her carry-ons from the overhead compartment and made her way down the aisle.

More than anything she wanted to stay on the plane and return to Portland. The recent development with Vanessa and Sebastian made it nearly impossible to leave, but she knew her family was waiting for her. She wished she could be there when Cami told Mitch what they'd overheard at the airport. While she hated to think how he'd feel being duped by Vanessa, she was extremely grateful he was finally going to learn the truth.

Arranging a smile on her face, she emerged from the plane with the rest of the passengers and looked for her family. A loud cry caught her attention and she looked up to see her parents, grandparents, and the rest of the family waving wildly at her and jumping up and down with excitement. They seemed so happy to see her, she nearly forgot how sad she was in the frenzy of hugs and wild chatter around her.

Miranda still looked tired from her pregnancy, but her tummy was beginning to grow rounder. Ashlyn had difficulty picturing her mother pregnant until now, but seeing her standing arm in arm with Garrett made the picture complete. She was so happy for them and so excited to have a little brother or sister. She received a second surprise when her Aunt Danielle, still a newlywed, told Ashlyn that she was also expecting. She'd just found out that week, and she and her handsome husband, Carson, were ecstatic with the news.

With less than an hour before Adam's plane would arrive, the family found an empty waiting area where everyone overwhelmed Ashlyn with questions about her summer in Oregon. They wanted to hear about everything she'd done while she was gone and all the places she'd seen.

Ashlyn showed them pictures of the coast and the city and the mansion. She had to swallow hard when several pictures of Mitch surfaced. Excusing herself to the bathroom, she allowed herself a few tears in the privacy of a stall and composed herself. She loved her family and was happy to see them. But she wished she could be back in Seamist just for a little while longer. There was going to be quite an explosion when Cami got home and dropped her bomb, and Ashlyn knew it would rock the entire town. She wanted so much to be there with Cami and Mitch to lend her support and help put things back together. But she knew she needed to be with her family.

Buck up, girl, she told herself as she walked back out to join them. *You can be strong for your family for a little while longer.*

As her brother's arrival grew near, Ashlyn was a bundle of nerves. She had to sit down often and take deep breaths she was getting so worked up. Although it was much too late now, she couldn't help wishing she'd written her brother more; she was awful at letter writing.

At last the plane arrived and people began exiting the plane, looking jet-lagged and beat. But one face stood head and shoulders above the rest of the crowd. It was the smiling face of her brother as he walked towards them.

"Adam!" Ashlyn screamed when she saw him. Without a second thought, she ran toward him. He dropped his bags and caught her in a hug. They started laughing and crying at the same time. He felt thinner and at least two inches taller. Now that he was home, they'd see to it that he was properly fed.

The next person to hug him was Miranda, grateful to welcome her son back home after two long years. He'd served an honorable mission; he'd been a leader and a hard worker. His mission president had even said in one letter that he wished all the missionaries who came to his mission were as dedicated and prepared as Adam had been.

While Adam made the rounds with the rest of the family, Ashlyn watched him, thinking how handsome he'd become. He was no longer her "little" brother. He was a man.

They drove in a convoy from the airport to Garrett and Miranda's house, where a huge sign on the garage greeted both of them. Adam teased that Ashlyn had only been gone two months and here she had received as big a welcome as he did when he'd been gone two whole years.

Ashlyn realized just how much she'd missed her brother's teasing and how selfish she'd been for even considering that she could miss this important moment in his life. She and Adam stayed up late that first night, talking about everything. She could relate to his ambivalence at being home. He was torn between the love he had for the people of his mission and his love for his family. He hadn't wanted to leave Portugal, but he knew it wasn't home. Ashlyn knew exactly how he felt.

As soon as she woke the next morning Ashlyn tried to call Cami but she wasn't home. She tried again several times throughout the day, but with no success. She wondered if Mitch would try to call her, especially since they hadn't had a chance to say good-bye, but she didn't hear from him either. As she waited, she tried to occupy herself around the house, examining and admiring all the changes her mother and Garrett had made.

Cami didn't call until later that night.

"It's about time you called," Ashlyn scolded her. "What have you been doing? How's Mitch? What's going on?"

"Whoa, slow down," Cami told her.

"Sorry," Ashlyn said, "but I've been dying to know what's going on up there. Did you tell Mitch about Vanessa and Sebastian?"

"Not exactly," she admitted.

"Cami, we have to tell him!" Ashlyn insisted.

"Oh, he knows," Cami assured her, "but I let Dallin tell him. I thought it might be easier to hear coming from Dallin than me."

Ashlyn released a sigh of relief. "How'd he take it?"

"Dallin said that he didn't believe it at first, but as they went over past events and conversations, Mitch finally began to realize that it all made sense. Last thing I heard he was going to confront Vanessa."

"And . . ." Ashlyn waited for the rest of the story.

"That's it. Neither of us have talked to Mitch since."

Ashlyn groaned in frustration. "This is driving me crazy. I hate being clear down here when so much is going on up there."

"I know," Cami sympathized. "And that's not all."

"There's more?" Ashlyn was beside herself. "I swear I'm getting on the next plane to Portland."

"No, no," Cami tried to calm her. "And this has nothing to do with Mitch and Vanessa."

"Then what is it?"

"Well," Cami drawled slowly, "I have something exciting to tell you."

"What?" Ashlyn exclaimed impatiently. "Tell me!"

"Dallin and I are engaged!"

It took a few seconds for the news to sink in, and when it did, Ashlyn nearly broke Cami's eardrum with her scream of delight.

"That is so great!" she told her friend. "I am so happy for you two." But then she sighed, thinking.

"What?" Cami asked.

"Oh, I don't know. I just hate to see everything change," Ashlyn admitted. "You'll get married and I'll be left all alone."

"I thought that was how you wanted it," Cami reminded her.

"I know," Ashlyn answered, suddenly wanting to change the subject. She had been thinking that her plan to stay unmarried and have a fabulous, interesting career wasn't such a good idea after all. "So, how's Grandpa Willy feeling about his granddaughter getting married?"

"He's really excited. He loves Dallin like a son. In fact, he's already talking about great-grandchildren. Says he wants us to hurry up and get five or six 'little buccaneers' here before he dies."

"Little buccaneers!" Ashlyn exclaimed and started to laugh. "Did he really say that?"

"Oh yes. He's determined to turn all of our children into little sailors. Our kids will probably say 'ahoy' before they say 'Mama' or 'Dada,'" Cami giggled happily. "So, tell me about you now. And how's Adam doing? And your mom?"

Ashlyn told Cami about her brother and her family, and what was going on with her, which wasn't much. Then Cami told her how renovations on the bed and breakfast were progressing. The electricity and plumbing on the house were finally completed, and the landscapers had cut back some of the trees, opening up a spectacular view of the coast in both directions, especially from the upstairs windows. The wallpaper and paint were going up inside, and three of the rugs, one for the dining room and two for the twin parlors, had arrived. Cami was thrilled to see that they were even prettier than they'd looked in the catalogue.

Everyone had gotten together for roadshow practice on Saturday, and George had resumed the role of Helaman. His wife, Gina, had brought the new baby to practice, and Cami made Ashlyn promise never to repeat what she was about to say but, sadly, the baby looked just like George! And she was a girl!!

"Well," Ashlyn said, "you'd better keep me posted on everything that happens. And when you see Mitch, tell him hello for me."

"I will. Do you know when you're coming back yet?"

"Not yet," Ashlyn said. "I'd leave right now if I could. I really miss all of you."

"We miss you, too," Cami told her. "Last night Grandpa said he wished I would have left and you would have stayed, because I've been so ornery since you left. He told me if I didn't quit moping around the house he was going to pack me up and ship me out to sea."

Ashlyn laughed. Good ol' Grandpa Willy, she thought. She missed the cranky, old sweetheart. She missed everyone and everything in Seamist.

Ashlyn soon decided that staying busy was the best way to keep herself from going crazy. Seeing that her brother needed help adjusting back to the "real" world, she volunteered for the job and took him shopping to get him some new clothes. Everything in his closet was old, out of style, and too big. He had lost almost fifteen pounds and had grown just over an inch. With Ashlyn's help, they found him a new wardrobe that at least helped him look like he fit in, even though his heart was a third of the way across the world.

Most of his friends were still on missions, so he needed a "buddy" just as much as she did. She found herself talking to him about her summer and her friends in Seamist. He was great at listening, and even though he never gave her counsel or advice, she realized as she explained her feelings about the town and the people—especially Cami, Grandpa Willy, Pearl, and Mitch—that the lines defining her emotions seemed to grow clearer, especially when it came to Mitch. Still, it didn't matter how she felt about him. He hadn't called and if that was any sign of how he felt . . . then what she felt for him really didn't matter.

Aside from getting new clothes, the next thing Adam needed desperately was a car. He'd sold his Jeep to help pay for his mission and now needed to buy something compact and practical, but still sporty and cool. Ashlyn hoped she wasn't making a mistake, but she called Jake to help her brother find a car.

After test driving a dozen cars and spending hours at the dealership, with Jake's help Adam finally found the car of his dreams, a snazzy Volkswagon Jetta that was a steal. Jake gave Adam the deal of a lifetime, which Ashlyn appreciated deeply. She wasn't surprised when he called later and asked her to go out with him Friday night. He had tickets to a new movie premier and wondered if she wanted to go with him.

She accepted although she had second thoughts.

"I just don't understand why, after all this time, he's gotten interested in me again," Ashlyn told her mother. "I mean, a couple of months ago I would have welcomed him with open arms, but now . . ." Her voice trailed off. She wasn't sure how to explain her feelings to her mother, especially when they were so tangled with thoughts and memories of Mitch.

"I don't understand either," Miranda told her daughter. "All you can do is listen to your heart and turn to the Lord for help. He will guide you, if you'll let Him. I know it takes a lot of faith and work and patience, but I promise you, He will help you."

Her mother's words sounded familiar. An image of the lighthouse formed in Ashlyn's mind. Yes, Ashlyn knew in her heart, the Lord would guide her.

Thursday afternoon the family got ready to go to the temple. Everyone double and triple checked to make sure they had their clothing and recommends. They were meeting Ashlyn's grandparents, as well as her aunts and uncles at the temple.

Everyone was already loaded into the car when Miranda realized she was missing her purse and sent Ashlyn back to the house for it. The phone rang just as she picked up her mother's purse, and for an instant, she debated whether or not to answer. The number on the caller ID came up "unavailable," but she knew she'd wonder if it was an important call, so she picked up the phone, half expecting a sales call or telemarketer.

The voice was heart-stoppingly familiar. "Ashlyn? Is that you?"

Her breath froze in her lungs.

"Ash?"

"Mitch, hi," she managed to say. Finally he had called, and her family was waiting just outside for her.

"Have I caught you at a bad time?" he asked.

"Actually, yes," she said reluctantly. "We're on our way to the temple. We're getting sealed today."

"That's today? Oh, I'm sorry, I didn't know," he said quickly. "I'll let you go."

"No, wait," she said, before he could hang up. "I want to talk to you. I can call you when I get back." She was tempted to call him back using the cell phone in the car, but then again, she dismissed the idea. There was nothing like having her family breathing down her neck while she was trying to talk intimately with the man of her dreams!

"I'd like that," he said. "I'll be around tonight."

"Are you okay?" she had to ask.

"Yeah," he answered, sounding a bit worn out. "I'm okay."

He left his phone number with her and said he'd look forward to talking to her later. She hung up the phone just as her stepfather honked the horn.

Her feet hardly touched the ground as she raced out to the car. At last, Mitch had called!

⊱⊰ ❀ ⊱⊰

The sealing was everything Ashlyn could have hoped for. The Spirit in the room had been so strong, Ashlyn was sure at any minute she would see spirits around her. She had been afraid that the image and memory of her dad would somehow surface and find a way to tarnish the experience, but nothing like that had happened. It had been a beautiful, spiritual, and memorable experience.

To kneel with her mother and Garrett and Adam around the altar, surrounded by the rest of the family, had been the sweetest moment of her life. Ashlyn knew that the minute she got home she needed to write everything down in her journal, because she didn't want to forget any of it.

But first, she had to make a phone call.

After four rings the answering machine picked up, and her mind raced for something to say. "Uh . . . this message is for Mitch. Sorry I missed you. I'm home now. Call me if you can. I'll be up pretty late." Hanging up the phone, she wandered into her room. She'd been looking forward to talking to him and was disappointed he wasn't home. She wondered if he was with Vanessa.

She waited for his call until nearly one o'clock, but he didn't call.

The next day Ashlyn and her family went to Temple Square together and out to lunch afterwards. She tried to call Mitch before they left but had no luck.

The family was still on a spiritual high from the day before. To know that their family was an eternal unit was the greatest blessing in their lives. Ashlyn couldn't have asked for a more loving mother or a more caring and devoted stepfather. He was a patient and adoring husband to Miranda, and he made an effort to involve himself in Ashlyn's and Adam's lives, but he didn't push them.

When they got home, Ashlyn rushed to check the answering machine, hoping Mitch had called. Instead, there was a message from Cami. "Ashlyn, call me as soon as you get home. You are never going to believe what happened."

Ashlyn placed the call immediately and was frantic herself to find no one home at Cami's house. She tried Pearl next, but she wasn't home either. Then she tried Mitch's house again. In a last-ditch effort to talk to somebody, she called Grandpa Willy's cell phone, but he didn't answer either. Instead, she heard, "The party you have called is unavailable at this time. To leave a message, press one."

She left a message, then hung up the phone completely frustrated. What was going on?

Her stomach was in knots the entire day. She had a date with Jake, but she hated to miss Cami's phone call and didn't want to leave the house. She tried calling almost every fifteen minutes, right up until the time Jake was supposed to pick her up. Still, no answer.

"Mom, I'm taking the cell phone with me, okay?" Ashlyn told her mother, who handed her a freshly ironed light blue blouse.

"Okay," her mother said, sitting on Ashlyn's bed with a groan.

Ashlyn sat down beside her. "You feeling okay, Mom?" As the pregnancy wore on, Miranda's morning sickness seemed to have worsened. She often spent the day in bed or hanging over the toilet. Ashlyn felt helpless seeing her mother feel so wretched, but except for bringing her drinks of ginger ale and saltine crackers, there wasn't much else she could do.

"I'm just tired. Wake me up when you get in tonight, will you?"

"Sure. And you'll call me if Cami calls? Or just have her call me on the cell. Or if Mitch calls, have him call me, too," Ashlyn insisted.

"Don't you think that's a little rude while you're on a date, honey?"

"No," Ashlyn answered pertly. Then on second thought, she added, "Yeah, maybe, but I don't care. Something's going on up there and I want to know what it is."

"I see," Miranda said. "Are you sure you want to go tonight?"

Ashlyn shrugged. "I've got a wedding dress in my closet that I was supposed to marry Jake in. And here he is over a year later picking me up for a movie. It's just too weird."

Her mother smiled at her. "I agree. But if he's changed as much as you say he has, then I think you need to make sure one way or the other how you feel about him."

Ashlyn nodded in agreement. It was time, once and for all.

She found Jake and Adam sitting in the living room, talking about Adam's mission. Adam was telling Jake about the time someone threw meat at him and his companion. A flank steak had slapped him right up side the head.

Jake stood up immediately when Ashlyn walked into the room. He complimented her on her appearance, noting her hair especially. She'd left it curly but had pulled back the sides with a clip.

"Where are we going to eat?" she asked curiously as they drove up Wasatch Boulevard along the east bench of the valley.

"You'll see," he said secretively. "It's a surprise."

They continued along the road until they came to the wrought-iron gate that led to one of the most expensive and elegant restaurants in the Salt Lake area.

"Jake! What are we doing here?"

"I remembered that you always wanted to eat here, so, here we are," he explained, pulling up the long drive to the parking lot near the restaurant. Peacocks strutted along the lane, fanning their tails in luminescent flares of color, and she even saw several lama in the distance.

The restaurant looked like a storybook chateau plucked from the countryside in France. Letting the valet park the car for them, Jake took Ashlyn's hand and led her up the cobbled drive, past a lovely fountain with the statue of a woman carrying an urn on her shoulder.

The restaurant inside was as quaint and timeless as the outside as the servers bustled around in peasant blouses and full skirts. Ashlyn wished she'd known they were coming here. She would have worn something a little dressier than the slim black slacks and blue cotton blouse she had on. At least they were better than the jeans she'd almost worn, she consoled herself.

Everything they ordered, from the appetizer to the dessert, was incredibly rich and delicious. The atmosphere was romantic and the restaurant was enchanting. Instead of monopolizing the conversation as he'd often done in the past, Jake asked her dozens of questions, appearing fascinated by everything she had to say. Ashlyn had to admit, she hadn't expected to enjoy herself so much. She liked this new Jake considerably more than the old one.

After dinner they headed into the city.

"I thought we were going to the movie," she asked, wondering why they were going downtown for a movie when the shows they had discussed were playing on the other side of the valley.

"Well, we kind of are," he said, pulling into a parking lot across from the Capitol Theater. "I just said it was a movie because I wanted to surprise you. We're really going to the ballet."

"Jake!" she exclaimed. He never cared for the ballet before. "I can't believe you. Why are you doing this?"

"Because you're worth it, and I want you to know how much I still care for you," he said, his voice quiet and sincere.

The ballet was wonderful and Ashlyn didn't mind too much when Jake held her hand the whole time. On the way back to her house, they talked about the performance and decided to get together the next day to play some golf. Ashlyn hadn't been for months and she was looking forward to it.

"It's been a lot of fun," she told Jake as they neared her home. "The restaurant, the ballet—it was fabulous. Even perfect."

It really had been a perfect evening. So perfect, in fact, that Ashlyn forgot all about Cami and Mitch. That is, until her cell phone rang.

CHAPTER TWENTY-NINE

She fished the cell phone out of her purse and held it to her ear, while Jake watched her curiously.

"Hello?" she said, expecting her mother on the other end. But it wasn't her.

"Ash, is that you?"

"Mitch!" she exclaimed. "What are you doing? What's going on up there?" She detected something strange about his voice and knew something was wrong.

"Can you talk?" he asked.

"I'll be home in ten minutes. Can I call you right back?" she said, not wanting to say anything in front of Jake.

He hesitated. "Um . . . okay. But call as soon as you can."

"Is something wrong?" Jake asked when she hung up.

"I think so," she said, "but I'm not sure what. I need to call Mitch as soon as I get home."

Jake gave her a sideways glance but didn't press her for more information, for which Ashlyn was grateful.

The last ten minutes of the drive home seemed like eternity. What was going on? She could barely stand the suspense. As Jake walked her to the front door, she felt like dashing inside. *If Jake thinks I'm going to invite him in, he's going to be disappointed.*

She opened the door, prepared to say good night quickly and end the evening. "It was a wonderful evening, Jake. I'll see you—"

Jake cut her off, trying to prolong their evening. "Really?" he asked hopefully. "I'm glad you had a good time."

"It was great, but you shouldn't have gone to all that trouble," she said, trying to be courteous and quick at the same time. "Well, I'll see you—"

Jake interrupted her. "I want you to know that you're worth it, Ash," he said for the second time that night. He took a step closer, gazing at her intently. Ashlyn opened the screen door and slipped behind it, using it as a shield. "I don't know about that, but I had a great time. Thanks, again," she said quickly. "See you later."

She reached behind her and found the doorknob, then turned it and slipped through the front door as well, shutting it firmly between them. She knew her actions had bordered on rude, but she wasn't ready for a good-night kiss from him. Right now she had something more important on her mind.

It took five rings for Mitch to answer the phone.

"What is going on, Mitch?" she demanded.

"Well, you remember that last morning we went running on the beach?" he asked. "I was late because Vanessa had called me and I'd asked her about the condominium and convention center."

"I remember," Ashlyn said. She and Mitch had returned to the Davenports' after their morning run, and Ashlyn had been completely bowled over to see Jake there waiting for her.

"Well, I decided to drive to Portland to see Vanessa and try to find out the truth. But I wouldn't have gone if I'd known you wouldn't be here when I got back," he said, which made Ashlyn feel a little better.

When Mitch had tried to pin her down about the supposed development plans, Vanessa had been elusive and prevaricating. He had returned to Seamist knowing little more than when he had left. But then Dallin had called to say they needed to talk and had told him what Cami and Ashlyn had seen and heard at the airport.

"I couldn't believe it," Mitch admitted, "but I had to. So I got back in my car and drove back to Portland. I went straight to the James Development office, planning to confront Vanessa, and what do you think I saw?"

Ashlyn had no idea.

"Right inside the front door, in the foyer, was a miniature display of the planned development for Seamist. Vanessa came out of her office and I couldn't even speak. I just looked at her. She said she'd meant to talk to me about the complex all along, but she wanted to wait until they had all the details ironed out. I was furious and I left right after that, but I tried to play it cool long enough to find out exactly what she and her father were up to."

Ashlyn had to ask. "When you say you 'played it cool,' does that mean kissing Vanessa on the main street of Seamist?" She knew there was an edge to her voice, but she couldn't help it. His actions didn't seem consistent with his words.

"What?" he exclaimed. "How . . . Who . . . ?"

"I saw you, Mitch," she told him tonelessly. "In the square."

He was silent. "You looked pretty happy together," Ashlyn added, wanting to make sure he understood what she had seen.

When he spoke, he was clearly miserable. "It wasn't what you're thinking. When I got back home, Vanessa called me. She was just leaving Portland and she wanted to meet me the minute she got back to town. I thought she had changed her mind, or if she hadn't that I could get her to see why the development would be a disaster for Seamist.

"Anyway, we met downtown," he continued, "and when she saw me, she immediately apologized, so I let her talk first. She said she was sorry she hadn't talked to me first about the resort, that if she'd realized how I'd felt she would never have done it. She almost had me believing her, and that's when she kissed me. And I knew then it was all just part of her act."

His voice relayed his utter disgust with her and with himself as well, Ashlyn thought. She could picture Vanessa doing exactly what Mitch had said.

"I believe you, Mitch. You don't owe me any explanations anyway," she said, though she was glad for his explanation.

"But I do," he countered. "I don't want you to think that I'm okay with all of this. Because I'm not."

"Did she tell you what their plans were?"

"Their planned development would cover the whole south beach area around the point."

Ashlyn had a sudden, stark realization. "But that's where the Davenports' home and mansion are," she protested.

"You're right. She and her father want to acquire that land and tear down all the existing structures to build this huge development," he said bluntly.

Ashlyn was horrified. "But that means tearing down the Davenport mansion! They just can't do that. And Grandpa Willy would never sell it to them anyway."

"No, of course not," he assured her, "and he won't have to."

"But what about Sebastian not signing the petition?"

"Believe me," he said. "That's not going to be a problem."

Mitch hadn't immediately told Vanessa he knew that Sebastian was her cousin, but he did demand that she level with him.

"I told her if she didn't tell me what was going on, our relationship was over." He paused. "To be honest, Ash, our relationship was already over. I realized when I was with her that we weren't right for each other and could never be. But that's beside the point."

That's the point I'd like to hear about, Ashlyn wanted to say, but Mitch went on.

"Knowing what you and Cami heard at the airport gave me some good leverage to make her talk. I guess they've had this whole thing planned for a long time. Then, when talk of converting the mansion reached them, they realized they had to move fast to prevent it from happening. That was when they involved Sebastian. She admitted to bringing him into the plan for two reasons—to hold up the business permit and to come between us."

"Us?" she exclaimed. "You mean, you and me, us?"

Mitch's tone was grim. "Can you believe it? She admitted that she saw you as a threat, and she thought Sebastian could entice you away from me."

So, Ashlyn thought, all her instincts and feelings telling her not to get involved with Sebastian were right on target. He hadn't been on the level with her. Not once, not ever. But she liked knowing that gorgeous, talented Vanessa had felt threatened by her.

"Oh, and one more thing," he said.

"There's more?" Ashlyn couldn't imagine what.

"From what you and Cami said, the fire department is reinvestigating the fire at the mansion on the Fourth of July to try to determine the cause of the fire. They're also going to question Vanessa, her father, and Sebastian."

"Sounds like things are going to get ugly for Vanessa and her father," Ashlyn commented.

"Things already are. With Sebastian's help in not signing that petition, Jonathan James had convinced the Zoning and Planning Commission not to grant the business permit to the Davenports. That is, until Dallin crashed the meeting last week. Apparently he's been doing some detective work of his own at the title company, and he uncovered the fact that the Davenport Mansion is just outside the Seaside city limits. Which means that they have no jurisdiction over the property. As Mr. James well knew. He nearly had a stroke when Dallin made the announcement. In fact, he caused quite a scene. Some of the men had to restrain him from attacking Dallin."

"Wow," Ashlyn breathed. "So, what happens now?"

"You mean aside from the fact that Jonathan James has put his house up for sale?"

"You're kidding?" Ashlyn responded, but she could understand why.

"I guess they don't feel comfortable here anymore. I have to admit I'm thinking of organizing a parade myself to escort them out of town," he said, half seriously.

On a happier note, Mitch reported that Willy and Cami had already received the permit, and they had even been approached by the Oregon State Historical Society, who wanted to make the Sea Rose one of their historical sites. Cami was ecstatic, since that would mean grants and funding, as well as plenty of free advertising.

The grand opening was set for Labor Day weekend.

"Wow," Ashlyn exclaimed. "Looks like I missed out on all the excitement. But I'm so happy this all worked out." Then she caught herself and said, "I mean, except for the part about Vanessa. I'm sorry it didn't work out, that is, if you're feeling bad about it."

"Are you kidding? I'm relieved it's over," he exclaimed. "I never had any intention of marrying her. I enjoyed dating her at first—there really isn't a large variety of datable women in Seamist, as you might have noticed. But as time went on she became more controlling about what we did and who we spent our time with. I admit, she's very pretty and she can be very charming when she wants to be. But I realize now that it was all an act. An act to help her get what she wanted."

"Well, I'm glad you're okay," she said softly, glad that he wasn't pining over Vanessa.

"There's one thing that would make it better, though," Mitch said.

"What's that?" she asked.

"If you were here."

Her heart fluttered around the edges, then it stopped completely. At least it felt like it did.

"What did you say?" she asked, wondering if her ears were working properly.

"I said, it would be better if you were here."

Ashlyn couldn't answer him. She was trying to remember how to breath.

"I miss you, Ash. I can't even go to the beach because I miss you so much. Everywhere I go there are reminders of you. Won't you come back? Please."

Ashlyn was speechless.

"Are you there?"

"I'm here."

"Are you okay?"

"I'm fine," she said. "And I'm thinking."

His voice sounded cautious. "That's a dangerous thing to do. You should do what your heart says, not what your head tells you," he told her. "Listening to your head can lead you astray. What is your heart saying?"

"It's saying to drop the phone and hop on the next plane out of here."

He laughed. "And what's your head saying?"

"It's telling me that I should at least call and get a reservation and pack some clothes first."

"That doesn't sound too unreasonable," he said, "if you're saying what I think you're saying."

Ashlyn's mind was whirling like a top. "I think I am," she said, carefully, not wanting to reveal more emotion until he did. Then she remembered this was Mitch she was talking to. Her friend, her running companion, the one she felt comfortable with, the one she could be herself with. "You bet I'm coming!" she hollered. "Just as soon as I can get there."

"Yahoo!" Mitch cried. "That's great! I can hardly wait to show you what I—" He stopped in mid-sentence. "Well, I'm not going to tell you. You'll just have to come here yourself if you want to know."

Her curiosity was piqued, but she was content just hearing the sound of his voice. She cradled the phone against her ear, smiling as if he'd just presented her with a beach full of long-stemmed red roses. "You're full of surprises, aren't you," she said softly.

"You have no idea," he said.

They said a hesitant good-bye, then Ashlyn hugged the phone close to her chest. She felt like shouting it from the rooftop. Mitch missed her! And Ashlyn was going to follow the whisperings of her heart and go back to Seamist, back to Mitch.

The next morning Ashlyn set her bags by the front door and kept a close eye on her watch. The plane left at ten-thirty and she didn't want to take a chance missing it. Her brother was driving her to the airport, so she gave him a running update on the time every few minutes.

"Adam, it's almost nine," she hollered down the stairs for the fourth time in the last half hour.

"Thank you, Big Ben," he yelled back at her.

As her mother helped her pack a few last-minute items, Ashlyn reminded her anxiously, "You guys are coming up for the Grand Opening, aren't you?"

"Of course," Miranda said. "Garrett has been to the Oregon coast several times, and he can't wait to go back. Adam is looking forward to it, too. I just can't believe you're leaving again so soon."

"You told me yourself that I needed to lean on the Lord and He would guide me," Ashlyn looked at her mother steadily. "And that's exactly what's happening. I know I'm supposed to go. I have never, ever been so sure of anything in my entire life."

Miranda stood in front of her daughter and rested her hands on Ashlyn's shoulders. "Then you need to go. But I'll miss you." She pulled her daughter into a hug.

"I'll miss you, too," Ashlyn said, then added reassuringly, "but everything's going to work out just the way it's supposed to, you'll see."

"I have a feeling there's more to you going back to Seamist than Cami, the beach, and the mansion," Miranda said with a knowing smile.

"What do you mean?" Ashlyn asked innocently as she checked her wallet for her credit card and cash.

"I mean this Mitch fellow. You haven't really told us much about him, but I get the feeling that he has something to do with this."

"I guess that's one of the reasons I'm going back," Ashlyn nodded, confirming her mother's suspicions. "To find out if there is something there. All I know is that he's one of the most wonderful men I've ever known. In a way, he reminds me of Garrett."

Miranda lifted an eyebrow. "Really? Then you know I would approve of him."

"And you'll get to meet him when you come up," Ashlyn promised as she threw the rest of her things into her bag. Miranda reminded her sternly to call from the airport in Portland as soon as she arrived so they'd know she got there okay. Cami was picking her up at the airport, if she could stop flipping out long enough to drive. She was crazy with excitement that Ashlyn was coming back. Ashlyn had nurtured a tiny hope that it would be Mitch who would be picking her up at the airport, but to get the "surprise" ready, he needed to stay in Seamist.

Ashlyn had everything ready and was about to holler for Adam yet again when the doorbell rang. A sudden realization hit her. "Oh no!" she exclaimed to her mother, horrified. "It's Jake!"

"Jake?" Her mother stared at her in exasperation. "What's he doing here?"

"We were supposed to go golfing," Ashlyn said, squeezing her eyes shut against the reality of the moment. Obviously she was going to have to face him.

"Ash," her brother called from the entry, "Jake's here."

Taking a deep breath, she braced herself for the confrontation, not knowing what to expect.

"Hi, Jake," she said brightly when she saw him.

Adam looked at her strangely, no doubt wondering how she'd managed to get herself in this fix, then he headed for the kitchen where Miranda was.

"Is someone going somewhere?" he asked, stepping over a suitcase.

"Um, yes," she said. "I am."

"What?" His face registered shock. "But we had a date to go golfing. Where are you going?"

"Back to Seamist," she stated.

"Seamist! Why? You just got home. You can't leave now. What about us? What about me?"

"What about us, Jake?" Ashlyn asked. "What exactly do you mean?"

"I thought we had something going again. Something really good. Ashlyn, I love you. You can't leave now."

Oh yes I can, she almost said. But instead she said, "Jake, can I ask you something? Will you be really honest with me?"

"Of course I will."

"Why did you come back to me? After all that's happened, why?"

He looked down at his shoes for a moment, then lifted his eyes to meet hers. "About four months ago I was in a relationship with a girl. Things were getting serious between us. We even talked about marriage. Then, out of the blue, she broke up with me. She'd met another guy," he said pitifully.

"So," Ashlyn helped him finish his story, "you came back on rebound? How flattering."

"No, that's not it at all," he said earnestly. "I remembered all the wonderful things about you. How sweet and thoughtful you were. How devoted and loyal and caring."

It sounded to Ashlyn like he was describing the family pet.

"I couldn't quit thinking about you, Ashlyn," he said. "I realized that you were perfect for me. And I wanted to kick myself for calling off our wedding. Please, Ashlyn," he begged. "Please forgive me."

She felt as if she were seeing him from a distance, as if she were a child standing on the roof of a stately Victorian house, with a spectacular view, and he was asking her to come down and play with him.

"You know, Jake," she said, "when you walked out on me, my whole world collapsed. Not only had you abandoned me, but I felt the Lord had abandoned me, too. These last few months have helped me realize that, no, the Lord hadn't abandoned me. It was a hard, horrible way to learn this lesson, but the Lord was helping me the entire time, and now I know just how much He loves me. He loves me enough to not let me marry you."

Jake's eyes were wide with shock and his mouth hung open. He seemed to be groping for a reply, but nothing came out.

"I forgive you, though. Okay? I really do. I have no hard feelings toward you," she assured him. "In fact, I have no feelings toward you at all. I'm sorry I can't keep that golf date with you, but I really don't have time to stand around talking. I have a plane to catch. And I wish you the best, I really do. I'm sure there's a wonderful girl somewhere out there for you. But it isn't me."

She turned around, looking for her brother. "Adam," she hollered. "Let's go."

"But . . . but . . ." Jake stammered. "Ashlyn, please, give me a chance. Give *us* a chance. Please?"

He was begging. He was actually begging.

"I appreciate your wanting to give it another try," she said honestly, unmoved by his pleas. "I think it was just what I needed to get some closure on our relationship. But you'll get over me. After all, I got over you."

Adam bounded in from the kitchen, took one look at Jake's dumbfounded expression, and said, "I think I'll load your bags."

Miranda followed right on Adam's heels and, putting an arm around Ashlyn, walked with her out to the car. Jake stood frozen in the entryway, an apparent victim of an acute case of reality shock.

"Call me," Miranda said, hugging her daughter tightly.

"I will," Ashlyn replied. Then she stepped back and patted her mother's tummy. "And I'll definitely be back for this little one."

"I'll move him out into the yard when I get home," Adam told Miranda as he nodded toward Jake, who still stood in shock in the hallway.

"Thanks, hon," Miranda said. She didn't really expect that her daughter's ex-fiancé would still be there when Adam returned.

Ashlyn was sad to leave her family, but she was definitely anxious to get back to Seamist. In a way she felt like she was going home.

CHAPTER THIRTY

Cami chattered excitedly nonstop on their way from the airport to Seamist. They caught up on each other's and everyone else's lives, then Cami told Ashlyn the latest happenings on the mansion.

"Since we found so much nautical stuff, we're going to make the west-facing room the 'Nautical Room,'" she explained. "And it has the best view of the ocean and lighthouse."

The room would be decorated with ship's anchors, sea shells from the South Pacific, and other treasures. They even had a wheel from a ship Grandpa Willy had sailed for many years as a young man, which they would mount on the bed for a headboard.

The Asian Room would have a rich silk bedspread and matching curtains and hand-carved ivory and jade elephants in a black lacquer curio cabinet. Pearl's gorgeous zebra skin would hang behind the bed, giving the room an exotic, oriental feeling of paradise.

The Victorian Room would use Pearl's cherry wood sleigh bed, and two Queen Anne chairs in deep burgundy, to recreate an eighteenth-century look. It would also contain antiques and treasures from years past—delicate doilies, lithophane lamps with thin sheets of hand-carved translucent porcelain lamp shades, and fringe-edged curtains.

Cami told about her favorite room last. This was the Rose Room, which was also called the Bride's Room. It had a small balcony overlooking the rose garden, the rocky point below, and the south beach, where Ashlyn and Mitch had gone horseback riding. From Grandpa Willy's storage had come a rich mahogany four-poster bed that would be draped with a gauzy sheer canopy. Cami had ordered two over-stuffed, floral upholstered chairs, and an elegant mahogany wardrobe for the room. But the crowning glory would be the delicate, hand-blown Venetian chandelier.

As if that weren't already enough, the room would also hold, encased in glass, an 1869 Victorian wedding gown of ivory satin, with lace-covered bodice and hundreds of hand-sewn pearls. Along with the dress would be an Edwardian corset cover, cap, camisole, petti-coats, undergarments, and matching gloves and leather boots, as well as a veil of sheerest chiffon.

By the time they pulled into the driveway, Ashlyn was worn out just listening to Cami. Her friend had definitely overloaded her circuits, but even so, it felt wonderful to be back.

"Why don't you go up to the mansion and I'll join you in just a minute?" Cami said. "You won't believe how much we've gotten done."

"Okay," Ashlyn said, tempted to ask what Cami had to do first. But Cami was acting a bit strangely, and Ashlyn decided to just do as she said.

"The door should be open," Cami told her, waving her on.

Ashlyn took a breath of the clean, fresh sea air and looked out toward the ocean. Enormous billowing clouds drifted above a lazy sea. The steady pound of the surf and the call of the gulls was like music to her ears.

She followed the well-worn path through the pines to the mansion, emerging into a clearing, where she stopped to admire the stately Sea Rose. The landscapers had done an outstanding job of laying out the yard. Blooms of color surrounded the wraparound porch. Geranium ivy hung from window boxes from the second floor, and all along the perimeter of the yard were rose bushes in full bloom.

She walked around to the west side of the house that faced the ocean, and gasped at what she saw there. There in front of her was a beautiful white gazebo surrounded by colorful flowers. Standing in the middle of it, smiling from ear to ear, was Mitch.

Even in a simple white T-shirt, jeans, and cross-trainers, he looked more handsome than ever. His unruly, golden hair, bronzed skin, and broad shoulders drew her gaze, but the way his green eyes sparkled and his smile lit up his face when he saw her captured her heart.

He held out his arms to her and she ran toward him. Catching her in a hug, he swung her around and she laughed through the tears that had somehow appeared the moment she had seen Mitch in the gazebo. Her gazebo.

"Welcome home, Ash," he said, holding her in his arms.

"It's good to be back," she replied, laying her head on his shoulder. The thought occurred to her that this was what heaven must feel like.

"So," he smiled, gazing down at her, "how do you like it?"

"Mitch, did you build this?" She looked around, admiring the structure with its lattice work and built-in benches all around.

"I did," he said. "I think it would be a perfect spot for a bride and groom to stand for a reception."

"Yes, it would be . . . perfect?" She choked on the last word and looked at him, wondering if his words held an additional message for her. He smiled devilishly at her, waiting for her to catch his meaning.

"Mitch . . . ?" She spoke his name as a question, not daring to presume what he might be saying.

"Ashlyn," he said softly, holding both of her hands, "I don't want to scare you, or rush you, but . . . I love you. I missed you so much while you were gone, I can't imagine not having you in my life."

"I love you, too, Mitch," she said, blinking back the tears that threatened to surface again. She had to know one thing, though. "Are you asking me what I think you're asking me?"

"I want you to take all the time you need," he reassured her. "I'm a patient man and I know that you've been through a lot. I wouldn't dream of pressuring you—"

"Mitch," she interrupted. "Shut up and kiss me."

There in the shadow of the Sea Rose, in Mitch's arms, surrounded by a place and people she loved, Ashlyn knew this was where she belonged.

ℰPILOGUE

"Today's been like a dream come true," Ashlyn told Mitch as they walked slowly around the grounds of the Sea Rose Bed and Breakfast. The roses, now in full bloom, filled the night air with their intoxicating fragrance. The voices and laughter of loved ones floated from inside the mansion.

Her parents and Adam had come to Oregon to not only celebrate the Grand Opening of the bed and breakfast as its first guests, but also to celebrate Mitch and Ashlyn's engagement. Pearl had prepared a royal feast of stuffed quail, steamed vegetables, an exotic rice dish, and mouth-watering dinner rolls. For dessert, Pearl's award-winning blackberry pie crowned the meal. In addition to Ashlyn's family, Mitch's parents, Grandpa Willy, Cami, and Dallin were also there.

"Look at that moon," Mitch said, pointing to the sky. Through the trees, a large, round moon climbed slowly in a star-filled sky.

Ashlyn rested her head on his shoulder, gazing at the moon and sighing with contentment. For her, life had never been better than right at that very moment.

They walked to the edge of the point where, below them the lapping and pounding of the surf could be heard along the rocky shoreline. A rustling breeze whispered through the pines, while crickets chirped their nightsong.

Mitch and Ashlyn stood arm in arm, enjoying the peaceful moment. No words were spoken, none were necessary. The night was clear and Ashlyn could see along the coastline the illuminated shape of the Misty Harbor Lighthouse.

The Lord's love had indeed lit the way for her. And now, with Mitch as her anchor, she would remain protected within the safety of the harbor. And no matter what storms came her way, with Mitch by her side and the Lord in her life, she knew she would weather them.

ABOUT THE AUTHOR

In the fourth grade, Michele Ashman Bell was considered a "daydreamer" by her teacher and told on her report card that "she has a vivid imagination and would probably do well with creative writing." Her imagination, combined with a passion for reading, has enabled Michele to live up to her teacher's prediction, and she loves writing books, especially books that uplift, inspire, and edify readers as well as entertain them. (You can also catch her daydreaming instead of doing housework.)

Michele grew up in St. George, Utah, where she met her husband at Dixie College before they both served missions, his to Pennsylvania and hers to Frankfurt, Germany. Seven months after they returned they were married and are now the proud parents of four children: Weston, Kendyl, Andrea, and Rachel.

Her favorite past time is supporting her children in all of their activities, traveling both inside and outside of the United States with her husband and family, and doing research for her books.

Aside from being a busy wife and mother, Michele teaches aerobics at the Life Centre Athletic club near her home. She is currently the Missionary Specialist in the Sandy ward where her husband serves as the bishop.

The best-selling author of *An Unexpected Love, An Enduring Love, A Forever Love, Yesterday's Love,* and *Love After All,* Michele has also published children's stories in the *Friend.*

Michele welcomes comments and questions from readers, who can write to her at P.O. Box 901513, Sandy, Utah 84090 or e-mail her at GPBell@msn.com.

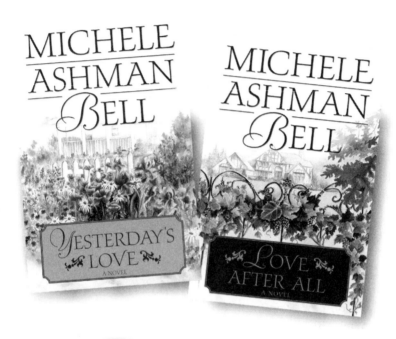

AN EXCERPT FROM THE NOVEL

Forgotten Notes

BY SIAN ANN BESSEY

15 May 1881

Dear Father,

I have only a few precious moments to write to you before our ship casts off for America. I could not leave without putting your mind at rest regarding my welfare. The thought of your distress over my sudden, secret departure has been the only thing marring my happiness. For I am happy, Father! And safe and well.

I hope you can find it in your heart to forgive me for leaving with no word of good-bye. It was perhaps the hardest thing I have ever done.

Glyn and I are married. We have loved each other since the first day we met. Our lives would have been forced to follow separate paths had we stayed in Pen-y-Bryn. I could not have born such a lonely, loveless life.

I have followed my heart, but I grieve for those I've hurt—especially you, Father, and Joseph Lewis. He is a good, kind man. I will always admire him and be flattered that he showed interest in me—but I could not love him as a wife should love her husband. And he, of all people, deserves that.

I have taken the small oval portrait of you and Mother. I will treasure it always. I have also taken the pearls that Mother gave me. It was all I had of my own to help augment Glyn's hard-earned savings. We will manage. We love one another dearly and look forward to our lives together in a new land.

I must go. My thoughts are with you.

Your loving daughter,

Mary

୭ ୭ ୭

Sarah Lewis sighed and tucked a stray wisp of long, chestnut-colored hair behind her ear. She sat up straight, stretched her aching shoulders and glanced longingly at the beam of bright sunlight pouring in through the small casement window above her head. After days of gray, wet weather the warm sunshine felt like a healing balm. She sighed again, and wished she could enjoy the beautiful summer day outside. But until inventory was complete, she was relegated to sitting in the chilly, uninviting back room of the shop, surrounded by dusty boxes and shelves of cans.

Sarah had been tempted to find a reason for doing inventory at another time. But then she would have had to face Aunty Lil. That was one of the disadvantages of working with family members—they knew you so well. Although she probably wouldn't have let on, Aunty Lil would have seen through any excuse she could have mustered. Then feeling guilty all day would have ruined Sarah's time off anyway. And so she found herself perched on the top of a rather ancient step stool alternately glaring at the rows of cans before her and the stack of papers on her knee.

It had been different when her dad was alive. She had always helped him do inventory. Perhaps that was why it fell to her lot now. Her father had made Sarah feel as though her assistance was invaluable, even as a young child. They had worked as a team. Sometimes she counted items and her father acted as scribe; sometimes they reversed roles. There were still pages in the old books on the office shelves with Sarah's large childish numbers meticulously listed in columns.

The shop had been in the family for almost three generations now. It was called "the shop" by everyone in the small Welsh village of Pen-y-Bryn quite simply because it was the only shop. Sarah's grandfather, Joseph Lewis, had been the first shopkeeper. Her father and aunt had taken over a few years before her grandfather's death. Now her aunt ran it alone with part-time help from Sarah and her mother.

The problem with being the sole retail establishment for the village was that it meant you had to stock everything from three-inch nails to cauliflower; pipe-cleaners to milk. As a child Sarah had always thought the back room of the shop was her very own

Aladdin's grotto. If you dug deep enough you could find almost anything. But now, as she sat chewing on her pencil and surveying the crowded shelves, it looked more like a lot of tedious work.

She heard the doorbell chime in the distance and the heavy tread of footsteps entering the shop. But Sarah didn't pay any heed to it until she heard her aunt's voice from behind the front counter.

"Can I help you sir?"

Sarah stopped tabulating numbers midstream, and raised her head with interest. A stranger? Having lived here all her life, Aunty Lil knew everybody in the community by name. They didn't get many visitors to Pen-y-Bryn. It was sufficiently off the beaten path to preclude the tourist traffic that frequented many of the other villages in mid-Wales.

"Sure! I'll take two of these candy bars please." He had a deep voice with a very distinct accent. Sarah heard the objects being placed on the counter and money exchanging hands. As the cash register rang out, the man's voice continued "I was also wondering if you could recommend somewhere my mother and I could stay near here? A guest house or bed and breakfast maybe?"

Sarah held her breath. There was only one bed and breakfast in the village. It was her house.

After her father's death two years before, she and her mother had been the only ones left at home. Her two brothers were already married. Kevin and his wife Mair lived on a farm about five miles away. John and Eileen were in south Wales for the time being. John was a banker and was transferred to a different branch of the bank every few years.

Since her sons were out on their own, Sarah's mother had decided to renovate their bedrooms. With some help from Kevin they added a small but serviceable bathroom to that part of the house, and listed the home as a 'bed and breakfast' establishment. Aunty Lil had clucked her tongue disapprovingly throughout the venture, but it had given her mother a much-needed diversion after the loss of her husband and, although the opportunities were infrequent, allowed her to use her abundant homemaking skills in making guests feel comfortable.

Sarah knew that if Aunty Lil had any hesitations about the character of the American in the shop, she would direct him to stay at the Black Swan Hotel in Llansilyn, six or seven miles away. The fact that he was American was not in question. Even if she had not heard his obvious accent she would have known. No one in Wales called chocolate a "candy bar"!

She heard footsteps again, this time her aunt's measured tread along with the man's. They were talking but Sarah couldn't make out what was being said. Overcome with curiosity, she inched her way down the step stool and quietly placed her papers on the floor. Quickly she tried to brush the dust off her pink T-shirt and faded jeans. The hair that had worked loose from her ponytail fell forward again. She brushed it back impatiently. She wasn't very presentable, so she would just peek.

She walked softly to the connecting doorway and was just in time to hear Aunty Lil say, ". . . and I'm sure you would find it suitable. If you follow this road just around the corner there . . . ."

They were walking towards the outer door and Aunty Lil was pointing down the lane that passed the shop and led to Sarah's home.

To her frustration, Sarah could see her aunt well, but her view of the visitor was obscured by shelves. She got an impression of blonde hair, long legs in blue jeans, and what appeared to be a tan, light-weight jacket covering broad shoulders.

". . . It's not more than a few hundred yards. A gray stone house with a navy-blue door. You'll see the sign in the front garden."

To Lil's obvious surprise, the man then grasped her aunt's hand and shook it. "Thank you so much. You've been very helpful."

Aunty Lil colored with pleasure. "Well, you're very welcome, I'm sure." The doorbell rang again and he was gone.

Sarah stepped into the shop. "Aunty Lil, who was that?"

"Well I never!" Aunty Lil was still slightly pink cheeked and looking a little bemused. "Umm, what was that dear?"

"Who was that man? You sent him on to our house didn't you?"

Aunty Lil ran her work-worn hands down her serviceable but faded floral apron, seemed to collect her thoughts, and finally focused on Sarah.

"Why yes dear, I did. He seemed to be a very nice young man. Yes indeed. Very polite too, and handsome. Didn't quite catch the name . . . Peterson, Pedersen, or something like that." She absentmindedly began rearranging the apples sitting in a box next to the counter. "Do you know, he reminds me of someone . . . perhaps . . . yes, y'know, I'm sure I've seen him on that *Dallas* program on the telly."

Sarah burst into laughter. "Aunty Lil, the only Americans you've ever seen are the actors on *Dallas* and the President when he's on the news."

Aunty Lil looked a bit sheepish. "Well, I dare say you're right dear. And he did look a bit young to be President."

Sarah grinned. "Oh well, if anyone can find out who he is and what he's doing in Pen-y-Bryn, Mam will!"

"You can be sure of that bach. The whole village will know within the hour." Aunty Lil gave a sniff that was intended to mean that she didn't approve one bit of her sister-in-law's tendency to chatter. Sarah hid a smile at the intentionally subtle reproof. She knew that beneath that prickly exterior beat the kind heart of someone who loved Sarah and her mother dearly. After all, they were almost all the family Aunty Lil had left.

Lillian Lewis was her father's only sister. She had never married and had lived in the flat above the shop ever since she was a young girl. She had co-owned the shop with her brother, Edward Lewis, and they had worked together daily. But each evening Edward, Sarah's father, had walked a short quarter of a mile down the lane from the shop to his own home, where his wife Annie and three children, Kevin, John, and Sarah were waiting with his dinner.

Mindful of his sister's single status, Edward and his wife had always tried to involve Lillian (or Lil as she was known by) in their family activities. She spent a great deal of time with Edward's family, and there could be no doubt that each of Edward's children held a special place in her heart. But she always found pleasure in returning to her own quiet haven above the shop. She was, by nature, fiercely independent and had capably taken control of the reins, running the shop quite successfully after her brother's death.

There was no question that she missed her brother. But in her mind, by continuing to operate the shop, she was showing her love for him, and doing what he would have wanted. She even felt it her duty to try and guide his widow against some of her more frivolous schemes (such as opening a bed and breakfast.) But to Lil's chagrin, Annie didn't give much heed to Lil's opinions unless they coincided with her own. Annie, it seemed, had her own share of the independent streak.

"How are you getting along?" Lil's question brought Sarah's thoughts back to the job at hand.

She groaned. "Oh, it's coming. But it's painfully slow."

Lil gave her a sympathetic nod and went back to rearranging apples. Her nonverbal message was clear. Time for pleasantries was over. It was back to work. Reluctantly, Sarah returned to the lists, ladder, and boxes.

ॐ ॐ ॐ